THE
HISTORY
KEEPERS
THE STORM BEGINS

DAMIAN DIBBEN

CORGI BOOKS

THE HISTORY KEEPERS: THE STORM BEGINS
A CORGI BOOK 978 0552 56413 7

First published in Great Britain by Doubleday,
an imprint of Random House Children's Publishers UK
A Random House Group Company

Doubleday edition published 2011
Corgi edition published 2012

7 9 10 8

Penguin Random House is committed to a sustainable future for
our business, our readers and our planet. This book is made from
Forest Stewardship Council® certified paper.

Printed and bound in Great Britain by Clays Ltd, Elcograf S.p.A.

Set in 13.5pt Garamond

Corgi Books are published by Random House Children's Publishers UK,
61–63 Uxbridge Road, London W5 5SA

www.**randomhousechildrens**.co.uk
www.**totallyrandombooks**.co.uk
www.**randomhouse**.co.uk

Addresses for companies within The Random House Group Limited can be found at:
www.randomhouse.co.uk/offices.htm

THE RANDOM HOUSE GROUP Limited Reg. No. 954009

A CIP catalogue record for this book is available from the British Library.

FOR CLAUDINE

And for Ali,
who she never met

1 THE MONUMENT STAIRCASE

The night Jake Djones found out that his parents were lost somewhere in history was one of the stormiest on record. Not since a long-forgotten hurricane in 1703 had London seen a night of such extraordinary weather, such torrents of rain and howling winds.

On Tower Bridge, at the raging centre of the tempest, an old Bentley, dark blue in colour, made its way unsteadily across the swelling Thames to the north bank. The front lights were on full beam and the wipers worked at double speed in the blinding downpour.

In the back of the car, sitting nervously on the great leather seat, was a boy – fourteen years old, with olive skin, curly dark hair and brave, intelligent eyes. He was wearing his school uniform: a blazer, black trousers and well-worn leather shoes. Next to him lay his old school bag, bulging with books and papers. Within the frayed tag, emblazoned in bold letters, was the name *Jake Djones*.

Jake's big brown eyes examined the two figures behind the glass partition in the front. On the left was a tall, haughty gentleman dressed in a sombre black suit and top hat. Beside him sat the driver in a chauffeur's uniform. The two of them were talking in hushed tones, but Jake could not hear what they were saying behind the glass anyway.

He had been kidnapped by these strangers just thirty minutes ago.

He'd been hurrying home from school across Greenwich Park when they had stepped out of the shadows just in front of the Royal Observatory. They'd explained he needed to accompany them on a matter of extreme urgency. When Jake had showed understandable reluctance, they'd told him his aunt would meet them at their destination. Jake had questioned this suspiciously, and then the rain had started to fall – first a few drops but quickly a deluge – and the men had taken action. The driver had lifted a handkerchief to Jake's face; Jake had inhaled something that smelled sharp and stinging and had felt himself falling. He'd woken shortly after and found himself locked in the back of this grand car.

Jake felt a surge of panic, just as a sudden clap of thunder seemed to shake the very foundations of Tower Bridge. He scanned the inside of the car. It was lined with dark silk and had obviously once been luxurious, though it was now past its best. The doors (he had tried to open them, to no avail, shortly after he had come round) had ornate golden handles. He leaned forward and looked more closely at one of these. In its centre was an intricate design: a symbol of an hourglass with two planets whizzing around it.

The top-hatted man, his face in shadow, looked round in disapproval. Jake stared resolutely back until the imperious head turned to the road ahead once more.

The old Bentley came off the bridge. It headed through the maze of city streets until finally it ascended Fish Hill and pulled into a small cobbled square, in the shadow of a great stone column. Jake looked up at the structure: from a solid, square base, a giant pillar, luminous in white limestone, soared into the stormy sky. Its apex, which seemed to Jake almost half a mile away, was topped by a flaming golden urn.

Jake remembered immediately that he had seen this curious memorial once before: he and his parents, returning from a disastrous trip to the London Dungeon (a clumsy ghoul had slipped on a pool of fake blood, and Health and Safety had to turn on the lights), had come across it by accident. Jake's father had suddenly become excited, telling his son the history of the building – how it was called the *Monument* and had been built by Sir Christopher Wren to commemorate the Great Fire of London; and how its gilded summit could be reached by a spiralling staircase inside. Jake had been entranced and longed to climb the staircase, and his father had agreed enthusiastically. But Jake's mother, usually so full of fun, had inexplicably become panicky and insisted they all go home before the rush hour started. Jake had been pulled away, still gazing back at the column.

The top-hatted man got out of the car and put up his umbrella. He had to hold on tight to prevent the wind from carrying it away. He opened the back door and looked Jake directly in the eye. 'Follow me. Do not consider escape.'

Jake surveyed his captor with distrust. He was elegantly dressed: as well as his silky black top hat, he wore a white collar, black tie, a dark morning suit fitted perfectly to his slim figure, narrow trousers with a faint stripe and immaculately polished boots. His face was distinctive, with a proud aquiline nose, high cheekbones and black eyes, impenetrable with flinty arrogance.

There was a flash of lightning and another surge of rain-tossed wind.

'Quickly,' the man barked. 'We are not the enemy, I promise you.'

Jake slung his school bag over his shoulder and guardedly climbed out of the car. The man held him tightly by the arm as he knocked on the glass to get the chauffeur's attention. The electric window descended.

'Go and pick up her majesty straight away.'

'Right you are.'

'And don't forget Miss St Honoré. She's at the British Museum; probably in Egyptian antiquities.'

'Egyptian antiquities.' The ruddy-cheeked chauffeur nodded.

'And, Norland – we set sail in an hour. On the dot, do you understand? No excursions to the betting shop or any of your other low haunts.'

The chauffeur was irritated by the gibe, but he covered it with a smile. 'Set sail in an hour, all clear,' he said, raising the window.

Jake's heart was beating at double speed. Suddenly he was overcome with a rush of adrenaline; he yanked his arm free and made a run for it, at full speed, across the square.

The tall man's reactions were instant. 'Stop him!' he bellowed to a group of office workers who were heading down the street towards the Underground. So authoritative was his voice that they did not even consider the boy's innocence. As they converged to intercept him, Jake turned on his heel, changed direction and smacked straight into his kidnapper. There was a loud crack as Jake's forehead collided with the man's jaw.

Jake managed to stay standing, but his pursuer was not so lucky: he tottered backwards, lost his balance, his umbrella took off, and his eyes went up, followed by his long skinny legs. He flew into the air before landing in a large muddy puddle. His top hat rolled down to the base of the Monument. Out of the corner of his eye, Jake saw the umbrella sail heavenwards, heading for the dome of St Paul's Cathedral.

Putting aside his own fears, he rushed across to the tangle of long limbs and spoiled clothes. The chauffeur had also left the car in panic; the office workers stood frozen in their tracks.

Jake looked down at the motionless figure. 'Are you all right?' he asked, fearing the worst. Despite his youth, his voice had a rich, low tone.

Finally the head stirred. Careless now of the driving rain, the tall man slowly sat up and swept back the hair from his forehead with a long, languid hand.

Jake breathed a sigh of relief. 'I'm sorry, I didn't know you were behind me. *Are* you all right?' he asked again softly, offering a hand to help the man to his feet.

The latter ignored the gesture and the question; instead he addressed the chauffeur. 'What's keeping you? I repeat, we set sail in one hour!' he hissed, before turning his venom on the assembly of gawping office workers. 'Never seen a man fall over before?'

His tone was unfriendly enough to send the group on their way. Meanwhile the chauffeur got back in the car and started the engine. It pulled away, turned a corner and disappeared, leaving Jake and his captor alone at the base of the giant column. For some reason Jake had lost his desire to run. He picked up the man's top hat, straightened it and offered it to him with an uncertain smile.

The man muttered through gritted teeth, 'I told you that *we* were not the enemy.' He pulled himself to his feet, snatched his hat back and placed it on his head. 'If you don't believe me, your aunt will clarify matters when she arrives.'

'My aunt . . . ?' Jake shook his head. 'What has she got to do with it?'

'Explanations later. Now follow me!' The tall man went over to the base of the Monument, produced a large key from his waistcoat pocket and inserted it into a hole concealed in the stone. Jake was wondering what on earth he was doing. Then he saw the almost-invisible edge of a doorway – a *secret* doorway at the very foot of the giant column.

The man turned the key and the stone door opened with an echoey thud. Within, there was a soft, flickering light from a taper. Momentarily Jake's anxiety was replaced by fascination. He craned his neck to see inside: there was a small chamber from which descended a wide spiral staircase of ancient stone.

'Quickly! Quickly!' the man barked. 'Inside, you will get answers to everything. Including the whereabouts of your parents.'

The blood drained from Jake's face. 'My – my parents?' he stammered. 'What's happened to my parents?'

'Follow me and you will find out,' was the only reply he got.

Jake shook his head and remained defiantly rooted to the spot. He took a deep breath and put on his deepest, most intimidating voice. 'You kidnap me in Greenwich Park. You bundle me into a car – you could be arrested twenty times over. Now I would like some answers! Firstly, what is it that you know about my parents?'

The man rolled his eyes. 'If you'll come out of the rain and allow me to change out of my ruined suit' – he indicated a great tear down the side of his jacket – 'I will tell you.'

'But who *are* you?' Jake persisted stubbornly.

The man took a calming breath. 'My name is Jupitus Cole. I have no intention of hurting you. Quite the opposite; I am trying to help. We were forced to kidnap you because it is safer for you to come with us. Now, would you please accompany me below?'

In truth, the adventurer in Jake was intrigued: by this eccentric man, by the secret door, by the tantalizing staircase. But he continued to stand his ground.

'I don't understand, what *is* below?'

'The bureau is below. The *bureau*!' snapped Jupitus. 'If you come, you'll see!' His eyes seared into Jake's. 'This is a matter of life and death, do you understand? Life and death.'

There was something about his solemn, determined manner that was compelling. He held open the door for the boy.

'You can leave any time you like, but I can guarantee it will be the last thing you want to do.'

Jake looked into the chamber and down the staircase. He could contain his curiosity no longer. 'I need my head examined,' he muttered as he stepped inside. The door closed behind them both with a resonant thud. The wind whistled down the spiral staircase.

'Now follow me,' said Jupitus softly, and he started to descend.

2 THE LONDON BUREAU

Jupitus glided down the stairs, his footsteps echoing around the space. Jake followed. The descent was lit at intervals by flickering gas lamps that illuminated a series of ancient murals. Now faded and crumbling, the paintings showed scenes from all the great civilizations of history: from Egypt to Assyria to ancient Athens; from Persia to Rome to Byzantium; from ancient India to the Ottomans to medieval Europe. Jake was transfixed by the pictures of kings and heroes, of epic processions, battles and voyages.

'They were painted by Rembrandt,' Jupitus explained in a matter-of-fact voice, 'when the London bureau moved here in 1667. Have you heard of Rembrandt?'

'Yes, I think so . . .' said Jake tentatively.

Jupitus looked round at him with his haughty eyes.

'I mean, I like paintings a lot,' Jake found himself explaining. 'Old paintings, where you can imagine how they used to live.'

He was surprised to find himself saying this. The truth was, he *did* love old paintings, but he was used to keeping it a secret: he felt that most of his friends at school – and all his enemies – lacked a certain type of imagination. Jake, on the other hand, often slipped off to the Dulwich Picture Gallery on his own, got up close to the paintings, half closed his eyes and imagined he was there, in another era. Often a sour-faced guard would tell him to stand back. He would wait until they had gone before immersing himself once again.

They arrived at the bottom of the stairs. Ahead was a single sturdy door. In the centre of this, engraved in brass, was the same design that Jake had seen in the car: the hourglass with two planets flying around it. It looked ancient, but it also reminded Jake of a diagram he had studied in physics: electrons revolving around the nucleus of an atom.

Jupitus looked at Jake solemnly. 'Not many people are brought to this door. And those who are find their lives changed incontrovertibly. Just a warning.'

Jake involuntarily swallowed a gulp of air.

Jupitus threw open the door and the two of them stepped inside.

'I will be with you presently. In the meantime, sit here out of the way.' Jupitus indicated a chair by the door and strode across the room and into an office. 'We have fifty minutes, everyone!' he announced, then slammed the door shut behind him.

Jake's eyes lit up in wonder.

The room had something of the look and dimensions of a great old library. Not a public one, such as Jake's local library in Greenwich, but one you could only visit by special invitation to look at ancient, precious books. It was two storeys high, with spiral staircases on each side leading up to a mezzanine floor packed haphazardly with shelf after shelf of ancient tomes. High at the top, above the bookcases, were mullioned skylights that rattled and whistled in the storm.

Along the entire length of the room was a great wooden table, lit by flickering green lamps. Old maps, charts, manuscripts, plans and diagrams were spread over it. At intervals amongst these ancient artefacts – and perhaps the most eye-catching feature of all – stood a series of globes.

The room was humming with activity. There were several men, dressed in what looked like sailors' uniforms, quickly but carefully packing items into wooden crates.

Ignoring Jupitus's instruction to sit, Jake, his school bag still over his shoulder, cautiously stepped over to the long wooden table and examined one of the globes. It was as old as anything he had ever seen. The names of the countries were handwritten in old-fashioned letters. Jake leaned right over to look more closely. He found Britain, a jewel in the North Sea. Below it, Spain covered a vast area nearly the size of Asia. In the centre of Spain was a faded illustration of an imperious-looking king. America contained nothing but drawings of forests and mountains. Jake looked closer still. At the bottom of the Atlantic Ocean, amongst the faint images of galleons and dolphins, was a date, only just discernible: 1493.

'If you wouldn't mind, sir . . .' One of the uniformed men had appeared with a crate. Jake stepped to one side and the man lifted the great old globe off the table and placed it carefully in the crate. Then he arranged a bed of straw around it, put the lid into position and hammered it shut with nails.

Jake watched as the man carried the crate towards a large open doorway at the opposite end of the room. He loaded it onto a trolley with a number of other crates. Then the trolley was pulled through the doorway into a corridor beyond.

Jake's eye was caught by something else. In a panelled partition, a boy sat working at a desk. He had rosy cheeks, unruly brown hair and thick spectacles that had been repaired with tape. Although he was Jake's age, he was dressed in a suit of brown check that looked like something an eccentric professor might wear. On his shoulder, sitting very upright, was a parrot. The bird's plumage of soft feathers was a kaleidoscope of colours, from orange to crimson to deep turquoise-blue.

The boy was typing quickly on an instrument that looked a little like a typewriter, though there were fewer keys, and in place of letters there were odd symbols. Sticking up out of the back of the apparatus like an aerial was a crystalline rod that fizzed and buzzed with electrical charges as each key was struck. After typing for a while, the boy quickly wound a lever at the side of the machine, then carried on again.

'Excuse me. You're blocking my light,' he told Jake without taking his eyes off the job. 'If this isn't sent within the next five minutes, I'll be done for.'

As Jake moved round to the other side of the desk, the boy looked up and scrutinized him; then he pushed his spectacles up his nose and returned to his work.

On the table next to the typewriter there was a plate of delicious-looking tarts. The boy reached out his hand, took one and popped it into his mouth. Jake's stomach was rumbling: he hadn't eaten since lunch time.

'Have one if you must.' The curly-haired boy could obviously sense Jake's hunger. 'They're pear and cinnamon. The pastry is as light as air.'

Jake looked at him quizzically; he had a correct, old-fashioned voice, like the people who read the news on serious radio stations. Jake took one of the tarts, and the multi-coloured bird watched him carefully as he bit into it.

'Is he friendly?' Jake asked, reaching out his hand to allow the bird to sniff it.

The parrot squawked like a banshee, puffed up

his feathers and flapped his wings. Jake jumped back in alarm.

'Mr Drake doesn't take kindly to strangers!' his owner pointed out. 'He was a rescue parrot, from Mustique. If I were you, I would follow Mr Cole's advice and take a seat.'

The boy carried on typing and muttering to himself as Jake retreated to the chair by the door. Mr Drake, the parrot, watched him very carefully as he did so.

Jake's thoughts turned to the events of the week. Up until an hour ago they had seemed in no way out of the ordinary . . .

Jake Djones lived in a small semi-detached house in an ordinary street in an unassuming part of South London. The house had three small bedrooms, one bathroom and an unfinished conservatory. There was a study that Jake's father amusingly called 'the communications room'; it was a dumping ground for old computers and a jungle of knotted cables. Jake's parents, Alan and Miriam, ran a bathroom shop on the high street. At the weekends Miriam would invent inedible dishes and Alan would attempt DIY. All would invariably end in disaster:

lopsided soufflés, burned sauces, burst pipes and unfinished conservatories.

Jake's school was a fifteen-minute walk across Greenwich Park. It was neither a particularly bad nor a particularly good school. There was a handful of interesting teachers and a smattering of vindictive ones. Jake was awful at maths, good at geography and excellent at basketball. He enthusiastically auditioned for every school play, but rarely made it beyond the chorus. He was intrigued by history; by the type of powerful, mysterious people in the murals he had just seen – rulers and emperors – but sadly his history teacher was *not* one of the interesting ones.

Jake had last seen his parents four days earlier. They had left him a message to pass by the shop on his way home from school. When Jake had got there, it had been deserted. He'd waited.

The bathroom shop was not a success. Jake often wondered how the business continued at all. His parents had started it up just after he was born and had struggled ever since. As one of the many unsatisfied customers had pointed out, 'They just have no instinct for ceramic!'

Jake tended to agree. Miriam manned the store

in a whirl of confusion, always losing papers and receipts, and sometimes entire bathroom suites. Alan worked mostly on site, overseeing the inevitable chaos of an installation. He was a big man, well-built and over six feet tall, and Jake always felt he just didn't fit into neat suburban bathrooms. Not just on account of his size, but also of his larger-than-life personality.

As he'd sat, waiting, two figures had rushed into the showroom.

'There you are, darling,' Miriam had puffed, trying to organize her cascades of dishevelled dark hair. She was an attractive woman with an air of voluptuous warmth and an olive complexion like Jake's. She had big eyes, long, curling lashes and a honey-coloured beauty spot just above the corner of her mouth. Alan was rugged and fair-skinned, with thick blond hair and the shadow of a beard. He looked as if he might give a mischievous grin at any moment.

'Disaster with Dolores Devises. Her overflow pipes weren't fitted properly,' Miriam had sighed with a glance towards Alan. 'I had to give her her money back.'

'I could spend all year fitting them,' Alan had

replied, 'but Dolores Devises will never be happy with her overflow pipes!'

There'd been a pause, as there always was – then Alan and Miriam had started giggling. They both had an infectious sense of humour. Anything could set them off, but usually it was a certain type of person: a supercilious bank manager or a pompous customer like Dolores Devises. They would rather laugh at things than let events get them down.

Miriam had turned to Jake. 'Now, we have something to tell you.' She'd attempted to keep things upbeat. 'We have to pop off for a few days.'

Jake had felt a pang of disappointment. Miriam had tried to carry on cheerfully. 'It's my fault – got the dates mixed up. Trade event in Birmingham. Boring beyond belief, but we need to – what was it the accountant said? – *broaden our range of merchandise*.'

'Granite and sandstone are very in at the moment,' Alan had added sheepishly.

'We're leaving today – straight from here.' Miriam had indicated a packed red suitcase behind the counter. 'Rose is going to stay while we're gone. Is that all right, darling?' she'd asked softly.

Jake had tried to nod, but it came out more like

a shrug. His parents had started going to these trade shows three years ago – just once annually to begin with, but this year they had already disappeared twice, on both occasions announcing their departure at the last minute.

'We'll be back by Friday afternoon!' Miriam had smiled, running her hands through Jake's thick curls. 'And you'll have our undivided attention then.'

'We have surprises planned,' Alan had chipped in. 'Big ones!'

Miriam had thrown her arms around her son and squeezed him tight. 'We do love you so much!'

Jake had let himself be squeezed for a short while before pulling away. He had just been straightening his school blazer when his father had also grabbed him in a bear hug.

'Look after yourself, son,' he'd told him, sounding like a father in a Hollywood film.

Jake had extricated himself. 'Thanks. Have a good time anyway,' he'd mumbled without looking at them. He'd then left the shop and headed into the windy street.

Jake had sulked all the way across Greenwich Park, and had sat on a bench until it started to get dark. He'd hated not saying goodbye to his parents properly, but he'd wanted to punish them.

It was not until an hour later that he'd had a change of heart. In an instant he'd forgiven them and felt a pressing need to get back before they left. He'd rushed up the high street, his heart pounding.

He'd arrived too late. The shop had been closed, the lights extinguished. The red suitcase had gone.

As promised, Alan's sister, Rose, had arrived that evening. She was one of Jake's favourite people – eccentric, outspoken and very entertaining. She always wore a mass of clanking bangles from her travels around the world. She was the type of person who happily talked to strangers, and she was always saying to Jake, 'Life's short, so have a blast!'

It had been fun with her looking after him, but this afternoon, straight after his last class, Jake had flown down the steps of his school. Friday had been the agreed time for his parents' return and he'd wanted to get home as fast as he could. Once again he'd hurried across Greenwich Park. As the whole panorama of London had opened up before him, he had seen the great black clouds approaching, war-like, from the horizon.

That was when Jupitus Cole and Norland the

chauffeur had stepped out of the shadows in front of the Royal Observatory.

Of course, Jake wouldn't realize until days later the pertinence of this location: the Royal Observatory was the place where, in 1668, Mr Hooke of the newly founded Royal Society, among others, had worked on linking space and time.

That encounter with Jupitus and Norland had taken place just a short while ago, and Jake was now sitting in this extraordinary room with his life, as Jupitus had warned him, about to change 'incontrovertibly'.

Jupitus's office door opened suddenly. 'You can come in now, Mr Djones,' he said tersely.

Jake stood up and approached the doorway. For a moment he was rooted to the spot. He looked back and found everyone staring at him. Rumbled, they quickly carried on with their tasks, and Jake went in.

3 Ships and Diamonds

'Shut the door,' barked Jupitus. Jake closed it carefully.

Jupitus was already seated behind his desk, scribbling furiously with his fountain pen. He had changed into new clothes almost identical to the ones he had been wearing before: white collar, black tie, a dark, tailed jacket, and trousers with a faint stripe. His wet clothes lay in a heap on the floor.

Jake looked around the wood-panelled office. It was a veritable treasure-trove of extraordinary objects. There was the marble bust of a Roman emperor, a cabinet displaying swords and antique weaponry, a tiger silently roaring, ancient paintings of noblemen and royalty, and yet more globes and maps. Next to the crackling fireplace was a large stuffed bird with a distinctive curved beak.

'Is that . . . ?'

'A dodo, yes,' snapped Jupitus, without even looking up. 'One of the last to walk this earth. Though obviously its walking days are now over. So, you're wondering what you're doing here? Who *we* all are?'

'That would be an understatement. How do you know my family?' Jake asked.

'I need to check your eyes first,' announced Jupitus, ignoring his question.

'My eyes . . . ?'

Jupitus opened a drawer in his desk and took out an instrument finely crafted in dark wood and silver. It was a loupe, an eyepiece such as jewellers wear to look at precious gemstones. Jupitus fitted it over his right eye and pulled the strap tight about his head. He came round the desk.

'Sit on that chair,' he ordered.

'There's nothing wrong with my eyes.'

Jupitus waited for Jake to do as he was told. Jake reluctantly sat.

'Put your bag there.' Jupitus waved his fingers at Jake's school bag. Jake took it off and placed it on the desk. Jupitus turned a dial on the instrument to switch on a circular light, then lifted Jake's chin.

'Eyes wide open, please.' He leaned in and examined the boy's right pupil through his device.

'What *is* this?'

'Ssssh!' Jupitus moved onto the left pupil, screwing up his face to focus on what he saw there. 'Now close your eyes, quickly.'

Jake obliged. Jupitus shone the light onto each closed lid in turn.

'Now tell me what shapes you see, in the darkness of your vision.'

'Shapes? I . . . I don't see any shapes.'

'Of course you do! There are shapes. Shapes of different sizes, but all of the same configuration. Oblongs, squares, circles? Look carefully. Which do you see?'

Jake concentrated hard – and indeed did start to see something. 'I suppose they look like . . . diamonds.'

'*Diamonds?* Really? Not rectangles? Not squares?' Jupitus demanded impatiently.

'Absolutely. Diamond shapes. I can see them everywhere now.'

Jupitus looked angry, as if he had been insulted. 'Are their shapes symmetrical, well-defined, or indistinct?' he persisted.

'Well-defined, I think.'

Jupitus took a deep, quivering breath. 'Lucky you,' he said, almost inaudibly, then pulled the instrument off Jake's head and threw it down on the desk. He returned to his seat.

'I'll get straight to the point. We are leaving for France. We are travelling by ship. We need you to accompany us.'

Jake chuckled in disbelief. 'Excuse me? France? *Tonight?*'

'I understand it is short notice. We will supply clothes, food, whatever you need. Do you suffer from seasickness? It will be stormy.'

'No, I don't. Sorry, this is . . . Who *are* you people?'

Jupitus glared at him. 'Perhaps you would like to stay in London – at that dull, insipid school of yours. Day after day of tedious study. Dates and equations.' With a leisurely hand, he opened Jake's bag and took out one of the books. He flicked through its pages. 'For what? To pass some pointless exams? To go on to "higher" education? To be rewarded with a tiresome, bland employment followed by a slow, meaningless death?'

Jake shook his head in utter bewilderment.

Jupitus snapped the book shut and threw it back into the bag. 'If you want education, the *world* is the place to find it. It's a richer, more complex place than you could ever imagine.'

Jake looked at the man in front of him. The phrase that he had just uttered somehow struck a chord within him. 'Well, it's not just school . . .' he began. 'Somehow I don't think my parents would really appreciate my disappearing with a group of strange people to France. No offence – but you all seem completely mad, dressed like that, talking in that old-fashioned way.' He tried to keep calm, but his hands were shaking.

'Your parents, you say? It is on their account that I am asking you to accompany us. They are missing, you see.'

'What?' Jake gasped. 'What do you mean?'

'The chances are that they will be safe. They are survivors, both of them. And certainly they have faced many perils over the years. But the fact is, we have lost contact. For three days. And we are concerned.'

Jake's head was swimming. 'I'm sorry . . . I don't understand. How do you know them?'

Jupitus Cole stared at Jake coolly before

answering. 'We work for the same organization.' He swept his elegant hand around the room. '*This* organization,' he added.

There was silence for a moment, then Jake laughed out loud. 'You've made a mistake. My parents sell bathrooms. Sinks, bidets, toilets. As we speak, they are returning from a trade fair in Birmingham. But of course you might know that *if* you knew them—'

'Alan and Miriam Djones,' Jupitus interjected, 'aged forty-five and forty-three respectively. Married on the island of Rhodes, in an orange grove by the sea. I was there. An unforgettable day,' he added without a hint of passion. 'The name "Djones" is, of course, unusual – the D being silent. One living son' – Jupitus pointed languidly at Jake – 'Jake Archie Djones, aged fourteen. Unaware of status. A further son, Philip Leandro Djones, died at the age of fifteen, three years ago.'

'Stop this!' Jake leaped to his feet, furious. Jupitus had touched, with sickening nonchalance, on the one subject that was sacred to Jake – his older brother, Philip. 'I'll leave the way I came in! Ships to France and staring into my eyes . . . You're all lunatics.' He glared at Jupitus as he grabbed his bag, then turned and stormed towards the door. As he crossed the room, his emotions got the better of him, and his lip trembled, but he regained control of himself.

'If you leave now, you may never see your parents again!' Jupitus announced – so forcefully that it made Jake stop dead in his tracks. Terror gripped him.

'As you were told, your aunt will meet us here,' Jupitus continued in a calmer tone. 'She will be joining us on our journey. She will reassure you. That's providing she arrives in time. Punctuality was never her strong point.'

Jake turned. He was now so confused, he was unable to process anything.

'*If* you want to find your parents, *if* you want to stay alive, you really have no choice but to come with us,' Jupitus concluded sombrely.

Jake spoke in a daze. 'Exactly where in France are you going?'

For the first time, Jupitus looked at him with just the faintest glimmer of respect. 'To a place you have certainly never been.'

There was a firm knock on the door and a business-like voice announced, 'Captain Macintyre.'

'Come in,' instructed Jupitus.

The door opened and revealed a sturdy, energetic-looking man wearing a sea captain's tunic. He nodded at Jake and then addressed Jupitus.

'Mr Cole. If you have a moment, we need to clarify co-ordinates.' Macintyre set down a map on Jupitus's desk. It was an old chart that showed the coast of Britain, the North Sea and the English Channel. 'I'm concerned, sir, that if we take our usual eastern horizon point' – Macintyre indicated a star-like symbol in the North Sea – 'we may be intercepted by anything heading this way. So I suggest we take *this* horizon point, south by south-east.'

There was another knock at the open doorway. One of the uniformed men was standing to attention with an empty crate in his hands.

'Sorry to disturb, Mr Cole, sir. What would you like me to pack from your office?' the man asked politely.

Jupitus went over to a glass cabinet containing large old books, opened it and pointed to specific volumes in turn: 'The Galileo, of course, the Newton . . . the Shakespeare.' He stopped and took an ancient manuscript down from the shelf. Jake craned his neck to see what it was. On the front he could just make out handwriting in faded purple ink: *Macbeth, a new play for the Globe.* Jake felt a shiver go down his spine when he realized that the author had signed his name in the same handwriting: *William Shakespeare.*

Jupitus handed the book to the uniformed man. 'Just take them *all.* God knows when we'll be back.'

He removed a painting from the wall and unlocked a safe. Reaching into the cavity, he took out a bundle of ancient banknotes and threw them into a suitcase. Then he removed a bulging leather purse and emptied the contents into his hand: glittering diamonds, emeralds and tourmalines. He replaced them in the pouch and flung it into the case.

Jupitus retrieved the last object – a small veneered box. *This* he handled very carefully. Snug within its velvet casing were three objects. In the middle was a device in gleaming silver, about the size of an egg cup, with many intricate dials and gauges. On either side of this were two miniature glass bottles. One bottle was plain and contained a grey liquid; the other was beautifully carved in crystal and contained a golden fluid. With the utmost care, Jupitus took out this second bottle and held it up to the light. It was a quarter full and glimmered with a faint spectral aura.

Jupitus realized that Jake was still in the room. 'That will be all, Mr Djones.'

'I . . . where should I . . . ?' Jake floundered.

'Wait through there for further instructions.'

Jake found himself nodding obediently. As he left the room he heard Jupitus booming, 'Right, Macintyre, where were we? Co-ordinates south by south-east . . .'

4 THE *ESCAPE*

Jake returned, dazed, to the library. His mind was in turmoil. Half of him, the logical half, wanted to get away from this crazy place – to call his aunt – to find his parents – to report the incident – to try and re-establish normality. The other half was urging him to stay: to find out who these people were; how it was that they knew so much about his parents; and, in particular, how they knew about his brother Philip.

Nearly three years ago, Philip had gone on a school trip – climbing in the Pyrenees. He had been fifteen. He'd loved expeditions more than anything – mountaineering, sailing, canoeing – and had an unquenchable passion for adventure. He longed to trek across deserts, through forests and jungles, discover unknown places.

On this particular trip he had disappeared on his own, without permission, to ascend a notorious peak. Night had fallen. Philip never returned. Exhaustive searches were made of many of the deep ravines, but his body wasn't found. The laughter that had always filled the house of the Djones family had stopped; instead there was only miserable silence. The sound of the phone ringing had been the only respite from the unbearable tension. For a moment, sleep-deprived eyes would come alive with hope . . . only to be disappointed when the call was answered. Jake had been eleven at the time and the loss had left a deep, irreparable wound.

Jake's parents were strong; after that first shock they had tried to hold things together. They were always coming up with novel ideas, oddball excursions and family competitions, to keep everyone's spirits up. But although Jake could appreciate their efforts to keep things upbeat, he couldn't stop feeling resentful that they had also thrown themselves into their work, frequently disappearing to those blasted trade fairs.

The door from the staircase opened and three people stepped into the room. The first was Norland, the ruddy-faced chauffeur. He was struggling with a number of smart suitcases and hat boxes. The second figure was new to Jake: a tall, haughtily elegant woman in a long fur coat with silky tails hanging from its hem. He guessed that this was the lady whom Jupitus had referred to as 'her majesty'. Norland escorted her across the room and into the corridor beyond.

The third was a girl, and the sight of her made Jake's throat go dry, his lips freeze and his eyes widen, without him even realizing it. She had a quizzical, playful smile, long golden locks tumbling about her shoulders, and her large eyes, shimmering somewhere between blue and indigo, sparkled with life. She was slender and also filled with restless, radiant energy.

With a few quick glances about the room, the girl seemed to compute everything that was going on. She spied Jake and swept over towards him.

'What's happening? Do we know? *Nous partons tout de suite?* Is it a mission?'

Jake's heart melted a little more: she spoke with an infectiously lilting French accent, asking these questions as if she had known Jake all her life. He struggled to force his face into a confident smile, but achieved only a tremulous grin.

'At first, when Mr Norland appeared in the British Museum, I was put out. I had so much work to do,' she continued, dazzling him with her eyes. 'My research on Tutankhamun had reached a critical stage. *Il a été assassiné* – he was assassinated – without doubt: the forensic evidence is undeniable' – Jake loved the way she struggled fearlessly with long English words – 'and I am certain it was at the hands of that glorified accountant Horemheb. Then Mr Norland told me we were leaving at short notice. Mr Cole has said nothing to you – nothing at all?'

'Er . . . not really,' Jake stammered, nervously running his hand through his thick hair. 'This is all a little new to me.'

But the girl wasn't listening. She was concentrating on the door to Jupitus's office, which was twitching as if someone was about to open it. She called over to the boy with the parrot, who was still typing furiously.

'Charlie, I don't suppose you can tell me what's going on?'

'If I told you, I'd have to kill you,' he replied dryly.

Suddenly a thought dawned upon the girl and

she turned back to Jake, her brow crinkling. 'You said this was new to you?'

Jake nodded.

She gasped and her smile broke out once again. '*Mon Dieu!* You're Alan and Miriam's son!' she exclaimed, looking him up and down and even walking round to examine him from all sides. 'I can see the similarity. You have your mother's eyes, no doubt about it.'

'Jake, yes. Jake is usually . . . what . . . people call me . . .' he offered in the deepest voice he could muster.

'Topaz St Honoré. *Enchantée,*' she said, shaking Jake's hand with warm confidence. Her tone changed. 'Norland told me the news of your parents on my way here. Please don't worry about them; they are the most resourceful agents in the service, as well as the kindest.'

'Yes . . . good . . .' Jake found himself saying.

'How old are you? I imagined you as younger.'

Now he felt his throat seizing up, but he straightened to his full height. 'Oh . . . I'm fourteen. You?' he asked.

'Fifteen, just.'

'And you're . . . French . . . ?'

'*Bien sûr.* Though from a different era.'

Jake nodded knowingly, not having the slightest idea what she was talking about.

The office door flew open.

'There is no more time,' announced Jupitus. 'Take whatever is at hand and board the *Escape*.'

'Mr Cole, sir. May I enquire as to the reason for our sudden departure?' asked the girl, Topaz, pursuing him across the room.

'Orders from headquarters. We are to return to Point Zero immediately.' Jupitus handed Charlie the message he had been scribbling in his office. 'Wire this to Commander Goethe – tell her we are on our way, then pack up.'

'Has our location here been compromised?' Topaz persisted. 'Is the present situation connected in any way to the disappearance of agents Djones and Djones?' she asked in a whisper so that Jake would not hear.

'I'm as much in the dark as you are.'

'Is it likely that we will be sent on a mission once we arrive at Point Zero?'

'I really can't say.'

There was a flurry of activity. The uniformed

men snapped into action, lifting the remaining crates and heading quickly for the corridor.

Amidst this mayhem, Jake was rooted to the spot, panic-stricken. 'Sorry . . . my aunt? Is she coming or not?' he asked Jupitus.

'She's late. And we're out of time. She was warned.'

'I can't leave without her.'

'Well, you have to. For your parents' sake. Anchor up in three minutes.' And Jupitus was gone.

The boy in spectacles came over, Mr Drake bouncing on his shoulder, the strange typewriter tucked under one arm. 'Charlie Chieverley – how do you do?' he said to Jake. 'Mr Cole is right – staying in London is not an option. Who knows what could become of you? Much safer with us.' Mr Drake squawked in agreement.

Jake felt as if he was on the edge of a precipice. He thought of his mum and dad, picturing their warm, loving faces. 'All right,' he agreed.

Topaz gripped Jake's hand and squeezed it. He was led quickly across the room, through the doorway, and into a long, winding passage. On the walls were more faded paintings like the ones on the staircase down from the Monument: moments of history, snapshots of long-gone civilizations. Jake's eyes were drawn to one painting in particular: a great galleon sailing through a storm towards a mountainous coast.

'No time,' Topaz said, pushing him on. Faster and faster he was led, racing towards a rectangle of hazy light. Finally they emerged into the blustery open air.

Jake took a moment to get his bearings. They had come out on an embankment overlooking the Thames. Foaming waves crashed against the banks. Jake's eyes widened at the sight of a ship docked beside the river, yanking violently at its moorings.

It was a sturdy, sea-battered vessel in the style of a Spanish galleon – similar to the ship in the picture. It was the type of ship that, hundreds of years ago, had set sail on heroic journeys of exploration to the New World. On the prow, a golden figurehead reached out her arms towards the sea, a warrior goddess with jewelled eyes. Below the figurehead, Jake could just make out the ship's name, in letters faded by many voyages: the *Escape*.

'All aboard!' shouted Jupitus.

Jake looked back down the corridor, desperate to see his aunt. For a moment Jupitus remained on the bank. He stared down the length of the storm-tossed Thames, its wild waters luminous under the black sky. 'Goodbye, England, for now,' he said under his breath. Then: 'Untie her!' And he jumped aboard.

At that very moment a black cab screeched to a halt on the north side of London Bridge.

'You'll be all right in this rain, will you, darlin'?' asked the driver.

A woman stepped breathlessly out of the car. She wore a long Afghan coat, and a silk scarf to tame a mass of reddish corkscrew hair; she carried a bulging carpetbag. She slammed the door. 'Believe me, I've known worse. You should try being in the middle of a battlefield in a storm like this, with half the Prussian cavalry about to charge. Then you really understand the meaning of hostile weather! Keep the change. No need for it where I'm going,' she announced, handing over a bundle of notes.

The cab driver's face lit up. 'Right you are, madam.'

But the woman was gone, charging down the steps to the embankment, her long coat trailing behind her. At the bottom, she stopped dead and the blood drained from her face.

'Stop!' she shrieked as the *Escape* cast off from the embankment. 'Wait for me!'

On board, Jake's heart missed a beat. That voice was unmistakable. He tore across to the side of the ship.

'Rose!' he shouted at the top of his voice. He held out his arms, nearly toppling over the rail and into the Thames. 'You have to jump!'

A handful of crewmen joined him, all shouting at once.

Rose took a deep breath. 'All right, all right, I'll try.' She tossed her carpetbag into the air. One of the sailors reached right out over the water and caught it.

Then she took a few steps back and ran. She shrieked as she took off from the pier and sailed towards the deck, but she landed short, her knees colliding with the ship's hull. She managed to grab hold of the rail, but her hand was slipping. In the nick of time, a sailor reached out and caught it. The veins in his neck bulged as he pulled her to safety.

Rose collapsed on the deck, where she lay for a minute, her chest rising and falling like bellows as she regained her breath. Then she looked up at Jake and burst out laughing. 'Thank God I made it in time. Thank God!'

The sailors helped her to her feet and she threw her arms around him. 'You must be so confused, my darling.'

Then her eyes shifted and she stiffened. Jake turned to find the cool figure of Jupitus Cole standing behind them.

'Rosalind Djones. There always has to be a drama, doesn't there?' He stared at her with his inscrutable eyes. 'We would have left without you.'

Rose stuck out her chin. 'It's nice to see you too, Jupitus – after fifteen years,' she replied pointedly. 'Considering I had just over an hour to pack up my entire life, I think I should be commended.'

Jake observed the pair of them. There was a current of antagonism flashing between them.

Not wishing Jake to hear, Rose drew a little closer to Jupitus and whispered, 'You couldn't explain over the phone, but you can explain now. Where were Alan and Miriam sent?'

Jake craned his neck, trying to make out what was being said.

'As I already pointed out,' Jupitus replied in velvety tones, 'that information is currently classified—'

'Classified? Rubbish! That act of yours never worked with me. Where *are* they?' Rose persisted. 'Of course it was *you* who signed the orders!'

'Signed the orders?' Jupitus exclaimed. 'Nothing could be further from my wishes than to have Alan and Miriam Djones working for the service again.'

'Just tell me where they are,' Rose repeated, rising up to her full height to look him in the eye. 'Tell me!'

Jake listened intently.

Jupitus took a deep breath. 'Venice,' he announced. Then added gravely, '1506.'

Rose dropped her head into her hands.

Jake's mind reeled in confusion. What on earth could Jupitus have meant?

Jupitus smiled thinly at Rose. 'Welcome aboard.' He looked at his watch. 'We dine in thirty minutes.' He climbed down the steps that led below decks. 'And you'd better tell the boy who he is and what he's doing here. He doesn't believe a word I say. Stations, everybody,' he ordered, and disappeared from sight.

As the *Escape* picked up speed down the Thames, heading for Tower Bridge, Jake stared at his aunt.

'Rose, what's happening? I don't understand – where *are* Mum and Dad?'

Rose fumbled in her carpetbag, produced an old tissue and wiped her eyes. She looked around the ship. 'I never thought I'd set foot on these creaky boards again. It's been fifteen years.'

'You know this ship?' asked Jake in amazement.

'Oh, yes – when I was just a little older than you, I spent a good deal of time looking out from this deck,' she remembered. 'My last trip was to Istanbul. Or Constantinople, as they called it then. A perilous voyage.'

She looked up. The wind was howling and the rain was starting to fall with renewed vigour.

'Let's go inside and I'll try and explain everything,' said Rose. She led Jake below decks as, at the helm, Captain Macintyre guided the *Escape* up the Thames towards the sea.

5 Dinner and Atomium

The main cabin was a warm, comfortable space. The old timber floors were strewn with a patchwork of rugs. The sturdy oak tables, lopsided by time, were covered with sea charts and navigational instruments. On the walls there were paintings of old seafarers and stern-faced explorers. Jake would later discover that the *Escape* was a galleon from the seventeenth century, but in Victorian times it had been lovingly adapted to the 'modern' world and a steam engine had been set into its core.

Rose led Jake over to sit on one of the sofas by the fire. She put down her carpetbag, arranged the bangles on her wrist, took a deep breath and began:

'Many years ago, Jake, just before you were born, your parents made a choice. Until then, they had lived a – how can I put it? – an unusual life. It was a life of adventure and discovery and excitement.' She paused for a moment, her eyes sparkling at the memory. 'But it was also a life of great, *great* danger. When Philip was born they started to wonder whether they should continue in this perilous world. Your arrival three years later sealed the matter once and for all. They chose – and it was the most painful choice they would *ever* make – to lead a "normal" life. And I supported them by choosing the same.'

Jake stared at his aunt, eyes narrowed in expectation of the next bombshell.

'They kept a secret from you. But it can be kept no longer. A situation has forced our hand.' Rose took a deep breath and proceeded in hushed tones. 'You have an ability, Jake. A skill, you might call it. A *power* that very few others possess. You have had it – without even knowing – since you were born. Your parents have it; I have it; and everyone on this ship, to a greater or less degree, has it.'

'An "ability"?' was all Jake could manage.

'First, tell me – did Jupitus use an instrument on your eyes?'

'Yes, just after I arrived.'

'And did you see shapes?'

'Diamonds – I saw diamonds.'

Rose gasped with excitement and clutched Jake's hand. 'Diamonds? Really? That's wonderful news! Wonderful! Were they sharp? Well-defined?'

'I think so, yes.'

'Grade one, no doubt!' Rose clapped her hands. 'Like your parents, and me. It is not always inherited, you know. It is rare, so very rare.'

'What does it mean?'

At this point, Rose glanced round to check that no one was listening. 'It means that the power is purer in you than in others. Diamonds are strong, the sharp ones the strongest.' Then she confided, 'What Jupitus Cole wouldn't give for diamonds!'

'So tell me – what is this ability?'

Rose looked at Jake gravely. 'You can travel *into history*. You can travel to it as other people travel around the world. And with diamonds, you can visit *every* destination, near and far.'

Jake looked at his aunt and burst out laughing. But it was a nervous, uncertain laugh: *was she completely crazy too?* he wondered.

'I'm not saying it is easy. No journey is easy. A simple journey across London can be full of complications. And a journey to another place in history is as fraught as anything you can imagine. But *you* can do what others cannot.'

Jake looked up at his aunt and shook his head. He wanted to tell her that he'd had enough of this nonsense, but the look on her face remained serious.

'I know you will have a lot of questions,' she continued. 'But soon you will see for yourself. Tonight we are going on a journey.'

'To France?'

'To Normandy, to be precise. Though it is not the Normandy of today. We're going to 1820; that's Point Zero, you see.'

'Point Zero?'

'The headquarters of the History Keepers' Secret Service. That's what all these people work for. These people and many more. The History Keepers' Secret Service has agents from every part of the world and from every corner of history. It's an important organization. Perhaps the most important that ever existed.'

Even though Jake felt a tingle go down his spine and the hairs stand up on the back of his neck, he continued to protest, 'Rose, really, as much I would like to *travel to history*, as you put it—'

'It all sounds ludicrous, I know. And don't ask me to explain the science of it, I'm useless at it. Jupitus could do a much better job. Or ask Charlie Chieverley – he's the real scientist. It is all to do with our atoms. They possess this memory of history – every single moment of it.'

Jake suddenly remembered the curious phrase he'd heard on deck. 'When Jupitus said *1506*, what exactly did he mean?' he asked nervously.

'What's that, darling?' Rose said vaguely, fiddling with her bangles and avoiding his eye.

'1506,' repeated Jake. 'Don't say he meant the year 1506?'

Rose gave a short laugh. 'I think that's what he did mean, but let's not worry about it now. Alan and Miriam were always disappearing. That was their style – instinctive.'

'1506?' Jake shook his head. 'You're trying to tell me that's where they are?'

Rose grabbed him by the shoulders and looked him straight in the eye. 'We're going to find them, Jake,' she vowed. 'We'll find them – I have no doubt about that!'

Jake knew, in that instant, that Rose was not lying. He understood nothing of why or how or who could travel to history, but he knew – he could feel it in the pit of his stomach – that it might all be true. In that moment, he also finally understood – and it was a startling revelation – that his parents were indeed missing.

One of the cabin doors opened and the lady in the fur coat swept into the room. She stopped when she saw Jake and Rose.

'Oh . . . isn't it dinner?' she asked, sounding irritated.

'Any moment, I think,' Rose told her. 'How are you, Oceane? You haven't changed a bit.'

'And you look . . . essentially the same,' was the best Oceane could come up with. 'Perhaps a little saggier under the eyes.'

'And *you* haven't lost your talent to flatter,' Rose giggled in reply. 'This is Jake, my nephew.'

'Oceane Noire,' the lady said dismissively. 'You don't mind if I linger. My cabin is like an icebox, as usual.' She installed herself on a chaise longue, then lit a cheroot and gazed with mournful theatricality through the porthole.

Presently two crewmen arrived and quickly laid the table in the centre of the room. Then the rest of the passengers assembled: Charlie Chieverley and his parrot, Mr Drake, the radiant Topaz St Honoré, and Jupitus Cole. Jake couldn't help noticing Oceane Noire perk up as Jupitus strode into the cabin. She stubbed out her cheroot, quickly checked her hair and crossed the room, throwing Jupitus an alluring smile before sitting down in front of him to show off her elegant back. Sadly the whole operation was wasted on Jupitus, who was lost in his own private world, examining charts.

Jake's attention was caught by a curious nautical instrument that was suspended from the ceiling above the table. It was composed of a sphere, encircled by three golden rings of different sizes that fitted perfectly within one another. On each ring was a different set of markings, some in numbers and some in indecipherable symbols.

'That's the Constantor,' whispered Rose. 'It guides us to the horizon point. Very important piece of apparatus. There's another one on deck. You can see it moving.'

Jake examined it more closely. Rose was right: he could just make out the golden rings turning, almost imperceptibly, on their axes.

'When all three rings are in alignment, we've hit the horizon point, and that's where the fun really begins. Your first time is unforgettable. It's like the best roller-coaster ride ever.'

Looking at his watch again, Jupitus flushed with irritation. 'Norland!' he shouted down the stairs. 'Is dinner being served or not?' The room fell silent as he muttered, 'Useless individual. What is the point of a butler who cannot keep time?'

Norland appeared from the galley below. He seemed quite unflustered. (He had learned from experience that the best way of dealing with Jupitus's temper was to pretend that no crime had been committed). He pulled on the ropes of the dumb waiter, opened the hatch and distributed plates of succulent roast chicken. Everyone sat down to eat, Jake with Rose on one side, Oceane on the other, and Topaz and Charlie directly opposite.

Oceane took one look at the platters of vegetables and sighed wearily. 'Dreadful English food.' No one paid her the slightest bit of attention.

Jake ate his meal, which was one of the tastiest he'd ever had, and listened in uncertain bemusement to the snippets of conversation around him. Topaz asked Jupitus about his experience in Byzantium defending the silk route from China. Jupitus played down the event in his usual deadpan style, but obviously relished the name he'd been given at the time: Hero of the Turks.

Oceane loved this story and offered one in return about her 'intolerable experiences' in Paris, where she'd found herself facing a horde of French revolutionaries 'without so much as a nailfile to defend herself'. Inexplicably this led to Norland, who sat down after he had finished serving (keeping the largest portion for himself), telling a long-winded anecdote about hearing Mozart playing the piano when he'd been sent to the Austrian court of Joseph II.

All these anecdotes were told as casually as if they had taken place on an ordinary holiday in the Costa del Sol. To Jake, it felt like a dream or an elaborate piece of theatre. And yet, what an entrancing, compelling idea it was – to actually travel back into history! Rose had told him that he would 'see for himself'. Jake was breathlessly waiting for this proof to materialize.

Every now and then he glanced over at the radiant, confident girl sitting opposite him. She was not like any girl he had ever set eyes on. On Jake's bedroom wall he had pinned up pictures of people he found interesting. One in particular, which he had cut out of a Sunday magazine, fascinated him: a portrait of a girl, a warrior princess – or so he imagined. Her face was pale and beautiful, her gaze both regal and uncertain. There were jewels in her long hair and she wore gleaming battle armour. Behind her lay a mysterious landscape of mountains and castles over which ominous storm clouds were gathering. Topaz reminded Jake of this figure: mysterious, beautiful, brave.

Brave? Jake wondered; he had never given a thought to whether someone looked brave before. As he watched Topaz chatting to Charlie, he lost himself in her blue eyes. They seemed to sparkle and shimmer with a thousand emotions at once: excitement, happiness, impatience and wonder. At one point, her concentration drifted and her eyes seemed to darken from indigo to deep ultramarine, filled with the deepest sorrow. A second later, she was roaring with laughter at Charlie's impersonation of a one-eyed parrot-whisperer he'd once met in Tangier.

During the conversation, expectant eyes would occasionally look up at the glistening Constantor that hung over the table. The golden rings were moving ever closer to their point of alignment.

At the end of the meal, Jupitus stood up and headed over to the sideboard. Everyone went quiet as he opened the veneered box that Jake had seen him remove with such care from his safe in London. He extracted first the gleaming silver device of gauges and dials; then the plain bottle of grey liquid; and finally, carefully, the fine crystal vial of golden fluid.

'What's going on now?' Jake whispered to Rose, wondering why everyone had fallen quiet.

'The little machine there is called the Horizon Cup', his aunt replied.

Jake watched as Jupitus carefully moved the device's gauges and dials to precise settings.

'He's entering the exact date we are travelling to,' Charlie explained. 'In a moment he will deposit a drop of each liquid into the cup. The cup then fuses the liquids at a certain ratio – an incredibly specific ratio. Then we drink it and it's hello, history.'

'It fuses the liquids?' Jake was struggling to understand.

'On a molecular level, naturally,' Charlie went on, pushing his spectacles up his nose. 'A certain percentage of the gold liquid will take you to 1750; quite a bit more, and you could be having breakfast in ancient Rome. That is, of course, providing you have the *valour* in the first place – that's the ability – the strength – to travel to history. Don't think just anyone can drink it and go tearing off into the past. Just a very select few of us, those of us with shapes in our eyes, diamonds or rectangles. An even smaller number can voyage any significant distance, to BC and beyond.'

'And what *are* those liquids?' Jake asked as Jupitus unscrewed both bottles and deposited a single drop of each into a funnel at the top of the device.

'The grey one is just some common tincture, but the golden one—'

Rose finished Charlie's sentence, speaking with profound reverence: '– is atomium.'

'Atomium?' asked Jake, fascinated.

'One of the rarest substances in history,' said Charlie. 'We couldn't operate without it. But be warned: it tastes like something you put in a car.'

Jupitus took a step back from the Horizon Cup. Everyone took a step back. Oceane Noire went so far as to shield her head with her porcelain-pale hands. Jake was utterly baffled as Rose guided him away.

'The Cup gets very hot!' she explained.

Then Jake noticed that it was changing – glowing red like molten metal; even from the other side of the cabin he could feel the intense heat coming from the tiny egg-sized machine. It rattled and whistled slightly as it returned to its normal state.

Jupitus waited a good three minutes before he returned to the device, using a napkin to pick it up. He unscrewed the top half (inside, the metal dazzled the eyes like sunlight) and deposited its contents, a dash of shimmering solution like a liquidized diamond, into a jug of water. This he stirred with a long spoon, then filled seven small crystal glasses. Norland put them on a tray and started handing them round.

'To the voyage!' Jupitus toasted, lifting his glass.

'To the voyage!' everyone repeated after him.

Rose looked at her glass. 'Nothing to lose now, I suppose. To my return to the History Keepers' Secret Service!' And she downed it in one.

Charlie left a sip in the bottom of his glass and held it up for Mr Drake. The parrot was clearly loath to drink; he sank his head down onto his chest.

'You know the routine by now,' Charlie told him, producing a peanut from his pocket. Mr Drake reluctantly drained the glass and received his reward with a muted *squawk*.

'Take the remaining solution to Captain Macintyre and the crew,' Jupitus instructed Norland, who disappeared with the jug of atomium.

Eyes gradually turned to Jake.

'*Bon voyage*, my darling,' said Rose. 'We all wish you the best of luck.'

There were calls of 'Here, here!' from around the cabin, though Jupitus only murmured his agreement, and Oceane remained silent.

As Jake lifted up his crystal glass, he saw that it was engraved with the emblem of the hourglass and the whizzing planets. He took a deep breath and drank the shimmering liquid. He immediately coughed and had to be patted on the back by Charlie.

'Mr Chieverley,' Jupitus called over, 'when we reach horizon point, make sure you stick with him.' He flicked his fingers towards Jake. 'It's his first time – we don't want any dramas.' He looked at the Constantor and then at his watch. 'One hour to the horizon point,' he announced, before leaving the cabin and slamming the door.

* * *

'Can you feel anything yet?' asked Charlie Chieverley as he came on deck with Jake.

Jake shook his head.

Charlie looked at his watch. 'It's nearly an hour since we took the atomium. You'll feel something soon.'

The *Escape* was now in the open sea, cutting through the waves towards a patch of moonlight that lay for ever beyond its reach. The rain had stopped, but the fresh wind persisted.

Jake was intrigued by Charlie: he was eccentric, with a dry sense of humour, more like a worldly-wise grown-up than a boy. If Charlie didn't like something, Jake reflected, he wouldn't hesitate in saying so. People who were brave enough to speak their minds had always appealed to him.

'So I just want to make sure I understand all this. There are two liquids, atomium and this tincture—'

'Atomium's the important one. Scandalously rare.'

'And the exact proportion decides the point in history we travel to?'

'In a nutshell, yes.'

'But what I don't understand is . . . how does the atomium work?'

'Ah!' Charlie exclaimed excitedly, pushing his spectacles up his nose. 'It reacts with our atoms, to take us into the time flux, that network of intangible pathways that connects all ages. The atomium wakes up every atom in our body and asks for an inventory of everything it possesses. Our bodies have more atoms in them than you could possibly imagine. In the breadth of a single hair, a hundred billion jostle for space. And these atoms are forever being recycled around the universe. You'll have a couple of thousand atoms that once belonged to Shakespeare, you'll have some of Genghis Khan's and Julius Caesar's, as well as some that belonged to a hedgehog living in Norway.'

Jake struggled to get his head around the notion.

His eyes bright with excitement, Charlie went on, 'That is one thing. But a single atom itself is extraordinary, like a mini-universe. Think of this: if the atom were the size of St Paul's Cathedral, the nucleus alone would be no bigger than a pea. So what about the space in between? What does that contain?'

'I don't know,' said Jake, half smiling.

Charlie leaned in close and took off his spectacles in order to make his point more dramatically.

'It contains *history*. The history of everything.'

Again, a tingling went down Jake's spine. More questions came immediately into his head. 'And the horizon point?' he asked. 'What's that?'

'There are *many* horizon points all around the world. Each one is a focus of intense magnetic activity . . . You know, of course, that the Earth has a magnetic field – the horizon points provide the *power* for the atomium to do its job. We invariably use horizon points that are far out to sea; the land-locked ones are fraught with complications.'

Again, Jake thought hard about this strange science. 'Rose said only a "select few" can travel into history. But we all have atoms – why can't everyone do it?'

Charlie smiled and took a deep breath. '*That* is the unanswerable question,' he said, relishing the mystery. 'No one knows where we get our valour from. But the fact is, if you do not have a shape in your eye, you will not be travelling to the past.'

'And what about the ship? The rigging? The cups and plates? How do they travel to the past?'

'Not to mention the clothes we're wearing. None of us would enjoy arriving in nothing but our birthday suits!' Charlie giggled to himself. 'As a group, we *extend our focus*. Telepathically, so to speak' – he swept his hand grandly around the ship – 'we carry all this with us: the *Escape*, everything in it and some of the water too. The most talented keepers, usually the diamonds – I myself am honoured to be one,' he added proudly, 'carry the most. Not just the inanimate objects, but the *other keepers* too, the less qualified ones.'

'That's why Jupitus Cole asked you to stick with me?'

Charlie whispered, 'With you also being a diamond – so I've been told – you should be a natural, but it's best to take precautions on the first voyage.' He looked round and dropped his voice further. 'When I said the diamonds "carry" the other agents, I meant more the oblongs and the mis-shapes. It's very hard to take any journey of note without at least one diamond on board.'

Although all these ideas were still abstract to Jake, he couldn't help feeling a certain sense of pride in his status. 'And if we are able to travel in time,' he asked, 'are we able to visit ourselves – you know, at a younger age?'

Charlie looked at Jake as if he were mad. 'You've been reading too much science fiction. Our lives are like everyone else's. They start at the beginning and finish at the end. We can only be in one place, in the present . . . wherever that present happens to be. Look . . .' Charlie held up his wrist and showed Jake his watch (which, like his spectacles, was battered and fixed with tape). 'The number there' – he pointed to a little window of numerals in the middle of the clock face – 'is my age. Fourteen years, seven months and two days. Wherever I am in history, it doesn't matter, this watch adds up the days. On my birthday it plays me a little tune – Beethoven's Fifth.'

He patted the watch fondly and whistled his birthday tune. He stopped when he saw that Jake's attention had been caught by something. Topaz St Honoré had appeared on deck. Jake's eyes flickered and again his throat dried as he watched her glide towards the prow of the ship.

'Oh dear.' Charlie rolled his eyes. 'Another heart stolen by *le sphinx français*.'

Jake blushed with embarrassment.

'Topaz has that effect on most boys,' Charlie went on.

'No, not at all, I . . .' Jake floundered. 'She just seems quite . . . mysterious . . . Does she live in

Normandy?' he asked, attempting to deflect attention from himself.

'Since she was adopted by Nathan's family, yes. Mostly she lives at Point Zero with them. Of course, she and Nathan fight like lunatics, just like any brother and sister.'

'Nathan?' asked Jake.

'Nathan Wylder. You'll meet him when we arrive. Actually, you'll *hear* him first. He has the loudest voice this side of Constantinople. American. A civil-war child.' Then Charlie added with more admiration than envy, 'He's the undisputed star of the service. A bona fide hero.'

Jake was still thinking about Topaz. 'Adopted? What happened to her own family?'

Charlie leaned in closer and whispered in Jake's ear, 'That is a long and sad story, and no one ever talks about it.' His eyes narrowed as he scrutinized Jake. 'Are you feeling the atomium now?'

Jake nodded. It had come upon him quite suddenly. His head had started to throb and he seemed to be floating in the air without actually leaving the ground. Within seconds the nauseous sensations had become ten times worse. He lurched forward; Charlie caught him and helped him over to a bench.

'Sit down, the worst will pass soon.'

Jake gazed out at the sea. He knew it was the sea, but at the same time he didn't recognize it. He didn't feel cold any more, and all the sounds around him seemed to come from far away.

One by one, the other passengers came up on deck to prepare themselves. Oceane Noire looked out at the sea as if she owned it. She took a deep breath and clutched Jupitus's shoulder, but he ignored her.

'Five minutes to go!' Captain Macintyre announced. Jake turned and saw the other Constantor next to the great wooden steering wheel; similar to the instrument in the cabin below, but larger, and forged from stronger metal. The three glinting axes had almost converged.

'Four minutes!' announced the captain.

Jake's headache and nausea had now passed and he felt only the sharp thrill of excitement. Topaz turned to him, smiled – and suddenly Jake could see things, extraordinary things: armies, kingdoms, great half-built cathedrals, shimmering palaces, moonlight, candlelight, mountain passes, heroic adventurers. Something had been unlocked inside him and he was overcome with a sense of the glory of the world.

'One minute . . .' the captain told them.

Silence fell. Charlie moved closer to Jake, while on his other side Rose clutched his hand firmly. All eyes were fixed on a moonlit point ahead of them. They waited.

'Ten, nine, eight, seven . . .' continued Macintyre almost inaudibly.

Jake's eyes opened wider. He held his breath. A whirlwind sprang up out of nowhere; a savage cyclone encircled each individual. Colours flashed. Rose and Charlie drew as close to Jake as they could. Then there was the sound of a slow-motion detonation – and suddenly he saw an explosion of diamond shapes shooting out in all directions, blasting from an epicentre within him. He seemed to be taking off like a rocket, above the ship, above the ocean. Jake had heard the term 'out-of-body experience', but, like most people, had never actually had one. He knew that he was actually still standing on the deck, but it was as if he were high above it and could see himself far down below. The diamond shapes flew to the far edges of Jake's vision, the colours flashed insanely – and finally there came the sound of a sonic boom.

And suddenly everything returned to normal. Jake was once again on the deck, with Aunt Rose at his side. A victorious cheer went up and everyone started congratulating each other.

Charlie turned to Jake and shook him by the hand. 'I hope you had a good trip. Welcome to 1820.'

6 HISTORY ALIVE

Although Jake was exhausted beyond imagining after the events of the last twenty-four hours, he was determined to stay awake until he had seen some sign that he was indeed breathing the air of a different century. He clung to the ship's rail, staring out to sea as his eyelids became heavier and heavier.

Everyone except the captain had gone below decks to get some rest. Rose had waited up with her nephew for a long while, but when she had started yawning uncontrollably Jake had kindly suggested that she lie down on one of the comfortable sofas by the fire. Rose had fetched a woolly blanket for him, kissed him on the forehead, then disappeared saying she 'probably wouldn't be able to sleep anyway'. A minute later, Jake had heard her loud snores from the cabin below.

With the blanket wrapped around him, he now looked out at the rolling sea and the faint light on the horizon, and thought again of his parents. A strange mixture of feelings churned around in his head. Of course, he was worried sick, but he was also haunted by a sense of betrayal. They had *lied* to him, pretending that they were going to a bathroom trade fair in Birmingham, when they had actually been heading not just across Europe, but across the centuries.

Jake shook his head to clear his mind. 'There's probably an explanation for everything,' he said out loud, and returned to scanning the ocean. Since the disappearance of his brother, Jake had learned, through painful trial and error, the trick of blocking out any dark thoughts that threatened him.

Slowly, the wind, which had been bracing and cool, started to die down. Within minutes it was replaced by a warm breeze from the tropics. Now an inescapable drowsiness took hold of Jake. First he knelt down on the wooden deck; a few moments later he lay on his side with his school bag under his head as a pillow, still staring out at the sea; then he fell fast asleep.

* * *

At the same moment, early that morning in 1820, near the Normandy village of Verre, a masked figure was making his way cautiously around the topiary hedges towards an imposing chateau set in grand, formal gardens. He stopped in the shadows and surveyed the building.

A guard with a lantern patrolled the grounds. The masked figure waited for him to disappear round the side of the chateau, before stealthily gliding across the lawn and scaling the wisteria until he was level with a first-floor window.

Inside the room, a girl was pacing anxiously to and fro. The intruder threw open the window, leaped inside and ripped off his mask.

'Nathan! Thank God! I thought you'd never make it,' the young girl exclaimed as she showered him in kisses. Nathan didn't react: he was used to young ladies throwing themselves at him. He was sixteen, athletic, strikingly good-looking, with a delightfully self-assured glint in his eye. He was also dressed in the height of fashion. He looked around the opulent bedroom; it was decorated with a ton of gilt and great festoons of lilac silk.

'Whoops – style overload,' he commented in his light American drawl. 'Isabella, your husband-to-be has clearly confused money with taste.'

'He will never be my husband! He said if I did not walk up the aisle tomorrow, he would force me. At gunpoint. And this is the horrible dress he wants me to wear.' She nodded disgustedly at an elaborate wedding gown hanging on a mannequin.

Nathan was appalled. 'The man is a monster! Isn't he aware that the Empire chemisette went out with the Ark? We need to get you out of here.'

He silently descended the wisteria, holding the breathless Isabella in his arms as if she were as light as air.

'I want to marry a man like you, Nathan, strong and heroic,' she sighed.

'Isabella, my darling, haven't we been through this? I'd be a terrible husband. I may be irresistible, but I'm unreliable, immature, infuriating. You'd be throwing yourself away on me.' Nathan set her down on the ground. 'Now, quickly – this place is swarming with guards.'

Minutes later, they were hurrying across a paddock towards Nathan's horse, which was waiting at the edge of the forest. Suddenly a voice came from beneath the canopy of trees.

'I had a premonition of your disobedience,' it growled in a low French accent. Isabella trembled as a sour-looking aristocrat, obese and ruddy-cheeked, stepped out of the shadows; at his side was a brutish-looking guard, holding the reins of his master's horse. 'So I took precautions.'

'Ah, Chevalier Boucicault . . .' Nathan beamed, unfazed. 'We're glad we caught you. Premonition justified: Signorina Montefiore is having second thoughts about the wedding. She has issues with your manners – not to mention your trouser size.'

The chevalier held out his hand, and the guard deposited a pistol in his palm. '*Très amusant*,' he sneered as he checked it was loaded.

'And on that subject, as much as I admire your brave sartorial efforts,' Nathan continued, indicating the chevalier's waistcoat, 'I have to point out that stripes are doing you no favours. They're merciless with a frame such as yours.'

Isabella's eyes went wide as the chevalier cocked his pistol and levelled it at Nathan. The boy's reaction was so quick it was almost invisible: suddenly his rapier was drawn, there was a flash of steel – then the pistol was whipped out of the chevalier's grasp; it flew up into the air and landed firmly in Nathan's hand.

'Let's go!' he shouted as he leaped onto his handsome black mare. He grabbed Isabella's hand and pulled her up behind him.

'*Arrêtez! Voleur!*' the chevalier bellowed as they tore off across the field. Within seconds he'd scrambled onto his own beast and was charging in pursuit.

'Hold on tight!' Nathan shouted back to his companion as he galloped along the narrow path that cut through the dense conifer wood.

A huge branch emerged out of the dawn mist right in front of them. 'Nathan, watch out!' Isabella yelled.

Nathan fired the pistol, and the offending branch was obliterated. They rode on at full speed. Nathan tossed away the gun, its cartridge spent.

The red-cheeked chevalier whipped his horse savagely until he was edging abreast of his prey. Nathan drew his sword again and checked his perfect white teeth in the glinting blade before turning to the chevalier. As both horses hurtled onwards, the two riders clashed swords, their blades flashing like lightning in the early morning sun. Isabella gasped, shielding herself from the whipping branches of the passing trees.

'I should warn you,' Nathan teased his adversary, 'I haven't lost a fencing bout since I was eight. And that was to the Chevalier d'Éon, considered by many to be the greatest swordsman in history. The odds are not on your side, my friend.'

With this, he delivered the decisive blow. Boucicault reeled, and there was an almighty clunk as his head collided with a thick branch. He flew through the air and landed with a thump on his derrière.

'*Adieu, mon ami*,' Nathan shouted, sheathing his sword. 'And once more – it's 1820, my friend: sleek is no longer a preference; it's a requirement.'

Half an hour later they stopped on a rocky outcrop suspended above the sea, where a local man was waiting with a carriage. Nathan dismounted, helped Isabella down and went to speak to him. For a moment he chatted jovially in broken French, then handed over his horse and a number of gold coins and returned to Isabella.

'Jacques here will take you back to your family in Milan. So this, as they say, is farewell.'

'But, Nathan,' Isabella pleaded, tears welling up in her eyes, 'I don't understand! Can't I come with you?'

'No can do, I'm afraid.' The soft Charleston twang in Nathan's voice was clearer now. 'I start work in an hour.'

'What is this silly job you do, anyway?' Isabella pouted. 'This big secret of yours . . . ?'

Nathan took a deep breath, but chose not to reply. He kissed her on the forehead. 'You'll get over me sooner than you think,' he said – and there was a hint of sadness in his eyes.

'Nathan, I love you,' Isabella told him.

'And I love an adventure!' he replied – then charged towards the cliff edge and dived, arms outstretched on either side, into the ocean.

Isabella watched in amazement, tears glistening on her cheeks, as he swam out into the mist.

The horizon was beginning to blush with dawn indigos and pinks when Jake awoke to the smell of freshly baked bread. A plate of croissants, still steaming, lay on the deck next to him.

'No doubt you feel like death . . . ?' a voice commented.

It was Charlie. He was looking out to sea with a telescope. 'Atomium leaves you groggy at the best of times, but the first experience is the worst. There's orange juice,' he said, indicating a china mug beside the croissants, 'and please help yourself to a pastry. They're almond and chocolate.'

Jake did indeed feel terrible: his throat was like sandpaper, his muscles ached and his head thumped. He reached for the cup and drank down the juice. It revived him enough to sit up.

'An East Indiaman, if I'm not mistaken,' Charlie muttered. 'Dutch, I suppose. Probably on its way to Ceylon or Bombay.'

At first Jake failed to register what Charlie was saying. Then, through the ship's rail, he saw a dim shape on the horizon. He leaped to his feet. 'Is that what I think it is?'

Gliding majestically across the crimson horizon was a ship. Its long sturdy hull was punctuated by a succession of portholes; three enormous masts supported steeply raked sails, each one billowing in the strong wind. Although it was some distance away, Jake could see activity on the deck.

'Could I please borrow your telescope for one second?' he asked his companion.

Charlie passed the eyepiece over. Jake took it excitedly and pointed it towards the ship. He gasped in astonishment at what he saw: a group of sailors were standing in the stern, hauling up the last of the sails. All wore the same uniform of flowing white shirts, narrow trousers and boots up to their knees. Overseeing the operation was a distinguished-looking man in a blue tunic and a triangular hat that made him look like Lord Nelson.

This was the proof that Jake had sought, and it left him spellbound. He eagerly examined other parts of the ship. Framed in a porthole was a cabin boy throwing out a bowl of slops; on a raised deck at the bow stood three gentlemen in long coats, holding canes; next to them, a lookout leaned over the side, scanning the horizon with his own telescope. Jake instinctively edged back into the shadow, aware that he might be discovered in his school uniform.

'You're treading on my croissants,' Charlie pointed out. Jake looked down to discover one of the pastries flattened under his heel.

'Sorry,' he said absent-mindedly, then immediately returned his attention to the East Indiaman, 'but this is amazing!'

'If you look in *that* direction,' Charlie said, indicating the bows, 'you'll get another surprise . . .'

'What surprise?'

'You'll see,' Charlie replied with a mischievous wink, and disappeared below.

7 THE CASTLE IN THE SEA

At the prow of the *Escape*, Jake waited patiently. Gradually he started to discern the faint outline of land, shrouded in early morning mist. Then, directly ahead, he spotted a faint triangular shape outlined against the rocky coast. At first it looked menacing, like a vast cloaked giant striding out from the shore. But as he looked more carefully, he realized that it was an island, cone-shaped, compact and granite-grey.

Jake remembered that he still had Charlie's telescope. He held it up and examined the curious triangle in more detail. Its wide, solid base was of natural rock, but on top of it stood what seemed to be a series of ancient *man-made* edifices – buildings erected upon buildings like toy bricks, rising up to a single tower and a sharp, pointed steeple.

'That's her,' said a soft voice behind him. 'Mont St Michel.' Topaz came to join Jake in the bows. 'Point Zero, the headquarters of the History Keepers' Secret Service.' She was eating one of Charlie's almond and chocolate croissants. French people always ate their pastries with such panache, Jake reflected, and Topaz was no exception. Even the simple action of catching crumbs and tipping them into her mouth he found inexplicably dazzling.

As the island continued to materialize out of the mist, Topaz told Jake all about it. 'Its history as a fortress dates back to the year 808; that's why the Secret Service chose it as their base. In over a thousand years its walls have never once been breached.'

She explained that the commanders of the History Keepers had not only chosen the safest *geographical* location for their headquarters; they also chose the safest *historical* location.

'The 1820s is a time of peace,' she told him. 'The bloody turmoil of the last two hundred years has passed its worst. The English civil war, the war of the Austrian Succession and the unforgettable French Revolution have all been resolved. The legacy of Napoleon Bonaparte, whether he wanted it or not, has brought a spell of harmony to this region of Europe.'

The decade was also free of the perils of the *modern* world, she went on: the coming Industrial Revolution would give birth to many necessary evils, and the development of the steam engine would lead eventually to the 'diabolical atomic bomb'.

'The modern times are *merveilleux*, full of magic, but they are also full of danger. The 1820s are safe from all that.'

Once Topaz had completed her whirlwind tour of history, she gave a quick smile. 'So now you understand the location of Point Zero.' And she popped the last piece of croissant into her mouth.

Jake didn't fully grasp it. 'So the headquarters remains in 1820 – *permanently*?'

'It stays for the decade – then, on New Year's Eve 1829, everyone gets on a ship, takes a horizon point back to the first of January 1820, and returns to the island, and so on for another ten years. I know it all sounds mad, but somehow it works.'

Jake decided he would wait and see if everything became clearer in time.

The island had now come into focus. He craned his neck to examine its impressive array of towers and peaks; of flying buttresses, colonnades and giant arched windows. From everywhere came the squawking of seabirds as they flew in and out of the shadows of the citadel. Mr Drake didn't care for them and kept a beady eye on them at all times.

On a promontory ahead of them stood a group of figures – a welcoming party. If the sailors of the East Indiaman had shown Jake that he was indeed in a different time, this collection of extraordinary-looking figures confirmed it. He had seen people dressed in old-fashioned clothes on television programmes or at fancy-dress parties, but somehow he had never felt convinced that they really belonged to a past era – they were always too neat and artificial. These were different; they looked right.

There were people dressed from every period in history, from the Victorian era back to the age of Elizabeth I and beyond. Amongst them was a middle-aged man in a flamboyant red velvet tailcoat with matching top hat. Clutching his arm was an elegant-looking lady, her skirts ballooning out with crinoline and ruffles. Another gentleman wore a black doublet, a white ruff framing his stern-looking face. However, for Jake the most eye-catching figure of all was a tall lady who stood at the front of the group.

She had large silver-blue eyes and long steely grey hair swept back from her proud face. Jake guessed that she must be at least fifty, but she still retained the fine features of her youth. A dark navy cloak hung from her proud shoulders. Standing perfectly still next to her was a greyhound with sleek grey fur and bright eyes.

A soft smile played across the lady's thoughtful face as, one by one, she took in the occupants of the ship. When those eyes rested briefly on Jake, he felt an uncertain thrill.

'That's a very old friend of mine,' said Rose, joining Jake and Topaz on deck. 'Galliana Goethe. She's in charge here, the commander of the History Keepers.'

The ship was moored at the pier, a gangplank was lowered and the passengers began to disembark.

'Would you mind?' asked Oceane, pushing through to the front. 'I have a fitting in the costumiery. I need to get out of these dreadful modern clothes.' She tossed her fox fur over her shoulder as she swept down the gangplank.

As Topaz followed her, the man in the red velvet coat boomed, 'There she is! There's our girl!' immediately jangling his wife's nerves.

'Truman, please don't shout!' she admonished him.

Topaz approached them, smiling warmly.

'They're the Wylders: Truman and Betty,' Rose informed Jake. 'Nathan's parents, and Topaz's guardians. Truman is just as much a vain peacock as his son, but *she's* charming. Of course, they're both from completely different centuries.'

Jake watched Topaz greet them with a hug.

'How are you, darling?' Betty gasped fondly as she clasped her arms around her. 'Good journey?'

Topaz nodded.

'Let's have a look at her,' Truman bellowed as he held her by the shoulders. 'You've grown. Hasn't she grown, Betty? So tall for fourteen.'

'Fifteen.'

'Fifteen? You're *not*!'

'I am.'

'How did that happen? You were just six a few years ago.'

Topaz and Betty shared a fond look.

'It's just occurred to me how quiet it is here,'

Topaz said, looking around at the rest of the welcoming party. 'Is His Loudmouth indisposed?'

'Nathan has disappeared on some mission to rescue his latest *amour fou*,' sighed Betty, with a shake of the head. 'No doubt she's fallen head over heels, blissfully unaware that she will be tossed aside like all the others.'

Jake followed his aunt down the gangplank. Galliana's face lit up as they approached. 'It has been an age,' she said, embracing Rose.

Jake could now see that Galliana's cloak was embroidered with an array of motifs: suns, moons, clocks and phoenixes.

'It might have been an age,' Rose replied, 'but you look as ravishing as always.'

'Are you sure you don't mean *ravaged*?' Galliana replied. 'I've hardly slept in three days. There are bags under my eyes.'

'But those cheekbones will never let you down.'

Galliana laughed, her face creasing around her twinkling blue eyes.

'Don't tell me that's still Juno . . .' Rose looked down at the bright-eyed greyhound.

'This is Juno's granddaughter, Olive,' Galliana replied, running her hand over the hound's silken coat. 'Every generation they get a little cleverer.' She turned to Rose's companion. 'And this, of course, is Jake.'

Although Jake felt unaccountably shy of this tall, stately woman, he smiled bravely, held out his hand and spoke in the most manly tones he could muster. 'Pleased to meet you.'

'*So* well-mannered.' Galliana enclosed Jake's hand in her own. 'I expect there has been an awful lot to take in. But don't worry – we are going to find your parents.' Suddenly her expression changed as she spied something approaching across the water. 'What on earth . . . ?'

There was a murmur of consternation as everyone caught sight of the swimmer churning his way towards the quay. Topaz knew who it was immediately; she shook her head and rolled her eyes.

'Ahoy there!' Nathan announced as he pulled himself out of the water with a beaming smile. He had swum fully clothed along the coast for over an hour, but looked as if it were the easiest and most natural thing in the world. He shook out his long hair and briefly checked his appearance in a vanity mirror produced from his back pocket.

Jake's eyes widened as Nathan swaggered along

the pier. He was intrigued. The boy could be no more than a year older than him, but he oozed confidence. Certainly there was an arrogance about him, but somehow he made the day seem brighter.

'I'm sorry I missed the arrival,' Nathan told them in a deep voice. 'I simply *had* to save a young damsel from a fate worse than death.'

Galliana was as unimpressed as Topaz. 'May I remind you, Agent Wylder, that this organization has no time for *personal* heroics. Risk is only acceptable in the line of duty, however glittering the prize may seem. Do you understand me?'

'Clear as crystal,' Nathan drawled, 'but I can assure you, this was for no personal gain. The lady was somewhat . . . over-enthusiastic. Like so many,' he added with a shrug.

'*Mon Dieu!*' Topaz winced. 'My brother's humility knows no bounds.'

Nathan's gaze alighted on her. 'Back in one piece then?' he asked casually.

'Looks like it,' Topaz replied with similar nonchalance.

'Your hair . . . different?'

'It's down.'

'Nice. Softer.'

That was the sum of the siblings' greeting.

Galliana announced to the whole company, 'I know everyone must be tired, but time is of the essence. I am calling a meeting in the stateroom at ten a.m. precisely. Everyone is to attend.'

The party started to disband.

'Agents Wylder and St Honoré . . .?' Galliana called over to Nathan and Topaz. 'Would you give Jake a tour of the castle and tell him something of what we do here?'

'Jake?' Nathan shouted. 'Jake Djones!' he repeated, clapping him warmly on the shoulder. 'Why didn't anyone tell me you were here? Nathan Wylder. You've probably heard all about me. And most of it is actually true!' Then he continued in a serious tone, 'We're going to find your parents if it's the last thing we do.'

'Commander,' Topaz interrupted, 'perhaps I should take Jake on my own. If we go together, I'm bound to cramp Nathan's style.'

'Please,' Nathan replied, 'you couldn't cramp my style if you locked it up and threw away the key.'

'That's enough!' interceded Galliana wearily. 'Both of you go. I want him to get a rounded view. And, Jake – come to the stateroom with the others at ten o'clock. I would like you to be there, so you can understand what is going on.'

Jake nodded. In truth, he wanted to ask Galliana all sorts of questions *right now*; but he realized he would have to wait. Topaz had already taken him by the arm and was leading him towards the castle entrance.

At the base of the Mount stood a pair of giant doors studded with iron rivets. On the front of them, an ancient plaque was engraved with a now-familiar emblem: the hourglass with two planets orbiting around it. This version of the symbol was much more ornate, and Jake realized that the two satellites orbiting the hourglass were both the planet Earth. To give an added, magical dimension to this particular design, the mound of sand in the bottom of the hourglass was shaped just like the Mont St Michel.

'Are you ready?' Topaz asked.

Jake nodded. He was feeling exhilarated.

Topaz turned the handle. The door was not locked; it opened with a hollow creak and the three of them stepped inside.

8 POINT ZERO

They ascended a wide staircase into the heart of the medieval castle. On either side was a succession of life-sized portraits from all ages of history, the faces staring down from the walls.

'Those are all the past commanders of the service,' Topaz explained as Jake examined their stern, important-looking faces. 'The man there' – she pointed to a mysterious figure in a turban in front of a dark, tropical landscape – 'is Sejanus Poppoloe, the founder of the Secret Service. He was a scientist and explorer from Bruges in Belgium, a real visionary. It was he who first discovered atomium and the time flux and drew the original map of Europe's one hundred and seven horizon points. He died in the English court of Elizabeth the First, two hundred years before he was born. He travelled back to that time by ship.'

Sejanus Poppoloe's searing eyes seemed to follow Jake as he passed.

At the top of the stairs they turned right, through an arch and then onto a balcony overlooking an inner harbour, a vast natural cave that was open to the sea on one side.

'This is where we keep the majority of the History Keepers' fleet. Regard' – she indicated each ship in turn – 'the *Campana*, Genoese merchant galley; the *Conqueror*, Byzantine dhow; the *Lantern*, Chinese junk, Yuan dynasty, built to endure the typhoons of the South China seas – worst in the world,' she added knowingly, her voice echoing around the cavern. 'The *Barco Dorado*, Spanish warship, one of the few survivors of the Armada fleet. And the *Stratagème*, a very early submarine. A Dutch ship and an Atlantic clipper are being repaired at the port of Brest. Shall we continue?'

As Topaz swept back through the arch, Nathan caught up with Jake and whispered loudly in his ear, 'In case you weren't sure, she loves the sound of her own voice.'

They crossed the landing and passed through a door into a large vaulted room.

'The armoury,' Nathan announced with relish, assuming the role of tour guide.

In the centre of the room stood two raised platforms like boxing rings, where agents in helmets and armour were practising combat. Every inch of the surrounding wall was covered in gleaming weaponry.

'Greek, Roman, Celtic, Byzantine' – Nathan indicated the various sections – 'Crusader, early medieval, Renaissance, Age of Enlightenment, Industrial Revolution, and so on. Catapults, slings, crossbows, longbows. Swords, sabres, long swords, broadswords. Axes, spears, lances, maces, daggers, glaives—'

'I think he probably gets the gist of it,' interrupted Topaz wearily. 'There's a lot of metal.'

'But you will notice a lack of firearms and explosive material,' added Nathan with an arch of his brow.

Jake hadn't noticed at all, but he nodded knowingly.

'You see, explosives cannot be transported in the time flux,' Topaz continued. 'If they somehow found their way onto a ship, the unstable elements could get mixed up with our atoms and . . .'

'. . . it would be goodbye tomorrow!' Nathan imitated an explosion. 'Any good with a longbow?' he asked Jake, taking one down from a rack.

'He wants to show off his somewhat limited skill,' explained Topaz.

'No, I – I don't think I ever . . .' Jake stammered.

Nathan primed his bow with an arrow and aimed for a target in the far corner of the room. They all squinted to see where it had hit. The arrow had found the bull's-eye, but not quite the very centre.

Topaz sighed, took a longbow herself, nocked the arrow and let it go. Her arrow hit the exact centre of the bull's-eye. But she did not stop there. She fired another arrow, then another and another and another. Nathan squinted at the target. With her perfect shots, Topaz had written the letter T.

Nathan scrutinized it, then turned to Jake. 'She's jealous, you see, as I am currently regarded as the Secret Service's most valuable agent.'

'So how many agents are there exactly?' Jake asked, trying to diffuse the tension.

'At any given moment,' Topaz replied, 'there are usually about forty actual *agents* working for the organization, although there are dozens more auxiliaries – like the crew on the ship, et cetera, et cetera. About a third of the agents are based in the Peking bureau in Ming Dynasty China. They report to the commander, naturally, but they're in charge of the eastern hemisphere.'

'And the agents here, from the western hemisphere,' Jake asked, 'they all live on the Mount?'

'*Ça depend.*' Topaz shrugged. 'Depends how much dangerous activity there is. In quiet times, most of them return to their own eras. Except Nathan and me, of course.'

'We're stuck with each other.' Nathan gave a wink. 'You should tell Jake that out of all those agents you've mentioned, only ten or so are *real* hot shots like us.'

Topaz explained. 'A small number, invariably us younger agents, have the greatest *valour* – hence our name: *Valiants*. It means we can travel further in history and with greater ease. As agents age, their abilities usually weaken – the diamonds much less so, of course, but even their valour coalesces and hardens over time. These *older* agents—'

'The has-beens,' Nathan teased.

'– are called *Advancers*. They're largely involved in the day-to-day running of things. But the strong ones, the diamonds – like your parents –

can continue on active duty if required.'

'Interesting fact,' Nathan butted in. 'Jupitus Cole, who's neither young nor a diamond, never lost his valour. He could still flip back to ancient Mesopotamia and not feel a damn thing.'

'Anyway, it's the Advancers,' Topaz resumed, 'who choose, by secret ballot, who is to be the commander of the History Keepers. Commander Goethe has held the post for three years.'

'Having narrowly pipped Jupitus Cole to the post,' Nathan confided. 'He was none too happy about it.'

The three of them left the armoury and climbed the stairs to the next floor.

'Communications,' announced Topaz, leading them through a door into another room. Along one wall, four people, two men and two women, all in nineteenth-century clothes, were working at antique desks. They nodded briefly at the youngsters. In front of each stood an instrument similar to the odd typewriter that Charlie Chieverley had been using in the London bureau, including the trademark crystalline rod that buzzed with miniature lightning flashes. Using quills and ink, they were noting down information on parchment.

'They're de-coding,' Topaz explained. 'Those devices are called Meslith machines, after Vladimir Meslith, the inventor. They're used to send and receive messages through time. Any *important* message, sent directly to the commander, arrives in the "Meslith nucleus", there.'

She indicated a thick glass cabinet in the centre of the room that contained yet another distinctive machine. This one was much larger and more intricate than the others, its crystalline rod sturdier. Emanating from the back of the device was a complex arrangement of miniature cogs and levers that led eventually to two quills, each poised over blank rolls of parchment, ready to print out an incoming message.

'When a message is received, two copies are transcribed. One is deposited in the box below the machine; the other is sent, by tube, directly to the commander's quarters underneath us.'

'By tube?' asked Jake, trying to keep up.

'That's right. Forget all about any modern communications systems,' Nathan added, inspecting his reflection in the glass cabinet. 'Null and void in 1820. We've fifty plus years before even the advent of electricity.'

'Though, personally,' Topaz commented, 'I find Meslith communication infinitely more magical. Look – there's a message arriving now.' She pointed to the machine. Its crystalline aerial was flickering with a light as brilliant as burning phosphorous. This, in turn, set off a chain reaction, which resulted in the two mechanical quills writing a short message on two separate sheets of parchment. One copy was deposited in a slot below the machine; the other was mechanically rolled into a tube and shot into a pipe that led down through the floor.

'The commander will receive it any second now,' said Topaz. She turned wearily to Nathan, who was still transfixed by his own image. 'When you've got your bouffant under control, perhaps we can continue . . . ?'

'It's that conditioner Father gave me,' sighed Nathan. 'I don't know what all the fuss is about jojoba.'

As Jake was led out of the room, he caught sight of a clock. There were just twenty minutes to go before the meeting in the stateroom and he felt a jolt of fear as he wondered what new revelations awaited him.

Nathan and Topaz led him down a set of steps and into another unusual space.

'The Library of Faces,' Topaz announced.

Jake gazed in awe down the length of the long gallery. On both the right-hand and far walls were shelves of vast leather-bound books. The entire long wall on the left was covered with portraits. Each one was a foot square and looked like an Old Master painting. Jake found the sight of a thousand faces staring out at him impressive enough, but the wall had another secret: after ten seconds a bell rang, there was a great creaking of machinery, and every single portrait turned on its axis to reveal another portrait behind it. After a similar interval the bell rang again, and the portraits turned once more to reveal a third set of faces. On the last revolution the portraits returned to their original setting.

'The faces on the wall,' Nathan told Jake, 'are people from history considered important or dangerous to the History Keepers' Secret Service at the present time. The books' – he took one down from its shelf and flicked through its stiff, crinkled pages – 'contain just about everyone else who's ever lived.'

'Ssssh!' The voice came from the shadows at the far end of the room. In the gloom Jake could make out a figure sitting at a sturdy desk behind a stack of books. She was in her fifties and wore a black dress from the baroque period, with huge puffy sleeves and a lace collar. Her hair was tucked neatly into her bonnet and she was reading with the aid of half-moon glasses.

'That's the head librarian, Lydia Wunderbar,' Nathan explained as quietly as he was able. 'She may look like a stickler for rules and regulations, but get her on a dance floor and it's a different story!'

The penultimate stop on the whirlwind tour of the castle was the costumiery. Of all the rooms Jake had seen since the evening before, this cavernous space was perhaps the most impressive.

The room was at least five storeys high, cylindrical in shape, with galleries on each floor. It was situated in one of the great round towers Jake had seen from the ship. Each floor contained an infinite number of clothes, hats and accessories, and was connected to the others by staircases and a somewhat rickety elevator set in the centre of the room.

'Here there are garments from every age in history' – Topaz was the tour guide now – 'from the nineteenth, twentieth and twenty-first centuries on the ground floor, and tracing back in time as you go up. Everything from ancient Egypt to Mayan Mexico to modern Moscow. And every single piece of clothing is entirely authentic. As you may guess, this is Nathan's favourite room. It has even more mirrors than his own suite.'

'What can I say? I'm attracted to beauty,' Nathan retorted.

Jake stared wide-eyed. On the next floor up he could see Oceane Noire being fitted with an extravagant dress. The assistants were fixing a pair of panniers to her skirt – hooped devices to extend the width on either side. Once they were in position, Oceane struck a pose and examined herself in the mirror. 'Mmm, I think we need to go wider, much wider!' Jake heard her say. The assistants patiently removed the offending articles.

'Good morning, Signor Gondolfino. My jacket fits like a dream,' Nathan was saying, his American tones ringing out. He was addressing a distinguished, beautifully dressed man who was emerging from amongst the rails of clothes, an eyeglass in his hand. 'Signor Luigi Gondolfino,' Nathan confided. 'Head of the costumiery. He's a genius.'

Gondolfino's old face creased into a smile as he

limped towards them. 'Miss St Honoré, is that you?' he asked in a quavering voice. 'I swear you become more exquisite with every passing month. How was London? How many hearts did you break?'

'All hearts in London still intact.'

'Nonsense, nonsense – you break some hearts. It's your duty.'

'How are you, Signor Gondolfino?' Nathan butted in. 'I just wanted to tell you that my new embroidered redingote jacket is perfection.'

The smile drained from Gondolfino's face as he turned to Nathan and examined him with his eye-glass. 'Oh, it's you,' he remarked. 'Are you returning something?' His refined European sensibilities clearly found Nathan's brashness too much to bear.

'No, I was merely . . . paying you a compli-ment . . . ?' For once Nathan sounded unsure of himself.

'This is Jake Djones,' Topaz interjected. 'Alan and Miriam's son. He has just joined us.'

Gondolfino held Jake's hand firmly in his frail fingers and whispered, 'It's a pleasure to meet you. Everything is going to be all right. Your parents are survivors.'

For some reason Gondolfino's comment made

Jake picture his parents in their kitchen at home. In his mind's eye they were no longer lost but waiting nervously for his return, clutching each other's hands as they stared at the empty garden path. Jake's trance was broken by Gondolfino's voice.

'Modern garments – so dull and charmless,' he murmured to himself, examining Jake's school blazer and trousers with his eyeglass. 'No offence, my boy,' he added with a smile.

'None taken,' said Jake, smiling back. He had always particularly disliked his school trousers; they were hot and itchy, whatever the weather.

'Later,' Gondolfino assured him, 'we'll find you something suitably elegant. You've the face for it. *Bel viso.*'

Suddenly bells started ringing from all around the Mount.

'Ten o'clock!' exclaimed Nathan. 'Time to go.'

The three of them said their goodbyes to Signor Gondolfino. As they left, Jake's eyes lingered on the rows of magnificent clothes. They retraced their steps, down staircases and along corridors, towards the stateroom. Jake's mind was now racing with many thoughts. Although he found it amazing that so many people knew his parents, and reassuring that they thought so highly of them, every new mention brought a fresh spasm of anxiety about them.

In truth, Jake was also struggling with the idea of the extraordinary organization for which his parents had covertly worked all this time. Certainly he had started to understand the details of how it operated, but one large, overriding question was not being answered.

'I don't wish to appear dense,' he said as they approached a set of double doors at the end of a corridor, 'but what exactly do you all *do*? I mean, the History Keepers' Secret Service . . . what is it *for*?'

Nathan stopped dead; Topaz too. They turned to Jake. Nathan was smiling proudly. 'That's a good question,' he said, nodding. Then he took a deep breath, squared his shoulders and announced in a dramatic whisper, 'We save history. We put our lives out on a limb to save history.'

'Yes, I think I understand that,' floundered Jake, none the wiser. 'But how? In what *way*?'

Topaz came to the rescue. 'You probably always imagined that history was something that was finished . . . done . . . in the past?'

'Isn't that the meaning of history?' asked Jake.

Nathan laughed and shook his head.

'*Pas du tout*,' answered Topaz in her softly accented tones. 'Not at all. History is *always* evolving. It's not a straight line, you see; it's a complex, ever-changing structure.'

Jake listened intently.

'And because history is never finished with,' she continued, 'there are some people who are always trying to change it. Change it for the worse. What if Tamerlane had succeeded in enslaving the whole of Asia, or Robespierre had turned Europe into a police state, or Adolf Hitler had won the last great war?' This was the first time Jake had heard Topaz speaking like this; her voice was solemn, hushed. 'As you may have learned at school, there have already been too many diabolical catastrophes. What we do is try and keep the rest of history as safe as we can.'

Jake found himself nodding passionately. He looked at Nathan: even *he* now looked sombre. Then his smile returned and he clapped Jake on the shoulder.

'Let's go in and see what all the fuss is about!' He pushed open the double doors and the three of them went inside.

9 CODE PURPLE

The stateroom was a large, bright room dominated by four gigantic windows that looked out across the sea. In the centre was a long conference table set with chairs. Norland was filling glasses with water and arranging them carefully at every place.

As they waited for the others to assemble, Topaz told Jake that the stateroom had been secretly designed and built in 1670 by the most celebrated French architect of the day, Louis Le Vau (who had also built the royal palace at Versailles), and how Magnesia Hypoteca, the elegant wife of the seventh commander of the Secret Service, once said of its famous windows, 'They are eyes from which one can see the world entire.'

Jake could see her point: the view was

spectacular. It felt as if he could see right across to the Atlantic and beyond.

One by one, the History Keepers filed into the room. Most of them had changed into new clothes. Charlie Chieverley was wearing breeches and a tail-coat, with a chequered scarf around his neck. It reminded Jake of the costume he'd once worn in a school production of *Oliver!* (Jake's trousers had famously caught fire during 'Consider Yourself'.) Jupitus Cole, a stickler for etiquette, had put on his most formal Victorian morning coat and tails. On his lapel there glinted a tiny golden badge: the History Keepers' familiar symbol. Truman Wylder had donned a silk smoking jacket, while Oceane Noire had been fitted with panniers so wide (extending nearly three feet on either side) that she had to come through the door sideways. There were another fifteen or so people, nearly all grown-ups, in outfits that spanned the centuries.

'At Point Zero, as we all live here covertly,' Topaz explained, 'people are allowed to wear clothes from their own times. *C'est jolie, n'est-ce pas?*' she added with a smile.

Jake was entranced as he watched them all soberly take their seats around the table. He was reminded once again of the collage of fascinating faces he had assembled on his bedroom wall at home. He had always thought that people who lived by their own quirky rules made the world a richer, more interesting place, and this was as strange and eccentric a group as he had ever seen.

'There's a free space here,' Nathan called up the table to Jake.

He sat down opposite Nathan, between Charlie and a distinguished man in a wide-brimmed hat and long lace cuffs like one of the three musketeers. Still dressed in his school uniform and wearing his school bag over his shoulder, Jake couldn't help feeling a little self-conscious.

'Nothing to be nervous about. They're all just pussycats really,' Nathan offered across the table in his version of a whisper.

'Sorry, have I missed anything? I didn't hear the bell. Was there a bell?' came a voice from the door. Aunt Rose hurried in, bangles jangling. In her Afghan coat and tie-dye dress, carpetbag over her shoulder, she looked even more out of place than Jake. 'Dear me, there's no room,' she muttered, surveying the table.

'Wait!' bellowed Nathan. He gallantly collected a

spare chair and inserted it between Jupitus and Oceane, much to the latter's annoyance. She stiffened as Rose sat down and started fishing around in her bag for an old tissue to blow her nose.

A moment later everyone turned as the greyhound, Olive, glided in; she trotted round the table, jumped up onto a raised bed beside the commander's chair and surveyed the company with her bright eyes. Now Galliana Goethe swept in and stood at the end of the table, holding onto the back of her seat.

'Good morning, everyone. Firstly, for those who haven't met, I would like to welcome the latest addition to our service, Jake Djones. Please, everyone, let's make the boy feel at home. He has a good deal on his plate already.'

There was a general welcoming murmur from the assembled company. Rose smiled at Jake proudly; Jupitus looked at him out of the corner of his eye.

'I will come straight to the point,' Galliana continued. 'As most of you now know, two of our agents are missing. For two weeks we had been following a thread of Meslith chatter. A "catastrophic" event was alluded to; the location

Venice, Italy, July 1506 was mentioned on a number of occasions.'

'And this chatter was fully credible?' asked Jupitus, not looking at anyone in particular.

Galliana paused and took a deep breath. 'I certainly felt that it was credible enough. I took the decision to send a small team to investigate. Alan and Miriam Djones were dispatched from here four days ago aboard the *Mystère*. It was to be a routine fact-finding mission, nothing more.'

Once again, Jake felt a stab of pain on hearing the details of his parents' deception. A few others around the table sensed his hurt and looked at him sympathetically.

'The day after they arrived in the city,' Galliana continued, 'we received this Meslith communiqué...' She put on her spectacles and read from a slip of parchment, '*Code Purple—*'

At this, a gasp went up, and startled glances were exchanged. Even the cool Jupitus Cole found himself choking on his water. Jake alone was unaware of the horrific import of the phrase.

Charlie whispered to Jake, 'Code Purple is the highest state of emergency, after orange and red.'

'*Code Purple* ...' Galliana repeated before

continuing with the message. '*Find the Summit of Superia. Extreme Danger. Repeat, Code Purple.*' She took off her glasses and passed the parchment to Jupitus. He scrutinized it without expression.

'That was received three days ago . . . We've heard nothing from them since.' Galliana paused, as once again Jake found himself the subject of everyone's sympathy. 'As a precaution,' she summed up, 'I have closed down the London bureau until we make contact with them.'

'You mean, in case they were forced to divulge secrets?' asked Jupitus mischievously.

'You know exactly what I mean,' the commander replied curtly. 'A Code Purple warning historically requires *all* European keepers to convene, and for associated bureaux to be temporarily neutralized. I am observing precedent, that's all.'

'Sir – may I?' asked Topaz, reaching for the communiqué. Jupitus passed it to her. '*Find the Summit of Superia?*' she repeated aloud, trying to decipher the puzzle. 'What is Superia? Is it a mountain?'

There were blank faces around the table.

'If it is, we have no idea where,' said Galliana.

'I, for one, have never heard of it,' announced

Jupitus haughtily, as if to say, *If I haven't heard of it, no one will have.*

'Is there anything to link this Code Purple, or the agents' disappearance, with Zeldt and the Black Army?' asked Nathan.

Jake happened to be looking at Topaz at that moment. It was almost imperceptible, but at the mention of the word 'Zeldt', her eyes flickered and she took a sharp breath.

'No tangible link, as yet. As you know, Zeldt has not been sighted for three years; that was in Holland in 1689, and he is still presumed dead.' Galliana carried on in a business-like tone, 'Having considered our position carefully—'

'But no doubt,' Jupitus interrupted her, 'agents Djones and Djones believed Zeldt was involved . . . Isn't that why they volunteered?'

'They did not volunteer. I offered them the commission' – Galliana fixed Jupitus with steely eyes – 'as I did on their previous missions. They remain two of our best agents.' She returned to her original subject. 'Having considered our position carefully, I have no option but to send a further team to Venice to investigate. They will be leaving this afternoon.'

Topaz was the first to put her hand up. 'Commander, I request permission to be part of that team.'

Nathan stood and tossed his mane of auburn hair. 'I naturally assume that I will be selected . . .'

'You will both be assigned, along with Charlie Chieverley,' Galliana announced. 'Topaz, you are group leader.'

Topaz felt a thrill of excitement. 'Thank you, Commander. I will not let you down.'

Nathan's jaw dropped open. 'You cannot be serious,' he drawled under his breath. He put his hand up. 'Commander, is that role in any way negotiable? I am, after all, more senior than Topaz, both in age—'

'All of two months,' Topaz pointed out.

'– and experience. I hardly need to mention the recent success of my Turkish mission.'

Galliana gave Nathan her most withering look. 'No, not negotiable.' She returned her attention to the rest of the table. 'Are there any questions?'

Although his heart was pounding under his school blazer, Jake found himself putting his hand up. All eyes turned to him.

'I – I would also like to volunteer for the mission,'

he said in a voice so quiet and uncertain that everyone struggled to hear.

Since he had been a young child, Jake had always worried about his parents, but in the last three years, since his brother's disappearance, his desire – his *need* – to help had increased a hundred-fold.

'Stand up!' bellowed Truman Wylder, waving his cane. 'Can't hear you at the back here.'

Jake stood up. He looked around at the serious faces. They in turn observed him coolly: a boy in his school uniform, with bright eyes and glowing cheeks. Jake took a deep breath and, knowing he had to show them that he was not a child, he spoke in the deepest tone he could muster. 'I said, I would also like to volunteer for the mission.'

A few people murmured in embarrassment. Oceane let out a tight little laugh – and was greeted immediately by a glare from Rose.

Galliana smiled at Jake. 'It is very brave of you to offer, Jake, but—'

'Seeing as it is my mum and dad who are missing, I really feel that I *should* be included. And I – I believe I could contribute to the endeavour . . .' He tried desperately to remember some lines from his favourite adventure films.

There were more murmurings. Jupitus was flabbergasted by Jake's boldness. But Galliana was unruffled. She continued in her calm, measured tones, 'Thank you, Jake. We appreciate your courage and concern, but the journey alone is exceedingly hazardous. We need to keep you safe here with us.'

Jake felt his cheeks flush with embarrassment as he reluctantly sat down again.

'Any further questions?' Galliana asked.

'I have one,' said Jupitus, taking another sip of water. 'Well, it is more of an observation than a question. Would you not agree that this incident clearly demonstrates that it is time to revoke Alan and Miriam Djones's licences to operate in the field? They may once have had a reputation, but at their age, and after a ten-year absence, they can hardly be considered "great" any more. Even as diamonds, their valour must have thinned and coalesced by now.'

Both Jake and Rose felt a surge of anger, but it was the latter who spoke.

'How dare you!' she exclaimed. 'My brother risked his life for this service. And once, you have perhaps conveniently forgotten, he risked it to save *you*! God only knows why.'

Jupitus stiffened, although he went on calmly, 'I'm just being practical. *And* voicing the thoughts of many others around the table. One can always rely on Rosalind Djones to turn it into a drama,' he added with barely concealed contempt.

'All right, that's enough from both of you,' Galliana interrupted. 'Alan and Miriam Djones have lost none of their valour – they were the only agents I considered for the mission. And, Jupitus, as I am sure I don't need to remind you, you are the same age as Alan.'

Jupitus pursed his lips in annoyance.

'*Je peux dire quelque chose?* May I say something?' Oceane had a languid, bejewelled hand in the air. Nearly everyone around the table braced themselves for some self-centred request. They were not disappointed.

'As everyone knows, there is to be a ball in celebration of *mon anniversaire* this week – my birthday. Will the Code Purple situation affect this? It's been six exhausting months in preparation. I even had to endure London on a jewellery-buying expedition.'

There were embarrassed murmurs, and Rose shook her head in disbelief, but Galliana did not react.

'In actual fact,' she said, 'the party will continue as planned. As we're all aware, we must open up the Mount occasionally for local inspection in order not to arouse suspicion.'

Oceane let out a squeal of delight. '*Parfait, parfait!*' she exclaimed, clapping her hands.

'This meeting is adjourned,' concluded Galliana. 'The selected team will set sail at two p.m. precisely. You will travel to Venice in 1506 and liaise with Paolo Cozzo, our man in sixteenth-century Italy, at the Quay Ognissanti. That will be all.'

There was a general hubbub as everyone stood up and started making their way out of the room.

'Jake, may I have a word with you?' Galliana asked softly. 'And you three' – she nodded at Topaz, Nathan and Charlie – 'can you wait over there? I wish to speak with you afterwards.'

They nodded obediently. 'Group leader! I suppose we'll never hear the end of it,' Nathan muttered as they waited to one side.

Galliana led Jake over to one of the great windows. 'Bearing up all right?'

Jake nodded bravely.

'There is something I must share with you in private,' she went on. 'I am telling you because I do not want you to think too badly of your parents. As you now know, they retired from the service after you were born. But there was a compelling reason why they chose to come back to us three years ago . . .' Galliana hesitated before continuing. 'They hoped they might finally understand what happened to your brother, Philip, and put his memory to rest.'

Jake gasped in shock. 'What do you mean? He died in a climbing accident.'

Galliana put a comforting hand on his shoulder. 'At the time of his disappearance he was working for us. Your parents tried to stop him. But we cannot deny our destiny. The pull is too strong.'

Jake felt faint; he gripped the window ledge tightly. 'So what happened?' he asked.

'Philip was sent to Vienna, 1689, to track down one of our oldest and greatest foes, Prince Xander Zeldt,' Galliana replied. 'He had uncovered a plot that involved the assassination of three European heads of state. No one knows what happened next – the plot never materialized and Zeldt was never heard of again. Unfortunately, neither was your brother. We think he lost his life in the course of duty, but no body was ever found:

history, as you can imagine, is a rather gigantic place to be lost in.'

There was a long pause as Jake tried to come to terms with this piece of news.

'So – so what are you saying exactly?' he stammered, trembling so much he could hardly get the words out. 'That Philip might be alive somewhere?'

'It's only a remote possibility,' Galliana told him.

It was too much for Jake; his lips trembled, his breath shook, and he couldn't prevent the hot tears from springing to his eyes. As soon as the three young agents noticed his plight, they hurried over.

Topaz put her arm round him. 'It's all right,' she said. 'It's going to be all right.'

Jake nodded. 'I'm fine, I'm fine,' he repeated through his sobs. 'I don't know why I'm crying – I'm not a baby any more . . .' He quickly wiped away the tears.

'You don't need to be grown up with us,' Topaz told him. 'We understand why you're upset.'

Charlie turned to Nathan and whispered, 'I don't have a handkerchief – do you?'

With only a hint of reluctance, the latter produced a beautifully embroidered silk square from his pocket. 'It's Chinese silk,' he explained as he passed it to Jake. As Jake blew his nose on it once, twice and a third time, Nathan flinched.

'Thank you,' said Jake, passing it back.

'Please, it's yours,' Nathan insisted. 'Something to remember me by.'

When Jake had finally got himself under control, Galliana spoke again.

'I'm sorry if I upset you by telling you this. The fact is, none of us know what happened. Maybe we never will. But your parents were drawn back to the service in the hope that one day they might discover the truth. Do you understand?'

Jake nodded. Galliana put a hand on his head. 'Now, you must be exhausted. Norland will show you to your room.' She led him to the door, where the smiling butler was waiting.

Jake was about to leave, but he paused in the doorway. 'This Code Purple . . . That's really bad, is it?' he asked.

Galliana was not one to sugar the pill: 'I'm afraid it refers to a threat of potentially cataclysmic proportions. I have known only one in my lifetime, and that did not end well.'

'And this prince . . . Zeldt, or whoever he is – what exactly did he do?'

Galliana took a deep breath and started to explain. 'It's a long story. For the moment, suffice it to say that once there were only *good* keepers. Long ago, Zeldt's family worked for this organization, but now they are the enemy.' She paused. 'If you choose to join us – and I can't really recommend it: you have to give it careful thought – you would learn all these things in good time.'

Jake nodded, and Galliana continued, 'One last thing, Jake: once it has happened, we must never try to *change* the past. We cannot, and do not, bring people back from the dead, or stop wars or undo catastrophes *once they have existed*. We cannot and should not stop the Great Fire of London or the sinking of the *Titanic*, no matter how we feel about those events.' Now her tone was sombre. 'History is sacred. The past may be littered with horrors, but remember, Jake, that those horrors could be a million times worse. Zeldt and his like desire that darker and infinitely crueller world; they wish to destroy our history.' Now her eyes shone with fire. 'That is why we fight them: to prevent *new* outrages, to *protect* what has gone before in our fragile past – that is why the History Keepers exist.'

She waited for Jake to soak up this information. 'Now, you go and have a rest.'

Jake nodded to the others.

'Make sure you come and see us off,' said Topaz with a smile.

Jake nodded again, turned and followed Norland out of the room.

Galliana stared after them for a moment, then closed the door carefully and came back to the other three, who were waiting by the window.

'Commander?' Topaz asked. 'What is it you wish to talk to us about?'

Galliana took a deep breath. 'Regarding your mission, I have one more important instruction. It mostly concerns you, Topaz, but all of you must understand it . . .'

10 DESTINATION: 1506

Norland led Jake up into one of the towers.

'As you might have noticed, there's an awful lot of steps on this little island,' he said cheerfully, pulling a face. 'It certainly keeps us older ones in shape.'

'You live here most of the time, do you?' asked Jake politely.

'Between here and London. Mr Cole likes me to be at hand. Make sure his head's screwed on in the morning.' Norland hooted with laughter and his ruddy cheeks went rosier still. Jake wasn't sure if it was particularly funny, but he smiled all the same.

'And do you go on missions – to other parts of history?'

'Oh no, not me, sir. I had a few problems with my valour when I was younger, you see . . . The shapes in my eyes were all at sixes and sevens. But don't get me wrong, I'm happy where I am. It's wonderful to be part of the History Keepers, in any shape or form.'

Jake remembered something from his trip across the Channel. 'Didn't you say you went to Austria once? You heard Mozart playing the piano . . .'

'Good gracious, you have got a good memory, sir. You're quite right, of course, but that turned out to be my one and only mission as a secret agent. It was simply magical, though,' he added, his eyes moistening at the recollection. 'All the pomp and circumstance of the Habsburg court; all the dances and balls and important people in their powdered wigs . . .' Norland imitated them with a flourish, then wiped the fond tears from his eyes.

'Anyway, here we are,' he announced as they arrived at an oak door. 'Always your mum and dad's favourite room. They loved the light.' He led Jake into a small, round room that occupied the top of one of the castle turrets. 'You'll be down, I expect, to see the others off. In the meantime, make yourself at home.'

Norland turned to leave, but paused in the

doorway. 'By the way, I'm sorry about the kidnapping in Greenwich. No harm was meant.'

'That's all right.' Jake smiled at him. 'It certainly wasn't my usual Friday afternoon.'

The butler was still looking slightly anxious. 'You forgive me then, do you? I was just following orders, you see, sir.'

'Of course – I haven't given it a moment's thought,' said Jake.

'Really? You're an absolute gent!' Norland exclaimed. 'I can see we're going to get on just fine.' He winked, then closed the door and made his way back down the steps.

Jake dropped his bag and looked around the room. There was just enough space for a four-poster bed, made up with new sheets and plump pillows, and an ancient painted cupboard.

He absent-mindedly bounced on the bed, then lay back and looked at the whitewashed ceiling. Galliana had suggested he should rest, but his mind was too full. He heard noises from outside: Nathan bellowing commands. Jake got up again, opened the window and looked out. The quayside was directly below his bedroom. The *Escape* was no longer there – presumably it had been taken into the secret harbour; but in its place was another, smaller vessel: the *Campana*, one of the ships that Topaz had pointed out. It was a distinctive yellow ochre colour, with a steep prow and square sails. Nathan, his voice sounding more American when giving orders, was overseeing a group of sailors as they loaded it up.

Jake left the window open and looked in the cupboard. The blood drained from his face. He had been expecting to find it empty, but it contained an item he recognized immediately: a red suitcase.

It was the suitcase his parents had brought to the bathroom shop when he last saw them. Jake seized it, put it on the bed and unzipped it, instantly recognizing his parents' clothes. As he rifled through the contents, hurriedly packed for a trip to a bathroom convention in Birmingham, he was once again engulfed in panic. He opened the front pocket of the case and received another appalling shock: inside were his parents' passports.

Jake took them out and opened them. The familiar pictures of his mum and dad posing self-consciously in the photo booth at Greenwich station stared back at him. He remembered the day perfectly. They had been laughing so much it had taken five attempts. A stern ticking-off from a sour-faced commuter had only made matters worse.

As Jake looked from one picture to the other, it hit him more acutely than ever before . . .

His parents were truly lost.

Not just lost in Europe somewhere, but lost in history. Of course, Jake knew they wouldn't need their passports in sixteenth-century Italy, but the fact that the documents were here in his hand emphasized their plight: what if they were imprisoned? What if they had been separated? What if they were already . . . ? Jake ran over to the window, desperate for air. Down below, the sailors were still loading up the *Campana*, although Nathan was no longer to be seen.

Jake suddenly yearned to sail on that ship – to join the others on their expedition and help to find his parents.

I'll go back and talk to Galliana, he told himself. *She'll understand how important this is. I've already lost my brother – how can they expect me to lose my parents as well?*

He shook his head as he remembered the embarrassed looks when he had suggested he should go too. He understood those looks: he knew absolutely nothing about the History Keepers and what they did. And yet he longed to go – perhaps even his brother might still be alive.

Then a notion took shape in Jake's head: 'I could stow away,' he whispered to himself. 'I just have to hide until we're far out to sea. They won't waste time bringing me back. I could persuade them to give me atomium and take me along.'

Jake hated the idea of tricking people, but the alternative was worse. He hurriedly put his parents' passports in the inside pocket of his blazer. At the doorway he stopped to pick up his school bag. He put it on the bed and took out one of his books: the volume of history that Jupitus had sneered at. Jake flicked through its pages, its illustrations of moments in history. He had always wondered what it would be like to live in the world of those illustra-tions. He threw the book down and ran, leaving his bag on the bed.

He navigated his way down the labyrinth of corridors and staircases, occasionally doubling back on himself when he went wrong, until at last he came to the armoury. He hurried across the room and down the main staircase. Once again, the inscrutable eyes of Sejanus Poppoloe, the History Keepers' long-dead founder, watched him as he passed. He opened the huge studded doors and stepped out onto the quayside.

Luckily, there was not a soul in sight: the *Campana* was now deserted. His heart beat at a rapid speed as he tiptoed towards it. He was about to step onto the gangplank when he heard a booming voice from above.

'Settling in all right?' Nathan asked as he emerged on deck, doing up the buttons of his tunic.

Jake did a double take: Nathan was now dressed in an entirely different outfit. He wore a tightly fitting jacket of dark navy suede, matching breeches and a pair of beautifully soft, worn boots. A glinting sword hung at his hip and a scarf was tied pirate-like around his head.

'Settling in fine,' Jake replied. 'That's what you're wearing for the voyage?'

'Italian fashion of the early 1500s is a very complicated animal' – Nathan fitted a tiny diamond stud into his ear – 'but I think I've hit the right balance, wouldn't you say?'

'Very authentic,' Jake agreed – though he hadn't the faintest idea what balance Nathan was talking about. 'And this is the ship you're taking to Venice?' he asked quickly to prevent the other boy from asking what he was doing here.

'She may not look like much, but this one's a survivor.' Nathan slapped the mast heartily. 'Rumour has it that Christopher Columbus taught himself how to sail on this very vessel.' He leaped down onto the quay. 'I have to collect the rest of my wardrobe. The secret of always looking great is simple: have options!' And he strode back into the castle.

Once he was out of sight, Jake took a deep breath and, pretending he was merely inspecting the ship, ascended the gangplank and stepped down onto the deck. In case anyone was watching, he made a show of examining the sails, the mast and the steering wheel, before taking one last furtive look around and disappearing down the steep, crooked staircase that led below.

Once out of sight, he immediately started searching for a hiding place. There was a tiny galley; the dining area had two doors – one leading to a neat cabin in the bows, where Topaz's single suitcase had been installed; the other to a messy cabin in the stern, containing a bunk bed and a huge mountain of Nathan's trunks.

Up on deck Jake heard a thud – more luggage

was being loaded; then Nathan's voice: 'That's the last of it. Leave it all in the cabin. I'll unpack it myself. Careful – that tunic belonged to Charlemagne!' The voice receded again. A moment later there was the clatter of footsteps down the stairs, then a cry as one of the sailors dropped a piece of luggage, followed by a mutter: 'Lucky his majesty wasn't here to see that.'

Jake quickly hid behind the door as they lugged the last of Nathan's heavy cases into the cabin.

'What does he need all this for?' one of them asked. 'He's all of twelve.'

They went back upstairs and Jake heard them disembark.

'This is ridiculous, I can't do it,' he said out loud as he emerged from Nathan's cabin. He went back up the stairs, then stopped, turned and came down again. He took his parents' passports out of his pocket and studied their pictures.

'What if they don't care enough about saving my family . . . ?' he said to himself – and once again his mind was made up. Just then, he noticed the hatch set into the floor. He opened it and saw a ladder leading down into the dark hull of the ship.

Like the *Escape*, this one had been converted to

steam: an engine resembling a large Aga range was discernible in the gloom. Amongst the piles of wood and crates of food there were shadowy places to hide, and Jake carefully descended the ladder and closed the hatch behind him. He felt his way through the blackness to the bow and settled down amongst a pile of boxes.

He realized he was still wearing his 'charmless' school uniform, and couldn't help feeling a twinge of regret at missing his appointment with Signor Gondolfino. He longed more than ever to belong to this more magical and elegant time.

Within a few minutes Jake heard the muffled voices of people assembling on the quay. Then the ship rocked as the crew climbed aboard. Nathan was giving some kind of impromptu speech, using phrases like 'for glory' and 'for the good of mankind'. Then Topaz issued the order to set sail, a cry went up and the ship lurched as she was untied from her mooring.

Jake was suddenly gripped with panic: he *must* make his presence known.

But he didn't move.

Even though it was pitch-black, he closed his eyes and thought of his parents, trapped in a dungeon, starving, awaiting their torturer. He thought of his brother, Philip – how he would ruffle Jake's hair when he was feeling down. On a wet camping holiday in the New Forest, Philip had once stayed up all night to protect Jake from the killer his little brother imagined lurking in the woods. Older brothers weren't usually so kind, but Philip wasn't like anyone else's older brother.

As the ship moved away from the pier, Jake felt his stomach turn over, and he was sure he heard his aunt say, 'Where on earth is Jake? I suppose he must have dropped off . . .'

An hour later Jake was feeling very cramped and more than a little seasick. In the dining area upstairs he could hear the muffled voices of Nathan, Topaz and Charlie Chieverley. Someone was cooking, and tempting smells were wafting down, making Jake's stomach rumble.

He had pins and needles down one leg, so he carefully shifted to a more comfortable position. When he saw the two tiny yellow eyes staring at him from the blackness, he shrieked out loud, shot back and knocked over a pile of boxes. Panting with fear, he gazed around, scanning the darkness. The eyes flashed again, and a rat scurried across the space into the shadows.

'Rats! I hate rats!' he found himself cursing.

Jake realized that the voices had stopped. A moment later the hatch creaked open, and in a flash Nathan was at the foot of the ladder, his drawn sword in front of him.

'Identify yourself or die!' he commanded in a deep, menacing voice.

Jake picked himself up and put his hands in the air.

'What the hell were you thinking?' Nathan demanded, banging his fist on the table.

Jake was standing uneasily in the dining area, facing three sets of unsmiling eyes (four, counting Mr Drake's). Like Nathan, Topaz and Charlie had changed into sixteenth-century clothes. Topaz looked beautiful in a creamy silk gown with a square neck and trumpet-shaped sleeves. Charlie, who managed to appear like a young scientist whatever he put on, wore a doublet and hose in small red check, along with a felt cap that had a feather in it.

'Do you think this is some kind of game?' Nathan continued. 'We are on a mission. There are lives at stake. Not just lives – civilizations!' he added dramatically.

'I was just—'

'You were just *what*?'

This was a very different Nathan to the playful joker Jake had met on his arrival.

'I just wanted to find my parents.'

'It's not your job. We have to take him back,' Nathan decided emphatically.

'*Ce n'est pas possible*. We're just twenty leagues from the horizon point.' Topaz gestured towards the Constantor hanging over the dining table. 'We'll lose a day.'

'Can't be helped. He'll jeopardize everything. Turn her round, Charlie.'

'Topaz is right. We'll lose a whole day,' Charlie said before slipping back to the stove, where he had three separate pans on the go. With a professional flick, he tossed some large field mushrooms.

Again Nathan struck the table in annoyance. 'Well, he can't travel the distance. A first-timer? This isn't a pleasant stroll to 1805. It's three hundred and fourteen years. If he detonates, we're all doomed.'

Jake looked up at Nathan in horror. Did he really just hear the word 'detonate'?

'Besides which – look at him,' Nathan continued. 'He's wearing school uniform. Think he might stick out a little.'

'Oh, really. You have enough clothes and accessories for an army in your cabin,' Topaz pointed out.

But Nathan was resolute. 'We put him out on the rowing boat – he finds his own way back.'

'Don't be absurd!' said Topaz. 'How will he make it alone?'

'Not our problem.'

'He's a diamond, Nathan. Grade one, according to Jupitus Cole. He'll survive. Anyway, as group leader, it's my decision.' Topaz turned to Jake. 'You can stay. But when we arrive in Venice, you remain in the background. Understand?'

Jake nodded. He looked at them all seriously. 'I'm sorry I came on board. I made a mistake. But now I promise to do anything I can to help.'

Topaz's face softened a little.

Nathan shrugged and slumped back in his seat. 'Grade one, huh?' he muttered to himself. 'Who would have thought . . . ?'

'What exactly does it mean . . . to "detonate"?' Jake wondered.

'If your body isn't prepared for high levels of atomium – which can take some practice,' said Charlie, turning away from the stove, 'you can stall in the time flux: your atoms split into millions of particles, making you explode like a hydrogen bomb, and taking us all down with you.' He took a dish out of the oven and tested its contents. 'This courgette soufflé is perfection. I may have surpassed myself.'

Though Jake now had no appetite, the dinner that Charlie had 'rustled up' would have won him an award in any top London restaurant. It included cherry tomato tartine, stuffed miniature peppers with marinated mushrooms à la Grecque and framboise torte with chantilly. Charlie, it transpired, had learned to cook in Napoleon's kitchen in Paris, but the experience had left him a firm vegetarian.

After the plates had been cleared away, Topaz placed a veneered box on the table. There was utter silence. She opened it and took out a vial of atomium and a Horizon Cup. For the last half-hour Jake had been imagining his detonation. He wondered how gorily explosive it would be.

The atomium was once again repulsive – like the liquid that seeps from old batteries, Jake imagined –

and its effect was quicker and more alarming than the first time. The moment Jake took it, he nodded unsteadily and passed out. He was woken up by Charlie jabbing a finger into his chest.

'Wake up. You mustn't sleep. Wake up.'

Jake tried to focus on the jumble of faces above him. He was slumped over the dining table.

'Wake up! It's dangerous to sleep.'

'Are we there? Venice?' Jake asked, drifting off again.

Nathan nodded at Charlie, who filled a glass with cold water and tossed it into Jake's face. He woke with a sharp intake of breath.

'I don't want to explode.'

After two minutes he collapsed again. It carried on like this for half an hour – until Topaz shouted down from the deck, 'Five minutes to horizon!'

Jake's state suddenly altered completely. A jolt of electricity threw him up out of his seat. 'We're flying!' he shouted – and started dancing around the cabin in what looked like an Irish jig.

Nathan was embarrassed, and Mr Drake squawked excitedly.

'I need to speak to Topaz!' Jake announced as he swept up the stairs onto the deck.

She gasped as he took her in his arms like some romantic movie hero, then laughed in confusion. Charlie appeared on deck, also shaking his head in amused bewilderment. Jake was about to kiss Topaz when the Constantor clicked into alignment and he seemed to shoot into the air like a bullet.

His alter ego – or whatever it was – hurtled to the edge of Earth's atmosphere where the blue turns to dark space. From here, Jake could see the ocean curving, the continent of Europe; France, Spain, the boot of Italy. Britain lay under a cloud of mist, just like the map on TV weather forecasts. He spun round, hurtling back towards the sea, and saw himself on the deck of the *Campana*, holding onto Topaz. Then he collapsed on the wooden boards, shaking and laughing.

Charlie looked at his wristwatch, tapped it with his fingers and smiled. 'We made it: 1506, July the fifteenth.'

Jake noticed a number of things at once. It was now dark and very hot; the ocean was as flat as a pancake and the sky shimmered with millions of stars. But his head throbbed as never before in his life and he felt he would rather die than look Topaz in the eye. He took off his blazer and carefully sat down facing the stern and the retreating sea.

It was the dead of night and everyone was fast asleep on the Mont St Michel. The occasional flickering taper was all that moved in the silent corridors and staircases. Outside, amongst the dark granite towers and turrets, the seabirds were quiet in their nests.

Then a figure in a dark blue cloak, carrying a candle, emerged from the gloom of an archway and tiptoed along the passage to the door of the communications room. The form – impossible to tell whether it was a man or a woman – stopped, looked around and, slowly and carefully, opened the creaking door and slipped inside.

The deserted room was bathed in ghostly moonlight. At its centre stood the glass cabinet containing the Meslith nucleus. Four further machines could be seen on desks along one side of the space. The figure approached the first of these, sat down and started typing, making the electric rod fizz with a brilliant light that reflected like shooting stars around the room. The intruder whispered the words of the message as they appeared:

'*Agents arriving July 15th, Quay Ognissanti, Venice . . .*'

Having completed the task, the figure stood, replaced the chair under the desk, dusted down the keys of the Meslith machine with a handkerchief and stealthily left the room.

As the person crept back along the passage and through the archway, the message started on its journey across space and time . . .

The flickering signal that had lit up the crystalline rod now jumped to the lightning conductor that jutted out from the steeple at the apex of the Mount. Here it flashed again, with greater intensity, lighting up the dark clouds, then launched itself into the time flux.

It made its journey through the dark matter of a trillion atoms, finding its route across the centuries.

The code, almost perfectly intact, arrived, still flickering, at a Meslith machine that sat on an old table in a high-ceilinged room. In front of the table a window opened out onto the rooftops of a dark and ancient Venice. A sleeping figure was woken by the glinting light, which picked out a great scar running down the side of his gleaming shaven head. He sat up, then dragged his bulky frame off his straw mattress and called out. Two guards, both clad in black breastplates and crimson cloaks, came into the room. The man with the scar pointed over to the desk. The light from the Meslith machine lit up their faces.

They smiled.

11 THE JEWEL OF THE ADRIATIC

The *Campana* sailed through the hot night, gliding effortlessly across the flat ocean. Topaz was at the helm, guiding its progress.

Charlie came on deck and spotted Jake sitting in the shadows of the rigging. He grinned at him. 'Feeling better now?'

Jake nodded sheepishly. 'How long will it take to get to Venice?'

'From Point Zero, usually four days, but we hurdled. That's why the atomium was so strong.'

'It certainly was,' Jake muttered, ashamed. 'What do you mean "hurdled"?'

'We jumped horizon points. Saved ourselves nearly three days. I think his highness may be ready for your fitting.'

Jake accompanied Charlie down the stairs. He

tried his best to look only at his feet, but he was unable to resist a furtive glance at Topaz. She stood at the wheel, scanning the horizon with her large indigo eyes, the great panorama of stars shimmering around her.

Ten minutes later, Nathan, Charlie and Jake were all squeezed into the boys' cabin. Jake was trying on one of Nathan's outfits. He'd already found a pair of breeches, some stockings and a voluminous white shirt gathered at the neck. Charlie helped him into a velvet doublet.

'Please be gentle,' Nathan begged. 'That piece is priceless. The velvet is finest Sienese and the fleur-de-lys were hand-embroidered in Florence with real gold thread.'

'The sleeves are meant to be like that, are they?' asked Jake, referring to the gaping holes down their length.

'They're slashed. That's the fashion,' Nathan announced in a voice as dry as dust.

'Shoes?' asked Charlie.

'These are a little outdated for 1506 – especially for Italy – but they'll have to do. I'm short on shoes,' Nathan lied as he presented Jake with a pair of boots.

Jake put them on and the other two stood back to inspect him. Inside, Jake may have felt awkward, but he looked the part. He seemed to stand up straighter.

'Do I get a sword?' he asked hopefully. He had noticed Nathan's extravagant rapier of ornate dark silver; Charlie and Topaz were also armed.

'I don't really see the need,' Nathan replied curtly. 'You'll be seeing no active duty.'

'But still, he'll need one,' announced Charlie as he tucked into his third bowl of framboise torte. 'In case of emergencies.'

Nathan grunted in irritation. 'I'll be left with nothing at this rate.'

He threw open one of his trunks. There were at least twelve swords carefully arranged in the velvet casing. Jake's eyes lit up at the sight of them. His hand instinctively reached out for the most impressive: a double-bladed duelling sword, the hilt crafted in the shape of a dragon.

'No can do,' said Nathan, removing Jake's hand. 'Reserved for special occasions only.' Instead, he selected the most basic, least interesting of the weapons. 'Ever handled a sword before?' he asked, passing it over carefully.

'Of course. Fencing club at school. I was commended,' Jake told him, lying shamelessly. He tried to show off with a few flamboyant thrusts, but the sword flew out of his hand and landed with a clatter on top of Charlie's framboise torte.

Charlie did not flinch, just carefully removed it from his pudding, passed it to Nathan and carried on eating. Nathan, unimpressed by the display, put the sword in its scabbard and fastened it around Jake's waist.

'That's where it stays. It's purely decoration, do you understand?'

'What are these?' asked Jake excitedly. Beside Nathan's trunk lay a large leather wallet containing a collection of fake beards and moustaches.

It was Charlie's turn to remove Jake's hand.

'*Ne touche pas!*' Nathan warned in a terrible French accent. 'Those rats' tails are Charlie's pride and joy. Personally I go *au naturel* – disguise myself purely with my facial expression.' Nathan demonstrated by narrowing his eye and furrowing his brow.

Charlie tutted and snatched up his prized collection. 'You know as well as I do, Nathan, that they've saved your skin on more than one occasion.'

He closed the wallet and fastened it to his belt.

Jake couldn't help but smile. He loved the way Charlie, though only fourteen, behaved like a mad old professor.

'Well, you'd better have a look at yourself.' Charlie held up the mirror.

Jake did a double-take. There was a bold adventurer staring back at him.

The *Campana* sailed on through the morning, across the endless calm of the Mediterranean. The hot sun rose high in sky, reaching its zenith before starting its slow summer descent.

Jake took in deep breaths of fresh sea air as he surveyed the horizon. He looked down at his sword and, checking that he couldn't be seen, surreptitiously unsheathed it.

'Stand back, villain!' he exclaimed, holding up the weapon to an invisible foe. 'It is I, Jake Djones of Greenwich—' He stopped – it didn't have quite the right ring to it. 'It is I, Jake Djones, special agent of the History Keepers' Secret Service, defender of good, nemesis of all evil. You have breathed your last—'

Jake stopped again, aware that eyes were upon

him. Charlie and Mr Drake were peering round the mast, watching the spectacle. He reddened in embarrassment and quickly sheathed his sword again.

At three in the afternoon, Topaz sighted their destination. Far in the distance, shimmering like gold in the afternoon heat, they could see the distinctive silhouette of Venice.

As they drew closer, the air started to fill with a cacophony of sounds. The quay was teeming with activity, with vessels of all sizes and types arriving or setting sail, unloading or stocking up. Jake had never seen so many ships in one place – a shimmering forest of rigging, masts, banners and flags, with sailors, merchants and traders all shouting for attention.

'The city of Venice, the Jewel of the Adriatic,' said Charlie, as if giving a guided tour. 'Originally founded in the sixth century, Venice inhabits a crucial position between Europe and Asia. And although recent Spanish discoveries in the New World have gone some way to diminish Venetian power, its merchants and bankers still dominate world trade. The candy-coloured building there,' he said, pointing at a glittering pink edifice, 'is the palace of the doge. The watch tower next to it is the Campanile, though of course it is yet to reach its full splendour.'

As their ship was moored between a small fishing boat and a vast Persian galleon, Jake gazed in wonder at the extraordinary sights that greeted him. He knew that he would never forget that moment: the sight of all those people teeming on the shore, all belonging to a different era from his own. It was as if one of the old paintings he loved so much had actually come to life.

There were rich merchants in doublet and hose, soldiers in armour, there were men in turbans and long robes and poor women in rags. There were dogs everywhere. An elegant lurcher belonging to an aristocratic lady was playing with the rough-haired terrier of a street seller. There were cats watching from wall tops or circling the people in search of fish heads. There were goats and horses and parrots in cages. (Mr Drake studied these with great interest and a hint of sympathy.) Jake was bombarded with smells – spices, crates of fresh herbs, fish and fried meats.

As he watched the scene, his heart thumped with

excitement inside his new adventurer's clothes. Suddenly he caught sight of a tall figure wearing a black breastplate and a crimson cloak and hood. The man stood perfectly still as the crowd surged around him. Although his face was not visible, Jake had an uncomfortable sense that he was staring directly at the *Campana*.

He turned to Charlie. 'Do you see that man there? I think he's looking at us.'

Charlie followed his gaze, but the man was no longer to be seen. Jake scanned the crowd for the crimson cloak, but he could not find it.

His eyes lit instead upon a skinny boy coming along the quay, surreptitiously reading the names of the ships as he passed them. He was red-cheeked, gawky and kept bumping into people and apologizing. When he saw the *Campana*, the boy stopped and checked the name against some writing on the parchment he held in his hand. He then looked at Charlie and, half reading his notes, announced stiffly, 'Welcome to Venice – what cargo do you carry?'

Jake guessed that this was some kind of code, as Charlie answered in the same deliberate way, 'We carry tamarind from the east.'

At this, the boy relaxed, grinned and waved at everyone on the ship. '*Buon giorno* – Paolo Cozzo, Italian liaison, sixteenth century.'

Nathan sprang down onto the quayside beside him. He was a good foot taller than the Italian boy. 'Why don't you use a loudspeaker next time, so everyone can hear?'

It took Paolo a moment to register that Nathan was being sarcastic. He grinned and nodded, then wiped the sweat off his brow. Charlie jumped ashore, followed by Topaz.

'*Bonjour* – Agent Topaz St Honoré,' she introduced herself. 'Agent Chieverley – and Jake Djones.' She turned to Jake, who had remained on the ship.

'He's just observing,' drawled Nathan.

Paolo blushed bright red at the sight of Topaz. 'Actually, Miss St Honoré, I believe we have already m-m-met?' he stuttered. 'In Siena, the spring of 1708? I was with my parents? I made you some lemonade?' He made every statement sound like a question.

'I do remember,' said Topaz, her face lighting up. 'It was the best lemonade I've ever had. You were going to give me the recipe.'

Paolo giggled and turned redder still.

'Where do Point Zero find these jokers?' Nathan rolled his eyes and muttered under his breath before asking Paolo wearily, 'So, are you based in Venice?'

'In Rome, actually . . . home is . . . Rome,' Paolo stammered. 'Although my aunt lives here. I came to meet the last lot of agents, the ones who disappeared.'

Topaz gave Jake a sympathetic look, embarrassed by Paolo's tactlessness.

'My brief,' Paolo went on, 'is to take you to the Venetian bureau and help you generally with all matters Italian.'

'The Venetian bureau then – let's go!' Nathan strode off along the quayside.

No one else moved.

'Actually it's this way,' Paolo pointed out nervously.

Topaz couldn't mask a sly grin as Nathan turned round sharply.

'Do I stay here on my own, or can I . . .?' asked Jake hopefully.

'Come with us for now,' Topaz said, relenting, 'but when work starts, you return to the ship. Understood?'

In a flash, Jake had leaped ashore.

* * *

Paolo led them along the waterfront through the bustling afternoon crowd.

'Crazy here during rush hour, isn't it?' said Nathan, as he lifted his hat to a pretty flower seller. 'Do we have time for a hot chocolate? If memory serves, Florian's in St Mark's Square do the best hot chocolate in the Adriatic.'

'You can try, but Florian's won't be open for another two hundred and fourteen years,' Topaz pointed out.

'The ship there' – Paolo stopped and pointed at a small caravel – 'is the one Mr and Mrs Djones arrived in.'

Jake's stomach lurched. Eagerly he inspected the small wooden craft: her sails were furled neatly around the boom and her decks were completely bare. Curling letters bore her name: the *Mystère*. The *Mystery*, Jake thought; the name couldn't have been more appropriate.

'Should we have a look?' he asked politely, wanting to jump aboard and examine it thoroughly for any signs of his parents.

But Nathan had already swung himself up onto the deck and jumped down into the cabin.

Moments later he reappeared, shaking his head.

'It's like the *Mary Celeste* down there,' he said, leaping back onto the quay. 'This was the only sign of life.' He opened his palm to reveal a handful of pips.

Jake was familiar with the sight – painfully so. 'Tangerines,' he murmured. 'My mum's obsessed with them.' He was about to reach out and scoop them up when Nathan tossed them over his shoulder into the sea, where they sank without trace.

'In case you hadn't noticed,' sighed Topaz, taking Jake's arm, 'his insensitivity is on a par with his vanity.'

They slowly made their way into the city. As they came into a square, they saw a crowd gathered around a man on a pedestal who was addressing them passionately, his voice hoarse. He had a long, unruly beard, wore torn velvet robes and was holding up a watermelon.

'What exactly is he saying?' Nathan asked Paolo. 'My Italian is a little rusty. I take it he's not selling watermelons . . .'

Topaz interrupted before Paolo got the chance to speak. 'He's saying, "This is the shape of the world.

It is not flat, but as round as this fruit. We are not the centre of the universe – the sun does not revolve around *us*, it is *we* who revolve around the sun!"'

Paolo nodded in agreement at Topaz's perfect translation.

'Actually, the gentlemen is way ahead of his time,' Charlie noted. 'Although the theory has been about since the Greeks, Copernicus doesn't set out his theory of Heavenly Spheres until 1542.'

Most people in the crowd just stared at the man, but some of them booed and whistled. Then a group of thick-set men in armour and spiked helmets pushed through and grabbed hold of the speaker; they pulled him down off the platform and propelled him, still shouting, out of the square. The crowd were ordered to disperse.

'That's become a common sight in the city,' Paolo noted. 'A lot of people are wary of the new philosophies.'

'The new philosophies?' asked Nathan.

'He's referring to the trend towards humanism that is starting to sweep across Europe,' Topaz explained.

'Really? I wasn't actually asking you, but . . . humanism – yes, I thought so.'

'He hasn't got a clue what that is, of course,' Topaz confided to Jake. 'He probably thinks it's something you catch in a swimming pool.'

'Humanism affirms the dignity of *all* people,' retorted Nathan in a studied English accent, 'regardless of the doctrines of religion and super-natural beliefs. In vocabulary you'll understand, it states that all men are equal.'

'All men *and* women.'

As Paolo looked between Nathan and Topaz, smiling unsurely, Charlie whispered in his ear, 'It's just an act. They love each other really.'

The young Italian led Jake, Topaz, Nathan and Charlie out of the square and along a canal. Jake caught a glimpse of a man training monkeys and another charming snakes out of a basket. Paolo took a furtive look around and climbed some steps to an old, shabby-looking building, motioning for the other agents to follow. On his way in, Jake noticed, carved into a wooden plaque beside the door, a very rough version of the History Keepers' symbol of the hourglass and planets.

They came into a bright, vaulted room, humming with activity. There were eight cooks at work, all covered from head to toe in flour.

Nathan's eyes lit up. 'A pizza bakery!'

'Actually it's *galette* flatbread, a new invention from Naples,' Paolo corrected him.

'Looks like pizza to me.' Nathan shrugged. 'Anyway, it's a great cover for a bureau.'

'Oh, it's not a cover,' continued Paolo. 'It's fully operational – the best in the city. As it is manned only sporadically, the bureau is in a rented room at the back.'

'I love the way Italians do business, it's so . . . *laissez faire*,' Nathan sighed as he scooped up a slice of flatbread fresh from the oven.

'Go ahead, just help yourself.' Topaz saw that that the head chef was not impressed by Nathan's pilfering.

'Emmental, if I'm not mistaken . . .' Nathan continued. 'Charlie – what would you say?'

Charlie tried a piece, chewing it pensively. 'I believe it's Gouda, though nuttier than usual,' he decided, 'with a hint of nutmeg. It's inspirational.'

The chef, who had been unimpressed by Nathan, recognized Charlie as a kindred spirit and gave him a genial nod.

Topaz quickly brought them back down to earth. 'When the feeding frenzy is over, perhaps we could discuss the small matter of the Code Purple and forthcoming world catastrophe.'

The young agents went into the little back room of the bakery. It looked to be, as indeed it was, a storeroom filled with boxes of fresh basil and tomatoes – a million miles from the grand austerity of the other History Keepers' headquarters that Jake had seen.

'I suppose *that* is the bureau?' asked Topaz, somewhat bewildered. She was pointing at a single lopsided desk at the far end of the room, where a tatty-looking Meslith machine sat amongst various cheeses.

Paolo's guilty shrug answered the question.

Topaz went to examine the desk. The Meslith machine, like all the others, had a crystalline rod protruding from its back. 'This must have been the machine that Alan and Miriam Djones sent their SOS from,' she concluded.

Jake was drawn to inspect it. He reached out his fingers to touch the crystalline rod and received a sharp electric shot.

'That's what happens when you do that. Lesson learned,' said Charlie, before turning back to Paolo. 'So where exactly did Alan and Miriam Djones go?'

Paolo took a messy bundle of notes from his pocket and tried to read his own writing. The first page confused him a good deal, but finally he worked it out: 'Oh, that's a shopping list from my mother. She collects Venetian glass. She loves the colours!'

'Fascinating,' muttered Nathan.

Paolo moved onto the next page. 'Here we are. They arrived in Venice on Tuesday night. On Wednesday they visited the house of a Signor Philippo in the north of the city; he is a famous architect who, earlier this month, disappeared quite suddenly on his way to work.'

'Disappeared? Might he just have slipped into a canal?' asked Nathan.

'No, that's the thing,' Paolo explained, suddenly animated. 'You see, at least ten architects have gone missing in recent months. Not just from Venice – from Florence, Parma, Padua. Everywhere. It's been the talk of the town.'

'Why would anyone want to do away with *architects*?' asked Nathan with a weary sigh. 'Quite a harmless race, I would have thought.'

'Maybe they weren't doing away with them,' Jake found himself suggesting. 'Maybe someone needed their services.'

Topaz looked at Jake, impressed. Nathan shrugged nonchalantly. 'So Djones and Djones returned . . . ?' he asked.

'Briefly,' continued Paolo; 'then, at seven in the evening, they set out for St Mark's Cathedral. I waited up all night. They never returned.'

There was silence for a moment. Topaz squeezed Jake's hand.

'They told you they were going to St Mark's?' asked Charlie.

'They asked for directions there,' Paolo told him.

'Religious, your parents?' Nathan asked Jake.

'Not unless eating mince pies at Christmas counts . . .'

'Mince pies are certainly sacred to me,' mused Charlie to himself.

'*Il y a quelque chose ici*,' announced Topaz, examining an apparently blank piece of parchment. 'Someone's written something on top of this. You can see – the inscription has come through.' Nathan reached out for it, but Topaz ignored him. She held it up to the light and made out the faint words. 'Do you recognize this handwriting?' she asked Jake.

Jake looked at it. He saw the ghostly writing – the big, cartoony letters, the endearingly clumsy mix of capitals and lower case – and his heart sank. Usually when he saw that writing, it was on a note warning him about the wet paint or explaining an absence to pick something up at the corner shop.

'It's my dad's.'

'Could I . . . ?' asked Nathan again.

Again Topaz paid no heed. She read the inscription:

CoNfeSs. St MaRK's. AmErIgo VeSPucCi.

'Ah, Amerigo Vespucci!' interrupted Nathan when Topaz read it out loud. 'I've heard of him. He was . . .' His voice trailed away. 'Who was he, again?'

'He was a renowned Italian explorer who gave his name to America,' Topaz informed him, 'but what has he got to do with St Mark's?'

'Obvious – he's buried there.' Nathan once again reached for the message.

'No,' said Topaz coolly, 'he was buried in Seville, Spain. I have visited his grave.' Finally she deigned to pass the message to Nathan. He tossed his hair out of his eyes as he snatched it.

'*Confess. St Mark's. Amerigo Vespucci*,' he repeated.

'Well, I'm sure a visit to the cathedral will make things clear. After dinner, obviously . . . Wouldn't want to work on an empty stomach.'

In silence the five agents made their way through the crowds back to the *Campana*. It was the time of the afternoon that the Italians called the *passeggiata*: everyone had finished work for the day and was sauntering up and down the streets, looking at everyone else. The agents forged their way through in single file. At one point, Jake sensed something behind him and looked round. He thought he caught a glimpse of crimson, but he was swept on by the surge of people.

At that same moment, the figure in the deep-red cloak and hood crept behind a pillar, where another red-cloaked form was waiting. From the shadows they watched the agents weave their way towards the quayside.

12 ALONE IN HISTORY

'We'll be gone an hour – two at most,' announced Topaz, coming up on deck with Charlie. She had draped a cloak around her shoulders as the evening was already becoming cooler.

Jake shrugged. 'Isn't it better to stay together?'

'It's better not to get killed in your first week.' Nathan had changed into a whole new outfit and was busy inspecting his reflection in a gilt mirror fitted to the mast (which he had installed himself 'in case of emergency'). 'Does this colour suit me?' he asked, referring to his doublet.

'Peacock green. What could be more appropriate?' offered Topaz.

Nathan was too taken up with his own reflection to realize that she was teasing him. 'It doesn't drain my eyes?' he asked, turning to Jake.

Jake was no fashion expert, but he remembered something his mother said sometimes. 'I think it . . . compliments your skin tone.'

Nathan beamed. 'I like your style.'

'Take this, Jake,' said Topaz, holding up a little silver chain with a vial attached to it.

'What is it?'

'It's atomium. The anti-ratio to return to Point Zero, in case you need it,' she told him. 'May I . . .?'

Jake's heart raced as Topaz put the chain around his neck and tucked the vial inside his doublet. 'Look after yourself,' she murmured. 'We shan't be long.'

'I left you some spinach quiche in the galley,' said Charlie, interrupting the moment. 'It's passable, but not my finest effort. I've literally over-egged it.'

Charlie, Topaz, Nathan and Paolo then jumped down onto the quay and disappeared into the crowd.

Four hours passed. Night fell and the moon rose. They still had not returned. Jake sat on deck, on the steps leading up to the prow. A chilly breeze now blew in from the sea. The old ship creaked and the sails flapped in the wind. The waterfront was almost deserted. Jake could see the silhouette of two young lovers sharing a secret kiss in a doorway. An old drunk stumbled along, cursing to himself. Then there was silence.

Jake reached inside his jacket and pulled out the silver vial that Topaz had given him. A minute rendering of the History Keepers' emblem was etched into the casing. He carefully opened it and inspected its glistening contents, then closed it and put it back.

He noticed something lying on the pile of ropes beside him: his school blazer, which he had discarded the night before. 'The passports!' he said to himself, suddenly remembering that they were still in the inside pocket. He took them out and gazed at the photos: his parents' smiling faces stared back at him.

Once again Jake pictured them in their kitchen, back when everything was normal: his father cheerfully but cluelessly taking apart a piece of machinery on the kitchen table; his mother frowning as she created another inedible catastrophe on the stove. During her last attempt at Chocolate Nemesis, Jake had had to put out the fire with the garden hose.

As the wind rustled the pages of their passports, Jake looked around at the city and wondered if they were out there somewhere in the darkness.

Suddenly there was an ear-splitting cry that made him jump up in alarm. He stuffed the passports inside his doublet and rushed to the ship's rail. Someone was coming along the quay towards him. It was Nathan. Although he was hurrying, Jake could see that he was limping and clutching his leg. He threw himself aboard, gasping for breath. 'Quickly! We don't have much time!'

Jake's eyes widened: Nathan was in a terrible state. His hair was dishevelled, his doublet torn, and thick blood dripped from his thigh.

'Pass me that! NOW!' he barked, pointing at Jake's school blazer.

When Jake handed it over, he tore it into strips. Jake knew he didn't have much use for it right now, but even so . . . But then he looked down at the wound in Nathan's leg. It was two inches wide and quite deep. 'What happened?'

'They were waiting for us. Someone must have tipped them off!' Nathan panted – and the South Carolina twang was clear now. He tied one of the strips tightly around his thigh.

'And the others . . . ?' Jake was almost too frightened to ask.

'Captured? Dead? Maybe they got away. We were split up, so who knows?'

Jake felt his stomach lurch in terror.

'Help me up!'

Jake supported Nathan as he got to his feet.

Nathan grimaced as he limped down the stairs. 'Quickly – we have one minute before they get here.'

'*Who* gets here?' Jake wanted to know.

But Nathan simply made his way through the galley and into his cabin. Jake watched in confusion as he opened his wardrobe door and pulled out a trunk from the bottom of a pile, sending the others clattering to the floor.

'Are you going to change again?' Jake asked in disbelief.

'Shut up,' snapped Nathan as he lifted the lid and started chucking the beautiful clothes all over the floor. Finally he found what he was looking for and shook it out. Jake could hardly believe his eyes: it was a deep crimson cloak with a hood. Attached to it was a breastplate in black enamel.

Finally Nathan grabbed one last thing – a pair of silver scissors. 'Quickly! Quickly!'

Jake shadowed him back up on deck. Nathan looked along the waterfront to see if anyone was coming. 'Hold these.' He bundled the cloak, breastplate and scissors together into Jake's arms and hobbled over to the Meslith machine that Charlie had left on the deck. 'Keep a look out. Shout if anyone comes.'

He wound the crank at the back of the machine. Once it was charged, he quickly typed a message. The light from the crystalline rod flickered over his anxious face. Halfway through his missive, the device ran out of power. 'Come on, come on!' Nathan shouted as he wound up the machine again.

Jake looked down at the shining black breastplate. It was lightweight, slightly battered, but forged from some strong metal. In its centre, picked out in silver, was the symbol of a snake twining around a shield. Jake heard noises from along the quay and looked out into the gloom. His stomach turned to liquid.

'Nathan, they're here!' he gasped.

Nathan turned to see a group of figures approaching. 'Let's go!' He picked up the Meslith machine and limped across to the side. As he climbed over the ship's rail, his injured leg clipped the top. He yelled in agony and the machine slipped from his grasp. It crashed onto the flagstones below, and flew apart.

Nathan had no time to despair: the cloaked figures were fast approaching. He jumped down onto the quayside and kicked the broken machine into the water. 'This way – or we're both dead!' he hissed, then limped off towards a shadowy passageway.

'Do I need to bring anything?' Jake was rooted to the spot.

'Yes – your overnight bag and a toothbrush.'

Jake was momentarily confused – before realizing that Nathan was being sarcastic.

'*Now*, you idiot!'

Jake jumped down and followed Nathan along the alleyway. Footsteps were approaching fast. Nathan pulled him into the shadow of a tree and motioned for him to be silent. They watched as twelve men came to a halt beside the *Campana*: all were tall and athletic, all had swords clanking at their sides, all were wearing the same crimson-hooded cloaks and black breastplates.

One of the men was accompanied by a dog, a strong, savage-looking mastiff. He issued an order in German, and six of the men boarded the ship, searching every inch and throwing anything inconsequential over the side.

Nathan winced and shook his head as his precious clothes were deposited in the water. 'Philistines,' he muttered.

The man with the mastiff turned towards the dark alleyway where Jake and Nathan were hiding. As he slipped down his hood, Jake gasped: he was tall and thick-set and his head was shaved; a deep, livid scar ran the length of his face. He wore a leather coat and high, mud-splattered boots. The man turned back towards the ship, but his dog, also battle-scarred, continued to stare into the darkness, sensing that something was there.

Nathan nudged Jake and whispered, 'This way – as quietly as you can.'

As they retreated and turned a corner, the dog started to growl. The two agents quickened their pace. They made their way along the side of a canal, Nathan clenching his teeth against the pain in his leg. He stopped and turned to Jake. In the moonlight Jake could see that his companion was as pale as a sheet, and he was gasping for breath.

'I've lost too much blood . . . You have to go on alone.' Nathan sat down and tightened the tourniquet around his leg.

'Go? Where?'

'Listen to me – it's our only chance.'

They could now hear the dog barking not far away.

'Those men back there – they're soldiers of the Black Army. The man with the dog is called Friedrich Von Bliecke. He and the others all work for Prince Zeldt.'

'Zeldt?' Jake exclaimed. 'The one my brother went to find?'

'That's right. We thought Zeldt was dead. In three years, not a single sighting of him. But he's obviously here in Europe somewhere. Whatever is happening, he is behind it.'

It was a terrible revelation for Jake, but he didn't have time to dwell on it.

'When I saw those red cloaks following us' – Nathan grimaced – 'I knew it was him!' He indicated the bundle in Jake's arms. 'This once belonged to one of them. This is Zeldt's symbol.' He pointed to the snake and shield.

'I saw a man in a cloak like this when we arrived,'

Jake confessed. 'I mentioned it to Charlie, but then the man disappeared.'

Nathan looked Jake straight in the eye. 'Zeldt is pure evil. Do you understand me? Pure evil.'

Jake tried to nod, but he was transfixed with fear.

'You *don't* understand! Think of the most depraved killer you have ever read about and multiply his depravity by a thousand – *then* you will understand!'

'Who is he?'

'Too much to explain now. There's a family, a royal family. He is not the worst . . .' Nathan was drifting out of consciousness, but he was roused by the sound of the dog barking again, much closer now.

He clutched Jake's arm. 'You have to go to St Mark's Cathedral. Find out whatever your parents discovered. *Confess, St Mark's, Amerigo Vespucci* – find out what it means.'

Jake's head was swimming.

'You wear the cloak to protect you. To disguise yourself as one of them.'

Jake nodded, blinking with apprehension.

'You have those scissors?' Nathan asked.

Jake held them up.

'Cut your hair short, as soon as you can – otherwise you'll stand out.'

Again Jake nodded. Everything felt like a dream.

Nathan reached inside his jacket and pulled out a small leather pouch. He opened it. Golden coins glistened inside. 'There's plenty of money there.' He gave it to Jake. 'And take this – it's a flint lighter,' he said as he pressed a small ebony device into Jake's hand. 'Keep it with you. History gets darker than you could ever imagine.'

'I don't understand . . . What about the others?'

'I don't *know* about the others! Listen to me – I'd slow you down, so you have to continue on your own. It's our only hope.'

The barking grew closer still. Nathan put his hands on Jake's shoulders and stared at him gravely. 'Look, Jake, you seem like a good man. They say your parents were two of the best agents this service ever produced. So you must be special – do you understand me?'

Jake assured him that he did – but they could hear men's voices now.

'I'll make sure no one follows you. They won't kill me – I'm too valuable to them.' Nathan managed to draw his sword. 'Look at my poor doublet,' he said, fingering a bloodstained rip. 'Florentine brocade, the best that money can buy . . . What a criminal waste.'

Jake looked along the canal at the route he would take to escape.

'One last thing . . .' Nathan panted; Jake stopped to hear what he had to say. 'What we do is important. Do you understand me?'

Jake nodded.

'No, you don't,' hissed Nathan impatiently. Once again Jake could hear his Charleston burr as he searched for the right words. 'History holds everything together – it's the glue that keeps everything intact. *Everything!* It keeps civilization civilized. And we *save* history – *us*, the History Keepers. We really do. It's not just talk. We are *vital.*'

'I understand,' Jake told him with calm certainty.

Nathan knew that he was not lying. 'Now go. *Go!*'

Just then the mastiff rushed round the corner, its mouth frothing, barking savagely, followed by the guards. Jake took to his heels, following the canal, then disappearing down one of the many alleyways.

Nathan got to his feet and stoically raised his sword. But the dog sprang up at him and knocked him to the ground. Moments later he was surrounded by the red-cloaked guards. Nathan looked up into the scarred face of Captain Von Bliecke before he slipped into unconsciousness.

Jake ran without thinking, without looking back. He hurtled down passageways, up steps, over bridges. After fifteen minutes he came to the Grand Canal and stopped. He was in a small *campo* edged with cypress trees and littered with half-cut blocks of stone destined for a new building. In his arms he still held the crimson robe, the breastplate and the scissors Nathan had given him.

His chest heaved up and down as his eyes scanned the little square. No one was following. The Grand Canal shimmered in the moonlight as it snaked its way through the city, the majestic palaces asleep on either side. To his left Jake could see the distinctive arch of the Rialto Bridge.

He sank down at the base of one of the trees. The full horror of his situation now started to dawn on him. He remembered how once, when he was eight, he had got separated from his parents on a trip to a huge shopping centre. He recalled the fear that had gripped him as he frantically searched through the maze of neon-lit shops. On that occasion, reason had prevailed and calmed him down: he knew he could find his parents, he knew where he lived in London, he knew everyone spoke his language.

This was different. He was alone. As alone as a person could ever be. In an unknown city, in a foreign country, in another era, abandoned by his parents, separated from his friends by a deadly enemy. Jake took out his parents' passports and looked at their pictures again. But he couldn't focus on them; they were a blur – panic was making him dizzy, his terror spiralling out of control. He opened his eyes wide and made a resolution to himself. He would not sink into despair. He would fight fear with reason.

Nathan had told him: *Go to St Mark's Cathedral . . . It is our only hope.* Right, he would go there; he would discover a way to find his parents, to find the others. Nathan had said he was too valuable to be killed. So they would *all* be too valuable. They would all be alive somewhere.

Jake was galvanized, but his head spun. As far as he knew, the other agents – who all had far greater experience than him – had been captured. What chance would *he* have? How would he know what to do? This Prince Zeldt, whom Nathan had spoken of, was evil incarnate. He was guarded by an entire army of soldiers. Jake was a solitary schoolboy, lost and alone in the sixteenth century. How could he possibly survive?

Stop it! Enough! Jake said to himself. *You have no choice.*

He defiantly seized the silver scissors and started to cut his hair. The thick brown curls that he knew his mother loved so much dropped silently onto the dirty ground. Within a minute his hair was cropped: he had transformed himself from a romantic into a young soldier.

He took a deep breath, stuffed the scissors into his pocket, scooped up the cloak and breastplate, straightened his shoulders and started to make his way along the canal towards the bridge. Keeping a sharp eye out, he carefully ascended the steps of the Rialto.

On the apex of the bridge, a group of people huddled together, drinking from flagons and talking in gruff voices. As Jake passed them, they all fell silent and stared at him.

He stopped and smiled uncertainly. 'Cathedral?

Duomo? San Marco?' he asked in his rudimentary Italian.

For a moment no one responded. Then a lady with a black eye and matted red hair pointed her finger southwards into a dark labyrinth of streets.

Jake nodded and carried on across the bridge. Silently, the group watched him go, then the conversation started up once again.

As Jake came into St Mark's Square, the bells struck five. The piazza was huge. On one side stood the Campanile watch tower; nearby, the golden, fairy-tale domes of the cathedral. Leading up to these was a long arcade of imposing, dark ochre buildings. At intervals along these, from arched first-floor windows, hung canvas awnings, billowing softly in the morning breeze, their stripes bleached and weathered by the sun and the salty Adriatic air.

Dawn was breaking, and sleepy-eyed Venetians were starting to go about their morning business. Jake looked around cautiously as he crossed the piazza. He passed an old bearded man in torn robes, who watched him through narrowed eyes; Jake quickened his pace towards the church and ran up the steps.

He was surprised to find the doors wide open; inside, the cathedral was full of activity. There were no rows of seating – it was an open space, with sawdust scattered over the marble floor and geese and sheep wandering around – even a cow munching its breakfast. There were people too, some bartering and exchanging battered coins for goods – cloth, spices and earthenware – chatting animatedly; others still sleeping in shadowy corners.

On one side, a timber scaffold clung to the wall. At the top of the precarious structure, a man in a square hat was working on a fresco. Jake could see that he had already drawn the outline of figures and was now painting brilliant blue sky between them. Jake was drawn towards the scaffold, wondering if this painter was someone famous. Perhaps it was Leonardo Da Vinci or Michelangelo, he thought.

The painter seemed to sense Jake hovering below him. He looked down and winked at him, then turned back to his painting. That was when Jake caught sight of someone out of the corner of his eye – someone who made him gasp in shock.

A figure in a deep crimson cloak was walking diagonally across the church. Jake lowered his head and turned away a little, but continued watching the man, who disappeared into a dark wooden structure by the far wall.

As Jake cautiously crossed the marble floor, a thought suddenly struck him: his parents' message had stated: *Confess, St Mark's, Amerigo Vespucci.* That wooden structure was surely a confessional box.

Jake edged around a stone pillar to get a closer look. The confessional was made up of two compartments. On one side there was a booth with a closed door where the priest sat. Next to it was an open booth with a curtain half drawn across. Behind this, Jake could clearly see the man's crimson robe.

Then it disappeared.

'What?' Jake said out loud as he craned his neck round the pillar to get a clearer view. He could see right to the back of the box: it was empty.

'*Per piacere.*' A thin voice spoke right into Jake's ear, making him start. He turned and came face to face with a wrinkled old woman holding out her hand. He saw that one of her eyes was dead white. '*Per piacere,*' she repeated, nudging him with gnarled fingers.

Jake smiled politely. He remembered the pouch that Nathan had given him. He cautiously took it out of his pocket, produced a single gold coin and gave it to the old woman.

For a moment she did not react, but disbelief soon turned to joy. Her face cracked into an extraordinary smile. '*Dio vi benedica,*' she whispered as she ran her ancient hand across Jake's glowing cheeks. Then she bowed, edged away and disappeared into the throng of people.

Jake turned back to the confessional. *There must be a doorway on the other side of the booth*, he thought to himself. *An entrance to somewhere.*

Although the idea terrified him, Jake knew that he must find his way through that doorway and see what lay beyond. His heart thumped: he looked down at the robe and breastplate in his arms. Now was the time to put them on.

The breastplate covered his chest and stomach. It was strong but light, and fitted him well. The long robe hung down to the ground. He lifted the hood over his head.

With a decisive step, Jake approached the confessional, pulled back the curtains and entered the booth. There were no obvious signs of a door. He pushed at the wall, but it wouldn't budge.

'*Chi volete vedere?*' a voice hissed, and Jake's

blood ran cold. He could see the faint outline of a face behind the grille.

'*Chi volete vedere?*' Strangely, the person was smoking a pipe. The smoke curled through the vent into Jake's compartment.

Jake had only the slightest grasp of Italian, but he was certain that *chi* meant 'who'. Then it came to him: the phrase that his parents had written down. The man who had given his name to America.

'Amerigo Vespucci . . . ?' he answered in his best Italian accent. There was silence for a moment. Then he heard a faint click and the back wall of the confessional slid open, revealing a passageway beyond. Jake stepped through, and the wall slid across behind him.

13 THE SHADOW OF EVIL

The passageway that lay ahead of him was gloomy and damp, with walls of thick stone. Jake saw the cloaked figure disappear through an archway at the far end and followed cautiously.

He came through the opening into a large, dark ante-room, circular in shape with a vaulted ceiling. The dim light came from an identical archway on the far side of the chamber. Jake saw a silhouette vanish through it.

He crossed the space, his eyes fixed on the archway. He stumbled over a ledge and heard a trickle of falling stones. He stopped dead, looked down and gasped: below his feet was a gigantic circular borehole that descended, a shadowy abyss, into the ground. An ancient stone staircase spiralled down into the darkness. Inside, it was damp and mossy;

the sound of dripping echoed up from the depths. Jake calculated that it must extend deep beneath the canals of Venice.

He quickly stepped back and skirted around the edge, still gazing down in awe. He went through the archway and into a large room: a double-height 'studio', with barred high windows extending from top to bottom. The cloaked man was crossing the chamber to another passageway beyond.

'I can't do this,' Jake suddenly said to himself, turning on his heel. Then he stopped, thinking. *You have no choice!* he realized. He clenched his fists and went back into the chamber. For a moment he stood there, frozen.

The room looked out onto a narrow canal. Dawn was only just breaking, so it took a moment for Jake to accustom himself to the eerie gloom. There were rows of long trestle tables, each with its own rough oak bench. At intervals hung low chandeliers, none of them lit. To his left was another passageway, but this one was sealed off by a sturdy iron gate.

As Jake approached one of the tables, he stubbed his toe on something metal and saw that a number of iron rings were set into the floor there.

His attention was then caught by a series of large

illustrations displayed on the tables, parchments inscribed with complicated diagrams. Next to these lay quills in pots of ink. Jake examined one of the drawings. The heading made him start – a word written in bold gothic type:

SUDERIA

'*Superia* . . .' Jake whispered the name to himself. '*Find the Summit of Superia.*' He clearly remembered the message his parents had sent to Point Zero.

Below it was a symbol like the one that was engraved on Jake's breastplate – a snake twining around a shield. The parchment was covered with intricate plans and elevations, showing a building of awesome proportions. It was as high as any modern skyscraper – at least forty storeys, Jake estimated. Yet the style was ancient, with its succession of arched gothic windows and details of gargoyles. It looked like a dark vision of the future seen through sixteenth-century eyes; it made him feel inexplicably nervous. Jake looked more carefully and noticed that every single window was barred.

At the next table, a drawing showed designs for a

giant archway, similarly austere and colossal, this one with hundreds of round windows, all barred.

Jake continued along the table, examining the illustrations. Each was headed with same phrase, the same symbol of the snake and shield; each showed plans for magnificent structures. Jake remembered their discovery in the pizza bakery. His parents' single lead in this business had been the missing architects. It could certainly be no coincidence.

Suddenly he heard footsteps approaching along one of the corridors. He quickly looked around for a hiding place, but there was no time. He sank back into the shadows as six guards, all dressed in the same crimson cloaks, marched into the room. They carried lit tapers and set about lighting the thick candles of the chandeliers.

Jake stopped breathing as one of the guards suddenly turned and approached him.

But the guard did not seem suspicious: Jake, after all, was dressed in the same way. He passed Jake a taper and issued an instruction – strangely, in English – for him to assist the others. As Jake took the torch, he caught sight of the face beneath the crimson hood: it belonged to a tall boy with cropped hair, cold eyes and a manner that was chillingly mature. He looked at the others: there were girls as well as boys, but their faces were all the same – tight-lipped, steely, expressionless. They were like robots. He knew instinctively that if he was to escape notice, he had to act in a similar manner.

As Jake started to light the candles, one of the guards took a large bunch of keys from his belt and unlocked the gate that barred the corridor on the left.

'*Svegliati!* Wake up! To work!' he ordered.

There was the sound of people stirring, chains clanking and voices murmuring. A few moments later a line of a dozen men, all shackled together by their hands and feet, shuffled into the room. It was a distressing sight. Jake realized that these had once been well-to-do people; their clothes, now in a sorry state, had been fine. They were herded into the room like animals.

In turn, each one was unlocked from the chain, led to his seat at one of the tables and attached to the metal rings on the floor.

Jake was in no doubt that these were the missing architects. His hands now free, one of them tried to pass a piece of bread to the old man who stood behind him. His neighbour smiled gratefully as he took it, but in a flash a baton came smashing down on his wrist, the bread dropped to the floor and was kicked into the corner next to Jake.

'Work now!' the guard barked.

The old man did as he was told. He went and sat at one of the tables, his thin, shaking hand lifted the quill and he started to draw.

'Everyone, work!' The guard brought his baton down hard on the table.

Jake strove to keep his face blank as anxiety raged inside him. He found himself feeling inside his cloak to check that his sword was still there.

As the architects worked, he observed them more closely: their faces were pale, their hollow eyes etched with despair. The old man who had been denied the bread was the most pitiful of all. As he worked, his eyes blinked and his bloodless lips muttered away quietly.

The sight of this poor man filled Jake with anger. Cruelty towards the weak was something he had always hated. Once, outside his school, he'd come across a group of bullies taunting a much younger boy whose leg was encased in a brace. Jake made a brave stand – only to be punched in the stomach.

The boy in the brace showed no gratitude – he told Jake that he'd only attracted *more* attention from the bullies – but Jake would have done the same again. His family were like that: they stood up for people.

All eyes turned as a door on the other side of the room was unlocked. Without thinking, Jake reached down, picked up the piece of bread and moved forward to drop it into the lap of the old man. He looked up in confusion; Jake responded with a stern look and stood to attention again.

Then a brutish figure strode into the room, followed by a savage-looking mastiff. Jake shivered: this was the scarred man from the quayside, Captain Von Bliecke. The captain picked up a great pitcher of water, took a gulp, and flung the rest over his head to wake himself up. His dog yawned and stretched, then wandered around the room, sniffing. Jake stood rigid as the beast approached him. He could now see the extent of his wounds: as well as his torn ear and scarred head, one of his eyes was half closed, and his flank was bare of fur. He smelled something interesting and pressed his cold wet nose into Jake's hand. Jake recoiled; then his blood ran cold as the dog's upper lip curled back and he gave a low growl.

'Felson!' Von Bliecke called. Grudgingly the dog turned away from Jake and trotted over to his master, who threw a bone into the corner. Felson pounced on it and started tearing off ribbons of flesh. Jake breathed a sigh of relief. Meanwhile Von Bliecke took a long cut-throat razor from his back pocket and started to shave away the faint growth of dark hair on his head, ignoring the nicks to his scalp.

Jake watched him out of the corner of his eye. He knew that this man could hold the key to the whereabouts not just of Nathan, Topaz and Charlie – if they were still alive – but of his missing parents. Perhaps this monster even knew something of his brother Philip.

After nearly an hour, with one eye on the architects and the other on Von Bliecke – who'd been polishing an array of eye-watering weapons – Jake noticed activity in the canal outside the window. A gondola with a black awning pulled up. Four red-cloaked guards disembarked, secured the craft and stood to attention with their heads bowed. A girl emerged from under the awning and stepped ashore.

Von Bliecke had also seen her arrive; his dark

brow furrowed as he announced in a quiet voice, 'Mina Schlitz . . .'

At the sound of her name, everyone – prisoners and guards alike – froze in terror.

A moment later there was a firm knock at the door.

Felson trotted over and sniffed the base of the door. Suddenly his tail curled under his body and he crawled beneath a table, whimpering. Von Bliecke strode over, unfastened the four great bolts and opened the door.

Mina Schlitz stepped into the room, followed by her retinue. She was a teenager of roughly Jake's age – chillingly self-contained, with dark eyes and long, straight, raven-black hair. She wore a neat pleated skirt and a tightly fitting doublet. A velvet cap topped her perfect white face, and a single pearl hung from a scarlet thread around her neck. Wrapped about her forearm was a thin, live snake with red markings down its back. It undulated as the girl stroked it softly with her pale fingers.

'*Guten Tag*, Fräulein Schlitz – a pleasant journey?' Von Bliecke murmured, with a bow of his head. He was a battle-hardened soldier, double her age, but even he looked timid now.

The girl ignored his question. She held up her serpent and kissed its head, then carefully placed it in a box at her belt. Still no one dared move as her sharp eyes darted around the room.

'Finish your drawings,' she instructed the architects – and her voice sounded like corrosive acid – before turning to Von Bliecke. She had a faint German accent but her English was clear and precise. 'Captain, you are to deliver the captured agents immediately to Castle Schwarzheim.'

Jake's ears instantly pricked up. Surely she meant Topaz, Nathan and the others. He took some comfort from the news that they must still be alive.

'*Und Doktor Talisman Kant – ein—*' Von Bliecke started – but was silenced by Mina.

'English!' she said firmly. 'The royal language is English.'

Von Bliecke took a deep breath and continued, 'And Doktor Kant? The rendezvous at Bassano?' he asked.

'You have been reassigned. *I* will rendezvous with Doktor Kant.' Mina looked at the guards. 'These soldiers will accompany me. Then I too will proceed to Castle Schwarzheim. That will be all.'

Von Bliecke scowled at Mina, then turned,

gathered up his weapons, whistled for Felson and left.

Jake's heart beat fast as he watched Von Bliecke cross the room in front of him. He desperately wanted to follow. If indeed this man was about to 'deliver the captured agents', he would lead him straight to the others. But he couldn't move. Instead, he made a point of remembering all the details of the conversation: *Bassano, Doktor Talisman Kant, Castle Schwarzheim* . . . He repeated the names over to himself.

Just as Von Bliecke reached the door, Mina spoke again. 'For your sake I trust there'll be no more mistakes.' The captain froze, his back to the room. 'It has been four years in preparation,' she said quietly and sharply. 'We have just four days now until apocalypse. Failure is not an option.'

Von Bliecke nodded soberly and left the room.

Jake went pale. Of all the pronouncements he had heard since arriving in Italy, this last one was the most alarming. *Just four days now until apocalypse*, Mina had said. What apocalypse? What had been four years in preparation?

'Stop working now!' Mina ordered. She swept along the tables and collected all the architects' drawings, placing them in a giant portfolio. Then she rang a bell and twelve more red-cloaked guards filed into the room.

'Attention!' she shouted, and the entire group, Jake included, formed a line. 'We leave by the Veneto Tunnel,' she continued. 'Make your way down to the carriages in single file.'

The other guards knew what to do: they turned on their heels and marched into the chamber where the giant borehole led down into the ground. Jake got into line and followed. Here they descended the spiral staircase into the subterranean world, their red cloaks streaming out behind them, their precise footsteps echoing around the cavernous space. As the extraordinary tunnel grew darker and hotter, its walls damp with moss, Jake wondered where it was leading. He glanced up to see the rigid silhouette of Mina Schlitz bringing up the rear.

After a long, dizzying descent they arrived at the base of the tunnel and marched through an arch towards three horse-drawn carriages, all with drivers at the ready. Two were open-topped with rows of rough benches, the third was sleek and black, decorated with the symbol of the snake around the shield.

As Jake turned to see where these carriages would be heading, his eyes widened in disbelief: he was at the end of a tunnel, perfectly round like those in the Underground back in London, and lit at intervals by gently flickering tapers, which receded into the distance, boring under the city of Venice.

One by one, the red-cloaked guards took their places on the benches of the two open carriages. Jake was the last onto his vehicle. As he climbed up, he heard a faint clang and noticed that the silver scissors had dropped out of his trouser pocket. He froze, wondering whether he should retrieve them or not. Mina Schlitz had now appeared through the archway, so Jake decided not to draw attention to himself. He took his place on the bench, accidentally sitting on his neighbour's cloak.

'Excuse me,' he said without thinking. The other guard did not react; he just looked at Jake blankly, then stared ahead again.

Mina Schlitz was scanning the carriages. Jake was terrified that she might catch sight of the glint of silver on the ground, but she merely climbed into the black coach and slammed the door behind her. A moment later the drivers cracked their whips and they set off. The big black wheels of Mina's carriage passed over Nathan Wylder's scissors and the vehicles rattled off along the tunnel.

Jake gazed at the walls, made of millions upon millions of bricks. He was so awestruck by this secret thoroughfare beneath the canals of the city that for a while he forgot his troubles. Enemy forces were clearly using this highway for dark purposes, but that did not detract from the astonishing achievement.

The tunnel gradually started to ascend. Thirty minutes passed before Jake finally spied a pinprick of daylight ahead. It was another twenty before they emerged into the open air. The tunnel had come out into a wood; as they left it and crested a hill, Jake looked back to see the Venetian lagoon spread below him. He let out a sigh. Despite all his fear and anxiety, suddenly he was thrilled by the prospect of adventure.

The three vehicles headed north in the direction of Bassano.

14 UNWELCOME NEWS

It was a bright, bracing morning on the Mont St Michel. Final preparations for Oceane Noire's birthday party had been underway since dawn. It was being held in the stateroom the following evening.

Oceane Noire had been born at Versailles, in the lavish court of Louis XV. It had been a time and a place of unparalleled extravagance, and Oceane had loved every indulgent second of it: the banquets, the clothes, the luxurious baths in jasmine water and rose petals.

When the French Revolution erupted, partly due to the behaviour of people like her, Oceane was extremely irritated: it interrupted a hectic season of coming-out balls. It was rumoured that she'd given Marie Antoinette her famous line, 'Let them eat cake,' but those who knew her claimed that Oceane would never have wasted pâtisserie on people who didn't fully appreciate it.

While most French aristocrats were fleeing across the Channel, Oceane's parents (now retired and living in the Cap d'Antibes, but very fine agents in their day) dragged their spoiled daughter across the remainder of the century to the safety of the 1820s and the Romantic period.

It had been all downhill from then on. Now Oceane felt that her life was commonplace; she longed in vain for those days of opulence to return. So for her party, although she didn't much relish turning forty, she decided that she would set new standards of luxury at Point Zero.

All morning an endless stream of merchants – florists, purveyors of game and, indeed, cake-makers – had been arriving from the mainland with their goods for the banquet: special linens for the tables; braces of pheasant and quail; chocolates, nougat and coffee from Paris; peonies and delphiniums for decoration.

It was only on very rare occasions that locals were allowed inside the Mount, so nearly all of them, though they affected an air of brisk efficiency, had their eyes peeled for anything worthy of gossip. Of course, no one knew what really went on here – that this was the headquarters of the History Keepers' Secret Service; they had been led to believe it was a community of painters and writers. This, of course, did not lessen their appetite for tittle-tattle.

The occupants of the island had to play the part and not arouse suspicion. That morning Norland had distributed a communiqué drafted by Jupitus Cole: as locals would be present today, he said, everyone must, 'without exception', be attired in the fashions of the time. To this end, Signor Gondolfino had opened the costumiery at dawn and had been run off his elegantly booted feet.

In the stateroom, Oceane was overseeing the florists, her eyes as hard and sparkling as the price-less diamonds that hung from her ears. Rose Djones came in, spellbound by the magnificent decor-ations, and made her way across to where Oceane stood.

'Looking very grand in here,' she told her. 'Will there be dancing?'

A cloud descended over Oceane's face. 'You're coming, are you?'

'Isn't everyone invited?'

Oceane tensed. 'There's a strict dress code, you know.'

'I've got the gown that Olympe de Gouges lent me somewhere here. I'm hoping I can squeeze into it. Amazing what you can do with a bit of invisible thread.'

'Or, of course, you may end up looking fat and feeling stupid,' replied Oceane helpfully.

Rose knew better than to take anything Oceane said seriously, but she couldn't resist a little bit of fun. 'So, fifty today? You look really great on it.'

Oceane's expression froze in horror. '*Comment?*'

'I hope I look as good as you when I hit the dreaded half century.'

'*Quarante,*' hissed Oceane. '*J'ai* quarante *ans!* Forty.'

'Oh, well, in that case' – Rose scrutinized her opponent's face – 'that makes much more sense.'

'*A vrai dire, je suis très occupée.* I'm very busy.' Oceane thrust her nose into the air, then swung round and demanded of the room, 'Has anyone seen Norland? We need to finalize menus *immédiatement!*' A servant who was in her way as she flounced out received a firm clip from her fan.

Rose left the room and made her way up the

stairs, her mind returning to more serious thoughts. Yesterday she had received the news that her nephew had disappeared to Venice with the others. The Meslith message from Charlie had arrived late last night: Jake had stowed away on the *Campana*. Rose knew why at once. He had gone to find his parents. She was, of course, terrified for him – but also immensely proud. If she herself had still possessed the strong valour of her youth, she would have done the same.

When Rose arrived at the door to Galliana's suite, Norland was leaving.

'Oceane Noire is looking for you. I believe it's urgent,' she told him.

'Urgent?' Norland replied with a mischievous grin. 'In that case, I think I might go and have a bath.' He hooted with laughter and disappeared down the corridor.

'Galliana? Are you there?' Rose called through the open door.

The greyhound, who'd been having her morning nap, pricked up her ears and wagged her tail. Galliana emerged from her bedroom. 'Rose, thank you for coming. I have Lapsang brewing.'

They sat on ottomans in Galliana's study,

drinking tea from bone-china cups. Rose had always loved this room. There were glass cabinets everywhere, crammed with objects assembled in the course of Galliana's many voyages to history: collections of marble busts, jade figurines, chess pieces, Spanish fans, limestone stalactites, dinosaur fossils, butterflies and beetles, duelling swords and ancient daggers. Amidst this treasure trove Galliana sat with her back straight, her smile warm and her eyes full of wisdom.

'You're the only person I feel I can trust absolutely,' she confided as she passed Rose a plate of cakes.

'*Real* French pastries – how did I manage without them?' Rose sized up the delicious-looking offerings. Her fingers hovered between a rum baba and a Mont Blanc, before finally settling for a millefeuille crammed with crème pâtissier. 'Dear me, it should carry a health warning,' she sighed as she took a huge mouthful. 'So, what's happened?'

'I think there is an informer amongst us,' stated Galliana coolly.

Rose stopped mid-swallow. Then she gulped the remainder of the cake down. 'Carry on,' she said seriously.

'Firstly, I received this from Agent Wylder late last night.' Galliana produced a Meslith message and passed it to Rose.

Rose read it out loud: '*Prince Zeldt alive!*' She gasped. Galliana motioned for her to carry on reading. '*They knew we were coming. Possible spy . . .* That's all it says? Is everyone all right?'

'We don't know. The message may have been cut short. We will have to wait to find out. But, Rose, if there *is* a spy, I have reason to believe that he or she may be amongst us at Point Zero.'

'Really? Good gracious me.' Rose reached for the rum baba to take the edge off her shock. 'What makes you say so?'

'As you know, any Meslith message that arrives from history is sent immediately, by tube, to my desk there.' Galliana indicated where the cylindrical packages were deposited on her bureau. 'Only *I* read these messages, and they remain top secret until I choose to disclose their contents. This is the communiqué I received yesterday from Charlie Chieverley,' she continued, passing Rose another piece of parchment. 'Look in the bottom right-hand corner.' She produced an old magnifying glass with a tiny candle attached to its base and gave the device to Rose.

Rose inspected it. 'Is that a fingerprint?' she asked.

'Certainly half a fingerprint. And it categorically is not mine.'

'But how could anyone else have got their hands on it?'

'I can only surmise that someone has entered my study illicitly. Only two people have access keys to all suites of the castle: myself . . . and Jupitus Cole.'

'You think he's the informer?'

'Let's say I would just like to eliminate him from my enquiries.'

'As you know, Galliana, there is little love lost between Jupitus and me – but a spy? Could that really be possible? Have any other messages been marked with fingerprints?'

'As yet, no. But that means nothing. I assume precautions would usually be taken – gloves and so on. The print on that message was probably an accident. Rose, this is what I need you to do. Tonight, during Oceane's party, I want you to search Jupitus Cole's chambers.'

'Really? Good gracious . . . Really?'

Galliana passed Rose a key. 'That will get you into his rooms. Firstly, you must obtain some papers from which we can cross-check the fingerprint. Secondly, you must seek out any evidence to link him to Zeldt, the Black Army or any other hostile organization. Understood?'

'I have a mission!' Rose gasped excitedly. 'After fifteen years, I have a mission!' She popped the key into her carpetbag. Then her face darkened with anxiety. 'What about Venice? Are we sending reinforcements?'

'Not until we know exactly what the situation is. Which brings me to my other question. In your opinion . . . your nephew – is he capable?'

Rose thought about it for a minute, then she looked at her old friend very seriously. 'Jake? He's a hero. I have no doubt of that!'

The convoy of carriages trundled on throughout the hot July day, rolling across the Italian countryside.

The young 'guards' – the boys and girls with whom Jake shared the carriage – were all roughly his age. Physically, they were a broad mix – dark, blond, petite, broad-shouldered – but it was as if their personalities had somehow been erased. None of them were friendly to each other and nobody spoke. Of course, this suited Jake fine – it meant he didn't risk saying the wrong thing – but he found it unnerving.

As the day cooled and the sun began to set, Mina shouted a command and the cavalcade drew to a halt. Jake watched her climb down from her black carriage and look around with her eagle eyes. They had stopped next to a small river in the centre of a broad valley. To one side a forest of dark fir trees stretched up and over the hill into the distance. Ahead and to the left, Jake could make out the silhouette of a town – Bassano, he assumed. Beyond that lay the dim outline of mountains, the Alps, their summits white with summer snow.

Satisfied that the place was safe, Mina issued an order to the waiting guards: 'We set up camp.'

There was a flurry of activity. A great mound of equipment was unloaded from compartments under the benches, and the guards erected a line of field tents beside the river. When Jake had gone on that disastrous camping holiday in the New Forest, he had learned how *not* to put up a tent. So now he was at least able to appear professional.

The first structure to take shape was Mina Schlitz's portable pavilion. It was jet-black, like her carriage, and double the size of the others. Once it was erected, she disappeared inside.

A fire was lit within a circle of rocks, and some guards set about cooking joints of salted meat. As they had travelled in silence, so they worked, speaking only when something was needed.

Suddenly Jake saw a falcon circling high overhead. It swooped down and snatched a fish from the river. The fish struggled in vain, flapping helplessly as the falcon carried it away to its lair at the top of the escarpment. Here, something else caught Jake's attention: a horse-drawn gypsy caravan of a distinctive yellow colour was snaking its way down the hillside towards the camp. One of the guards, who'd also seen the vehicle, went to the entrance of Mina's tent and announced, 'Miss Schlitz, Doktor Kant is arriving.'

A moment later Mina emerged from her tent and observed the caravan with her black eyes. She took her snake out of its box and gently stroked its head. It curled itself around her forearm like a giant bracelet.

As the caravan drew closer, Jake noticed that it was covered in all sorts of paraphernalia that made it rattle and jangle: instruments, tools, pots and pans. Also hanging from it was a grisly collection of dead game: rabbits, hares and even a whole deer swaying from side to side. The vehicle pulled up and stopped in front of Mina Schlitz. The driver was a boy of no more than twelve; a sulky adolescent with a dirty face and squinting eyes.

Behind him, a curtain was pulled back; a tall man appeared and descended the caravan's three wooden steps. He immediately made Jake feel uneasy. He had a thin sunburned face that glistened with sweat, and a long, untidy beard. Despite the heat he wore a fur hat and a thick robe fastened with a belt around his skinny frame. From this hung more instruments: spyglasses, measuring cups, daggers and pistols. On his bony fingers he wore a number of large jewelled rings.

Seeing Mina, his face crinkled into a sinister smile, revealing blackened teeth. 'Miss Schlitz.' He bowed his head.

'Doktor Kant,' she replied. 'How was Genoa?'

'Like every other city in the world – full of dirt, stench and idiocy.' He grimaced. 'But let's leave the small talk for later. Business first. Hermat – the merchandise!'

Hermat, the driver, was distracted, observing a butterfly that was fluttering past. In a flash, he had caught it in his hand and held it firm as it struggled to escape. Carefully he pulled its wings off.

'Hermat, you imbecile! Bring me the box,' Kant snapped, then turned to Mina. 'My son, you may remember, has the mental capacity of a fish. Were it not for the fact that he makes a perfect subject for my experiments, I would probably have put him out of my misery by now.'

Hermat paid no attention; he went round to the back of the caravan and returned with a small silver box. Jake, sensing that this was important, edged a little closer. Hermat placed the box in his father's gaunt, bejewelled hand. The latter thanked him with a swift cuff around the head.

Kant in turn passed the case to Mina, handling it as if it were a priceless *objet d'art*. 'The fruits of fourteen months' hard work—' He froze when he saw the snake on Mina's wrist undulate and flick out its tiny tongue.

'He won't bite,' Mina reassured him; 'unless I ask him to . . .' The serpent hissed at Kant then curled back around her forearm. She opened the case and inspected its contents. A smile played across her face.

Jake edged forward, trying to see what lay inside; but Mina snapped the box shut.

'You and you,' she said suddenly, pointing to Jake and another guard. 'Retrieve the coffer from the back compartment of my carriage for Doktor Kant.'

Jake, his heart pounding, headed across to Mina's jet-black carriage; he and the other guard opened a wooden compartment and lifted down the coffer. Jake gasped when he felt the weight of it and almost dropped his end. Using all their strength, they heaved it over to where Mina was standing and put it down. She flipped open the lid with her foot, and Kant's face lit up: it was filled, almost to the brim, with gold coins. He leaned closer, quivering with delight as he dug his hand deep in amongst the treasure.

'There's nothing more reassuring than the cold touch of money,' he said, laughing. 'As always, such a pleasure trading with you, Miss Schlitz . . . I have venison' – he pointed to the dead deer hanging from the back of his cart – 'well matured. Let's celebrate with dinner. Hermat! Load the coffer and unfasten the animal.'

Hermat did as he was told: he replaced the lid and effortlessly lifted the coffer up onto his father's caravan. Then he untied the ropes from the deer's hooves and let it drop, with a thump, to the ground.

Jake watched Mina lead her guest into the black pavilion, the silver case clutched firmly in her hand. He thought to himself . . . Mina had travelled a whole day with a platoon of guards to meet this man, and then paid a fortune for a single silver box. Jake knew that his first job was to find out what that box contained.

15 ENTER THE DARK PRINCE

Night was falling as a carriage wound its way up a narrow rocky road towards a castle perched high up on a mountaintop, an ominous silhouette of soaring turrets. In the back seat sat Friedrich Von Bliecke, with Felson asleep at his feet. The captain grimly contemplated his fate. His mission had been to intercept and capture four enemy agents in Venice. He had only half succeeded: he was painfully aware that an incomplete mission would be viewed as a failure.

Attached to the rear of the carriage was a sturdy wooden container on wheels. It was chained and locked, and contained two cramped and hungry human beings – Nathan Wylder and Paolo Cozzo.

Nathan was barely conscious. His head rolled around as the carriage negotiated the rocky path.

Paolo, who for twelve hours had worn a look of horror on his young face, was gazing through a crack in the wood.

'We're arriving somewhere!' he announced breathlessly. 'I think it's a castle. A *horrible*-looking castle. This is it, isn't it? This is where they're going to kill us.'

'If they were going to kill us,' Nathan managed in a broken whisper, 'I think it might have happened already. What's in store for us could be worse than death.'

'Worse than death? What could possibly be worse than death?' It took Paolo only a moment to answer his own question. '*Torture?* You mean *torture*?' he asked in despairing tones.

'Fingers crossed for the rack.' Nathan attempted a grin. 'I'm in desperate need of a stretch.'

Paolo shook his head. 'This is no time for jokes, Nathan.'

'Who's joking?'

The carriage rattled on towards the castle.

On the first floor of the castle was a library – a long, dark room filled with shelves of ancient tomes. In every shadowy recess – and there were many in this ghostly space – stood statues on pedestals: warriors, rulers and tyrants, their powerful faces frozen in time, captured in marble. Down the length of the room was a succession of chimneypieces with crackling fires. A colossal table occupied the centre. In a throne at one end sat a figure.

He was pale-faced and perfectly still. Over his shoulders hung a long cloak of lustrous dark fur, from which stared out the occasional pair of dead eyes. Underneath this lay more layers of black: a tight-fitting doublet of velvet and brocade, encrusted with ebony jewels, surmounted at the neck by a white ruff.

The doors at the end of the chamber creaked open, and Von Bliecke entered. He strode towards the man on the throne, Felson padding obediently at his side. He stopped in front of the table and clicked his heels.

'Prince Zeldt,' he murmured with a bow of the head. 'I come from Venice.'

At first sight Zeldt looked like a boy – a slight, pale boy. His features were fine and colourless, his eyes a dim, watery blue, his neat hair silvery blond. But as the firelight played on his face, a different picture emerged. It was clear that he was far from youthful. The layers of translucent skin on his face hid an incalculable age: he could have been forty, fifty – or older still.

Zeldt scrutinized Von Bliecke with expressionless eyes. 'The prisoners?' He spoke in a clear, precise voice.

'Outside.'

The prince signalled with his fingers and a guard brought in Nathan and Paolo, chained together. Paolo was almost hysterical, but Nathan took it all in his stride.

Zeldt gazed at them, his face blank. 'Just two?' he asked. 'Where is Miss St Honoré? Didn't I make it clear that she was our priority?'

Von Bliecke cleared his throat. 'Miss St Honoré managed to evade capture, sir, along with Agent Chieverley. It couldn't be helped.'

Zeldt pushed back his chair and stood up. He approached Nathan and Paolo and examined them from all angles. Paolo whimpered in terror, but Nathan gave him a cheeky smile.

'Evening,' he drawled. 'Warm in here, isn't it?'

Zeldt ignored him. He approached Von Bliecke like a dark shadow. 'And what about the *fifth* agent?' he whispered.

'The fifth?' The captain gulped. 'No. Four agents. The mission was to intercept *four*.'

The prince held up his thin hand to silence him. 'We received intelligence from our contact at Point Zero that a further agent had joined the mission. The Djones boy.'

Nathan and Paolo looked at each other out of the corner of their eyes. Von Bliecke was starting to sweat.

'Of course, you were unaware of this development,' Zeldt continued in sepulchral tones, 'but if you had done your job properly, you would have intercepted *all* the agents.'

Von Bliecke nodded in agreement. 'Your Highness is right. It was an oversight on my part.'

For a moment Zeldt's rigid expression did not alter. But then he seemed to relax and a faint smile lit up his face. 'You're right, it couldn't be helped.'

The captain let out a sigh of relief: his life might be saved after all.

Zeldt walked slowly to a door on one side of the room. It was made of metal, like a safe door, and on its front, as on a safe, was a wheel, and a single bronze handle fashioned in the shape of curling snakes. He turned the wheel and the door opened with a heavy clunk, revealing a small chamber beyond.

'You have travelled all day. Dinner is served through there.' The prince motioned for Von Bliecke to enter.

The captain nodded eagerly and crossed the room, his dog at his side. 'Thank you, thank you. Next time, no mistakes, I promise.'

'You can leave the dog.'

The blood drained from the captain's face. 'Sir?'

'The dog. Leave him.'

'Yes . . . of course.' Von Bliecke wiped his brow and looked down at Felson in terror. He ran his scarred hand over the dog's head and nodded at him. Felson whined, but his master continued through the door into the chamber. It appeared to be empty.

'There's an exit on the other side,' said Zeldt with an enigmatic smile. He closed the door and turned the bronze snakes until it locked tight.

Von Bliecke gasped as he was engulfed in pitch darkness. His chest rose and fell. Then he heard the sound of grinding stone, and the back wall of the chamber started to move apart, revealing another dark space beyond. The walls stopped moving and the captain stepped over to investigate.

'God save me . . .' he whispered in horror as he looked down into the void.

He had heard about this diabolical place but had always assumed it was a myth to frighten Zeldt's Black Army. The spot where he stood was roughly halfway up a wall overlooking a vast space that contained a Byzantine maze of old staircases and landings, juxtaposed in seemingly illogical configurations. Some staircases went up; others went off at right angles, while some looked as if they were upside down.

On the opposite wall the captain thought he could make out a faint rectangle of light. This, he calculated, was the 'exit' that Prince Zeldt had referred to. It was his only chance – though Von Bliecke was smart enough to know that this chance was close to zero.

He carefully set his foot down on the nearest set of steps. But the staircase, set at an unnatural angle, was cruelly deceptive, and his foot came into contact with nothing but air. He fell twenty feet to the floor, yelling in agony as the bones in his ankles splintered.

He turned to see three serpents, their bodies as

thick as lampposts, slithering over the floor towards him. The snakes reared up and unlocked their inky black jaws.

In the library above, Zeldt listened carefully to the cries of agony. Felson shuddered and Paolo hyperventilated.

When the screams finally stopped, the prince returned to his throne. 'When I said dinner was served, perhaps he didn't understand . . . He *was* the dinner.' He looked at Nathan and Paolo. 'Life is so fleeting,' he reflected in a melancholy voice. 'One must enjoy every moment.'

'I just wanted to tell you about the agent you *failed* to capture,' Nathan told him. 'He's probably the best agent this service has ever had. You're doomed – you're totally doomed.'

Zeldt smiled thinly as he issued his instruction to the guard. 'Take them down into the mountain. Lock them in the dark.'

Paolo snivelled helplessly as he and Nathan were dragged out of the room.

Nathan was still shouting, 'You don't believe me? You wait. Jake Djones is our *star* agent. He's already on to you. And be warned – he's fierce, agile, *sleek*, like a jaguar!'

16 FOREST ENCOUNTER

J ake tripped over one of the guy ropes and went sprawling. As his knee smashed against a rock, his face twisted in silent agony. He looked around to check that no one had seen him, then picked himself up.

It was nearly ten at night, and most of the other guards were asleep. Clearly visible in the moonlight, three sentries, each with a lantern, stood on watch at the edge of the camp. Jake stood in the shadows behind the tents, observing the activity in Mina's pavilion.

There was candlelight inside, and he could clearly see the projection of Talisman Kant and Mina Schlitz finishing their dinner. Finally Kant stood up, bowed and left. Jake watched the doctor's silhouette cross over to his caravan, climb up and slam the door behind him.

Now was the time to act.

Jake's hand was shaking as he retrieved the flint lighter that Nathan had given him. He knelt down, lit it and held the flame to the bundle of dried grass that he grasped in his other hand. The fire crackled into life as Jake placed it at the foot of the nearest tent. The dry canvas caught instantly and was soon engulfed in a brilliant blaze.

Everything happened at once: shouting guards emerged in confusion, the look-outs came running from their posts, and everyone started to gather water from the river. The fire spread rapidly, engulfing the row of tents.

When Jake saw Mina stride out of her pavilion in her dressing gown and march towards the burning wreckage, he darted through the shadows, around the edge of her tent, and ducked inside.

Jake's heart beat at double speed as his eyes darted about the room in search of the silver box. The tent was sparsely furnished: a work desk, a small chest and a number of animal furs spread across the floor. On top of the desk there was a quill in a small china pot of green ink and a sheet of parchment, inscribed with neat, fresh script. The page's heading contained familiar words:

GUESTS AT THE SUPERIA CONFERENCE, CASTLE SCHWARZHEIM

Below this was a long list of names of every nationality: Italian, Spanish, Russian, Dutch ... Next to each name, words were written: *gold*, *tin*, *grain*, *fur*, and so on. Jake quickly folded the parchment and wedged it in his inside pocket.

He realized he was losing focus: it was the box he'd come for. The drawers of the low chest revealed nothing. Jake swung round in desperation, and then his eyes found it, sitting in the centre of Mina's camp bed. He opened it up and revealed two glass containers. One was a sealed capsule, with no obvious top or bottom, containing a quantity of a sticky yellow substance. The other was a corked bottle filled with a white powder. Jake took this out and examined it more carefully: the powder had the same consistency as bathroom talc.

Suddenly Jake noticed another small box by Mina's pillow, out of which a thin, deadly red-backed snake emerged noiselessly. He gasped and dropped the bottle of powder.

Luckily, it didn't break. Jake froze. He wanted to reach down and pick it up, but the snake hissed a diabolical warning. Then he heard footsteps approaching. He dived into a corner and covered himself with a fur rug just as Mina stepped in.

She retrieved a pair of leather gloves from the oak chest and quickly headed back outside. But in the doorway she paused, sensing that something was amiss. She turned slowly, saw the bottle on the ground and the silver box open on her bed. Then she discovered her red-backed snake dropping to the floor and setting off towards a mound of fur in the shadows.

From his hiding place Jake had a view of the serpent slithering towards him. Then he heard the chilling sound of Mina's sword being unsheathed.

He gave a yell as he tossed the rug to one side, then overturned the chest in Mina's direction and ducked under the bottom of the tent. He yanked out the main guy rope and the tent started to topple. He ran, but fell immediately: one leg was tangled in the ropes. He freed it, got to his feet and sprinted away from the camp towards the dark canopy of forest across the valley.

'Stop him!' Mina let out a bloodcurdling cry as she emerged from her collapsing pavilion.

Five cloaked guards rallied immediately; they armed themselves with bows and set off in pursuit of Jake's retreating silhouette. At the edge of the wood he stopped, breathless, and looked back. Figures were approaching from three directions across the moonlit field. His hand shaking, he drew his sword from his scabbard. The weapon became entangled in his cloak and he struggled to release it.

Suddenly he heard a sharp noise and an arrow whistled past his head and struck a tree. For a second Jake was rooted to the spot; another quick salvo followed the first. His eyes went wide as the next missile flew straight towards him. With the force of a hammer it struck the centre of his breast-plate, denting the metal and bouncing off with a hollow clang.

Jake turned and charged into the forest, his feet automatically finding their way through the trees, his hands shielding his face from the branches that whipped back at him. Still the arrows hissed past from every direction. Then there was a rush of air closer than the others; he heard the sound of tearing and felt a stab of pain. An arrow had grazed the side of his arm and sliced open the flesh above his elbow.

He felt the wound with his hand and found a rush of hot blood.

His adrenaline kept him moving, his feet sure on the rutted forest floor. Then he heard a hunting horn and turned to see a group of mounted riders charging through the trees. All at once Jake's foot caught on a root and he went flying. There was a crunch of branches as he struck the ground and somersaulted through the thorny undergrowth. Finally he hit a tree and his sword flew from his hand.

Jake opened his eyes and saw the moon shining brightly down through the awning of fir trees. He heard footsteps closing in on him and knew that this was the end. He felt so stupid. He wondered how he'd ever imagined that he could survive on his own against an army from another land and another time. The steps drew closer and a cloaked figure emerged from the dark undergrowth. It was the guard Jake had sat next to on the journey from Venice.

The boy's eyes were blank, expressionless. He drew his sword and readied it for the kill. Then Jake's instinct to survive kicked in. He leaped to his feet, reached for a fallen branch and hurled it at his assailant's head. There was a hollow crack, the guard's eyes flickered and he fell back, his skull hitting a tree.

Jake's first impulse was to check that the boy was all right. As he looked down, he noticed the eyes flicker and half open. He was still alive.

This is war, Jake reminded himself. 'I'm sorry,' he muttered as he picked up his sword and took off. Once again his weapon became entangled in his cloak. 'What is *wrong* with me?' He cursed, this time ripping the material from his shoulder and discarding it.

The hunting horn sounded once more; the horses were gaining on him, snorting savagely, their hooves echoing through the dark conifers. Jake ran, blood pumping, breath rasping. The galloping drew closer. Within seconds the ground behind him was pounding, and the sweating flank of a stallion was at his side. Jake looked up and saw the rider's ghostly silhouette against the moon. The shadow raised an axe and swung it down towards him.

Jake's eyes went wide. In a flash, his mind filled with a kaleidoscope of visions: his mum and dad, his brother Philip, his house, his bedroom, his last birthday, the corridors of his school, and again his mother, father, brother. The axe swung down towards his face.

Time stopped.

The blade froze in mid-air, hovering above Jake. He looked up at the rider: he was falling sideways, his eyes empty. A dagger had struck him in the back.

A voice came out of nowhere. 'Quickly! Here!'

Jake turned to see, behind him, another figure on a white horse, reaching out a gloved hand. '*C'est moi*, Topaz,' he heard.

Jake's heart leaped. She was wearing a cape and a hood that masked her face, but the golden hair was unmistakable. He jumped to his feet, grabbed her hand and sprang up onto the back of the white horse.

'Hold on tight,' Topaz cried breathlessly as she dug her heels into the horse's flanks. It galloped on through the forest. Jake was no expert at riding, but a friend of Philip's had horses of his own, and he had picked up the basics: how to sit on a horse, to canter and gallop. Even so, Jake had never done any jumping or gone at such a breakneck speed. He concentrated on keeping his balance.

The remaining riders were closing in on them, and Jake could hear their shouts.

'In the saddlebag there are fireworks,' Topaz shouted back as her horse soared over a fallen tree.

'Fireworks?' he exclaimed.

'It's a long story. Light one – it'll scare the wits out of them.'

Jake reached down and grabbed a bundle of rockets.

'There are matches in there too.'

'I have a lighter.' Jake produced the device that Nathan had given him.

Topaz slowed down as he lit one of the fuses and hurled the firework towards their pursuers. With a loud whistle, the rocket exploded and a bolt of light shot through the trees in a brilliant cloud of indigo. Two of the horses reared up, whinnying and throwing their riders to the ground. Topaz's horse, also startled by the explosion, quickened its pace, and she struggled to retain control. Jake lit another rocket and let it go. This one erupted even more dramatically into myriad blue and white stars. The flash of the third rocket was so dazzlingly intense, the remaining guards were blinded completely.

The terrified white mare was now bolting through the trees. Topaz calmly brought her under control, and they emerged from the forest and raced across the tapestry of moonlit fields, jumping hedges and streams. Once again Jake felt the thrill of adventure as the wind whipped past.

'Charlie and I have been following you since the Veneto Tunnel,' Topaz panted. 'We were trying to choose the right moment. Mina Schlitz is not someone you want to mess with.'

'You know her?'

'We have history,' Topaz replied enigmatically as she flicked the reins and they headed down into a valley.

Finally they reached a cluster of old farm buildings. They both dismounted, Topaz checking carefully that no one had followed them.

'Are you badly hurt?' she asked Jake, removing her scarf and passing it to him. 'Tie it with this!'

Jake hesitated.

'Take it!' she insisted. 'I've no social engagements this evening.'

Jake obeyed: he looped it around his elbow and pulled it tight.

'Follow me,' Topaz ordered, striding into a barn. 'You look different with short hair,' she commented. 'Bolder.'

'I'm so happy to see you alive,' Jake gasped,

secretly hoping that Topaz might stop and give him a welcoming hug. She didn't. Instead, she swiftly made her way through the towers of hay bales.

'We have no idea what happened to Nathan,' she told him as she gave a series of knocks on the wooden wall in some kind of Morse code.

'He came back to the ship – he gave me these,' Jake replied, indicating what remained of his red cloak and breastplate.

'We were wondering how you got your hands on them.'

Topaz's taps were answered by coded knocks from the other side of the wall.

'He was badly injured,' Jake continued. 'He gave himself up.'

'I suppose they got Paolo as well.' Topaz sighed. 'Can't see him putting up much of a fight.' Again she tapped the code, and again the wall replied. 'Just open the door, Charlie!' she groaned in exasperation.

A panel of wood slid back, and Jake was greeted by the excited cries of Mr Drake, who flapped his multi-coloured feathers and did a circuit of the little storeroom.

'I'm afraid I had you down as a goner,' Charlie Chieverley told him, pushing his spectacles up his nose. 'Though Topaz had money on you pulling through.'

Jake turned to her, a smile on his lips. She removed her hood and loosened her cape. He could see her clearly now. After nearly two days' absence, she seemed more like a goddess than ever: her brilliant indigo eyes sparkled and her cheeks glowed with the thrill of danger. More than anything, Jake wanted to throw his arms around her, but decided it might be better to show his delight to Charlie instead. He hugged him with all his might. 'Thank you for saving me! Both of you!' he exclaimed.

Charlie pulled a quizzical face at Topaz as he was nearly choked to death.

'I've been very busy,' Jake informed them, finally releasing his friend. 'You'll be impressed. I've found out all sorts of information.'

'First tell us,' interrupted Topaz. 'Have you seen Prince Zeldt? Was he in Venice? Have you heard any mention of him?'

'I haven't *seen* Zeldt,' Jake continued as if he had been a spy all his life, 'but Captain Von Bliecke is taking Nathan and Paolo to him now. He is at a place called Castle Schwarzheim.'

'Castle Schwarzheim! I knew it!' said Charlie, banging the wall. 'Didn't I say so?' He turned to Jake. 'You never know where he may be hiding. He has strongholds in every corner of history. They say Castle Schwarzheim, "the black home" – that's the name *he* gave it, of course – is the most diabolical of them all.'

'What else did you find out?' asked Topaz.

Jake took a deep breath and looked at the other two gravely. 'Mina Schlitz said it was "four days until apocalypse".'

For a moment there was silence. Mr Drake screwed up his eye, and looked from one to the other.

'What apocalypse?' Topaz wanted to know.

Jake shrugged. 'I have no idea.'

'And she said that yesterday?' she asked.

Jake nodded.

'So now there are only three days . . .'

Topaz exchanged a serious look with Charlie, then turned to Jake. 'You'd better tell us everything you know.'

17 THE DIABOLICAL TRIBE

Jake recounted every detail of his adventure –
from the guards storming the *Campana*, to the
discovery of the secret door in the confessional in St
Mark's Cathedral, to finding the architects' drawings and the arrival of Mina Schlitz. He told them
about the escape from Venice through the subterranean tunnel, the journey to Bassano, the
rendezvous with the unnerving Talisman Kant and
the discovery of the glass bottles. Finally he showed
them the parchment he had taken from Mina's desk
– the list of names that was headed: *Guests at the
Superia Conference, Castle Schwarzheim.*

After Jake had finished, Charlie and Topaz
pondered everything for a while before speaking.

'So, these building plans in Venice . . .' Charlie
finally asked. 'What did they look like?'

'Scary, like medieval science fiction,' said Jake.

'Those poor architects.' Topaz shook her head. 'We'll have to get them out of there.'

'And each of the drawings had the heading *Superia*?' Charlie continued probing.

Jake nodded.

'And did a mountain feature in any of the drawings? The summit of *Superia*?'

'Not that I could see.'

'And what about Talisman Kant?' Topaz joined in the cross-examination. 'You say Mina gave him a whole casket of gold for the contents of two glass bottles.'

'Some honeycomb and some talcum powder,' added Charlie dryly.

'That's what they looked like,' Jake insisted.

'*Very* expensive honeycomb and talcum powder,' Charlie sighed.

'So you know Talisman Kant, do you?' asked Jake.

'Never been formally introduced,' Topaz replied, 'but his reputation goes before him. Excessively nasty piece of work – not a moral bone in his body. He calls himself a "scientist" and conducts experiments on his own family, which explains that son of his. Still, his wife was even worse off: she ended up having her legs dissolved in acid.'

'So does he work for Prince Zeldt?'

'Long ago,' Charlie said, 'he was a member of the History Keepers. After it was discovered that he had been corresponding with Ivan the Terrible, suggesting methods of mass torture, it became clear that he didn't have the interests of the world at heart and he was unceremoniously dismissed. Now he'll work for anyone, anywhere in history, providing the price is right. Let me see that list of names again.'

Jake passed him the piece of parchment he had stolen from Mina's tent.

'*Guests at the Superia Conference . . .*' Charlie mused. 'This is an impressive line-up.'

'Who are they?' asked Jake.

'I recognize some of them. Sixteenth-century billionaires, merchants, traders, mining tycoons . . . The notes by their names give us clues as to where they made their money. What on earth is Zeldt up to? The whole business is as clear as mud.'

'Wait a minute – let me have a look,' said Topaz, taking the list. A thought had suddenly occurred to her. '*Mon Dieu!* We've been so stupid,' she announced. 'The answer's right here. *Guests at the*

236

Superia Conference . . . Find the Summit of Superia.
The summit is not a mountain, it's the conference
itself!'

Charlie took the list and cast his eyes over it
again. 'Miss St Honoré, you surpass yourself.'

'Now we have double the reason to reach Castle
Schwarzheim – and quickly,' Topaz said decisively,
gathering up her belongings.

'Where is it?' Jake wondered.

'*En Allemagne* – Germany. It's a two-day journey
over the Alps. There's not a moment to lose.
Charlie, have you fixed the axel on that cart?'

'I may not have solved the riddle of the Superia
Summit' – Charlie shrugged – 'but I am still an
engineering genius.'

'You wouldn't need to be an engineering genius if
you hadn't been conned by that dealer in Padua.'
Topaz turned to Jake. 'He spent all our money on a
glorified wreck.'

'*And* two of the finest horses I have ever set eyes
upon,' Charlie defended himself.

'I have money,' said Jake helpfully, trying to ease
the tension.

Topaz checked through a spy-hole that the coast
was clear, slid the door back and led the way out of

the barn to the offending cart. Jake actually thought it looked quite good. Two sturdy-looking bay horses were drinking from a water trough – along with Topaz's white mare.

She ran her hand fondly through the horse's mane, then led her away and clapped her firmly on the rump. 'Go on! Home you go,' she instructed, pointing towards a house on the hill in the distance. 'I "borrowed" her for the night from a somnolent ostler,' she explained to Jake. 'I needed a very particular animal for your rescue.'

The mare did not move, just blinked her big eyes at Topaz. 'Go now!' she shouted, and this time the horse took off, still tacked up, across the field. Charlie and Topaz busied themselves harnessing the remaining horses to the cart.

Jake's mind was whirling with a torrent of thoughts, but one question nagged him incessantly – not least because of the connection with his brother Philip.

'Everyone has been talking about Prince Zeldt,' he said, 'but I still have no idea who he is. What exactly has he done?'

Jake's enquiry was met by silence. Topaz continued to fasten the straps of the harness.

A good minute passed before Charlie finally answered, 'We probably shouldn't discuss it on an empty stomach.'

A few moments later the three of them climbed aboard. Topaz took the reins, and the cart set off up the road towards the distant mountains.

It was a bumpy, noisy ride, but Jake was surprised how quickly they sped along. Within half an hour they'd found a Roman road that cut straight across the countryside. Its tightly packed stones had been flattened from centuries of use, and their pace picked up still more. Topaz's golden hair flew about in the breeze and Mr Drake's feathers were ruffled as he gazed serenely at the passing landscape from Charlie's shoulder.

'How did you escape in Venice?' Jake shouted over the noise of the wind, the wheels and the galloping hooves.

'Mr Drake saved the day,' Charlie announced proudly, feeding the bird a peanut. 'We were being led away, when my feathered friend created the most spectacular diversion. A great flock of pigeons were sleeping on a rooftop – Venetian pigeons are famously fat and ill-tempered – when Mr Drake dived in and forced them to take flight. You've never seen so many angry feathers. We took advantage of the moment and leaped into the nearest canal. After some very unpleasant underwater navigation, we found our way onto a Chinese trade ship.'

'That's where the fireworks came from!' Topaz shouted from the front as she flicked the reins.

Jake looked at the rolling hills, now bathed in morning sunshine, and wondered what lay ahead; what dangers they would encounter when they reached their destination. Charlie had described the stronghold of Castle Schwarzheim as 'the most diabolical of them all'. Jake thought about the castle's fierce inhabitants, most particularly the infamous Prince Zeldt – 'a thousand times more evil' than the worst killer he could imagine. More than anything, Jake wondered if the castle would reveal the whereabouts of his parents.

All day they swept along the Roman roads, stopping briefly at roadside inns to change horses, then carrying on. The sun travelled across the sky; the passengers in the back played cards or chatted – Charlie, to Mr Drake's embarrassment, even sang some songs. Late in the afternoon Jake was entrusted with the reins. To begin with, he had some teething problems, and Topaz and Charlie had to give him a lesson. In a short while, however, he was handling the horses with confidence.

As evening approached, they started to climb the slopes up to the Brenner Pass. The horses panted with exertion, but soon the road began to even out. They stopped at a tavern in a mountain village to change horses again, and ate delicious local sausage and sauerkraut.

After dinner they returned to the cart. It was Charlie's turn to drive. He lit the lanterns. 'Why don't you join me at the front?' he asked Jake, who jumped up next to him, while Topaz climbed into the back. Charlie shook the reins and they set off again, the lanterns flickering as they trundled out of town.

In the half-light, Topaz once again examined the guest list for the Superia Summit. She couldn't stop yawning.

'I know you're officially in charge,' Charlie told her, 'but I really must insist you have a rest. You haven't slept in two days.'

'No need, I'm wide awake,' Topaz insisted, but her heavy eyelids told a different story. '*D'accord* – ten minutes,' she agreed. She put the list to one side and gathered up some hay for a bed. 'I'll just doze,' she said as she lay down, falling instantly into a deep slumber. Mr Drake, who was also exhausted, fluttered off Charlie, perched next to Topaz, fluffed up his plummage, dropped his bill onto his chest and closed his eyes.

It was a calm night. After travelling in silence for a while, Charlie cleared his throat and whispered, 'We don't usually talk about the Zeldt family in front of Topaz. We all have reasons to hate them, but Topaz more than most. It's to do with her parents.'

'Did they kill her parents?' Jake asked bluntly.

'Sssh . . .' Charlie turned to check that Topaz was still asleep.

'Sorry,' whispered Jake.

Charlie thought about how best to answer his question. 'They didn't actually kill them, but it was something along those lines.'

Jake nodded seriously.

'The Zeldt dynasty goes back to the very beginning of the History Keepers,' Charlie continued, 'before they were even called *keepers*. Rasmus Ambrosius Zeldt, born originally in the frozen wilds of northern Sweden, was a close contemporary of Sejanus Poppoloe, who discovered atomium and drew the first maps of the world's horizon points. They were firm friends, visionary scientists and great adventurers. Their goal was to explore history, to understand it, but *never* to change it. However, Rasmus grew increasingly unstable.'

'Unstable?'

'Criminally unstable,' Charlie reiterated solemnly. 'Around that time he met his wife, Matilda, on a voyage to England during the civil war of the seventeenth century – and by the way, *she* was the reason why the Zeldt family still speak in English. Drunk with the power of time travel, Rasmus descended into madness and split from Sejanus and the other time observers who had joined the society. He proclaimed himself King. Not of Sweden or Europe or the world even, but of Time itself. Really it was more *talk* and bravado than any-thing else. Many generations passed. The self-declared "royal family" lurked around history like a bad smell. Then King Sigvard was born and nothing was ever the same again.'

'Sigvard?'

'The grandfather of all our troubles,' Charlie said ominously.

'What did he do?' asked Jake.

Charlie paused for effect. 'He declared *war* on history.' At these words, a shiver went down Jake's spine. 'He vowed to *change* the world, to *ruin* the world, to steep it in evil. In order to learn his diabolical craft he took a grand tour of history's greatest atrocities. He observed, at first hand, the Spanish Inquisition, the witch hunts of Salem, the persecution of the Jews, of the Christians, of the Huguenots, the murderous rampages of the Thugees in India, the Islamic holy wars . . . King Sigvard watched it all from the shadows, influencing it where he could, learning his craft and planning his domination. He started a campaign of horror. The History Keepers' Secret Service have been fighting the Zeldts ever since.'

'Is he still alive?'

'He died decades ago, in ancient Mesopotamia. Would you believe – a roof tile fell on his head! He suffered internal bleeding and died soon after. After his extraordinary reign, his malevolent career, his lifetime of evil, he dies in a household accident.'

'I suppose that's fate having the last word,' Jake mused.

'Not the last word at all, I'm afraid. He left three

children. Xander was the oldest – the Dark Prince, as he is known, the one we're on our way to see. The second, Alric, disappeared when he was fourteen. He has never been seen since. The third was Agata, and she was the worst of the lot.'

'Worse than her father?'

'To give you some idea, when she was five she tried to drown Xander, her elder brother, in a freezing lake. That's why, to this very day, he's unable to feel warmth. Or anything else for that matter. On another occasion she discovered her lady-in-waiting trying on one of her gowns. She forced her to sit on a throne of red-hot iron, with a red-hot iron crown on her head and holding a ret-hot iron sceptre, until she was scorched to death. No, Agata Zeldt is categorically the most evil woman in history.'

'What are you two talking about?' came a soft voice from the back of the cart. Jake turned to see Topaz, bleary-eyed, looking up from her bed of hay.

'Nothing!' Charlie declared flatly. 'Just soufflés.'

Topaz smiled warmly at Jake, lay back down and drifted off to sleep again.

Jake looked around at the moonlit landscape, at the snow-peaked mountains on either side. He was suddenly filled with a sense of foreboding as the

cart flew on into the night towards Castle
Schwarzheim.

18 THE CHEQUERED ROSE

Back at Point Zero, Oceane Noire stood at the entrance to the stateroom, greeting her party guests. Only once did she lose her composure. '*Mon Dieu!*' she exclaimed as a figure stumbled into the room. 'She's carrying that *bag*.' She was referring to Rose Djones, who looked quite beautiful in the Empire gown that Olympe de Gouges had bequeathed her – though the effect was spoiled by her jangling bangles and ubiquitous carpetbag. That and the fact that the dress was so constricting she could barely move in it.

At seven forty-five precisely, a gong sounded and the guests took their seats for dinner. There were place names set out so that Oceane could control exactly who sat where. The hostess put herself next to Jupitus Cole and sat Rose in a draughty corner at the far end by the kitchen door. Oceane had no idea that this suited Rose perfectly – at some point she planned to make a casual exit and set off on her secret mission.

During dessert, there was an excited commotion over the clementine and fig jelly that had been cast in the likeness of the hostess. As the occupants of Rose's table (all of whom were black sheep in Oceane's eyes) diverted themselves by wobbling their miniature Oceanes into a frenzy, Galliana surreptitiously nodded to her old ally. Rose nodded back, stood up and slipped unnoticed from the room.

As quickly as her dress would allow her, she hurried up stairways and along deserted corridors until she came to the entrance to Jupitus Cole's suite. Here she put on her gloves, unlocked the door and slipped inside.

The rooms were just as formal and austere as Rose had imagined, with heavy pieces of furniture, dark portraits of glum-looking people and a faint but all-pervading odour of stale potpourri.

'Dear me,' she said, taking it all in, 'it's like a tomb.'

She started searching the bureau, carefully going

through a pile of perfectly stacked papers. From the bottom she retrieved two sheets to give to Galliana to check for fingerprints. As she folded them and put them in her pocket, she saw something inside the bureau that made her heart stop. She reached out and carefully withdrew a small glass box, beautifully crafted, with fine gold joints. It was not the box that she recognized; it was what lay inside – a single dried rose which, though long dead, still retained its distinctive red and white chequered pattern. At the bottom of the box there was a tiny drawer. Rose opened it to discover a bundle of handwritten notes. She gasped in disbelief and sank back onto one of the chairs.

In the stateroom the party was in full swing. After dinner had finished, the tables had been cleared to create a dance floor, and the hitherto restrained orchestra had picked up their pace dramatically. The dancing had become more and more high-spirited as the band worked their way through the hits of the 1820s, from the Regency quadrille, to the exuberant *danse espagnole* and the positively racy waltz.

Into the melee strode Rose, ashen-faced. She manoeuvred herself past Norland (who was dancing so energetically with Lydia Wunderbar, the librarian, that they both threatened to do themselves an injury) and cut around the dance floor towards Galliana.

'Here. You can check these for fingerprints,' she said as she subtly passed the commander the two letters she had retrieved from Jupitus's bureau.

'Did you find anything else?' asked Galliana, without looking at her accomplice.

'I went through every single drawer in his apartment. Nothing suspicious at all.'

'Rose? Are you all right? You look pale.'

'Not really,' Rose replied, her brows knotting. 'I found something else that rather alarmed me. Do you remember, years ago, when I lived on the Mount, I took up gardening for a while? I tried to cultivate my own rose. I only managed to produce one rather lacklustre plant, which lasted all of three weeks and never bloomed again. The roses were red and white in a chequered pattern.' Rose continued as if in a trance, 'In Jupitus's rooms, I have just discovered one of the flowers, preserved in a glass case.'

Galliana turned to her friend, arched her eyebrow, then looked back at the dancers again.

'Not only that,' Rose continued. 'But I also

discovered a drawer containing old notes of mine – shopping lists, memos, irrelevant scribblings that must surely have been taken from my waste-paper basket.' Her voice strayed into a high, slightly hysterical register.

'Good God, he's clearly in love with you.'

'Don't be ridiculous,' Rose announced. 'We hate each other!'

Half an hour later, Rose received her second shock of the night. As she went to the bar to get another calming glass of rum punch, a low voice announced behind her, 'It is not I, the spy.'

She turned, to be confronted by a very serious-looking Jupitus. 'Excuse me?' she replied innocently.

'I know you were in my rooms. I have just been there and I smelled your perfume. Believe me or don't believe me, it makes no matter, but if you are looking for a double agent, your time would be better spent elsewhere.'

'I don't understand . . .' Rose mumbled.

'Don't be obtuse,' said Jupitus, fixing her with his most piercing stare. 'If you wish to find out what I know on the subject, follow me.' He turned, strode across to the door and left the room.

Rose stood there for a second, dumbfounded.

Her eyes darted from side to side as she decided what to do. Then she drank down the entire glass of punch in one and followed Jupitus out.

He was waiting for her nonchalantly at the foot of the grand staircase, holding a lit candlestick. 'This way,' he said coolly, heading up the steps. He led her silently up two flights and along the corridor until they came to the doorway of the Library of Faces. They could still hear the distant sound of the party.

'I couldn't sleep last night,' Jupitus explained. 'I came this way to the kitchens. I find a hot chocolate usually takes the edge off my worries. As I rounded the corner there, I saw a figure in a navy-blue cloak emerge from the Library of Faces. I couldn't see his face, but he had the bearing of a man. 'He closed the door and quickly disappeared along the corridor in a manner that I found suspicious.'

'Did you follow him?'

'I chose rather to investigate the library.'

Jupitus opened the door and led Rose inside. The candles illuminated the room only dimly. It was fifteen years since Rose had set foot inside and she had forgotten how eerie it was: the long high wall composed of nothing but portraits. The faces of the

History Keepers' many friends and foes, dating back centuries, stared down at her. After a minute, a bell rang and the machinery clicked into motion, turning every painting on its axis to reveal another wall of faces.

'I found this door ajar,' Jupitus continued in a whisper, making for a concealed entrance in the far corner of the room. He pushed it open and ushered Rose into the pitch-black area that lay behind the portraits.

'Take my hand,' he whispered. 'It's easy to trip over the machinery.'

Rose stopped. Her eyes flickered with apprehension before she tentatively held out her hand. It was clasped by Jupitus's. Rose was surprised at how warm it was; somehow she'd expected him to be cold-blooded.

Jupitus led her deep into the dark space. The Library of Faces, indistinguishable in the gloom, still watched them. The light from Jupitus's candlestick picked out the room's secret mechanics, the hundreds of levers and pulleys that turned the faces.

In the blackest corner, Jupitus finally lighted upon a length of piping that ran down the wall and through the floor.

'This tube,' he explained, illuminating it with the candles, 'comes from the communications room above us and runs down into the commander's private suite below.'

Rose was beginning to grasp Jupitus's meaning. 'This is the way the Meslith messages are sent to Galliana?'

'Affirmative. And yesterday I made an alarming discovery.'

He held the candlestick close to the tube, and Rose gasped. She could see that it had been cut and its path blocked with tape.

'Messages are being intercepted,' Jupitus explained, 'before they continue on their way. We need to find out who is responsible.'

'You mean the man in the navy-blue cloak?'

'Exactly, Rosalind,' Jupitus whispered. 'Tomorrow we need to conceal ourselves in this place in the hope that our "interceptor" returns.'

'W-we? *Together?*' stammered Rose.

'As I am evidently under suspicion, I would feel more comfortable. Or are you busy tomorrow?'

'No, I . . . of course . . . if you think it would be helpful.' Rose floundered, suddenly inexplicably nervous. 'A stakeout, huh? It'll be like old times.'

Jupitus stared at her. The candlelight flickered over his face. Rose looked into his eyes. For the briefest moment the person staring back at her was not the cold, irritable, unknowable Jupitus Cole, but another man altogether – a sensitive, almost fragile soul. Then his gaze hardened once again.

'Why couldn't you sleep last night? What – what were you worried about?' Rose found herself asking.

Jupitus took a while to respond. 'Dull matters of work, nothing more.' He shrugged and offered Rose the curtest of smiles. 'We should return to the party before we are missed.'

He headed back towards the door at the far end of the room. Rose, feeling totally discombobulated, followed.

19 VILLAGE LIFE

Jake weaved through the crowds of commuters and holidaymakers hurrying across the forecourt of Euston Station. He navigated his way to platform five just as the Birmingham train was arriving. It slowly snaked into the building and pulled up with a whine of brakes.

Jake's face lit up at the thought of seeing his parents again. They had only been gone four days, but it seemed much longer. He had never missed them so much as he had this week: their cheerful banter; their mischievous sense of humour; the displays of affection that Jake had taken so much for granted.

For a while there was no movement on the train; no passengers disembarked. Then, at the near end, a door creaked open. Jake's heart soared with excitement as an unseen hand passed out a red suit-case and deposited it on the platform. He waited for his parents to follow.

But no one stepped down from the train. The red suitcase stood alone on the empty platform.

Gradually Jake's excitement drained away, replaced by a creeping sense of foreboding. He walked down the ramp towards the suitcase, expect-ing a sudden rush of travellers; but still no one emerged. Jake stopped and looked at the red case suspiciously, then glanced at the single open door and cautiously stepped aboard the train. The glass door into the compartment opened automatically and Jake went in.

There was no one there. Jake moved up the aisle looking at the rows of empty seats. There were signs of occupation: luggage bundled onto racks, news-papers open on tables, even a steaming cup of coffee, but there were no people. Then Jake caught a glimpse of crimson and he froze. At the far end of the carriage, sitting perfectly still, his back to Jake, was a figure in a hooded cloak. Against his will, Jake found himself drawn towards the motionless silhouette, whose face was shrouded in shadow. The figure did not turn to look at him, but gazed ahead.

And now, as Jake swivelled round again, he realized that there were crimson-cloaked figures everywhere, all rigidly still. Through the glass doors he could see the same chilling spectacle in the next compartment.

Jake was finding it difficult to breathe; he had to leave the train immediately. Focusing only on the exit, he retraced his steps. This time, the glass door did not open for him. He pulled at its handle, but it was locked.

The cloaked figures now slowly turned and fixed their gaze on him.

Through the train window Jake saw a guard pick up the red suitcase and drop it into the back of a rubbish cart. The man gave a signal and the cart pulled away.

'Wait! Stop!' Jake cried out in vain. 'That belongs to my parents!'

He tugged hard at the door handle, but still it did not shift. He heard movement behind him and saw one of the cloaked figures advancing slowly up the aisle. Then another rose to his feet, and another and another. The ghost-like crimson forms swept towards him, enveloping him in shadow. Jake shielded his eyes as he fell to the floor . . .

* * *

'Jake, wake up!' a familiar voice called out.

Jake opened his eyes and found himself in the back of the hay-strewn cart, with Topaz leaning over him.

'You were having a bad dream,' she said softly.

The cart was travelling along a country road under a canopy of trees. Charlie was at the reins, with Mr Drake perched on his shoulder.

'How long have I been asleep?' asked Jake, his mind full of fog.

'Nearly five hours,' Topaz replied. 'We've crossed southern Germany – we're almost there.'

'We're almost there! Really?' Jake exclaimed breathlessly, sitting up and eagerly scanning his surroundings.

The road emerged from amongst the trees and curved round to reveal an immense valley bordered by mountains on either side. A wide, placid river wound its way through the centre.

'The Rhine,' said Charlie in his tour operator's voice. 'The old frontier of the Roman Empire; one of the longest rivers in Europe – after the Volga and the Danube, of course.'

Jake could see the great waterway twist its path

far, far into the warm, hazy mist of the distance. Then the cart rattled back under the trees and the view was gone.

They passed through a small, neat group of thatched houses. A cluster of old villagers watched them, their attention drawn to the multi-coloured Mr Drake (one of the old men dropped his walking stick). Then, a mile out of the village, Charlie spied a grey shape amongst the trees in the distance.

'I think we might be approaching a gatehouse of some description. Reconnaissance required.'

He veered off the road and pulled up in a small clearing. The three of them got down and crept through the undergrowth into the shadow of a sturdy oak, from which they could examine the scene.

'If I'm not mistaken,' whispered Charlie, 'that's the entrance to Castle Schwarzheim.'

Jake frowned. 'How are we supposed to get in there?'

It was a forbidding structure of two granite towers enclosing an archway sealed with a mighty iron portcullis. On either side, high walls curved into the distance, enclosing the vast estate. To add to the sense of impenetrability, a group of bearded sentries – crimson-cloaked like all Zeldt's staff – stood guard.

'Actually that's probably just the first hurdle,' said Charlie, pushing his glasses up his nose. 'At the top of the mountain, the entrances will doubtless become even more impassable.'

'So do we have a plan?' Jake was trying to contain his sense of urgency. On the one hand he knew they could be tantalizingly close to uncovering the mystery of his parents' whereabouts; on the other, the task seemed more impossible than ever.

As the three of them pondered in silence, they heard a rattling sound, and a farm cart emerged through the trees from the direction of the village. The driver pulled up in front of the gatehouse and stopped. Jake could see that the vehicle was laden with an unwieldy tower of produce: crates of vegetables, huge sides of meat, and basket upon basket of squawking fowl. A guard sullenly inspected the goods, ignoring the driver's nervous chatter. At length he gave a signal to a figure inside the building and, with a grinding of metal, the portcullis slowly rose. The truck entered the grounds and the barrier inched back down again.

'We need to return to the village,' said Topaz decisively, 'and find out what other vehicles are heading this way.'

They crept back to their cart and retraced their steps. As they rattled along the high street, Charlie spotted a young girl seated on a stool in front of the village inn, cheerfully plucking a chicken. Her frizzy curls were almost identical to Charlie's, but for the bright red colour.

'She looks the helpful type,' he said. 'I'll go and enquire.' He leaped down and addressed her in perfect German.

The girl looked up, saw Mr Drake, let out a yell, threw down her half-plucked bird and leaped to her feet in alarm. The parrot replied by squawking loudly, fluffing out his feathers and flapping his wings. There was a duel of shrieking between both parties – until eventually, when she realized that the strange bird was harmless, the girl's screams turned into whoops of uncontrollable laughter.

Charlie picked up the chicken, dusted it down, laid it on the stool and started questioning the girl. At first she seemed wary, but Charlie was so charming and persuasive that within moments she was revealing a torrent of information, giggling coquettishly at his jokes. When she started winding her hair around her finger, Jake and Topaz shared a look.

'He's certainly on form today,' Topaz commented. 'There's no one like Charlie Chieverley for getting you to reveal your deepest secrets.'

With the interview complete, Charlie ran back to the others. 'Well, there's good news and there's bad news.' He was brimming with excitement. 'The young lady there – Heidi is her name – was extremely helpful.'

'So we noticed,' said Jake, raising his eyebrows.

'Hairstyle-wise, Heidi and you are a match made in heaven,' added Topaz playfully.

Charlie went bright red and stammered on, 'Well, yes – anyway . . . the bad news is: that was the last delivery of food to the castle. Apparently they put in an order of astronomical proportions – a hundred brace of pheasant, thirty boxes of truffles, fifty crates of mead, et cetera, et cetera.'

'Quite a summer barbecue,' Topaz mused. 'And the good news?'

'From dawn tomorrow morning,' Charlie continued, 'they have been told to expect up to thirty groups of foreign dignitaries, from Portugal, France,

Flanders, Greece – even as far as Asia Minor . . .'

'Our guests at the Superia Conference,' Topaz noted.

'And they'll all need refreshments before the ride up the mountain, which apparently is gruelling.'

'Well, that's our way in,' said Topaz conclusively. 'We catch a ride with one of them. We have until dawn to think how.'

'Dawn?' Jake was surprised. 'That's twelve hours away!'

'Eight, to be precise,' Charlie corrected him.

'But isn't it less than a day and a half until the apocalypse?' Jake persisted doggedly. 'Shouldn't we be trying to find a way *now*?'

'We're all concerned' – Topaz's voice was calm yet firm – 'but we have only one opportunity to get this right and this is our best chance. We cannot fail.'

Jake held his tongue and nodded.

'On a lighter note,' Charlie announced, 'the travelling players are in town. Tonight, there is to be a candlelit performance of *Oedipus* on the village green.'

'Greek tragedy – that'll raise our spirits . . .' said Topaz with a smile.

They took a room at the inn. A rosy-cheeked landlord escorted them up a winding staircase to an oak-beamed set of rooms; there was a good deal of lopsided furniture and a pot of wild flowers in the sitting-room window.

The three of them washed and had something to eat. After the sun had gone down, a throng of locals emerged from their houses carrying candles and headed for a clearing on the banks of the Rhine, where the travelling players were due to perform. The three young agents were eager to enjoy a little local entertainment and, keeping to the shadows, followed the villagers to the edge of the fast-flowing river. Here a rough stage had been erected, lit on either side by flickering torches. At the back was a tapestry screen, behind which the players changed their costumes. To the right, three musicians sat on a bench, fiddles and drums at the ready.

Charlie was entranced by the romance of the setting. 'This is how it all began, show business!' he exclaimed with a flourish of his hand across the heavens. 'Just the bare stage, the words and the sky.'

Topaz saw two figures waving as they approached through the throng of people. It was Heidi, the helpful redhead, and her friend, a girl with buck teeth whose face was fixed in a permanent grin. Heidi flirted outrageously with Charlie, tickling him under the chin, before heading off into the crowd.

'Charlie Chieverley, *je suis impressionnée* – you have them falling at your feet,' noted Topaz.

'They were asking about Mr Drake, that's all,' Charlie mumbled, going bright red. 'I told them he was taking a nap.'

There was a drum roll, and the players, all dressed as ancient Greeks, came out from behind the screen and took their positions on the stage. A blanket of hushed excitement descended across the audience and the play began.

Jake was transfixed. Of course, the play was in German, and he didn't really understand the details of the story (Charlie explained the bare bones: a man ends up marrying his mother by mistake and killing his father), but the actors spoke with such gravity, their movements were so graceful and expressive, their torch-lit faces etched with such passion, that he could not help but be mesmerized.

An hour seemed to pass in an instant. The audience hung on every word, sometimes in silence, sometimes exclaiming out loud at the action. All the while, the musicians accompanied the unfolding drama. Jake glanced at Topaz, her eyes wide and sparkling with excitement. Without looking away from the stage, she reached for his hand and clutched it tightly. Jake felt his heart soar. This balmy summer evening was full of magic: the players in their Greek costumes, the moon over the Rhine, the mission that lay ahead of them.

When the play was finished and the actors had taken their bows, the musicians jumped up onto the stage. The fiddle player stamped his feet three times and the band started to play. There was a cheer from the crowd. Some of them stood up and started dancing in circles and clapping their hands.

Charlie's two admirers reappeared, then dragged him to his feet and into the dancing circle.

'No, it's out of the question – can't dance for toffee – two left feet,' he protested as he was twirled from one to the other. But he threw himself into it all the same.

Jake and Topaz watched the festivities, smiling broadly. Nearly all the villagers had now got to their feet. The young and the old danced together, whooping with joy. One couple in particular drew Jake's attention: a young boy was dancing with an older lady. The former was shoeless – he looked as if he had been working in the fields all day, while his partner was elegantly dressed. But they danced together expertly, laughing and taking it in turns to show off their dazzling footwork.

Jake turned to Topaz, raised his eyebrows and opened his mouth to speak. He meant to invite her to dance, but found himself asking something altogether different: 'The tune's surprisingly catchy, isn't it?'

Topaz merely nodded. Jake reeled in embarrassment, wondering how he could possibly be so banal. He attempted a second time: 'I don't suppose you would like to—'

Too late: a tall, handsome youth had approached Topaz and was holding out his hand. He had long blond hair and a cloak thrown dashingly over his shoulder. His ear was pierced with a diamond stud. Two fresh-faced friends (also wearing cloaks, though not quite as dashingly) were watching with keen interest to see if he would be successful.

Topaz looked up at the gallant and smiled. 'You don't mind, do you, Jake?'

'Not at all,' Jake lied, shaking his head a little too enthusiastically.

Topaz was led away from him. Her beau guided her into the centre of the throng and they started to dance. Topaz was not familiar with the steps, but she picked them up quickly and added flourishes of her own that set Jake's heart racing once again. She and her partner, with their striking looks and long blond hair, were the golden couple. The young man's two sidekicks watched their friend with envy and admiration.

'*The tune's surprisingly catchy?*' Jake repeated to himself. 'How could I be so stupid?'

He stood up and wandered over to the river. The immense expanse of water flowed silently by. It reminded Jake of the Dordogne in France, where he and his family had gone on holiday four summers ago. Jake was eleven at the time and Philip was fourteen. Older brothers often have little time for their younger siblings, but Philip was different: he always treated Jake as an equal.

One day, Philip was going canoeing and Jake begged to accompany him. Philip was a little uncertain about his younger brother's skill on the water, but he agreed to take him. It was a still, hot morning and the river had been placid to begin with. But an hour into their journey, a black cloud came over the mountains. There were deep rumbles of thunder, torrential rain started to pelt down and the current quickened alarmingly.

'I'm heading for the bank,' Jake shouted.

'No!' Philip yelled. 'Stay in the middle – it's dangerous!'

Jake did not heed his brother's advice; he turned his canoe against the current, and a surge of foaming water capsized it immediately, sending him into the river. The current dragged him under.

Philip did not hesitate. He dived in and fought the swirling eddies to reach his brother and pull him to safety. They both sat on the bank, getting their breath back. Jake was mortified that he had let his brother down.

'I'm sorry,' he said quietly.

Philip smiled and put his arm around him. 'If the river goes crazy like that, always go with the flow. And if a wave comes at you, go straight into it, even if that seems like the maddest thing in the world. Understand?'

Jake nodded. He traced an imaginary shape on his soaking trousers. 'I suppose that's the last time you're going to take me . . .'

'Are you joking?' Philip replied. 'Next time,

you're leading the way. You're my protégé, remember.' He ruffled his brother's hair affectionately.

The holiday to the Dordogne was the last trip the whole family had taken together: Philip had disappeared the following winter.

Suddenly Jake heard a cheer from the river.

'Look at that,' said Topaz, appearing at his side. She pointed to a large boat that was gliding downstream. Lanterns were twinkling on its decks and crewmen waved at the villagers on the bank.

'Cargo ship by the looks of it,' she told him. 'Probably on its way to Cologne or Düsseldorf – maybe even to Holland. The Rhine is quite a river . . .'

Jake nodded, then glanced at Topaz before turning back to the water. 'What happened to the hunk?' he asked as nonchalantly as he could.

'Put it this way,' she replied. 'The type of boy you meet at a summer dance in Germany rarely changes through the ages.'

'The curse of the holiday romance,' Jake agreed. 'Actually, I've never had a holiday romance, but I thought the phrase might make me sound wise and worldly.'

Topaz turned and beamed at him.

'That's not quite true,' Jake suddenly remembered. 'I was forgetting Mirabelle Delafonte. She proposed to me on the Ghost Train at Alton Towers.'

'Mirabelle Delafonte? *De vrai?* That was her real name?'

'I'm afraid it was worse. Mirabelle Portia Svetlana *Ida* Delafonte. Her parents were involved in amateur dramatics, to put it mildly.'

Topaz giggled. 'Did you say yes?'

'As I was "thinking" about it, she glued her mouth to my face and my cheek got caught on her brace. We almost had to have it surgically removed.'

Topaz burst out laughing: for almost five minutes, the image of Mirabelle Delafonte's cumbersome brace played over in her head, and she couldn't stop laughing. Just as she got it under control, it would start up again. Eventually she took some deep breaths and confessed, 'I'm terrible when I get started.'

Jake felt brave enough to ask her some questions. 'So, bringing things down to earth, how long have you been . . . doing this kind of thing? In the History Keepers' Secret Service, that is.'

Topaz gazed out across the river. 'Well, I was born during the battle of Poitiers in the Hundred Years War. And when I say "during", it was apparently in the ammunition tent in the middle of the battlefield. Thankfully I have no recollection of it. But I do remember my first Crusade, at the age of four. My mother took me to eleventh-century Jerusalem "to show me the ropes", and things never really changed much from then on.'

Jake detected a certain brittleness in Topaz's tone. He wasn't sure if he should continue, but found himself asking one more question: 'And would it be rude to ask – what happened to your parents?'

Any trace of a smile now vanished completely from Topaz's face. The dark shadow of sorrow had taken over.

Jake felt terrible. 'I'm sorry, I shouldn't have asked.'

'It's all right, I understand. You're worried about *your* parents,' Topaz replied bravely. 'Alan and Miriam are wonderful people, Jake. I am sure they are safe somewhere. I can feel it here,' she said, touching her heart. She looked deep into his eyes. 'The story of my parents was very different.'

And that was all she would say on the matter.

She gazed out at the river a little longer, then turned and took Jake's hand. 'Let's go and find Charlie before *his* holiday romance gets out of control.'

Jake laughed and followed her into the crowd.

The sound of fiddles drifted across the valley and along the Rhine. It became fainter and fainter as a warm breeze carried it through the night clouds to the castle perching high on the nearby peak. Here, behind granite walls fifteen feet deep, two figures sat forlornly in a dungeon . . .

'I wonder what his last meal was,' pondered one.

Nathan Wylder and Paolo Cozzo were leaning against a damp stone wall in a prison cell lit only by a single ray of moonlight that came through a barred loophole window. One of the walls consisted of a partition of thick iron bars, through which the rest of the murky dungeons could be glimpsed. Nathan still had a steely glint in his eye, but Paolo was a picture of despair.

'Whatever it was, his last meal, I am categorically not going to order it,' Nathan declared. The object of his musings was a skeleton propped against the opposite wall of the cell.

Paolo rolled his eyes. His stomach made a strange

rumbling sound. A minute passed before he muttered morosely, 'How do you know it's a man?'

'Was that a question?' Nathan gasped. 'This is exciting! We're having a *conversation*! You said we weren't going to have any of those again. Hmmm – you're right, maybe it is a young lady. That might change things.' He rearranged his matted hair and torn jacket and winked seductively at the skeleton. 'Doing anything tonight?'

Paolo sighed. The faint sound of music drifted up from the village below. As Nathan hummed the tune, suddenly an idea struck him and he clambered to his feet. 'I know . . .'

'What?' Paolo asked excitedly.

'Why don't we dance?'

Paolo gritted his teeth. 'You really are hysterically funny,' he muttered, and slumped back down again.

'Actually I wasn't talking to you. I was talking to my new friend here, Esmerelda.' He held out his hand to the skeleton. 'Esmerelda, do you fancy a waltz with me? Or a polka – or I can go more baroque if you like? I promise not to tread on your bones.'

'Shut up, Nathan!' Paolo finally exploded. 'I'm sick, I'm tired, I haven't eaten in three days – we're going to starve to death, or be tortured or cut up into pieces, and all you can do is make stupid jokes!'

'Haven't eaten? Your memory is playing tricks: we had those delicious cockroaches this morning. I thought the texture was revelatory. And as for making jokes, we have to, don't we? Humour is what sets us apart from the animals.'

'SHUT UP!' Paolo yelled. 'OR I WILL NOT BE RESPONSIBLE FOR MY ACTIONS!' In frustration, he scooped up a pile of hay from the ground and threw it at Nathan.

Nathan crouched down beside the skeleton, sharing a guilty look with it. 'Sorry about my friend,' he whispered confidentially. 'Italian – very dramatic.'

His eye caught something on the ground: a tiny piece of material that he'd uncovered with his foot. Nathan reached forward and picked it up. An inscription was sewn onto it. He read it quietly to himself: '*Marks and Spencer?*' He rubbed the material with his fingers. 'Synthetic, obviously twentieth century.' Then a terrible thought struck him. 'Miriam and Alan Djones.'

'What's that?' Paolo looked up.

'Nothing,' replied Nathan breezily, slipping the

tag into his pocket. He covertly scanned the floor for any other signs of previous occupants.

Suddenly they heard the distant sounds of keys jangling and a door being unlocked. Paolo gasped and sat up, not knowing whether to feel delight or terror. Heavy footsteps approached. Candlelight flickered on the vaulted roof beyond the bars of the cell, and finally the elegant figure of Mina Schlitz glided into view, accompanied by a single guard carrying a lantern.

Mina stopped and stared down at the two prisoners. In her hand she held a great domed pewter charger. She lifted the lid to reveal a magnificent array of food: cuts of cold meat, fresh bread and a mountain of fruit.

'Food? You've brought us food?' Paolo stammered in disbelief, pulling himself to his feet.

Mina replaced the lid, put the platter on the ground and, pointedly, pushed it away from them with her heel. She withdrew her red-backed snake from the box at her waist and wound it around her wrist. 'The prince would like to know if you are hungry enough yet to strike a deal.'

'A deal – of course,' Paolo exclaimed. 'We'll do a

deal. What does it involve?' He clung to the bars excitedly.

'My friend is dehydrated and not thinking properly,' interjected Nathan. 'We don't negotiate with the enemy.'

'Really?' purred Mina. 'That's very odd. You're given two alternatives: a slow, lingering death or a purposeful and glorious career with the very creators of history.'

'Purposeful career! I'd go for that every time,' enthused Paolo. 'Where do we sign?'

Nathan removed him from the bars and steered him to the back of the cell. 'I'm warning you – *no more*.'

He turned to face Mina. His expression was no longer playful: his face was grave and his eyes alert.

'History has already been created, Miss Schlitz,' he said in a deep, forceful tone. 'It's had enough problems already. We don't wish to make things worse.' His expression hardened another notch. 'There are no deals to be made.'

A smile played across Mina's face. 'The last people who were locked in this cell said the same thing.' Her voice dropped to a teasing whisper. 'I've heard that their demise was wonderfully unpleasant.' Again, she kicked the pewter platter yet further from the prisoners' grasp. 'There's still time for second thoughts.' She nodded to the guard, and they both turned to go.

'But if I may make so bold, Miss Schlitz . . . ?'

Mina stopped and looked round hopefully.

'Red isn't your colour at all,' Nathan teased. 'I dare say you think it goes with that friendly viper of yours, but actually, they're different tones: your dress is magenta, the markings on your serpent are vermilion. Subtle clashes can be a sign of confidence, but in your case, I think it's verging on the vulgar.'

Mina's face darkened angrily. She turned and strode away, the guard and the light vanishing with her. There came the sound of a door slamming shut and keys turning.

'Don't you feel better for that? More alive?' asked Nathan, turning to his companion.

But Paolo merely shuddered with misery.

20 THE RUSSIAN VISITORS

'Someone's here,' whispered Jake as he patted Topaz on the shoulder.

It took her a moment to surface from her deep sleep, but suddenly her eyes flashed open; she pulled back the covers and leaped out of bed, already fully dressed. Charlie also surfaced and sat up quickly.

'Down there,' Jake whispered. He pointed through a gap in the curtain. In the street below, like an apparition emerging from a blanket of morning mist, stood a carriage.

The three of them had discussed their plans just before going to bed, and now they snapped into action.

'You're clear about what you're doing?' Charlie asked.

Jake nodded confidently. 'At school I went down a storm in *Oliver!*' he lied.

'Here are your props . . .' said Charlie, handing Jake a bowl of bloody offal. 'Entrails, compliments of the chef.' Then he added dryly, 'And you two wonder why I'm a vegetarian.'

'Let's take our positions, everyone,' instructed Topaz.

They all crept down the stairs.

In the street, a young couple descended from the carriage and took a disdainful look around the village. The gentleman was tall and chinless; his companion was sour-faced and haughty. Both were dressed in the fashions of the period and, even though it was July, draped with a veritable menagerie of fur: dead minks, ocelots and martens. The lady withdrew a whip from her belt and cracked it at the ancient driver, barking an order at him. As the poor man was feeling his way down from his seat, coughing and wheezing, Charlie came out of the inn and rushed over to the pair with an expression of panic on his face.

'Castle Schwarzheim?' he asked them.

Their faces were momentarily blank.

'English? *Deutsch? Français?*' asked Charlie.

'*Russki*,' the lady replied indignantly.

From then on Charlie and the couple spoke in fluent Russian. 'I believe you may be on your way to Castle Schwarzheim . . .' he said.

'Castle Schwarzheim, yes,' answered the man.

'Your names, please?' Charlie asked. He was holding the guest list that Jake had found in Mina's Schlitz's tent.

'Mikhail and Irina Volsky,' the lady answered with a sigh of irritation.

'From Odessa,' her husband added.

Charlie scanned the parchment and found their names near the bottom of the list. 'Yes, of course. Thank God I found you in time – thank God!' He breathed a sigh of relief. 'You must take cover immediately. It's dangerous!' he said, sweeping his hand around the entire valley. 'Highwaymen! An army of them.'

Irina gasped as she gazed around. The driver, who was still standing there, looked terrified.

'Where?' the husband asked.

'On the road ahead – on the road behind. Everywhere. A gang of fifty of them! All savages! This very morning four people were killed and dis-membered.' Charlie did an impression of throats being cut that made Irina clutch the pearls around her neck in alarm.

Red-headed Heidi emerged from the inn, rubbing her eyes sleepily. She had come out to see to the new arrivals, but Charlie intercepted her.

'Friends of mine – I'll deal with them. You go back to bed,' he whispered, switching to German. He ushered her back into the inn, closed the door behind her and returned to the Volskys.

'If you follow me, I will show you to your room.'

'Room?' Irina asked.

'You'll need to stay here until the danger passes. You will be safe.'

Charlie tried to usher them towards the inn, but the Volskys were evidently appalled by the idea.

'At a common tavern? Impossible!' Irina exclaimed, shaking herself free.

Just then, the expression on the old driver's face changed. He saw a figure approaching along the street. It was Topaz, running towards them at full tilt. 'Help! Help!' she wailed.

Irina's jaw gradually dropped as Topaz drew closer. Her dress and hands were covered in blood.

'They're coming! There's so many of them! They killed my husband! They're coming!' Topaz gasped as she flew past the astonished Russians and into the inn.

But the show was not over yet: another figure was limping towards them. Jake took the role of the dying husband, and he made sure that it was the performance of his life.

He was drenched in blood. He held one hand dramatically aloft; the other clutched a gory fistful of entrails to his stomach. If Topaz's act had been all about the voice, Jake's was pure mime. He staggered towards them, his head shaking as if in shock. Irina recoiled in disgust as he held out a bloody hand towards her face. He tried to speak, but could not form words, instead moaning piteously. Then his body stiffened and he crumpled to the ground. His body shook a little and then was still.

As Charlie caught a glimpse of Topaz in the doorway of the inn, he shook his head, worried that Jake's performance had blown their cover. But the Russians were now convinced of the danger. Irina immediately headed for the inn door, her husband following close behind. Charlie took them upstairs and showed them into the suite they had just vacated. Irina Volsky had never been so pleased to see a low-ceilinged room full of rustic furniture. She dashed over to the window, threw the flowerpot out and closed the shutters.

'You'll be safe here until further notice,' offered Charlie.

Irina slammed the door in his face and bolted it.

Charlie came downstairs to find the poor driver shaking with anxiety in the hallway.

'Come this way.' Charlie showed him into the comfortable downstairs room and produced two gold coins. 'Buy yourself a feast and the best room for the night.' Then he added in a mischievous whisper, 'No bandits.'

The driver was nonplussed. Charlie pointed out of the window. In the street, Jake stood up, wiped the mess from his clothes and took a bow for his own amusement. The driver's face was transformed by a huge smile.

They wasted no time: they quickly drove the Volskys' carriage away from the village and headed for the copse from which they had scouted out the gatehouse. On the back seat of its sumptious interior, Topaz found the couple's invitation to the 'summit'. The phrase *It will be a pleasure to finally meet* . . . provided the agents with an invaluable piece of information: namely that the Volskys had never actually met their host. The invitation was signed, in blood-crimson, by Prince Zeldt himself.

They quickly removed eight trunks from the carriage roof and started searching through their contents. The first six they opened were devoted solely to Irina. She was obviously a woman of quite astonishing vanity. Two trunks contained her dresses, another two her shoes. All of the above contained endless detailing of fur, and a disgusted Charlie guessed that the Russian couple had made their fortune in the trade of 'poor dead animals'. Another trunk contained jewellery and fans, and a sixth was full of exquisite china pots of powders and bottles of perfume. Most girls would have been in seventh heaven at this discovery, but Topaz was unimpressed: clothes and make-up held little magic for her.

The seventh trunk contained the entire wardrobe of Irina's husband. Certainly there were fewer items, but each was just as beautifully crafted.

'Nathan would have an absolute field day with all this,' exclaimed Topaz as she took out a velvet cap adorned with a green peacock feather and put it on her head. 'Does this colour enhance my eyes?' she said in a shameless impersonation. 'I rather think it makes them pop.'

Next Charlie retrieved a velvet doublet studded with emeralds. He held it up to his chest and pulled a face. 'Too big for me. You'll certainly have to be the husband,' he said to Jake, 'though I think you should anyway – you look more the part. I'll have to be the driver.'

Charlie was right about Jake: although he was the same age as Charlie, he was a good two inches taller and had a certain confidence, a bearing that made him look the part. Charlie helped Jake into the doublet. It fitted him like a glove.

Topaz was impressed. '*Merveilleux*. You look like a prince.'

Jake bowed theatrically again.

'Though try and keep it a bit more authentic this time,' Charlie said wryly. 'This is the real world, not musical theatre.'

Jake nodded seriously. Then a thought came to him: 'Will I need to speak in Russian? That could be a problem.'

'Fortunately the royal language is English – everyone is required to speak it. So just a Russian accent will suffice.'

'What about Mina Schlitz and the others?' Jake asked. 'They'll recognize me immediately.'

'Don't worry about that, either,' said Charlie, producing the wallet that Jake had seen aboard the *Campana*. 'Mr Volsky didn't have a beard, but who knows that, apart from us?' He opened the pouch, and his face lit up at the sight of his beloved beards and moustaches. He selected one of them and held it up to Jake's face. 'Ravishing,' he said, shaking his head proudly.

Topaz was struggling with the catch on the final trunk. 'This one's locked for some reason.'

She took a pin from her hair, straightened it and introduced it into the lock. A moment later there was a click and Topaz lifted the lid; all three of them gasped at once.

It was full of treasure. On top was a velvet-lined tray with compartments like a specimen box, each one containing a large and beautifully cut jewel. Beneath this lay another tray of priceless diamonds, emeralds and rubies. Below that, a third, and a fourth. Finally, in a large compartment at the bottom, there were neatly stacked bundles of ancient banknotes and at least a dozen gold ingots.

'Now, why on earth would they be carrying this amount of money around?' Topaz pondered.

Charlie raised his eyebrows theatrically. 'I have a feeling that this riddle, and all others, will be solved once we penetrate the walls of Castle Schwarzheim.'

21 INTO THE LION'S DEN

Half an hour later the Volskys' carriage was rolling along the road towards Castle Schwarzheim's imposing gatehouse. Charlie was driving, with Mr Drake perched on one of the trunks at his side. The former wore the black cloak and cap that he had found stuffed into a tiny trunk at the back of the coach, along with the driver's other meagre possessions. He was wearing a blond beard that made him almost unrecognizable.

In the luxurious, silk-lined interior of the carriage Jake and Topaz sat side by side, impeccably dressed as the Russian millionaires. Topaz looked exquisite in her corseted gown and golden headpiece, but it was Jake who had undergone the most startling transformation: in his fine suit and neat moustache and beard, he looked every inch the dashing young tycoon.

'Charlie,' Topaz called out of the window, 'I hate to say this, but I think it's time Mr Drake went undercover.'

Charlie nodded reluctantly, opened the trunk and guided the parrot inside. 'It won't be for long,' he assured him, giving him an extra-large handful of peanuts. 'Quiet as you can, now.' He felt awful shutting his pet in the dark – though for a handful of peanuts Mr Drake was happy to do anything his master asked of him.

As the carriage pulled up in the shadow of the gatehouse's granite towers, Jake noticed Topaz's eyes flicker nervously. Her hand went to her throat as if to control her tremulous breathing.

'All right?' he asked softly.

'It's funny,' Topaz sighed. 'You would think the fear would lessen over time, but it seems to get worse.'

One of the sentries strutted out of the lodge, held up his oversized hand and enquired, with a nod at them, as to the identity of the new arrivals.

'Mikhail and Irina Volsky of Odessa,' said Charlie in English – with a perfect Russian accent – and handed the guard their invitation to the summit.

The sentry examined it without expression, then looked through the carriage window and scrutinized the occupants through narrowed eyes. Jake and Topaz gazed back at him haughtily. At last he returned the invitation to Charlie and signalled to his accomplice in the tower. The creaking iron portcullis ascended and the carriage entered the vast walled estate of Castle Schwarzheim.

Jake looked out of the window. Rising up in front of him was a great mountain of rock, towering through ghostly swirls of mist to a sharp peak. At the summit, far in the distance and almost hidden in the gloom, stood Castle Schwarzheim, a dark grey silhouette.

As the road rose around the base of the mountain, Topaz spied something through the trees. 'Down there! Look.'

Charlie stopped the carriage. Down below, where the Rhine snaked round to one side, lay a harbour set in a steep-sided inlet. Moored within it was a black galleon with shimmering red sails.

'Our old friend the *Lindwurm*, if I'm not mistaken,' said Charlie in an ominous voice. He took his telescope out of his pocket and peered through it. 'Not a ship you forget in a hurry.' He passed the eyepiece to Topaz, who studied the craft, pursing her lips.

'What's the *Lindwurm*?' asked Jake.

'Zeldt's warship of choice,' explained Charlie. 'The legend goes that he stained her timbers with the blood of his enemies, which accounts for their luminous black hue. The *Lindwurm* takes its name from a creature of the deep, half snake, half dragon.'

Topaz passed the telescope to Jake and he surveyed the vessel. She was a handsome craft, splendid and awesome in equal measure. Her three gigantic red sails had the lustrous sheen of velvet. Emblazoned in the centre of each, in a yet deeper shade of crimson, was Zeldt's symbol of a snake and a shield.

'It looks like they're getting ready to leave,' said Jake, pointing to the guards loading crates onto the deck.

'Not too soon, I hope,' said Charlie as he cracked his whip, urging the horses on towards the castle.

The carriage zigzagged up and up. For stretches they would lose sight of the castle. Then, as they turned a corner, it would loom above them once again, each time a little closer and more distinct.

The weather started to change. Below, it had been a warm, sunny day. But now, halfway to the mountain's peak, the air cooled and thinned. Charlie started to shiver.

Suddenly the horses stopped; one of them whinnied with fear, stamping its hooves and shaking its head.

'What is it?' Charlie asked the animal. He was perplexed: the road ahead was empty. The lid of the trunk next to him lifted slightly, and Mr Drake's eyes darted keenly from side to side, also sensing danger.

Jake leaned out of the window, glimpsing movement amongst the trees. He peered into the darkness of the forest; a chill wind rustled through the branches. Then he caught sight of a darting shadow.

Charlie saw it at the same time; he gasped and dropped the reins.

The figure flew through the trees, its footsteps silenced by the mossy ground; it wore a pointed black hat and a long black gown billowed out behind. Fifty yards ahead, it left the trees and came to a stop on the road, its back to them.

Jake craned his neck out of the window to get a better look. He had seen people dressed as witches before, usually at Halloween, but everything about this figure had an eerie look of authenticity; the gown was torn and muddied, but the material was fine, with complicated patterns woven into its blackness.

The figure remained motionless. The horses continued to snort and stamp their hooves anxiously. Charlie slowly unsheathed his sword while, inside the carriage, Topaz's sharp dagger was already drawn.

The black form slowly turned its head. The face – what could be seen of it – was oddly beautiful: through the pale layers of transluscent skin, a network of blue veins pulsed. For a second the eyes made contact with Charlie's; then the figure flew off again. The occupants of the carriage watched as it darted through the trees as if pulled by an invisible thread. In the distance it met up with two similar dark shadows. All three looked round at the carriage one last time, then fled into the wood until they were out of sight.

Everyone breathed a sigh of relief, and Charlie and Topaz re-sheathed their weapons.

'Nothing to be frightened of – they're basically glorified scarecrows,' said Charlie, trying for nonchalance, although his heart was thumping.

'Scarecrows?' questioned Jake.

'An old medieval custom. Rich landowners use them to scare off intruders. They're just actors.'

'Still, I don't fancy seeing the full performance,' said Jake.

As the track led them closer to the peak, it steepened dramatically and the temperature dropped further still. The horses were again apprehensive, and Charlie had to encourage them in a bright, breezy voice that failed to mask his growing sense of unease. Out of the window Jake could see the edge of the precipice just below. Some rocks disappeared into the cloudy void.

As they came round the final bend, Castle Schwarzheim loomed into sight in all its terrifying glory. It looked as solid as the mountain itself; an immense puzzle of towers, turrets and stone staircases soaring up into the cloud. Jake noticed a succession of gargoyles jutting out from the closest tower. There were beasts of every kind: dragons, two-headed gorgons and fierce monkeys, mouths wide, as if silently screaming. The whole scene reminded Jake of another favourite painting of his – a tableau of high Victorian gothic: riders approaching a windswept castle, walls luminous in the twilight.

The horses struggled up the last stretch, until finally the carriage rolled through an archway into a large courtyard.

Jake gazed with keen interest at the sights that greeted him. A few other vehicles had recently arrived, the bright, rich liveries contrasting with the sombre granite of their surroundings. Their finely dressed occupants were being helped down by castle servants, all of whom wore the familiar red cloaks of Zeldt's army. The new arrivals were offered cups of hot spiced wine served on pewter trays. They took them and drank, paying no heed to those who served them.

'I find it strange,' Topaz observed, 'that whole families have been invited.' She was referring to a group of people descending from another carriage. A youngish couple were accompanied not only by their two sulky-looking daughters, but also an ancient lady, evidently the girls' grandmother. The grand old lady studied her surroundings as the luggage was unloaded and taken off into the castle.

During the ascent, Charlie had slowly become accustomed to the cold, but Jake and Topaz did not notice the dramatic change in the weather until they set foot on the cobbles. It was positively wintry: the occasional flake of snow drifted by.

'Good afternoon, welcome to Castle Schwarzheim,' a voice announced in English. It belonged to a red-cloaked attendant – a blue-eyed Teutonic beauty with a smile as tight as the blonde braids knotted across her head. Jake found himself involuntarily checking his fake beard and moustache as she continued, 'I trust your journey was satisfactory. Mikhail and Irina Volsky of Odessa, if I'm not mistaken?'

'How did you know?' answered Topaz, also in English but with a perfect Russian accent.

'By the coat of arms on your carriage, of course,' the girl replied as if it were the most obvious thing in the world. 'You are in the east tower, in the Suite Charlemagne. Dinner is at seven in the banqueting hall. Enjoy your stay.'

Another carriage rolled into the courtyard, and the German goddess smiled insincerely and took her leave. Jake and Topaz watched her retreat.

'Friendly.' Jake was dazzled by her cool confidence.

'As a box of snakes,' commented Topaz.

'Don't look now,' muttered Charlie as he started

to unload the luggage from the roof, 'but there's another box of snakes. Eleven o'clock.'

Jake and Topaz turned nonchalantly and glimpsed a figure on the first-floor balcony. It was Mina Schlitz, coolly surveying the scene below her.

'She doesn't frighten me,' Topaz murmured. 'It's all an act.'

She and Jake were shown across the courtyard. Charlie followed behind, doing his best to balance the large collection of cases. He was conscious of poor Mr Drake rattling around in one of the trunks – so much so that he tripped and dropped everything. Two servants came to his rescue.

Jake couldn't resist teasing: 'He's new. We're just breaking him in. It's so difficult to find the staff these days.'

Charlie shook his head and muttered under his breath, 'I offered to play this part – I think I deserve a little respect at least.'

As they climbed the steps to the front entrance of the castle, Topaz suddenly stopped. 'Wait!' She clutched Jake's arm tightly. He was alarmed to see that she was as white as a sheet. Suddenly her eyes rolled up in her head and she collapsed into his arms.

'Topaz!' Jake cried as her eyelids flickered. From all over the courtyard, people looked in their direction. Concerned servants soon surrounded them.

'You mean *Irina*,' Charlie muttered under his breath, aware that Mina Schlitz was now squinting down from the balcony.

Topaz came to her senses and pulled herself to her feet.

'Are you all right?' Jake asked.

'Of course – it's the altitude, that's all,' she said breezily. 'Shall we . . . ?' She continued up the steps into the castle as if nothing had happened.

Jake was confused and unnerved by the incident, but quickly resumed his role of aloof young tycoon.

They found themselves in a baronial entrance hall. Groups of guests were being led towards their suites. It felt like a busy hotel lobby in a smart ski resort – except, of course, that everyone was dressed in the fashions of the early 1500s, and downhill skiing had not yet been invented. There were great fires crackling on every side, and macabre hunting trophies – antlers and stuffed heads of deer and bear – hung from every inch of wall.

'That's really charming,' Charlie muttered. 'The

sight of dead animals really does endear our host to me . . .'

The hunting theme continued: two 'sofas' were fashioned out of more antlers; on a series of pedestals, stuffed eagles, falcons and ospreys were frozen in time; and bearskin rugs were spread at intervals over the stone floors.

Jake, Topaz and their 'manservant,' Charlie, were escorted by a red-cloaked servant up the grand central staircase, along a succession of corridors and more stairs, and finally through a set of double doors into the Suite Charlemagne.

The young agents did their best to conceal their amazement. It was an extraordinary room, occupying the entire top floor of one the round towers. There were huge sofas, and rich tapestries hung from the walls.

'There is hot chocolate for your pleasure . . .' The servant pointed – without the slightest hint of pleasure – to a coaching table set out with cups and a steaming pewter jug. 'And a bath has been filled for you. Dinner will be at seven.' Of course, this information was for the benefit of Jake and Topaz; Charlie waited by the door, his head bowed.

The man nodded, walked backwards out of the room and closed the door behind him.

Charlie immediately dropped the luggage and released Mr Drake from his silk-lined prison. The parrot squawked, flapped his wings excitedly and did an elegant circuit of the room to stretch them.

'Was it really the altitude?' Jake asked Topaz, relieved to be able to drop the pretence.

For a moment she did not reply. 'Not really,' she said quietly. 'It's been a while since I was actually inside one of Zeldt's castles. Memories got the better of me . . . But I'm perfectly calm now.'

'Memories . . . ?' Jake asked.

'Why don't we explore the suite?' she suggested, ignoring the question, and disappeared into the next room. Jake followed her, understanding that the subject was now closed.

The bedroom was quite as large as the living room. The huge four-poster bed was draped with extravagant swags of velvet. The bathroom was lined with terracotta-coloured marble. A giant steaming bath in the centre gave off magical odours of roses and bergamot.

An archway led onto a terrace. As Jake and Topaz emerged outside, they were filled with awe.

It was freezing cold and the wind whistled, but they did not notice.

'*That* is a view.' Jake said in awe. He could see for an eternity: the Rhine wound its way far into the distance between the forested hills. Nestling amongst them were little towns and villages, and more castles sprouted from mountaintops near and far. This would be an awe-inspiring view at any time in history, but Jake knew that now, in 1506 – way before the modern age of cars and aeroplanes and new towns – it was at its most remarkable. He turned to look at Topaz: she too was lost in wonder.

'*C'est incroyable, non?* History is amazing,' she said as if reading Jake's own thoughts. 'It's like the stars: the more you look, the more you see.'

After they had taken it in turns to soak in the marble bath (which was way ahead of its time and fitted with working taps in the form of golden dolphins), they selected their evening outfits. They were somewhat lost without Nathan's sartorial eye to guide them, but Jake chose a smart Maltese doublet in sapphire velvet and accessorized it ('one of Nathan's favorite words', Topaz pointed out) with a great clunky gold chain. Topaz selected a long cream gown of brocade and silk organza. Charlie remained in his plain gown and breeches.

At seven sharp, a servant came to collect them. He escorted them silently back down the maze of staircases and landings, until they arrived at an enormous set of double doors.

'You are not permitted,' the servant told Charlie curtly. 'You wait with the other staff,' he said, indicating the narrow staircase down to a servants anteroom where various sombre-faced valets had taken up residence to await a summons from their masters.

'I usually accompany them everywhere,' Charlie floundered, letting his accent drop slightly in his anxiety.

The man was unmoved. 'You are not permitted,' he repeated, this time holding up a hand to make his point.

Charlie realized he had no choice but to comply. He whispered into Jake's ear, 'I want a full report on dinner. I need to know everything that's on the menu. Everything! Understand?'

Jake nodded and Charlie reluctantly turned and headed down towards the anteroom. He was met by the unfriendly gaze of forty surly-looking servants.

His attempt at a broad smile and an affable wink did absolutely nothing to endear him to them.

Jake and Topaz, the Volskys of Odessa, were led towards the double doors, which opened as if by magic. They stepped into the room.

The sight that greeted them made their hearts pound. For a moment they both found it difficult to breathe, but they kept their composure. The double doors closed behind them.

22 THE VEILED EMPIRE

Just as Charlie had been met by the staring eyes of many strangers, so had Jake and Topaz, but *these* eyes were far, far more unsettling.

The banqueting hall of Castle Schwarzheim was a large, dimly lit circular room, around which a succession of fires blasted out a fierce heat.

In the centre was a vast table. Hewn from white marble so translucent it resembled crystal, it seemed to hover, phantom-like, above the stone floor. Around it, fifty people, their backs in shadow, were already seated. They were, without doubt, the most chillingly magnificent group of individuals that Jake had ever set eyes on.

These were medieval millionaires: Charlie and Topaz had learned from Mina's list that they were not neccessarily famous, nor aristocratic, but their self-made fortunes gave them huge power. Amongst them, Jake knew, were traders of grain and livestock from eastern Europe, mining barons from the Baltic, timber and wax dealers from Scandinavia. There was a salt merchant from Asia Minor, a silver tycoon from Bavaria, and an ivory dealer from Africa. There were bankers from Germany and Italy, and insurance brokers from Amsterdam and Copenhagen.

Jake and Topaz were shown to two vacant seats on the left. They sat down, their composure imitating that of the guests around them. But inside, they were both quivering with fear. Jake looked around at the sea of faces. It was as if a whole gallery of old portraits had come to life.

Some were old, some young, some middle-aged. Some were upright and respectable-looking; others had sinister faces, sullen and scarred. There were more men than women, though the latter were possibly even more impressive than their male counterparts (one imperious lady in an African headdress looked about seven feet tall). All radiated an arrogant power. They wore the finest clothes, the most sought-after jewels, the rarest perfumes. They had no doubt come from some of the largest mansions in the world, filled with wonderful, price-less things and scurrying staff.

Jake had never felt so intimidated in his life. This was the second time in three days that he had sat at a table of extraordinary people. The first time, in the History Keepers' stateroom on the Mont St Michel, had been intriguing: the room was full of light and the conversation sparkled. This was another matter entirely: the chamber was dark, almost silent and charged with malevolence.

Jake stole a sideways glance at his neighbour. The man's small head and sharp nose were directed straight ahead, his plump hands clenched together on the table. A sumptuous purple doublet was tightly fitted to his narrow shoulders.

Jake surveyed the room in more detail. Of the four remaining empty chairs, one was larger and more important-looking than all the others. It was the only seat with armrests, which were carved in the form of entwining snakes. In the centre of the table a crystal hand held up a mysterious sphere of sapphire blue that emitted a soft light – evidently a representation of the planet Earth. In front of each person stood a glass goblet of transparent liquid and a tiny tortoiseshell box. There was no sign of dinner.

The double doors opened and two more guests came into the room: an older man and his young, aristocratic-looking wife. They were red in the face and frowning, as if they had been arguing. They strode – the man with a slight limp – across the stone floor and took their places.

Finally, on the far side of the room, a low door opened. Compared to the grand main entrance, this one was inconsequential-looking, almost hidden in the wall. Jake froze as he saw the figure of Mina Schlitz step through it. She circled the room, scanning the backs of all the guests. They half turned their heads as she passed. Finally she took her place beside the large unoccupied chair, removed her red-backed snake from its box and stroked it.

Another figure emerged from the small doorway. From a distance he looked almost unremarkable, but Topaz's face told another story. Her eyes became steely and her jaw clenched.

'Is that him?' Jake whispered to her. 'Prince Zeldt?'

Topaz nodded, and he noticed that her hands were shaking. She held them together firmly under the table and edged her seat back a little until she was partially concealed behind Jake.

'It'll be all right,' he whispered in her ear.

The prince took his seat. 'Welcome,' he announced in a thin, barely audible voice. Some people struggled to hear, but kept that to themselves. 'Welcome to the Superia Summit. For many of us, it is our first meeting,' he whispered. 'For many of us, it will be our last . . . but the bonds between us will endure.'

There were murmurs of agreement. All eyes were fixed, like magnets, on Prince Zeldt. He continued:

'Fourteen years ago, in the spring of 1492, Marsilio Ficino, a trite, whey-faced intellectual, wrote this – and I quote . . .' He affected a slightly nasal voice: '*If we are to call any age golden, it must certainly be our age. This century has restored to light the liberal arts that were almost extinct: science, oratory, painting, sculpture, architecture, music . . .*'

Zeldt scanned the mesmerized faces around the table. 'No longer God's playthings, this age has placed humankind centre stage. Now the people begin to understand the universe and take control of their fate . . .' He paused momentarily before spitting out the next sentence with such extraordinary venom that it sent a chill down everyone's spine. 'This age has seen the birth of modern man.'

The prince suddenly stood up and glared at his guests, as if *they* were responsible for the concoction of this repulsive phrase.

'*The birth of modern man?*' he hissed again.

Thirty seconds passed before his sneer relaxed into a sinister smile. 'I don't think so.'

There was a murmuring of approval that turned into a soft round of applause.

'I am a man of actions, not words,' said Zeldt, 'so I will get straight down to business. I am sure you are all dying to know what our new world is going to look like.'

Jake turned to Topaz. He wasn't sure if he'd heard correctly. 'Our new world . . .?' he asked. Topaz shook her head and shrugged.

The prince nodded at Mina. She returned her snake to its case, stepped back and pulled a lever. There was a whir of machinery and, behind Zeldt, a long thin section of floor slid back. Jake craned his neck to see: through the slim aperture rose up a wall of smoke. Mina crossed to the back wall of the room and turned a dial. A ray of brilliant light, as sharp as a laser, illuminated the smoke (as well as the faces around the table). A ghostly image started to take shape behind Zeldt's throne: the symbol of a snake and a shield and, in giant gothic letters, the familiar word . . .

SUPERIA

These millionaires were rarely impressed, and if they were, they seldom showed it. This was different: Zeldt's state-of-the-art 'camera obscura' made them all gasp in wonder.

The image gradually changed to one of a dark, imposing city containing a series of skyscrapers and encircled by a huge impenetrable wall.

'Here is a blueprint,' said Zeldt, his eyes now glittering, 'for the first of our *secure* cities.'

'That looks like the drawings I saw in Venice,' Jake whispered to Topaz.

So began Zeldt's medieval 'slide show'. Images followed one after another, showing every aspect of the ghastly metropolis: a 'secure city' with high, ugly buildings, each with its endless succession of barred windows. Vigilant, crimson-cloaked guards were stationed at every corner, and lookout towers soared up from the city's walls. The Black Army's symbol of snakes on a shield was everywhere: surmounting every window, engraved into every door, and looming, supersized, above the giant gates of the city.

'It looks like a prison camp,' Topaz whispered, aghast at the collection of pictures.

One image showed the city's downtrodden occupants being herded like animals through the gates; in others, people were farming the fields in supervised groups or being forced down mines.

A map of Europe now appeared before them.

'I am proposing eight such communities, all self-sufficient, in the *old* continent,' Zeldt continued. 'For that's what Europe is – old, tired and bloated.' The locations of these cities were marked on the map with a pulsating symbol of the snake and shield.

Topaz shook her head in disbelief. 'Those are the sites of every major capital city,' she whispered. 'Look . . . London, Paris, Rome, Madrid, Athens. What on earth is he proposing?'

The map of Europe changed into one showing two great land masses. The outlines were rough, but Jake recognized them as North and South America.

'But it is in the *new* continent on the other side of the Atlantic where most of our progress will be made,' announced Zeldt with pride.

The guests gazed in awe and fascination at the

uncharted lands.

'Since its discovery fourteen years ago, America has proven to be a land of unparalleled potential. There is gold beyond your wildest imaginings; copper, mercury and iron in abundance. Below the ground is a secret substance that has the power to transform us completely. Here is paradise on Earth, and we will control every square inch of it.' Zeldt's voice became loud and shrill. 'Here, I propose to build at least fifty secure cities!'

The spectral map of the Americas began to pulsate with images of the snake and shield. All the guests, their faces glowing in the light from the image, watched with eyes full of greed. Only Jake and Topaz were blank-faced.

Slowly this picture of America disappeared, and the image that had begun the demonstration – the single word *Superia* in giant gothic letters – returned. It loomed over Zeldt's head, before finally melting away into the darkness.

The light dimmed. Mina closed the gauge on the wall and pulled the lever to replace the section of floor. The last of the smoke rose up into the vaulted ceiling. The presentation was over.

Zeldt scanned the faces around the table.

'Tomorrow I must leave the country on a private family matter. But I would encourage all of you, and whatever family you have brought with you, to remain in the castle until the worst has passed. Of course, you will be safe anywhere, but it is best that you stay here. We have enough food and drink to last a year. And naturally, all my staff are at your disposal.'

Jake and Topaz once again exchanged a sidelong-glance with each other.

'So this leaves only the final matter . . .' Zeldt murmured. 'Please open your boxes and charge your glasses.'

The occupants of the table seemed to know what to do. They reached forward and opened the small tortoiseshell box in front of them. Jake and Topaz followed suit. Jake was amazed to discover a quantity of white talc-like powder.

'I recognize this,' he whispered in Topaz's ear. 'It looks like one of the substances Talisman Kant sold to Mina Schlitz for the casket of gold.'

The guests started emptying the powder into their crystal goblets of water, as did Zeldt and Mina Schlitz. The glasses were fizzing and bubbling as the water reacted with the agent. Jake and Topaz had no choice but to copy everyone else. Soon the liquid in each goblet became still again.

Zeldt held up his glass. Once again his voice was loud and rousing. 'TO THE FUTURE. TO THE FUTURE OF *OUR* WORLD!'

Everyone was about to drink, when a voice called out, 'One moment.'

The man with the sharp nose sitting next to Jake put up his hand. 'Pieter De Smedt of Ghent,' he introduced himself. His voice was nasal, high-pitched. Jake had stopped breathing, aware that eyes would now be looking in his direction.

Zeldt stared at the man, his eyebrows raised in anticipation.

'I am sure I am not the only person around the table who is thinking this . . .' The man indicated his goblet with tiny, bloated hands, his jewelled rings catching the light. 'But how do we know that this "potion" of yours is going to work? All this could be an elaborate trick to get hold of our money.'

Mina's lips tightened in annoyance. Pieter's other neighbour, the tall, haughty lady in the African headdress, surveyed him with distaste.

Zeldt took a deep breath and smiled thinly. 'Isn't it obvious that I need all of you, just as much as you need me. I thought I had made it quite clear that we were working together. But there is no compulsion.' His voice was now clear and sharp as a razor. 'Would you like to leave now?'

There was a long pause. As he thought it through, Pieter De Smedt's thin red lips pursed and his nose twitched. 'The fact is . . . I don't trust you.'

There was an astonished murmur amongst the guests. All eyes flashed in Zeldt's direction to see how he would react. The prince's expression remained inscrutable. He simply lowered his eyelids at Mina. She did not hesitate, but swept round the table to Pieter. She quickly deposited her snake on the table, then unclipped a whip from her belt, looped it around Pieter's neck and pulled it tight.

The effect was shocking. He gasped helplessly, giving a high-pitched whine; his face turned pink, then crimson, his eyes bulging; he reached out his stumpy hands in vain, knocking over his glass. The snake thrashed with delight as Mina effortlessly tightened her grasp. Jake, whose hands were shaking under the table, had one eye on the serpent, the other on Pieter's face. He wanted to stand up, to put a stop to it *now*! But Topaz took hold of his leg firmly. The lady in the African headdress watched the spectacle, her eyes glinting sadistically. Pieter let out a final twisted glottal stop, Mina released the whip – then his head thumped forward onto the table, the serpent deftly coiling out of its way.

Mina reached over, straightened the goblet, then took Pieter by the collar of his purple doublet and deposited his limp, lifeless body on the floor as if discarding yesterday's rubbish. Jake wondered if the man had any family with him; it was impossible to tell as not a single guest dared show any emotion. Finally Mina retrieved her beloved pet, kissed it and placed it back in its box.

Suddenly Jake caught sight of Pieter's vacant staring eyes and he was seized with panic. Topaz, aware of Mina nearby, clutched his leg even more firmly under the table.

'Be strong, Jake, I beg you, be strong,' she whispered, trying to reassure him. A red-headed man who had been sitting next to Pieter turned his head questioningly – but at last Jake managed to get his breathing under control. Pieter's body was dragged out of the room by two guards. The double doors closed behind them.

'Anyone else . . .?' asked Zeldt.

The guests shook their heads eagerly, held up

their goblets again and started, one by one, to drink. Jake looked at Topaz, his anxious eyes asking her what to do. Topaz was aware that they could be found out if they did not comply, and she could already feel Mina's gaze heading in their direction. She nodded at Jake and drank; he did the same. He braced himself for something nasty like atomium, but this tasted only of water.

Zeldt stood up. 'Miss Schlitz will supply you with enough elixir for the rest of your families.'

Mina pulled back his chair and he made for the hidden door. He turned and looked at the occupants of the room. 'Now, you are my guests – enjoy your dinner,' he said enigmatically before vanishing into the darkness.

Moments later, the double doors swung open again, and an army of servants swarmed in to serve the food.

As one might have guessed from the décor in the entrance hall, the general theme of the meal was meat. There were hams baked in cloves and cabbage, poule au pot Henri IV, Michelmas goose in almond sauce, roast duckling with spice rub, and a red deer pie that was so enormous it was decorated with its own set of antlers.

Topaz had no appetite, Jake even less, but they realized they had to go through the motions of eating in order to not arouse suspicion. Conversation started up around the table, but it was desultory: a tableful of arrogant medieval millionaires, each one thinking themselves better than the next, does not make for a convivial party. As Jake forced down his food, all cloyingly rich, he glanced at the place where Pieter De Smedt had been sitting just twenty minutes before. Nathan had spoke about Zeldt's capacity for cruelty. Those were just words; that empty chair was a fact.

Just when Jake and Topaz thought they might be able to slip away, the desserts arrived.

'Frangipane pie, lemon posset, prunes in syrup, almond jumballs with orange sauce,' the waiters announced. Jake and Topaz chose the smallest and forced it down, wondering whether they should try and sneak one out for Charlie. In the end they decided that with Mina still scanning the room, it was far too risky.

Finally the meal ended and people started to disperse. Jake and Topaz stood up, made their way cautiously towards the door and slipped out.

* * *

'Soup! I had *soup*,' Charlie complained as the three of them made their way back towards the suite. 'And not interesting soup, like pea and thyme or porcini mushroom, but cabbage soup – or rather, cabbage floating in tepid water. That was the only vegetarian option – pig's trotters weren't really doing it for me. Though even cabbage soup was more scintillating than the conversation. I now know just about everything I will ever need to know about carriage axels and their provenance. In short, don't buy a carriage from north-eastern Europe. Anyway, if you refuse to tell me about your desserts – "for my own good", as you put it – at least tell me what went on.'

Jake and Topaz gave him a synopsis of everything they had witnessed earlier, ending with the unpleasant demise of Pieter De Smedt of Ghent.

'Good grief,' said Charlie, unnerved. 'I saw him being carried out. Presumed he'd overdone it on oysters or some such.' His face could not get any paler. 'Whatever Zeldt is planning, this is the big one.'

'Look!' Jake exclaimed, glancing down the corridor.

Mina Schlitz had appeared round the corner and was striding towards them. They retreated into the shadows and hid behind a statue of a Roman warrior.

Mina stopped in front of a stone wall-fountain. She looked from side to side and, confident that no one was in the vicinity, did something with her hand (the agents were unable to see exactly what, as Mina herself was blocking their view). A thick panel of stone on one side of the fountain creaked open, revealing a dark cavity within. She stepped inside and disappeared down a staircase before the wall closed behind her.

The three agents looked at each other.

'I'm guessing there'll be some answers through that doorway,' whispered Charlie. 'We need to come back after dark and investigate.'

23 UNMASKED

Rose Djones did not sleep a wink that night. She was disturbed by her discovery of the chequered rose and the bundle of notes, and haunted by the image of Jupitus staring at her behind the Library of Faces. She wondered if she had really glimpsed 'the look of love' in his otherwise inscrutable gaze. She wondered also why she had butterflies in her stomach. 'It can't be possible,' she exclaimed out loud to herself, 'that I could have feelings for that rotter!'

In the twenty-five years that Rose had known Jupitus (when they were younger they had been forced to go on missions together), he had not once shown her the slightest sign of affection.

The following day Jupitus ignored Rose at lunch, taking a seat next to Oceane Noire, who was dressed, with attention-grabbing theatricality, in black. (Norland asked her if anyone had passed away, and she replied, 'I'm in mourning for my thirties.') It was only when Rose was leaving the room that Jupitus pushed in front of her and spoke: 'Four-thirty sharp, the eastern battlements. Don't be late.'

By five o'clock, freezing by the windy parapet, Rose was ready for an argument. 'About time,' she muttered when he finally appeared. 'It's cold out here, you know!'

Jupitus made no attempt to apologize. 'You see the metal shaft on that sharp pointed steeple . . .' He indicated a rod attached to the highest tower.

'Yes,' sighed Rose wearily. 'That's where the Meslith messages arrive. I first came to the Mount as long ago as you, Jupitus.'

'Our spy no doubt has his eyes on that steeple. When that conductor fizzes with electrical current, he will know that a message is being delivered and will make his way down to the Library of Faces.'

'Obviously that could be anyone.' Rose swept her hand around the castle. 'So many rooms have a view of it.'

'As we are not able to fake the arrival of messages, we will just have to wait patiently in the library until one arrives. I have given Miss Wunderbar the day off so we will have the place to ourselves. Follow me,' Jupitus barked. 'At a distance. We don't want to be seen together.'

Rose reluctantly did as she was told. She shadowed him down the maze of stairs and corridors, occasionally pulling faces at him behind his back. *What is going on in that very odd mind of yours?* she mused to herself.

Eventually Jupitus came to the library door. Here he checked that no one was around and slipped inside. A minute later Rose followed him.

'Sssh!' Jupitus snapped as Rose, her bangles jangling, picked her way through the minefield of ropes and pulleys that lay behind the façade of faces.

'Good gracious,' she remarked, on arriving at the hidey-hole that Jupitus had created for them. There were two comfortable chairs and a little table set with a plate of sandwiches.

'We may be here all day.' He shrugged. 'No point in being uncomfortable. I know that you like Lapsang . . .' he said, unscrewing the flask.

'I love it, thank you,' said Rose, settling herself in a chair.

'Well, I can't bear it, so Oolong will have to do. You see, we have a clear view of the tube.' Jupitus shone his light into the far corner. 'We'll see him, but he won't see us.'

'Perfect,' replied Rose with a weary smile.

They sat in silence for nearly an hour before Jupitus finally spoke. 'This reminds me of our last mission together, back in the day.'

'Byzantium, 328,' replied Rose. She had also had time to remember it. 'We waited all night in the sewers under the hippodrome. They were going to destroy the city with a plague of flies and destabilize the whole of Asia Minor.'

'It was locusts, not flies,' Jupitus corrected. The brief sentence masked the faint sound of a message arriving in the pipe. Consequently neither he nor Rose noticed it.

Another ten minutes passed in silence. With nothing else to talk about and the events of yesterday still preying on her mind, Rose suddenly announced, 'Jupitus, it's ridiculous of me not to mention it . . . I found the flower in your rooms yesterday, along with all those old notes of mine.

Why do you have them?'

'I have no idea what you are talking about.'

'The flower, Jupitus – my chequered rose.'

'This was a mistake,' said Jupitus, standing and picking up the lantern. 'There is no point in *both* of us being here.'

'No, I wish to discuss this with you!' Rose insisted. As she grabbed his arm, she knocked the lantern to the floor, extinguishing the candle and plunging them into darkness.

'Now look what you've done!'

They both heard it at once: the soft sound of a door clicking shut. They froze. From the other side of the wall of faces came the sound of footsteps slowly crossing the room. There was a creak as the second concealed door was opened, and a silhouette holding a lantern slipped into the space. The figure carefully made its way over to the pipe in the corner and retrieved the new message.

Jupitus felt carefully along the ground for the lantern. 'Argh!' he yelled as boiling-hot wax spilled over his hand. The intruder immediately halted; then turned, hurled his lamp at Jupitus and Rose, and leaped through the nearest section of wall.

The face of Stede Bonnet, the infamous

'gentleman' pirate of 1770s Barbados, split in two as the spy tumbled through onto the floor. He picked himself up, charged across the room and was gone.

'After him, quickly!' shouted Jupitus as he too threw himself through the pirate's broken portrait, followed swiftly by Rose. They dashed across to the library door. The spy was disappearing up a stair-case, his distinctive navy-blue cloak trailing behind him. They charged after him.

At the top of the stairs, the corridor split in two. The cloaked figure was nowhere to be seen. They both listened intently to see if they could hear his retreating footsteps; there was no sound but the ticking of a grandfather clock.

'I'll go this way, you go that,' said Jupitus firmly. 'Are you armed?'

Rose rummaged in her carpetbag and produced a letter opener.

Jupitus rolled his eyes. 'Take this,' he commanded, drawing a small pistol from a holster inside his jacket.

'What about you?' Rose asked as he passed her the gun.

He took Rose's letter opener.

She felt a stab of affection. 'That's so gallant of you!'

'The bullets are expensive. Only fire if you absolutely have to,' he retorted brusquely as he set off.

'I know you're gallant, even if you won't admit it!' Rose called after him as she headed the other way.

Jupitus followed the corridor round to the communications room. He opened the door and looked inside; the workstations were empty and the large Meslith machine sat motionless inside its glass case, its quills poised over blank sheets of parchment.

Meanwhile Rose stopped at the entrance to the stateroom. The door was wide open. She held up the pistol and went in. The room was deserted, the lights extinguished. The moon was beginning to rise through the giant windows, casting four long rectangles of light across the floor. From behind a screen in the corner, she heard a dumbwaiter rumbling and a hatch opening. She swung round. She could see the outline of two feet at the bottom of the screen.

'Who's there?' she demanded, pointing the pistol directly at the partition, her arms rigid.

There was no reply – only the clink of crockery being loaded into the dumbwaiter.

'I asked, who's there?' Rose repeated in her most commanding voice as she headed towards the screen.

'What's that?' came a voice from the corner.

She recognized it immediately. She relaxed and lowered the gun as Norland put his head round the screen.

'Miss Rose, I didn't hear you come in.'

Norland was innocently loading dirty plates into the dumbwaiter. 'Afternoon tea. Should have done it hours ago. Clean slipped my mind. Don't get old is my advice to you. Off to target practice?' he chuckled, glancing down at Rose's pistol.

'Did anyone just come through here?' she asked.

'Not seen a soul.'

Rose sighed and put the pistol down on the table. 'I'd forgotten what it's like to hold a gun. Not an altogether happy memory.'

Suddenly she caught a glimpse of dark blue under the table. It took a split second for her to register the information – it was the spy's navy cloak. She reached for the pistol, but Norland got there first. She gasped as he pointed it directly at her.

'It was *you*! *You* were in the Library of Faces?' she gasped.

Norland's expression had altered completely: the jovial smile had been replaced by a contemptuous sneer.

'I don't understand,' Rose stammered, edging backwards towards the open door.

'Forty years I've been here,' Norland snarled, advancing threateningly. 'Does anyone care? "Norland's not important. He just cleans up other people's mess".'

'No one thinks that. You've always been a valuable member of the team.'

'Don't patronize me! One mission! One miserable mission – then never trusted again. Just because of the shapes in my eyes. "Poor old Norland – he can barely cross the road to the eighteenth century." You diamonds make me sick. You're so smug and self-important.'

Rose reached the doorway and turned to run, but Norland was one step ahead of her. He slammed the pistol in her face, knocking her to the floor. He kicked the door shut, turned the key in the lock and threw it across the room.

'Zeldt has promised me a new beginning.' Norland's eyes flashed wildly as he spoke. 'He'll take me to history – to wherever I wish to go. Get up!' he hissed.

Rose, trembling, picked herself up. Blood was trickling down her face.

'Over to the window,' he barked. Rose did as she was told.

There was a knock on the door – someone tried to turn the handle. 'Rose, are you in there?' Jupitus asked from the other side.

Rose shrieked as Norland raised the gun, pointed it at one of the huge windows and fired. The glass shattered, and wind gusted into the room.

'Rose!' Jupitus shouted from the other side of the door, shaking it violently.

Norland took hold of Rose's dress and pushed her through the open window, holding her over the precipice. He was much stronger than he appeared; the muscles of his forearms bunched and the veins throbbed on his big hands. Rose teetered on the ledge. Below her was a sheer drop down the side of the Mount into the foaming sea.

'Ancient Greece, Mesopotamia, Minoan Crete, Babylon – I will travel everywhere!' Norland shouted over the gale.

'Rose!' a voice cried from above. A great shadow

descended, and Jupitus, hanging from a curtain tie, swooped down and crashed through the adjacent window. Amid a shower of glass, he landed gracefully on the stateroom floor. Norland let go of Rose. As she fell, gasping, she hooked the handles of her carpetbag onto a spike of broken window frame. One of the handles tore, the bag split apart, and a cascade of belongings – lipsticks, old tissues and dentist reminders – showered down on her.

Jupitus advanced on Norland, punching him square in the face. The butler raised his pistol and fired, but Jupitus, with the toe of his perfectly polished boot, sent the gun flying through the open window and into the sea beyond. Norland lunged at his opponent, but in a series of expert manoeuvres, Jupitus chopped him in the throat, smashed his arm, dislocated his ankle and deposited him, half-dead, on the floor.

He ran over to the open window and grabbed Rose's hand just as her carpetbag gave way. Pulling her back into the room, he helped her onto a chair to regain her breath, took off his jacket and put it round her shoulders. Rose looked up at Jupitus: his eyes were bright, his cheeks flushed, his hair wild and dishevelled like a romantic hero.

'Exciting enough for you?' he asked breathlessly.

Suddenly Rose leaped to her feet, threw her arms around him and kissed him passionately. Jupitus made no attempt to stop her.

The door was unlocked and Galliana flew into the room, followed immediately by Oceane Noire – who halted in shock and fury at the sight of Jupitus and Rose in a passionate embrace. The pair broke apart as an assortment of other panicking keepers came into the room.

Galliana went over to inspect Norland, who was lying comatose on the floor.

'Your spy,' Jupitus announced coolly. He put his hands on Rose's shoulders. 'This is who you have to thank for catching him.'

Later that night, after the semi-conscious Norland had been locked away and the furore had died down, Oceane made her way to Jupitus's suite and knocked firmly on the door. Jupitus appeared in his dressing gown.

'We need to talk,' Oceane announced, sweeping into the room without waiting for an invitation. 'Rose Djones and you in a tawdry clinch was not a sight to warm the heart.' Her voice was as sharp as vinegar. 'I will make it clear to you, Jupitus – again: as agreed, our "friendship" is going to develop, whether you like it or not. Neither Rose Djones nor anyone else will interfere with that development. That is, of course, if you do not wish me to reveal your precious secrets to the commander. It's a wild guess, but I think she might have some difficulty in accepting your grubby past.'

Jupitus locked eyes with her. Fiercely independent, he hated to be blackmailed, but he knew that the alternative was worse. 'I understand,' he said coolly.

Oceane smiled curtly and left the room, slamming the door behind her.

24 CASTLE SURPRISES

After everyone, first the guests and then their servants, had gone to bed and the flickering candles had been extinguished, Charlie said goodbye once more to Mr Drake (he promised 'for the last time today'), and the three agents, dressed in the darkest clothes they could find, set off down into the heart of the castle.

As they reached the wall-fountain, the clocks struck four. The solemn sound of the bells echoed around the stone passageway; then there was silence again.

First they tried to push on the wall-fountain, but were not surprised to find it immovable.

'So how do we get in?' whispered Jake as they all examined the wall for some mechanism to open the chamber.

'Perhaps it's something to do with these characters,' suggested Charlie. He was referring to a series of Roman numerals engraved into the stone below the fountain: I, VIII, VI, III, IV, II, and so on.

Topaz knelt down and looked at them more carefully. 'There's no logic to these numbers. One, eight, six, three, four, two, seven, five, nine . . .' she counted. 'Mean anything?'

Charlie shrugged. Jake took the candle from Topaz and studied them closely. As he ran his fingers across the numerals, he noticed something.

'Look, they move!' he exclaimed excitedly – and demonstrated how the rectangle of stone surrounding each numeral could be depressed.

'There must be some particular code,' mused Charlie.

All three of them stared at the numbers to try and solve the puzzle.

Suddenly Jake's eyes opened wide and he exclaimed, '1492 – the year America was discovered. Shall I try it?'

Topaz shrugged. 'What's the worst that could happen?'

'Well, the *worst* that could happen,' said Charlie,

pushing his spectacles up his nose, 'is that the mechanism is booby-trapped and a wrong number releases hidden blades that decapitate us. But feel free . . .'

Jake tried the sequence of four numbers. The door did not open. Charlie scratched his head while Topaz stared at the numbers.

'1649,' she murmured – so softly that the others didn't hear at first. 'It's 1649,' she repeated more clearly. 'I've seen it before.'

Topaz didn't wait for their approval. She simply pressed the numbers, and the panel of stone opened with an echoey clunk. Taking the candle out of Jake's hand, she went inside. A stone staircase went down towards a distant pool of light.

'Shall we?' she asked as she fearlessly started to descend. Jake and Charlie followed, closing the door behind them.

'How did she know that number?' Jake asked Charlie.

'1649 is the year Zeldt was born,' Charlie whispered. 'He was born in London on the thirtieth of January of that year. The legend goes that his birth coincided with the beheading of Charles the First. Creepy,' he added, a chill going down his spine.

'The execution of Charles the First? I've read all about it!' said Jake excitedly. 'He wore three shirts so that he wouldn't shiver.'

'It was certainly a cold day,' Charlie replied solemnly. 'A cold day for history.'

They joined Topaz at the bottom of the staircase. A landing lit with lanterns led into a cavernous space: the castle's catacombs. These were supported by a series of mighty pillars.

'Take cover!' Topaz ordered suddenly – something was happening. The three agents hid in the shadows behind one of the columns. Standing in a pool of light in a large space ahead of them was a large piece of machinery; around it stood an assembly line of workstations, with people rushing around, toiling flat out.

'What is that thing?' asked Jake.

Charlie had recognized it immediately: the sight had brought a smile to his face. 'That, my friend, is one of the world's first printing presses.'

'Really?' asked Jake, suddenly intrigued. 'It's huge.'

'In 1455, Johannes Gutenberg devised his mechanical method of printing,' Charlie explained in an excited whisper. 'Apparently inspired by the humble wine press. Before Gutenberg, books were either written by hand or printed from laboriously carved blocks of wood. Very long-winded and ruinously expensive. Gutenberg's revolutionary notion—'

'Was to use molten iron to produce metal type-faces,' Topaz interrupted, 'thus giving a limitless supply of letters.'

'In reality Gutenberg wasn't the first. There was a Japanese prototype early in the thirteenth century, but it was Gutenberg who patented the first oil-based ink, without which the machines never worked properly.'

'You see' – Topaz smiled – 'you learn something new every day with us.'

'That's the understatement of the century,' Jake commented.

'The question is,' mused Charlie, 'what is Zeldt printing so urgently?'

They watched the frenetic activity. As the newly printed pages, with their bright colours of black, red and gold, came off the press, they made their way down the production line. Some workers carefully folded the paper into reams; others expertly sewed these together; others still used glue and metal pins to bind the giant tomes. At the final workstation the front of each volume was expertly fitted with an elaborate clasp-and-key mechanism. The finished books were finally placed carefully in wooden crates.

One such crate, being full, was loaded onto a trolley and dragged out of the room by two workers. On seeing Zeldt's men heading in their direction, the three agents edged further round into the shadows. They came to an archway that led to a further wing of the catacombs.

'Shall we investigate?' Jake asked.

Charlie stared at him, then turned to Topaz. 'How long has he been working with us . . . ?' he asked. 'All of three days, and now, apparently, he's running the show.'

They disappeared down the passageway and into another huge chamber: this one was unoccupied and a good deal darker than the first. It took the agents a full minute to accustom their eyes to the gloom. Finally a repeating pattern of shapes came into focus.

'What are those things?' asked Topaz, unnerved by the strange atmosphere.

On either side, as far as the eye could see, was a series of rectangular containers such as you might find on a cargo ship. Each one was raised at least six feet above the ground on sturdy legs; from its base emerged a thick funnel that curved round into the wall.

'You're the tallest,' said Charlie to Jake. 'What are they made of?'

Jake went underneath one, reached up and rapped the bottom. 'Wood,' he whispered.

Jake's knocks had started some kind of reaction. Charlie listened carefully. 'It sounds as if there's something alive in there.'

They all listened: from the container came a muffled scratching noise.

'That crate has a crack in it,' said Topaz, pointing to another container: there was indeed a narrow opening towards the top of the box.

'I'll look,' said Jake bravely. He grinned at Charlie. 'What's the worst that could happen? It's full of killer scorpions? Give me a leg up.'

'I think I prefer the old, unassuming, I couldn't-possibly-board-a-ship-without-my-aunt Jake,' said Charlie, making a cradle with his hands and hoisting his friend upwards. 'What about you, Topaz?'

'Actually, I think Jake was *always* brave,' said

Topaz with a smile. 'That's what I like about him.'

Jake felt such a thrill of joy at this pronounce-ment that he shot up the outside of the container like a professional climber. He managed to clamber up so that his eyes were level with the crack.

'Careful . . .' warned Topaz. Jake was now a good twenty feet from the ground.

'Can you see anything?' asked Charlie.

'I can smell something,' replied Jake. 'It smells like the pet shop in Lewisham that was closed down by the authorities. Hold on – I can get a bit closer.' He put his hand into the crack and climbed further so that he could look down into the container.

There was a splintering sound, and a section of wood came away in his hand. He managed to balance himself by gripping the top of the structure. There was a sudden loud rumble from within. Jake could see an undulating blanket of shapes advancing towards him. Suddenly rats started pouring out of the opening, across his head and shoulders, and dropping to the floor below.

Jake was seized with choking terror. He hated rats at the best of times, but this was disgusting. Fat rats, with thick tails longer than their bodies, were scrabbling across his hair and face. He wanted to cry out, and needed every ounce of self-control to stop himself.

Topaz and Charlie could see a stream of rodents heading towards the passageway they'd come from.

'We'll be discovered,' Charlie whispered. 'Plug up the hole now!'

Jake tried to replace the broken piece of timber, but the tide was unstoppable. More and more rats spilled out. A long hairless tail flicked into his mouth – he could feel it against his tongue. Then a rat slipped right down Jake's neck, inside his shirt. It struggled to claw and bite its way out.

Jake could contain his revulsion no longer. Suddenly he lost control. He gave a blood-curdling yell and dropped to the floor; the rats continued to shower down on him and he screamed again.

From the other side of the room, Topaz heard the sound of rushing feet; then a group of guards burst in, approaching them with swords drawn. They soon surrounded the agents, who had no choice but to drop their own weapons and put up their hands.

'I'm sorry – I'm so sorry,' Jake muttered to the others. He was overcome with shame.

'Don't worry: adrenaline does that sometimes,' said Topaz kindly. 'It happens to the best of us.'

The words were of little comfort to Jake. He was painfully aware that he might have ruined everything.

Mina Schlitz strode into the room, and pushed through the guards until she was facing the three of them. Behind her the rats were still dropping from the hole in the container. The guards shrank away from them, but Mina did not flinch. In fact, when one rodent took an interest in her feet, she flipped it over, under her shoe, and, without even looking, stabbed it with her heel.

She studied Jake's face. His beard was coming away and she ripped it off. This hurt a good deal, but Jake decided he would rather die than reveal either pain or fear again. Mina glared at Charlie. Charlie attempted to glare just as fiercely back. Finally she turned her attention to Topaz, and removed her headdress. First, she frowned as if in recognition. Then her eyes suddenly widened in astonishment.

'Am I mistaken,' she cried, 'or might it be the one and only Topaz St Honoré?'

'You managed to miss me in Venice,' taunted

Topaz, 'so *deuxième fois la chance*, second time lucky.'

'I never miss!' hissed Mina. 'Incompetence is as vile a notion to me as' – she chose her word carefully – 'mercy.' Her composure returned. 'Take them to Zeldt!' she commanded.

25 BOOKS, RATS, CATACLYSM

They were led up a back staircase into the castle above. The journey was made in unsettling silence. Soon they reached the large library of Zeldt's private suite.

This was the same long room to which Nathan and Paolo had been summoned two days earlier, with its succession of fires, book shelves filled with ancient tomes, and Renaissance statues set in every shadowy recess.

Jake, Topaz and Charlie were pushed roughly onto chairs at one end of the long table. With a firm signal, one of the guards indicated that they should wait. To ensure their obedience, guards stood behind each of their seats. Zeldt's throne at the other end was empty – for the moment.

'Mr Drake will be worried beyond belief,' whispered Charlie.

Topaz squeezed his hand. 'He'll be fine. He's resourceful,' she replied softly.

They waited in uncertain silence. Through the casement windows they saw the sun come up over the Rhine valley, the rays searing into their eyes. Occasionally one of them would turn round, only to be met by the steely gaze of the guards.

As the clock struck seven, two servants appeared with silver trays of food. Charlie, in particular, perked up in anticipation: all he had eaten in nearly twenty-four hours was a bowl of tepid cabbage soup.

Unfortunately the food was not for their consumption. It was set in front of the empty throne. Tantalizing wafts floated over in the direction of the prisoners.

The next arrival was a familiar-looking beast: Felson, the savage dog that had belonged to Von Bliecke. He strode down to the end of the table and, recognizing Jake's scent, started to growl.

'Long time no see,' Jake offered mischievously.

Felson bared his teeth, but then heard another set

of footsteps. He quickly retreated to the nearest fire-place, where he sat down, quivering.

Mina Schlitz stepped into the room. She ignored its occupants and went over to check the windows and fireplaces; she felt under the rim of the table and inspected the silver trays of food. Satisfied that all was well, she returned to the door and nodded a signal.

It was opened by an unseen guard and Prince Zeldt glided in.

It seemed to Jake as if the temperature had suddenly dropped – as if the prince emitted an invisible icy aura.

Zeldt also seemed to feel the cold. He pulled his fur cloak tightly around him and went over to one of the fireplaces. He carefully positioned his slim leather boot against a burning log and gave it a kick. New flames flickered into life.

The prince turned and stopped dead. Immediately, instinctively, his eye went to Topaz, and his lips curled into a malicious smile. For her part, Topaz stared fixedly down the length of the table. Mina watched them both with interest. She took her snake out of its box, wrapped it around her forearm and stroked it under the chin.

Zeldt sat down on his throne, opened out a napkin on his lap and perused some papers while one of the servants served him with food.

Jake glared at him as he ate his breakfast with slow deliberation but little appetite. For Zeldt, eating was a vulgar chore. It was this, in part, that gave him such a pale, bloodless complexion. He put his plate to one side and poured a cup of weak jasmine tea, pursing his lips to take a sip, then replacing the cup carefully on its saucer.

'At two o'clock this afternoon there is to be a solar eclipse,' he said finally, in a voice so quiet that the others weren't sure if it was directed at them. 'Being trespassers in this corner of history, you are doubtless ignorant of the fact.' He took another measured sip of tea.

'Of course, I haven't arranged it myself – that would be impressive; no, "the heavens" will provide it for free.' Once again the prince's eyes rested on Topaz, with what seemed to be a mixture of fascination and disgust. 'An eclipse is one of the few things in history that can be depended upon absolutely.'

Charlie looked quizzically at Topaz and Jake.

'Such a spectacle is always memorable, and no

doubt the gullible masses will be quaking with fear,' Zeldt continued in a monotone, 'but I have a feeling that *this* eclipse will be more memorable than most.'

'Where are my family?' Jake found himself demanding. 'My parents – where are they?' he repeated, getting to his feet. The guard behind him immediately stepped forward, smacked him hard across the back of his head and pushed him down again. Topaz gave him a concerned sideways glance.

Zeldt calmly took another sip of tea. 'What do any of you know of the Renaissance?' Receiving no reply, he looked up and stared at them directly with his cold grey eyes. 'I understand that the phrase is not in common parlance at this particular moment of time,' he continued, 'but that is neither here nor there. The Renaissance – what is your knowledge of it? You on the left,' he said, pointing to Charlie.

'The Renaissance . . .?'

Zeldt hissed with irritation. 'Ignorant people. You, then, Topaz St Honoré,' he sneered.

For a moment he and Topaz locked eyes. Then she looked away. 'The Renaissance refers to a period of history,' she replied matter-of-factly; 'the present period – during which various classical doctrines and philosophies are rediscovered—'

'Insipid!' Zeldt silenced her with a snap of his fingers. 'Do none of you have any character?'

Charlie reddened angrily as Zeldt stood up, went over to the fire beside him and kicked it again with his boot. Felson flinched, but dared not move from his position. The prince stared into the flames with his back to them.

A good three minutes passed before he sighed and went over to one of the bookcases. 'The printed book . . .' he said finally, brushing his pale hand along the shelves. 'The invention of the century – of the millennium, perhaps.' His expression soured. He pulled back the seemingly immovable bookcase to reveal, behind it, the entrance to a secret chamber. 'Bring them,' he whispered as he disappeared inside.

Jake, Topaz and Charlie were dragged to their feet and escorted through the doorway onto a stone bridge that looked down onto the catacombs where they had just been captured. Mina followed closely behind.

'I believe you have already seen my printing press,' Zeldt said, pointing into the space below. 'Quite the stupidest and most dangerous device ever invented,' he muttered. 'Once only a handful of chosen people were endowed with knowledge. The printing press wishes to give knowledge to *all* . . . Enlightenment even to the slaves who wipe the stench from our gutters?'

His eyes darkened. 'Enlightenment for everyone? Most repulsive of notions. What next? The beasts are enlightened too? The spiders and worms learn philosophy?'

'If it's so stupid and dangerous,' asked Jake, 'why do you have one?'

Zeldt smiled malevolently before answering. 'Oh, I intend to give the people what they want for a little longer.' His voice dropped. 'Just long enough for them to . . . die. Come and see my laboratory.'

The prince led them across the bridge and into a large room filled with gleaming scientific apparatus: measures, test tubes, calibrators and square clocks with complicated dials. Technicians were at work here. In the centre of the chamber there was a room-within-a-room: a cube of thick glass where two further technicians, both dressed in protective armour, were engaged in some careful operation.

Zeldt led the others over to a table and picked up a large tome. 'This is a copy of the book we are printing downstairs. *The Book of Life*, I've called it – which amuses me no end.' He flicked through the crisp pages of newly printed gothic type and intricate illustrations. 'It contains all the branches of new learning: science, astronomy, mineralogy and that most invisible of evils, mathematics. The book is a complete compendium of modern learning.' His voice fell to a whisper. 'But it also has a sting in its tail.'

An icy smile played across Mina's face as he said this.

'When the book is unlocked,' Zeldt continued, 'a surprise is revealed.'

The front of the tome was surmounted by an ornate golden lock with a key. With his fingertips Zeldt extracted a tiny glass vial from within the mechanism. He held it up to the light. His prisoners saw that it contained a viscous black liquid.

'When the key is turned,' the prince explained, 'the glass vial will be snapped and its contents released.'

'What *are* its contents?' asked Charlie.

'The fruits of many years' hard work,' replied Zeldt proudly.

He led them over to the plate-glass cube where the armoured technicians were working. Inside, a cabinet, also of plate glass, stood on an iron table. Here, using layers of pigs' intestines as protective gloves, the two workers were distilling a quantity of that same black substance.

'What is it?' asked Topaz, almost afraid to know the answer.

'You are witnessing a unique operation. The substance on the left,' said Zeldt, indicating the contents of a small container, 'is a paste of infected flea guts. It took a billion fleas harvested from a million rats to produce even that small amount of usable material.'

'Rats . . .' Charlie glanced at Jake.

'The matter with which it is being combined' – Zeldt pointed to the contents of another container – 'is an ingenious agent that increases the efficacy of the other by at least a hundred times.'

Jake immediately recognized this as the substance in the *second* bottle that Talisman Kant had sold to Mina Schlitz: the honeycomb-like material.

'Infected fleas?' asked Charlie. 'Infected with what?'

Zeldt couldn't suppress a mischievous chuckle.

'Oh, really. You must have guessed by now.' Then the smile vanished from his face. 'The plague.'

For a second all three of the agents stopped breathing.

Zeldt's eyes glittered with the fervour of a true fanatic. '*Yersinia pestis* is the deadliest killer in history. In its first wave, medieval Europe was decimated: seventy million deaths. First fever, then vomiting, then agonizing, stinking boils, and finally blackened skin as death takes its grip. That was *then*. Thanks to the efforts of Talisman Kant, *this* edition – if you will pardon the pun – will be ten times more lethal. You shouldn't stand too close. Those insatiable germs would love to get their teeth into you—' He stopped mid-sentence. 'But I was forgetting. You two meddlers' – he nodded to Jake and Topaz – 'are already protected with my antidote, my . . . What's that vulgar word you use for it in the modern age? My *vaccine*. But please don't worry.' The prince addressed his last phrase solely to Jake. 'I will find an equally revolting way for you to die.'

The three agents stared in horror as the technicians filled a number of minute glass vials with the deadly black matter. These were sealed with a red-hot torch and transported to another workstation.

Here they were inserted into the lock mechanism of the books, which were then packed into crates and, at the far end of the room, loaded into the back of an armoured carriage forged in blood-red iron.

'In twenty minutes that carriage will leave here with five hundred of these books and head south. Over the next forty-eight hours every town and city in southern Europe will receive its free publication. Innsbruck will be the first port of call' – Zeldt indicated it on a map that hung on the wall beside him – 'then Milan, Verona, Genoa, Florence, and so on. The people will receive their gift in awe, they will wonder at its magic, *ignorant* of the fact that they have welcomed death itself into the heart of their communities.' The prince's eyes were now blazing. '*Ignorant* that anarchy will already be descending, decay already setting in. *Ignorant* that their meaningless lives will already be over.'

Mina Schlitz smiled gleefully at the thought of such delicious destruction.

'So my books will eventually ensure the annihilation of Italy and all the arrogant countries of the Mediterranean – the worst criminals in the great fiasco of the Renaissance,' Zeldt continued, 'but the master stroke of my design, the *prologue* to my apocalypse, will begin, with a bang, this afternoon in northern Europe.'

He nodded at Mina, who produced a wooden box. She unfastened the latch, and from its padded lining lifted out a heavy golden contraption, placing it carefully on the table. It was a clock-like instrument comprised of tiny gleaming dials, levers and pulleys. On top of it was etched the same emblem of the snake and shield.

'Such beautiful craftsmanship,' Zeldt sighed. 'It seems a pity that no one will be alive to appreciate it. Please – take a closer look,' he instructed his prisoners, repeating with menace, 'Take a closer look *inside*.'

Their attention had already been drawn to the curious inner workings of the device. Although it pained them to follow Zeldt's orders, they leaned down and examined it more carefully. Encased in the heart of the machine lay a king-size vial of the same viscous black liquid. On either side of this, two miniature golden fists, each also engraved with the Zeldt symbol, were poised to strike and smash the bottle in two.

'This literally world-shattering device,' the prince continued, 'will shortly be deposited on the unfinished spire of Cologne's new cathedral, a vulgar and ostentatious edifice if ever there was one. At precisely three minutes past two this afternoon, when the eclipse is total, those golden hands will do their work and release the contents of the glass vial. What glorious poetic licence: as the dark starts to engulf Europe, my *super* plague is released. Within days, half the continent will be extinct. The survivors will fight over the putrid bones of Europe, until they too succumb to the might of King Death.'

Zeldt stared at them, and his voice rose as he proclaimed: 'The Renaissance will be destroyed before it has even begun.'

'So that's your grand plan?' Charlie tried for his most cutting tone. 'Advancement? Progress? The sciences? The arts? They're no use to you?'

Suddenly the blood rose in Zeldt's face. 'I'm cleaning up the stinking mess of history!' he roared. 'You're not so stupid that you do not know what becomes of it! Giving knowledge to the masses brings nothing but catastrophe and despair! Human beings are animals, and that is how they should be treated.'

'Except for the select few . . .' offered Topaz with a sneer. 'You and your millionaire investors.'

Zeldt glared back at her before speaking. 'Someone will have to be in charge: slaves do not drive themselves.'

'But if you plan to kill everyone,' Charlie enquired, 'who exactly is going to man your prison camps?'

'Those slaves, as I said,' Zeldt answered with a shrug. 'Selected and imported from every corner of the Earth. I will have the world at my disposal because I will *own* the world. And I will rebuild it, *stronger* than it has ever been before – a marvellous, awe-inspiring creation such as history has never seen!'

Mina Schlitz silently packed Zeldt's time bomb back into its wooden box and fastened the catch.

The prince took a deep breath and settled down again. 'Now, if there are no more questions . . .'

'I have a question,' Jake persisted. 'Where are my parents?'

'Tiresome individual,' Zeldt sighed. He turned to Mina. 'Take them back to the library. I shall join you presently.'

As the prince went to speak to one of his scientists, Jake, Topaz and Charlie were escorted back across the laboratory and over the bridge.

'Your friends are already waiting,' Mina announced. 'We thought it would be charitable to dispose of you all together.'

As they entered Zeldt's library, they immediately recognized the two sorry-looking figures who awaited them there.

'Nathan!' Topaz exclaimed.

'Don't say you've missed me!' said Nathan with a twinkle in his eye as he limped towards her. Behind him, cowering helplessly, was Paolo Cozzo. All five agents were herded together.

'Charlie, Jake – good to see you both alive,' Nathan said, nodding to the others. He stopped and did a double-take at the sight of Jake. 'Don't tell me you put that outfit together yourself?' He squinted to get the full effect. 'Great silhouette! And nice work on the hair. A style rethink during a world catastrophe takes a special kind of courage.'

Paolo shook his head in bewilderment. 'How can he talk like that – as if nothing's happened?'

Zeldt came back into the room, carrying his time bomb. He closed the bookcase behind him. 'I have a ship to catch,' he said, rounding on the agents, 'so I'm sorry to report that the time has come to say our goodbyes.'

He nodded at Mina, who went over to the metal door through which the unfortunate Friedrich Von Bliecke had been sent to his death two days earlier, and turned its distinctive bronze handle of curling snakes, then rotated the wheel.

'On the other side of that chamber is a door. In one hour exactly it will open and take you into a labyrinth. In the labyrinth there is a single exit that will take you out of the castle.'

'An exit?' exclaimed Paolo. 'You're really going to let us go?'

'Idiotic simpleton,' Zeldt said with a curl of his lip. 'I am telling you this not because you will ever reach it – it is impossible – but to prolong your exquisite agony a little longer.'

'How thoughtful you are,' Nathan drawled. 'It's a mystery that you've remained unmarried all these years.'

Zeldt turned to Topaz. He stared at her long and hard. 'I think this lost little soul should come with us,' he whispered with a nasty glint in his eye.

Topaz's eyes widened in trepidation.

'You take your hands off her!' roared Jake, momentarily freeing himself from the guards and taking her arm. She looked back at him as if trying to tell him something. Whatever it was she wished to impart, he failed to understand it.

Nathan whispered urgently into Jake's ear, 'Let her go – at least *she* has a chance.'

Zeldt nodded, and the guards herded Jake, Nathan, Charlie and Paolo across the room towards the open metal door.

'One last thing.' Zeldt held up a hand to stop them. He touched Jake's sleeve. 'You were asking where your parents were . . .'

Jake held his breath and gazed at Zeldt in terror.

'Once you get into the labyrinth,' the prince continued, 'you'll find out soon enough. You'd better prepare yourself.'

Jake yanked himself free and flew at his captor. As his hands closed around the prince's neck, the guards delivered an agonizing punch to his kidneys.

'Take them!' Zeldt hissed as he straightened his collar, and Jake and the others were dragged into the chamber.

'Human beings are stronger than you think!' Jake shouted defiantly. His last sight was of Zeldt reaching out a gloved hand and taking Topaz's face in it; then the metal door slammed shut behind them.

Nathan couldn't resist a final taunt: 'And Miss

Schlitz,' he shouted through the door, 'you really should take my advice about red – it totally drains your skin tone.'

Zeldt descended the great sweeping staircase towards the main doors, Mina at his side, the bubonic bomb clutched firmly in her hand. A pale-faced Topaz was dragged along behind them. As the prince reached the foot of the stairs, he stopped, and a number of footmen snapped into action. They fitted a brilliant silver breastplate to his chest and armoured gloves over his thin, pale fingers; a helmet with a plume of black feathers was placed on his head, and a magnificent fur cloak, with a tiger's head roaring silently from each shoulder, was carefully fastened around his neck.

The principal footman made the final checks. He removed a tiny piece of stray lint from the fur cloak before all the servants bowed their heads and withdrew.

As Zeldt swept out onto the steps of the main entrance, a courteous round of applause echoed around the courtyard. His accomplices had come to bid their respectful farewells. Their young sons and daughters, dressed in fur against the chill morning, gazed wide-eyed at the resplendent figure of their commander-in-chief.

Also assembled there were Zeldt's guards. They stood to attention, backs rigid, swords drawn and held aloft.

The prince made a gesture to the assembled crowd, then stepped down towards the blood-red carriage and inspected its load. It was neatly packed with its crates of books: five hundred volumes whose deadly contents would shortly strike Europe. He cast his eye around the cargo and nodded in satisfaction. The door of the carriage was closed; Mina gave a signal to the huge, ugly beast of a driver and his equally ugly companion, and the vehicle set off through the archway, heading down the mountain on its journey south.

Immediately an open-topped carriage drew up. Zeldt climbed in and took his seat with great solemnity. Mina, still clutching the box, joined him. Then she signalled to a guard, who had Von Bliecke's dog, Felson, on the end of a lead. The dog yelped as he was bundled into the carriage, then crouched down, cowering away from both Mina and the prince.

Topaz was now ushered to move towards them, but she remained where she was.

'Come and sit here, my dear,' Zeldt hissed, patting the seat next to him, 'and tell me *everything* you've been up to. It's been *epochs*.'

Still Topaz did not move. Two guards forced her up into the vehicle. She sat beside Zeldt, but did not look at him; Mina studied her with a sinister smile.

The carriage set off out of the castle, heading for the harbour and the red-sailed warship, the *Lindwurm*.

26 SNAKES AND LADDERS

'Is everyone all right?' Nathan's voice echoed around the pitch-black space.

Charlie just grunted and Paolo replied, 'I'm locked in a stone box with no food or water, apparently about to die . . . I've never felt better.'

'That's the spirit!' answered Nathan, ignoring Paolo's sarcasm. 'Jake? Are you all right?' He waited for an answer. 'Jake? Can you hear me?'

Jake could hear Nathan perfectly (it was physically impossible *not* to hear him), but he didn't feel like talking. The truth was, he was very far from all right. His mind was awhirl with fears and worries. Zeldt had told him that he would 'find out' about his parents in the labyrinth, and that he should 'prepare' himself. He knew this could mean only one thing. He was desperate both to find out

367

and *not* find out what awful secrets might lie beyond the chamber.

On top of all this, Topaz had now been abducted. The fact that Jake had known her for only a matter of days – that he was unable to explain or understand his feelings for her – was neither here nor there. Jake felt a deep attachment to her, as though, somehow, she was a part of him. His need to find her again was almost as strong as his need to find his family.

'If you're worried about what Zeldt said,' Nathan persevered, 'we shouldn't jump to conclusions.' The truth was, after finding the clothing tag in the dungeon, Nathan himself feared the worst, but he felt it was his duty to keep morale as high as possible.

'He's right,' Charlie added cheerfully. 'There's no point in worrying until we find hard evidence.'

'Like Alan and Miriam's severed limbs,' Paolo suggested unhelpfully. 'Ow!' he cried as he received a clip on the back of the head from Nathan. '*Ow!*' he yelled again as Charlie gave him another for good measure.

'Let's not talk about it,' Jake decided grimly. 'Let's just get out of here!'

'I like your style!' drawled Nathan.

'Spoken like a true History Keeper,' Charlie concurred.

'Zeldt said that a door would open into the labyrinth in an hour . . .' Nathan set about feeling his way around the walls. 'I'd say ten minutes has passed already. We need to find that door and force it somehow. What's this . . . ? Charlie, does this feel like something?'

Nathan directed Charlie's hand to a groove in the back wall. 'Can you get any purchase on it?' he asked.

They both groaned and grunted as they tried to force the wall apart.

'Oh, thank God!' Nathan cried suddenly.

'You've opened it?' Paolo exclaimed.

'No, I thought I'd cracked my nail, but it's all right – disaster averted.'

'How can you care about your *nails* at a time like this?' murmured Paolo in despair.

'I'm not going to dignify that question with an answer. My nails are perfect in all respects: tone, colour and contour. There exists no time or circumstance in which I would lose interest in them.'

Even with all four of them pulling with all their

might, the stone wall refused to budge. Eventually, with reluctance, Nathan suggested that they conserve their energies and wait until the chamber opened of its own accord.

As they sat there in the darkness, Charlie told Nathan and Paolo about Zeldt's plan to destroy Europe and the Renaissance. With every new twist, from the prince's use of genetically modified plague, to the books with their vile secret, to the time bomb to be detonated in Cologne Cathedral, Paolo uttered a single phrase over and over again: '*Oh, mamma mia! Oh, mamma mia!*'

Finally there was a sound of grinding stone, and the back wall of the chamber split in two.

'It's opening! The wall's opening!' Paolo gasped as pale light crept into the room. Jake's heart started pounding like a bass drum.

Nathan limped over to the aperture and peered inside. 'The labyrinth, I assume. Very welcoming.'

'Is anyone in there?' Jake shouted out into the void. 'Anyone at all?' His voice echoed around the space. There was no response.

'Jake, do you still have that lighter I gave you?' asked Nathan.

Jake took it out of his pocket and passed it over.

Nathan turned to Paolo, and with one tug ripped the sleeve from his jacket.

'What are you doing? Mamma made me that.'

'Sorry – cheap material burns well,' Nathan replied as he set light to Paolo's sleeve.

He was right: it produced a bright flame, and he hurled the burning sleeve into the centre of the space. It landed on the edge of a wooden gantry, revealing Zeldt's labyrinth with its endless puzzle of staircases going off at every conceivable angle.

'Exit?' Paolo wailed. 'Where? How on earth are we to find the exit?'

'Hello!' Jake called again, scanning every inch of the murky space.

All four agents listened intently. Eventually they heard an odd noise like shifting sand.

'Wh-what is that?' asked Paolo, wondering if he really wanted to know the answer.

'It sounds like it's coming from the floor,' said Charlie.

Nathan turned to Paolo and ripped off his other sleeve.

'Nathan!' he exclaimed.

'What? You want to go around with one sleeve?

You've got four hundred years until asymmetry becomes fashionable.'

Nathan lit the second sleeve and flicked it into the centre of the space. It was a good shot. It fell between the various staircases and landed on the floor far below. The others craned their necks to see what lay there. The burning sleeve illuminated a large circle of empty stone.

Then the tail of a snake slowly curled out of sight. Paolo gasped. There was stillness again.

'I don't want to be the voice of doom,' said Charlie, 'but that looked suspiciously like a black mamba.'

'A black mamba?' whispered Paolo. 'That's bad, is it?'

'One of the deadliest creatures on earth,' Nathan confirmed. 'It can deliver up to four hundred milligrams of venom in one bite. You're dead in twenty minutes, if it doesn't strangle you first.'

'And it's long,' added Charlie. 'Fifteen feet. That's nearly three of you put together.'

It was impossible for Paolo to go any paler, but he said nothing. Jake continued to search the chamber for any sign of his parents.

'Of course, the "black" refers not to its skin

colour,' added Charlie, 'but to the inky interior of its mouth.'

'Which they say is blacker than a black hole.' Nathan raised his eyebrows.

'All right, that's enough!' snapped Paolo. 'We don't know what it is for sure, so lesson over!'

'Not quite . . .' Charlie had seen something else. The head of another terrible serpent appeared in the illuminated circle. For a moment it did not move. Then it gradually started to slither across the space. In unison, all the boys' eyes widened in horror: it was, at the very least, fifteen feet long.

'That'll be a black mamba then,' said Nathan.

'And all its black mamba friends,' Charlie added chillingly.

'Let's go then,' said Jake, swallowing his fear and descending to the first step of a staircase leading away from their chamber. But his foot came into contact with nothing but air. He lost his balance and fell forward. In a flash, Nathan had caught him and pulled him back up.

'Those steps are not what they seem to be. None of them are. It's a puzzle – a trick with mirrors.'

He demonstrated by dropping a small stone onto the 'apparent' staircase in front of them. There was actually a sheer drop into the great abyss below.

'So how do we know which way to go?' asked Paolo desperately.

'Well, mirrors can play tricks, but gravity can't,' said Charlie as he scooped up a handful of grit and scattered it in front of them. Amazingly it settled on a flight of stairs that appeared to go in completely the wrong direction. The others were puzzled, but the truth was there to see in front of them. Charlie took a pace forward. It seemed as if he would step into nothingness, but he landed on firm ground.

'You see? Simple really,' he said, secretly drawing a sigh of relief. 'Everyone get some grit and follow me.'

Jake, Nathan and Paolo each scooped up some dirt and cautiously set off. Charlie led the way; Nathan followed Jake, holding onto his shoulder so as to avoid putting pressure on his leg. A whimpering Paolo brought up the rear.

They cautiously made their way down to a landing at the bottom of the first staircase and stopped. There were now three staircases going off at wildly divergent angles. Charlie scattered some grit and identified the correct path – a much narrower staircase that ascended high into the chamber.

As the four of them climbed the steps, they gradually got a clearer view of the space below. It was large and uneven, punctuated by clusters of shadowy rock, amongst which they glimpsed a spine-chilling undulating movement.

The agents carefully found a way through, up and down staircases, moving forward, doubling back and moving on again. Jake's eyes still darted everywhere. After twenty minutes of slow, nail-biting progress, Nathan spotted a small rectangle of light.

'Look! There!' He pointed up to a doorway at the top of the winding staircase ahead of them.

Paolo gasped and his face lit up. 'That's it! That's the exit!' He pushed past the others and started up.

'Wait! Come back,' barked Nathan. 'It might be a trap.'

'No, I can see sky! I promise I can see sky,' replied Paolo, rushing towards the light. 'We've done it, we've done it!' he exclaimed. He was running so swiftly that he did not notice one of the steps moving as he trod on it.

This set off a chain reaction in the mechanism below the labyrinth of stairs.

Paolo was four steps from the top when the

staircase started to tilt. It creaked over onto its side, further and further, until, with a cry of terror, he lost his footing. The other three watched helplessly as he flew past them and crashed to the ground below in a cloud of dust.

For a second Paolo lost consciousness. When he came round, his mouth opened to scream, but nothing came out. Staring back at him were the dead eyes of Captain Von Bliecke. Next to his head was the captain's half-eaten forearm, still gloved and clutching his sword. His legs were nowhere to be seen. Once again Paolo screamed soundlessly.

'Back this way! Quickly!' shouted Nathan, retreating to the previous landing.

But it was too late.

From all around came the sound of mechanical clunks, and gradually every staircase started to shift on its axis. Nathan, unable to balance on his bad leg, was the next to fall, hitting a gantry on the way down.

Jake and Charlie managed to switch to an upright staircase – only for that to start turning until it was almost upside down. Charlie fell; Jake managed to catch the ledge of another staircase, but this too was moving – and not in his favour. He held on with all his might, but at last his fingers slipped and he was forced to let go.

As he hit the ground, Jake heard a faint crack beneath his feet. He lost his balance and his back thumped onto the ground. It was covered in dark, dusty sand – much softer than it had appeared from above – but his body still trembled with shock. Voices seemed to be coming from all sides and blurred together in an indecipherable buzz.

Jake sat up and tried to focus. There were white shapes on the floor beside him. It took him a moment to realize what they were. They were eggs, black mambas' eggs, and Jake had destroyed two of them when he fell.

He felt a pop in his ears and his hearing returned. 'To your left!' Nathan roared. '*To your left!*'

Jake saw the creature out of the corner of his eye: the mother of the smashed young mambas, a snake as thick as a human leg, was slithering towards him across the dark sand. He tried to get to his feet, but he was frozen with terror. The snake reared high off the ground and opened its inky black jaws. It hissed savagely as its lips curled back to reveal poison-drenched fangs. Like a possessed demon, it flew at Jake. He flinched away and was only half conscious of the sweep of metal and a sound of slicing.

A twelve-inch tranche of the mamba's head flew across the chamber. The rest of its body seemed to freeze for a moment before collapsing in a lifeless coil.

Charlie stood there, breathing a sigh of relief and holding the sword taken from Von Bliecke's severed forearm. 'All right?' he asked.

'Up here! Now!' Nathan shouted. He and Paolo had taken refuge on top of the largest rock. Charlie pulled Jake to his feet and they hurried across, dodging more furious snakes. Nathan held out his hand and pulled Jake up. As Charlie followed, another snake, smaller but more nimble, reared out of the shadows and sank its needle-like teeth into the thick leather of his boot.

He let out a cry and stabbed the sword into the snake's trachea. There was a wheezing of escaping air, then the snake's whole body juddered violently and went limp. Charlie had to shake his boot several times to release the dead clenched jaw. He joined the other three at the apex of the rock.

'Nice work,' said Nathan, patting his comrade on the back. 'I bet you're glad I insisted on the bullhide boots.'

Tears were streaming from Paolo's eyes. 'Why did I join this service – *why*?' he moaned. 'I could have been an accountant. My mother wanted me to be an accountant. I was offered a position at the Medici Bank in Florence. I could be working with an abacus at a little desk, with a view of the peacocks in the garden. My life could have been full of sunshine and *torta della nonna*, but here I am, perching on a rock in a dungeon, with no sleeves on my jacket, surrounded by black mambas!'

'Look on the bright side,' said Nathan. 'We're still alive, aren't we? And we have Von Bliecke's sword. Where would we be without that?'

'Hurrah, hurrah! We have a sword!' Paolo sounded half demented. 'Let's all dance to celebrate!' He stood up and started to do a jig. 'Can't you see, you idiot – we're all about to die!'

Snakes had now gathered from every dark corner, from under every rock; through the numerous holes that littered the ground, more and more appeared. Twelve-foot leviathans were heading straight towards the four boys.

Despite his bravado, Nathan knew that they had little hope, even with Von Bliecke's sword. Three or four they could probably handle, but this many . . .

Paolo closed his eyes and said his prayers. The others huddled closer and closer together. As the first group of snakes reached the base of the rock, their tongues darted in anticipation and they hissed at each other, their anger sharpened by hunger.

Suddenly, from beyond the walls of the dungeon, the boys heard a distant sound of rushing air, followed by a thunderous *crack!* Splinters of rock fell from the far wall and a cloud of dust spread out across the room. They stood there, stunned. Then there was a second almighty crack, and a shaft of light appeared as a vast boulder, the size of a cow, flew into the chamber. It soared across, obliterating two wooden staircases on its way, and crashed to the floor. It careered on, squashing every living thing in its path: there was a strangled cacophony of hisses. The boulder struck the rocky wall and came to a halt. Nathan grabbed the sword from Charlie and, lunging, his eyes bright with determination, despatched the remaining snakes.

Bright light now streamed through the hole, illuminating Jake's astonished face. A moment later, the silhouette of two heads appeared in the opening.

'Jake? Are you in there?' A voice echoed around the space.

Jake's heart stopped beating. 'Mum . . .?' he asked, hardly daring to believe his ears.

'Jake!' the other figure exclaimed. 'It's really you?'

'Dad?' Jake now called out loud. 'Mum! Dad!' he bellowed as he jumped off the boulder and ran along the carpet of flattened snakes. He hurriedly picked his way from rock to rock, climbed through the hole, leaped down into a courtyard – and came face to face with his parents.

For a moment Jake froze in wonder. He stood there, trembling, as he inspected them from head to toe. Both were dressed in Renaissance clothes, Miriam in an elaborate (though torn) velvet gown, Alan in doublet, hose and strong leather boots. Both looked exhausted, bruised and battered – and utterly ecstatic.

'I thought I would never see you again,' Jake cried as threw his arms around them and held them with all his might. 'I thought you were gone!' he blubbed into their chests.

'How on earth did you get here?' said Miriam, wiping away tears of relief. 'To the sixteenth century of all places! Your father and I nearly died of shock when we saw you come through that gatehouse yesterday. Though we hardly recognized you at first

– your lovely curls are all gone.' She sighed as she ran her fingers through his short dusty hair.

'Well, whatever happened – however you got here,' added Alan proudly, 'you look every inch the adventurer now.'

'I thought we'd *agreed*.' Miriam looked daggers at her husband. 'No encouraging him. *Remember?*'

Jake laughed with pure joy as he stood back and admired them. 'You saw me come through gate-house yesterday?' he asked. 'Where have you been?'

Miriam sighed. 'It took us four miserable days to get out of that ridiculous snake pit.'

'With just this to dig a tunnel!' added Alan, producing an old penknife from his waistcoat (like a fisherman's jerkin, its various pockets were bulging with paraphernalia). 'Your mother immobilized the vipers with one of her more antisocial perfumes.'

'I learned that in Alexandria, 200 AD,' chipped in Miriam. 'Snakes hate a citrus top note.'

'We barricaded ourselves under a pile of rocks and dug down until we got into the drainage system. A tunnel took us all the way to the foot of the mountain. We were just planning our attack . . .'

'. . . when we saw the three of you coming in,'

Miriam finished her husband's sentence. 'So are you going to tell us why on earth you're here? I suspect Jupitus Cole.'

'I came to find you,' Jake answered simply.

'You see, a hero!' declared Alan triumphantly, clapping his son on the shoulder. 'A bona fide hero! It's in his blood, Miriam – nothing we can do about it.'

'And I heard about Philip,' Jake added nervously. 'Is there really a chance he's still alive?'

Alan and Miriam looked at each other gravely.

'We *feel* he's alive,' she said softly, 'but we didn't find anything this time.'

'Mr and Mrs Djones, your timing is impeccable!' Nathan boomed in his brash South Carolina accent, leaping down beside them. 'So you found Zeldt's arsenal then?' he said with a nod towards a series of giant catapults that filled the courtyard, one of which had pierced the dungeon wall.

'It was facing the other way,' explained Alan. 'Nearly gave myself a hernia trying to turn it round.'

'Mrs Djones, may I say how much I like your hair like that,' Nathan continued charmingly. 'Up with cascading curls is very *à la mode*, very *early baroque* – it takes years off you.'

'That's funny,' said Miriam, impervious to his charms, 'you said the same thing when I had it straight and down.'

'Really . . . ?' Nathan floundered. 'Then you are obviously eternally youthful. Perfect.'

Charlie helped an ashen-faced Paolo down into the courtyard.

'Here he is – Charlie Chieverley.' Alan beamed. 'Someone's been rather worried about you.'

There was a flash of colour, and Mr Drake flew down from the courtyard battlements, alighting on Charlie's shoulder, shrieking and fluttering his wings in excitement.

'I know, I've missed you too,' said Charlie, welling up with tears. 'You're a very brave parrot indeed – you deserve a medal.'

'I hate to be the one to bring everyone down to earth,' Nathan announced, 'but this is how matters lie: firstly, in the absence of Miss St Honoré, and being the most senior agent now present – no offence, Mr Djones, Mrs Djones: I believe you're not, strictly speaking, "fully operational" at present – I offer myself as group leader. Any objections?'

They all shook their heads impatiently. Miriam rolled her eyes at her husband, making him chuckle.

'Secondly,' Nathan continued, 'we have approximately four hours before the total eclipse.' He turned to Jake's parents to explain. 'I'm not sure how *au fait* you are with Zeldt's plans for world catastrophe, but you will be briefed in due course. In the meantime, I propose that myself and Agent Chieverley go south in pursuit of the carriage of books, while the remainder – Agents Djones, Djones, Djones and Cozzo, under the leadership of Miriam Djones' – Miriam gave a little wave – 'will head north to Cologne, where you will disarm the bubonic bomb before it destroys northern Europe. This leaves only the matter of our transportation.'

'Group leader Wylder, if I may make a suggestion on that score . . .' Miriam enquired, curtseying mischievously.

'Carry on,' answered Nathan stiffly.

'We have already at our disposal two good horses,' she said, pointing at them. 'You and Agent Chieverley could perhaps take these to follow the books south. Regarding *our* mode of transport north, I would suggest the following: Zeldt left in his galleon, the *Lindwurm*, over an hour ago, travelling down the Rhine. Evidently he will stop briefly in Cologne, roughly a hundred miles north of here, before continuing along the river to a horizon point in the North Sea. In Zeldt's boat-house below, there are three fast vessels disguised as fishing boats. We can appropriate one and make it to the city in record time.'

'Sounds like a plan. I concur,' announced Nathan. 'Any questions so far?'

'Yes,' Jake found himself saying. 'Topaz? Will we be trying to rescue her?'

'That's a negative,' replied Nathan firmly. 'Zeldt is not to be intercepted. The mission is to disarm the bomb and nothing more.'

Jake was thunderstruck. 'But I don't understand . . . surely it's our duty to—'

'Our duty,' interrupted Nathan, 'has been stated quite clearly!'

'How can you be so cold-blooded?' Jake felt his anger rising. 'You grew up with her, and she means nothing to you?'

'*How can I be so cold-blooded?*' repeated Nathan in a suddenly chilling tone. As always when he was angry or nervous, his deep American twang became far more noticeable. 'I'll explain. Zeldt wishes to destroy Europe. He wishes to end the Renaissance before it begins. He wishes to halt the progress of civilization, to turn the clock back to the Dark Ages and enslave the world. Perhaps you don't believe this can happen? Perhaps you once saw a Michelangelo or a Leonardo in your National Gallery, and you're thinking, *Well, I know the Renaissance happened, because I've seen the paintings*. Think again!' Nathan shouted, his eyes blazing.

Everyone, even Alan and Miriam, was frightened when Nathan got worked up like this. Mr Drake started fluffing out his feathers nervously.

'I will say it clearly so you understand,' continued Nathan, looking Jake straight in the eye. 'Zeldt has the power to change history, to alter its course. If there's no Renaissance, there's no learning, no science, no progress, no cures for illnesses, no music, no painting . . . no understanding. That world that you've come from, where you turn on lights and play with your electrical devices and enjoy your friends' company – *it won't exist*. There'll be *nothing* to go back to! Nothing but a dark age.'

Jake had gone very pale. 'I'm sorry. I understand,' was all he said.

'Agent Djones' – Nathan turned to Miriam – 'I repeat, on no account will there be a mission to save Agent St Honoré, even in the event that you succeed in your task. There are reasons. Is that clear?'

'It is,' Miriam replied softly.

Jake closed his eyes in despair. *What reasons could there possibly be for not helping another human being?* he thought to himself.

'Good,' concluded Nathan. 'After both groups have completed their missions, we will all reconvene in Venice, on the Rialto. Whichever group arrives first will wait there at noon every day until the other appears. The best of luck to everyone!' he finished in his most stirring tones. 'Now, are there any final comments?'

'Yes,' said Paolo. 'How do I officially hand in my resignation? It's clear that I have become a burden to the service and I would like to return to Italy forth-with. My poor mamma will be beside herself with worry.'

'Resignation denied,' barked Nathan. 'However ludicrously inept you may be, we need all available hands. Let's go! There's not a moment to lose.'

27 THE DEADLY BOOKS

Nathan and Charlie took Alan and Miriam's horses. They opened the gate on the far side of the courtyard, shouted their goodbyes and rode off. Keeping a lookout at all times for Zeldt's guards, they cantered round in the shadows of the outer walls of the castle until they reached the main drive and set off down the mountain.

The horses galloped fearlessly down the steep rocky slope. They navigated the sharp twists and turns, heads down, nostrils snorting. Within five minutes, they had reached the edge of the forest. Here, the path was wider, enabling the horses to pick up speed. The two riders flew through the dark wood.

Eventually they came to the gatehouse. As they approached, the portcullis was just being lowered.

They accelerated, ducking right down over their horses' necks. The metal tips of the gate grazed their backs as they flew through. The sentries barely had time to register their presence as the agents emerged through the archway and turned south. They galloped on towards the mountains far in the distance.

Jake, his parents and Paolo quickly descended an endless flight of crumbling, moss-covered steps. Miriam led the way through the conifer wood to a crumbling section of perimeter wall. They helped each other scale the stones, leaped off on the other side, then wound their way down the mountain towards the banks of the fast-flowing Rhine.

'That's the boathouse there,' whispered Miriam, indicating a low wooden building beside the river. She motioned for everyone to take cover in the shadow of a large oak. Through the undergrowth they could see two of Zeldt's red-cloaked sentries guarding the entrance.

'Alan, what do you think? The damsel and the drowning child?'

'Perfect,' her husband concurred.

Miriam pulled down her gown and loosened the laces of her bodice to give herself a more voluptuous air.

Jake could hardly believe his eyes. 'Mum, what are you doing?'

'I'm the decoy – I need to have a certain . . .' She didn't finish her sentence, but continued shaking out her hair and applying lipstick from a tiny wooden box. 'It's how we do things around here,' she told him. 'If we needed a male decoy, your father would do the same.'

'Though I probably wouldn't wear the lipstick.'

'All right!' Jake winced, blushing. 'Just do what you have to do.'

Miriam winked at her husband and sashayed through the wood towards the guards.

'Doesn't she look great?' said Alan proudly, watching her go. 'She's like a fine wine – just gets better with age.'

They all looked on as Miriam rushed up to the guards and started yelling in German, gesturing at the water, at the same time making sure she appeared as attractive as she possibly could.

'*It's a tragedy!*' Alan translated with relish. '*My little boy fell in the river and he can't swim!*'

'Are they really going to fall for that?' asked Jake dubiously.

The guards leaned right over the bank to see where Miriam was pointing. She delivered two brutally efficient karate chops and dispatched them, one by one, into the torrent. They tried to swim back to the bank, shouting and clutching onto the reeds – but the current carried them rapidly downstream.

'That's our cue,' said Alan, leading the others out of the undergrowth.

Unfortunately the commotion had brought two more guards out of the boathouse.

'Miriam!' Alan shouted as they came at her in a pincer movement. Her reactions were lightning fast: she cartwheeled out of their path, and the guards collided with a crack of skulls. By the time they had picked themselves up and drawn their swords, Alan had caught hold of an overhanging branch. He launched himself into the air and felled the first guard with an expert jab of the heel.

'Here!' shouted Miriam, tossing him a rapier. He caught it in one hand and fought off the second guard, parrying with a flamboyance that left his son slack-jawed with amazement. Finally he knocked his adversary off balance with the flat of his blade, caught hold of his ankle and pitched him into the river.

'Mum, Dad . . . ? Did you just . . . ?' Jake's mouth was still open: could this really be his scatty shopkeeper parents?

'We haven't even got warmed up yet,' said Alan, dusting down his doublet.

The four of them rushed into the boathouse. Inside, they saw three small vessels bobbing in the water. These looked like ordinary fishing boats, but they were evidently part of a special fleet: each had a funnel, cleverly disguised as a cooking pot on deck.

Miriam jumped aboard one of them, which she noticed was called the *Aal*. Jake and Paolo followed while Alan loosed the moorings. He pushed the vessel out into the river and leaped onto the deck as she took off downstream. The three guards, who had managed to grab onto an overhanging branch, swore at the Djones family as they sped past. Miriam gave them a cheery wave as Alan went below decks and fired up the engine.

Within ten minutes, steam was billowing from the funnel and the *Aal* was speeding up the Rhine into northern Germany.

* * *

Nathan and Charlie galloped side by side down the relentlessly straight road that led south to the Alps. They sped through Mannheim, Heilbronn and Metzingen. Mr Drake perched, shielded from the wind, behind Charlie's back, clearly happy to be reunited with his master. Occasionally he would crane his neck round to inspect the open road in front of them and the blast would ruffle his many-coloured feathers.

In each town the two breathless agents drew up beside a group of locals and asked if they had seen a carriage pass by – windowless and blood-red in colour. Every time, the wide-eyed townsfolk pointed south towards the mountains, and Charlie and Nathan continued on their way.

The *Aal* powered up the river through the echoing shadows of the Rhine gorge, which rose up three hundred feet on either side. They sailed past castles of every shape and size – the turreted strongholds of Asterstein, Hammerstein and Stahlberg, and the towering bastions of Rolandseck, Linz and Godesburg.

Once they had passed the walled town of Bonn,

they reached the wide northern stretch of the river, where traffic was heavier; soon they were weaving their way through ferry boats and trading vessels carrying goods to the booming medieval towns of northern Europe.

Much to the bemusement of the many traders and sailors, the Djoneses' small craft overtook them all. As they passed a galleon, her decks piled high with great chunks of black and white marble, the crew whistled at the occupants of the swift fishing boat. Miriam Djones whistled back and blew kisses at the sailors, making her husband chuckle.

At intervals Alan took a small telescope from his jerkin and scanned the horizon. (The instrument, Jake noticed, bore the familiar image of the hourglass and planets.) Then he checked his timepiece, an intriguing pocket-sized cube that contained a compass and a sundial, and glanced up at the sky. Every time he looked, the moon, a faint, almost imperceptible disc high in the firmament, had drawn a little closer to the sun.

Still Jake could think of nothing but Topaz. His eyes were fixed on the river ahead, in the hope that he might spy the red sails of Zeldt's ship. Of course, he knew that, even if he saw the galleon, he would be powerless to act. This did not stop him looking. No doubt Topaz would have passed this same stretch of river no more than an hour earlier, a prisoner. He was tormented by the notion that she was already suffering some unimaginable cruelty at Zeldt's hands. The knowledge that she would face such horrors with composure did not lessen Jake's distress; it made it worse.

Charlie and Nathan finally spied the red carriage as they came over the brow of a rise. It was cresting the summit of the next hill, just half a mile away. They had ascended nearly two thousand feet of winding mountain roads and were now crossing a gently undulating plateau. A breeze had risen and brought with it a white mist.

As the carriage – no more than a flash of scarlet – disappeared over the hill, the two boys looked at each other and urged their horses on.

When it came into sight again, it was a good deal closer. It had started to climb steeply. Nathan and Charlie spurred on their horses, faster and faster. At last they were almost upon the red vehicle, with its four snorting horses, as it hurtled along the narrow road, its wheels flicking up stones like rounds of ammunition.

As Nathan and Charlie came round a corner, the whole mountain range suddenly opened up before them. Beside the road was a sheer drop into the cloudy abyss.

Suddenly they were within touching distance of their goal. The heads of two brutish-looking guards could just be made out at the front of the carriage.

'We need to get the driver to stop,' Nathan shouted.

'Understood . . . How?' Charlie shouted back. 'They don't look like the types to respond to polite requests.'

'Physical persuasion!'

As they spoke, a windswept and nervous Mr Drake was looking from one to the other.

'You've finally lost your mind!' Charlie yelled back. Nathan smiled again. 'The things we do for history . . .'

Charlie sighed as he took Mr Drake from inside his jacket and passed him to Nathan.

Mr Drake averted his eyes as Charlie set off on a death-defying stunt: spurring his horse on, he carefully stood up and balanced precariously on his saddle. He crouched down, and as he drew level with the red carriage, sprang into the air and landed on top of it. The roof was wet with condensation and he lost his footing, sliding down over the side, but managed to claw his way back to safety.

Nathan was gesticulating wildly, and Mr Drake flapped his wings in frenzy.

Charlie turned to see one of the red-cloaked guards climbing up onto the roof – a fearless mountain of a man. The carriage hurtled on, its wheels just inches from the precipice. The monster lunged for Charlie, closed his huge fingers around the boy's neck and lifted him into the air.

Mr Drake had seen enough. He took off and flew into the bully's face. The guard lost his balance and slipped on the wet roof. As he flew off, he grabbed hold of Charlie's breeches, threatening to take the poor boy with him. Just as Charlie managed to cling onto the roof, the breeches ripped. His attacker carried on over the edge, a piece of Charlie's trousers still in his hand, and down into the abyss.

Charlie hung on, his feet trailing almost to the ground. Nathan shook his head at the sight of his companion's exposed underwear: a pair of bizarre shorts – pantaloons embroidered with birds of paradise. 'A little unnecessary, aren't they?' he commented with a mischievous smile.

'They were in honour of Mr Drake!' Charlie yelled back. 'Besides, I didn't realize I would be doing a striptease when I last got dressed!'

As the carriage bounced its way along the twisting mountain road, Nathan could see that his companion had no chance of clawing himself back up. So he urged on his horse and, favouring his good leg, stood on his saddle and sprang onto the roof.

He screamed in agony as his bad leg thumped against the metal. Suddenly a whip cracked down on his fingers. The lone driver, holding the reins in one hand, was attacking Nathan with the other.

But Nathan had unfurled his scarf from around his neck; he lassoed the driver and tightened it about the man's throat until he'd pulled him up out of his seat. The huge guard snarled like an animal. He flicked his whip at Nathan's head, the wet leather slicing into his cheek. Electrified by anger, Nathan swung his fist, thumped his opponent in the solar plexus and upended him. His back came down with a crack on top of the carriage.

With the reins flapping uselessly, the horses galloped uncontrollably along the sheer twists and turns of the mountain pass.

Meanwhile Charlie was still hanging on for dear life, his pale legs sticking out of his brightly coloured undershorts.

As Nathan tightened his scarf around the driver's neck, the man in turn took hold of Nathan's head, digging his black nails into his skull.

Nathan's eyes suddenly widened in alarm. They were approaching a sharp bend at a speed that could only spell disaster. Charlie stopped breathing. The driver turned. With a last desperate cry, Nathan pushed him towards the edge of the roof. As he fell, the scarf tightened around his fat neck.

'That neck tie is woven from Indian spider-silk from the Jiangxi province!' shouted Nathan over the furious wind. 'One of the rarest materials on earth. It was given to my father by Shi Huang the Great, Emperor of the Qin Dynasty. Frankly, it cost more than you've earned in your lifetime.' The driver's face was now going blue as he dangled from the priceless scarf. 'I'm just telling you this so you know . . . It hurts me much more than it hurts you.'

With reluctance Nathan let go of the scarf – and the driver, who tumbled down two hundred feet of sheer rock.

Nathan picked himself up, leaped into the driver's seat and yanked on the reins until he had brought the horses to a standstill. He looked down: the whole of southern Europe seemed to lie before him.

'Italy,' he sighed. 'You'll never know how close you came . . .'

'It's not over yet, Nathan,' said Charlie, jumping down. 'If they don't get to the cathedral in time, we're all history.'

28 THE INESCAPABLE ECLIPSE

The *Aal* tore round a bend in the river. Jake stood up slowly as the medieval city came into sight: an endless panorama of timber houses, their roofs like witches' hats. At its heart, dominating the entire valley, was a gargantuan structure, so high it cast a shadow over a quarter of the city.

'Cologne Cathedral,' Alan said, gazing in wonder. 'At this moment in time, the highest building in the world.'

'Really?' said Jake, impressed.

'Oh yes – round about now Cologne is possibly the richest place in Europe. It's a "free city", its own sovereign state. That, along with its location on the Rhine, slap-bang in the centre of Europe, is the key to its success.'

'Your father, he's not just a pretty face,' Miriam teased. 'He's a mine of information.'

The harbour was bustling with activity.

'It's like boat soup,' Miriam gasped as Alan tried to manoeuvre his way to the shore through the myriad vessels and shouting traders. Jake winced as the boat narrowly missed a load of anxious-looking donkeys. Two small craft were not so lucky and thumped together. A heated argument ensued between an unshaven grain trader and a grand lady in a velvet headdress and cloak.

As they approached the quay, Jake stared up at the huge cathedral. It was a fantastical construction of soaring steeples and flying buttresses. He could see now that the building, vast as it was, was incomplete. High on its roof were the bases of two half-built spires. Between them, a colossal timber crane reached up into the sky. Jake was awestruck. He had seen a few cathedrals in his short life, but had always taken them for granted. Seeing this building in the throes of construction made him wonder at the sheer scale of human endeavour.

'The unfinished spires . . .' he said. 'That's where Zeldt is planning to leave the bomb.'

Alan looked at his timepiece. 'Five past one. We

have an hour to spare before the eclipse. Almost time for a coffee,' he joked.

'If it's five past one, why does that clock say five to two?' asked Paolo, pointing to a clock tower beside the harbour.

Alan looked at it, and then at his timepiece, which he jiggled vigorously and checked again. The blood drained from his face.

'I told you not to buy Italian.' Miriam shook her head. 'Everything in that country runs late.'

The eclipse of 20 July 1506 had already started.

Gradually at first, the frantic cacophony around them started to subside. Above their heads there was a confusion of squawking birds, then complete silence. In the shadows under a nearby pier a flock of lapwings huddled together, cooing nervously. Jake saw a little girl point up into the heavens. Then, from all around, came gasps of disbelief. All along the quayside, people began to stop in their tracks, bumping into each other. One by one, every face turned skywards.

Jake looked up and saw that the brilliant disc of the afternoon sun was being consumed by a sliver of black shadow. The eclipse was beginning.

'Don't look at the sun, Jake!' Miriam cried. 'It's dangerous.'

Mothers pulled their children close. A group of market traders gazed up in disbelief. An ancient nun pointed a shaking finger at the sky, muttering prayers. Dogs barked in confusion. Boats, un-piloted, crashed into one other.

'Coffee after then,' said Alan, jumping ashore and mooring the *Aal*. 'Quickly, everyone,' he said, helping his wife and Paolo onto the quay.

'Shall I just hang around here?' Paolo suggested. 'I wouldn't want to get in anyone's way.'

Alan laughed heartily and pushed him into the crowd. 'You wouldn't want to miss all the fun! It's going to be dramatic.'

'That's what I'm worried about,' the Italian mumbled to himself.

Jake would never have seen the caped figure if everyone had not come to a standstill. In the grand square between the river and the cathedral there must have been more than five hundred people, but only one of them was running. A compact figure, all in black, her cloak billowing behind her, rushing across towards the far end of the harbour.

It was Mina Schlitz.

Jake saw her run up the gangplank of the *Lindwurm*. As she leaped aboard, the red-cloaked guards cast off and the ship headed out into the river.

'Dad . . .' Jake cried, stopping Alan in his tracks. 'It's Zeldt! He's still here.' He pointed towards the retreating galley.

His father spotted it then, but he also remembered Nathan's strict orders. 'Nothing we can do about it now,' he said firmly. 'We have less than five minutes to diffuse a bomb.'

Jake had no choice but to jump ashore. He followed his father through the crowd and caught up with the others. Jake's mind was in turmoil. He knew that his duty lay in the cathedral, but something almost as strong was pulling him in another direction: in pursuit of the *Lindwurm* and Topaz St Honoré. As he pushed through the throng of gaping townspeople, Jake's eyes kept turning to watch the red sails in the distance. But by the time he'd reached the steps of the cathedral, they were lost from view.

The congregation, having heard about the eclipse, were rushing out to see the apocalypse for themselves. Alan, Miriam, Jake and Paolo had to fight their way through the melee. At last they were in the great nave, an endless succession of arches upon arches upon arches. The huge stained-glass windows were darkening gradually as the sun was slowly blotted out.

'That scaffold will be the quickest way.' Alan pointed towards a vast timber structure that stood in front of the central window. The steps climbed the entire height of the cathedral. Beside it was an arrangement of buckets and pulleys that brought materials up from ground level.

Jake led the way through the sea of people still charging for the door and was the first to reach the scaffold and leap up onto its timber steps.

The rough staircase ascended floor by floor, spiralling up towards the vaulted ceiling. At each pass, a gantry ran beside the multi-coloured window, affording an ever more panoramic view of the city. Through the tinted panes, Jake could still just make out the silhouette of Zeldt's ship.

'Did you know that the Three Wise Men are buried here?' Alan asked as he pounded up the creaky steps. 'That's why the largest bell in the tower is called the *Dreikönigenglocke* – the Bell of the Three Kings. It's the heaviest in Europe.'

'Fascinating,' Miriam shouted back. 'I'd say we have two minutes before the end of the world.'

They picked up their pace. Soon they were at a dizzying height. The people in the nave below were now just moving dots of colour fanning out from the main door.

On the eighth turn, Jake saw the *Lindwurm* disappearing round a bend. On he hurried, his parents close behind him, Paolo panting at the rear, following the timber scaffold until it spiralled through the roof of the nave and into the bell tower.

Jake looked around the cavernous space; it was half open to the elements and dominated by four vast iron bells, each as big as a small house. His eyes met those of an owl, huddled in a dark corner, *twoo*ing uncertainly, thinking night had come. Then there was a hollow creaking of ropes, a great pulley stretched backwards, turning a giant wheel and setting one of the bells into motion. As it smashed against the giant clapper (itself the size of a person), a peal rang out, so deafening that it hurt Jake's ears and reverberated through his very bones.

Then more pulleys tightened, wheels spun, until every piece of apparatus in the room was in motion and, one by one, all the bells started to chime.

'Two o'clock!' Alan shouted as he climbed up, followed by Miriam and the hapless Paolo.

Jake ascended the last section of scaffold, through the ceiling of the bell tower and out onto the wind-battered roof. In the five breathless minutes it had taken him to get here, the sky had darkened beyond all logical comprehension. Only a sliver of sun now remained behind the black moon. Jake looked over the parapet; far below the large jutting gargoyles of devils and vengeful creatures he could see the crowds standing motionless and awestruck in the square.

Once again he caught sight of the *Lindwurm*, now just a tiny shape on the horizon. Another image of Topaz's terror-struck face flashed into his mind, but he forced it away.

Jake cast his eyes around the roof. On either side rose up the foundation stones of the cathedral's two unfinished spires. Perched between them, reaching up into the dark heavens, was the colossal wooden crane, constructed from a million criss-crossing timbers. Jake started to scan it from top to bottom.

'Good gracious me!' gasped Alan as he emerged onto the roof. The sheer drama of the landscape, along with the wind and the tolling bells, took his breath away.

But Jake's eyes were darting across every inch of the crane. 'There! *There!*' he suddenly yelled hysterically as Miriam and Paolo heaved themselves onto the roof.

For there, halfway up the crane, he'd caught sight of the tiniest glint of gold. If anything, the eclipse had helped to pick it out, for it was almost the last of the sun's swiftly vanishing rays that struck Zeldt's golden bomb.

Alan pulled open his telescope and inspected the glimmer. Jake was right: the bomb was sitting there, balanced on a wooden girder.

Jake was already clambering up the crane, feet and hands moving at double time. The wind gusted around him, the terrifying vortex of space yawned below. Just as the moon consumed the last feeble ray of sun and plunged them into blackness – and at this moment there was a howl from the people below – Jake reached out and took hold of the bomb. With a sharp *whoosh*, a pale shape suddenly emerged out of the gloom, flying towards him. It was the owl from the bell tower, hooting with fear and confusion. It thumped into Jake, he lost his balance and the bomb slipped from his grasp.

Miriam was the closest. She lunged towards the falling golden clock and caught it, then plunged over the edge of the parapet.

'Miriam!' Alan swung round, expecting to be met by the horrific sight of his wife falling to her death. His face told a different story. 'Miriam . . .?' he repeated softly.

His wife had landed sprawling on top of one of the huge gargoyles – a satanic beast, half lion, half bat, with a snarling mouth and outstretched wings.

'My – my guardian angel,' Miriam stammered with a half-delirious smile.

'I'm coming to get you,' Alan cried as he started to lower himself over the edge.

'Bomb first – we need to defuse it,' gasped Miriam. Breathlessly, she examined the golden device. 'But how?'

'Mum,' Jake shouted down as he descended the scaffold, 'inside, there's a glass vial between two golden fists. Can you see it?'

Miriam scrutinized the inner workings. The light was so dim she could barely make it out. 'I think so.'

'You need to reach inside and remove it,' Jake commanded.

Miriam probed with slender fingers. 'I can justify that manicure now!' she joked – then saw that the clock was seconds away from alignment. 'Ow!' she cried, quickly withdrawing her hand. 'It gave me a shock.'

'Careful, my darling – careful!' Alan urged her.

'Mum, you have to try again,' Jake yelled. 'We have *seconds*!'

Miriam inserted her fingers again; again she received a jolt of electricity. The clock ticked, the cogs turned. She gritted her teeth and plunged her hand in for a third time. Just as the mechanism clicked into position, she retrieved the glass vial. She was breathing a sigh of relief – when suddenly the marble beast gave a huge crack. Everyone shrieked at once as Miriam slipped, losing her grip on the golden clock, but managing to catch the gargoyle's wing in one hand and cling to the glass vial in the other. The clock struck a gargoyle below and smashed into a thousand glittering pieces.

'I'm coming for you, Miriam – I'm coming!' Alan shouted, but when he put his weight on the marble, it cracked again.

'This doesn't look too good,' Miriam breathed, contemplating the sheer drop below.

'You're too heavy, Dad. Let me go,' said Jake, who had climbed back down to the roof. He did not wait for permission. He stepped carefully onto the gargoyle's back. But the crack widened and the gargoyle moved alarmingly. 'We're *all* too heavy,' he murmured to himself in despair. Then an idea occurred to him. He turned to the small figure who had been keeping very quiet in the background. 'Paolo Cozzo, this is your moment!'

Jake was right; he was their only hope.

'*Che?*' Paolo stammered, edging away. 'No, I don't think I'm your man. I'm terrible with heights.'

'Not negotiable,' barked Alan sternly as he dragged him back. 'If you don't do the right thing and save my wife, I will throw you off anyway.'

'You can't do that,' whimpered Paolo. 'You'd be reported. You'd be decommissioned instantly.'

'*Not negotiable!*' Alan pushed him to the edge of the parapet. 'We'll hold your legs. You crawl down and reach out for Miriam.'

Paolo snivelled with fear as he lay flat on his stomach. Alan and Jake took a leg each, and the boy started to reach down over the edge of the building towards the gargoyle. The moon had now passed over the sun, and the sky was bright again, illuminating the void below.

'There *must* be an alternative,' said Paolo, trying to pull himself back onto the roof.

'*Do it!*' barked Alan. He could see that Miriam was starting to lose her grip.

Paolo lowered his body onto the gargoyle and held out his shaking hand for Miriam. The stone creaked again.

'You're nearly there,' Alan encouraged him. 'Just a little further.'

Paolo's eyes streamed with tears. He reached out, not daring to look down. He had never wanted anything more than to abandon this appalling adventure.

Then something strange happened to him. Time seemed to stop. Silence suddenly descended. He could hear neither the wind, nor the bells, nor his companions. All he could hear was his own breathing. He opened his eyes wide and looked down. He was hanging from the edge of a great cathedral, the tallest building in the world. Below him lay a city, and a woman hanging from a gargoyle with enough death in her clenched hand to destroy Europe. Within him, Paolo felt a sudden surge of courage: he *could* be a hero.

'*Not on my watch!*' he roared, and thrust out his hands. Miriam carefully placed the vial between her lips; she reached for his right hand, then let go of the gargoyle and grabbed his left.

Paolo gasped in agony as he bore her entire weight. His back was stretched to the point of dislocation. But his desperate tears were replaced by a defiant glare of resolution. He held on with all his might as Alan and Jake slowly reeled him back onto the roof – until at last Miriam could clamber to safety. She held the terrible vial triumphantly in the air.

Alan threw his arms around his wife and hugged her. Paolo, still dangerously close to the edge, squared his shoulders and took the glass vial from Miriam's hand to examine its deadly contents. Immediately it popped out of his fingers and flew up into the air. Everyone gasped at once. Images of instant death flashed before their eyes. But Paolo caught it neatly in one hand.

'Relax,' he told them. 'I'm using humour.'

Alan's mouth curled into a quizzical smile and he laughed out loud. But he still took the vial carefully from Paolo; they could afford to take no chances now.

The four of them climbed back down into the bell tower. With the present crisis averted, Jake's mind turned immediately to Topaz.

'I'm going after her,' he declared, resolution shining in his eyes. 'Zeldt's galleon is no more than five miles away. I will take the *Aal*. If I go alone, I will make up the time quickly.'

'The *Lindwurm*? No, Jake, it's not a good idea,' said Miriam.

'We've completed the mission. What's to stop us?'

Miriam and Alan looked at each other. She continued in a tone that was both soft *and* firm. 'Well, amongst other things, we have orders. Nathan Wylder was very clear: we were not to rescue Agent St Honoré, "even if we succeeded in our task".'

'Orders?' Jake shook his head in disbelief. 'I, for one, won't be able to live with myself if I don't at least *try*.'

'You won't be living at all!' Miriam turned to her husband. 'Tell him, Alan.'

'She's right. A very bad notion.'

'Topaz is not your concern,' Miriam added. 'Her situation is very . . . complicated.'

'It's not *complicated*!' Jake felt a tide of emotion rising within him. 'It's *simple*: she'll die if no

416

one saves her. And when did you ever obey orders? Did you obey orders when you went looking for Philip?'

He took advantage of the sudden silence that followed his question. He had calculated that there would be resistance, and had already formulated a plan. First he plucked his father's telescope from his leather jerkin. Then he leaped over to the large basket of rocks that had been winched up to the top of the scaffold. Jake tossed out its contents, quickly checked the pulley, then kicked the basket over the edge of the scaffold and jumped inside. Miriam and Alan shrieked in unison as he started to descend at breakneck speed. As he went down, a counterweight shot up from the ground.

'I'm sorry,' he yelled back as he flew through the air. 'Wait for me here.'

'Jake!' his parents shouted helplessly.

He hurtled downwards. Just before he landed, he grabbed hold of the rope to slow his progress. Below him, the basket shattered as he dropped down and set off along the long nave.

Miriam turned to Alan. She was expecting a face like thunder, but was met instead by a look of fatherly pride.

'You can take that expression off your face right now,' she threatened.

'Are you forgetting how we first met? The Egyptian mission, 872?' asked Alan. 'You crossed two enemy lines and burrowed twenty metres under the great pyramid of Giza to reach me. History seems to be repeating itself.'

He looked down at his son as he dashed out through the main door, heading for the quayside. 'He's an adventurer, all right,' he said, shaking his head. 'Nothing we can do about it.'

29 THE TERRIBLE TRUTH

Jake powered down the Rhine, navigating the bends and eddies of the huge river. He wove his way between the galleons, trade ships and ferries, surfing the waves of the larger vessels. His determined gaze was fixed firmly on the horizon, searching again for the red sails of Zeldt's warship.

Every twenty minutes, ensuring that all was clear ahead, he dashed below deck and tossed wood into the furnace. The huge pile of fuel was steadily diminishing, but Jake did not consider failure.

He raced past the towns of Düsseldorf and Duisburg. Around the ports, the townspeople seemed to be moving slowly and cautiously, as if expecting some horrific consequence of the eclipse.

Then, suddenly, just past the village of Dämmrich, Jake was plunged into a dilemma: half

419

a mile ahead of him, the river split into two tributaries, its traffic dividing equally between them. Jake opened up his father's telescope, but there was still no sign of the red sails. As he advanced uncertainly towards the wave-tossed headland between the two rivers, he made a snap decision and took the right fork, which looked slightly wider.

It was the wrong choice. Just as he steered into it, he finally caught a glimpse of the *Lindwurm* steaming along the other tributary. Jake yanked the rudder round; the *Aal* swerved dangerously, and was suddenly awash with foaming water that drenched Jake and almost swept him overboard. But he clung onto the rudder with all his strength. It shook crazily as he steered around the headland. At the mercy of the choppy waters, the boat suddenly lurched round, into the path of an approaching ferry. The passengers on deck cried out angrily, there was a hollow splintering sound, and the ferry carried on. The *Aal* was damaged, but still seaworthy, and Jake finally found himself in the calm reaches of the left-hand tributary.

From here the river widened as it drew closer to the sea. Jake was now quickly gaining on the red sails. At last he glided into the magnificent bay at Hellevoetsluis. The North Sea opened out before him. The sun was starting to set over the horizon, colouring the sky in hues of pink and vermilion. It had become a still, hot evening.

Jake scanned the darkening horizon. There were maybe fifteen ships dotted around, each a distant silhouette. Jake identified the *Lindwurm* at the far end of the bay. She was moored just offshore, near a fishing village.

Jake studied her through his telescope. There was a rowing boat moored to her stern, and provisions were being loaded up onto her decks. With the task completed, the smaller boat turned and headed back to shore. The *Lindwurm* bustled with activity as the crew made hurried preparations for the voyage ahead.

Now the great barnacle-covered anchor was being hauled up from the sea bed, and Jake, under cover of the swift-descending darkness, drew closer. He slipped below decks and turned off his engine, and the *Aal* glided noiselessly across the water.

As he approached the *Lindwurm*, Jake could see how large and handsome she was. Her sturdy timbers still smelled of the great Rhineland forests from which they had been hewn. Her gigantic sails, the same rich red as the sunset, had the lustrous sheen of velvet.

The great hull was punctuated at intervals with rectangles of warm light; these were the windows of the many finely appointed cabins. It was in one such aperture at the stern – this one protected by bars – that Jake spied a familiar silhouette. He examined it with his telescope, and saw, staring forlornly out to sea . . . Topaz.

A stern voice shouted orders from the deck. There was a low rumble as the engine started up, and a moment later the still water behind began to bubble as the propeller rotated. The wooden behemoth started to move towards the open sea.

Jake wanted to cry out to Topaz, but there were too many guards on deck. Then he spied two ropes that had moored the rowing boat earlier; they were still hanging over the side, not far from Topaz's window.

He drew alongside the ship and launched himself off the side of his boat, his legs pumping, and crashed against the hull, grabbing hold of one of the slimy ropes. He turned to watch the *Aal* drift on towards the harbour, coming to rest beside some other fishing vessels.

Jake looked down and saw that he was positioned immediately above the gigantic propeller, an indistinct shape moving just below the surface. It had been turning slowly, but now its revolving blades whipped up the water into a frenzy. Mesmerized, Jake lost concentration: his hand slipped on the wet rope. He gasped as he plummeted towards the water, the rope tearing the skin from his hand. He caught himself just in time and felt the chilling pulse of the propeller sweep past below his foot.

He wrapped the rope around his forearm and pulled himself up again. His forehead was wet with sweat, his feet drenched by the churning sea.

Jake now lunged across and took hold of the second rope. He had to summon all his strength to hang on with his bleeding hands; he worked his way along the side of the ship until he drew level with Topaz's window.

Holding onto the metal bars outside, his chest heaving with exhaustion, he peered in. The cabin was now empty.

It was furnished with dark antiques and forbidding portraits of Zeldt's aristocratic and murderous family. Jake noticed a picture of Zeldt himself, dressed in shimmering black, his face stern, his white hand clasping a globe. The image sent a shiver down his spine, reminding him that he was an intruder in this private, forbidden world. In front of the fireplace stood two high-backed chairs, and, from behind the nearest of these, a pale hand reached out and took a book from a side table.

'Topaz,' Jake whispered.

The pale hand froze.

'It's me, Jake!'

Topaz leaped to her feet, startled. She gasped as she saw Jake clinging onto the bars outside her window, then threw down her book and ran over to him.

'*Que fais-tu ici?* What are you doing here?' she asked, almost angrily. Her long black cloak accentuated the paleness of her face.

Jake was taken aback by her apparent hostility. 'You're not hurt?' he asked softly, hoping he had misinterpreted her tone. He had not.

'Why are you here?' she barked again, her eyes burning with fury.

'I came to save you,' he declared breathlessly. 'The bomb in the cathedral – we stopped it, Topaz!

So I came to get you. As soon as I could.'

At this, Topaz gave a glimmer of a smile, but her eyes swiftly became resolute again. '*C'est très dangereux!*' she whispered with a terrified glance round at the door. 'We're still close to shore. You can swim back from here. But you must go now!'

Jake was perplexed. 'You don't want to be saved?'

'I am not thinking about myself, I am thinking about you. I can handle myself, but you will be killed. There is no question. So, please, I beg you, swim back to shore.' Then, perhaps to mask her true feelings, perhaps to show more gratitude, Topaz tried a softer approach. 'It's such a relief to know you are safe. And Nathan, Charlie . . . ?'

'They went after the books. We don't know if they were successful. But my parents are safe.'

'You found them? Jake, I'm so happy for you! I knew it!' Topaz clutched his hand through the bars and dropped her head so that he would not see the tears in her eyes.

Jake continued in his deepest, firmest voice, 'Topaz, I have come here to rescue you and I do not intend to leave empty-handed. I'm coming aboard!'

'No! That's an order, Jake, and I am still in command.'

'Well, I disobey,' he said resolutely. He hitched up the rope and clambered onto the window ledge.

'Jake, go back – go back immediately!' Topaz demanded. 'You mustn't come in here.'

But Jake wasn't listening. With new resolve, he scaled the side of the ship and pulled himself up onto the deck, ducking into the shadows behind the boxes of provisions. Most of the crew had gone below, but a group still remained in the bows. Jake picked up two of the boxes and, concealing himself behind them, headed for a staircase that led below.

Meanwhile, outside Topaz's cabin, a guard was waiting with a tray of food. Holding the tray in one hand, he took a key from his pocket, unlocked the door and went in.

As he set down the tray, Topaz glanced fearfully towards the unlocked door. Feigning interest in her food, she approached the guard. In a lightning manoeuvre, she winded him with a thrust of her elbow, twisted his arm and brought him to the floor. She silenced his mouth with a firm hand as she took a small dagger from his belt.

'Not a word!' she commanded.

The guard looked sideways at the sharp blade, held an inch from his eye.

Jake burst into the room, quickly kicked the door shut behind him and threw down the crates he was carrying.

'Help me, quickly!' ordered Topaz. 'The curtain ties – there!'

Jake whipped two lengths of cord from the window.

'Tie him up,' instructed Topaz.

With one of the cords he bound the guard's feet. Topaz took the velvet belt from around her waist and fastened it over the man's mouth as Jake used the other cord to tie his hands together.

'Here!' Topaz motioned for Jake to help her lift the body. They carried the wriggling, kicking guard over to an oak chest and shoved him inside. He was still struggling and protesting as she shut the lid.

Topaz turned to Jake. She was panting, her eyes glittering. 'It was very brave of you to come here, but you must leave immediately!'

'No. You're not making any sense. We can both escape.'

'It's too late. I have already drunk atomium.

It was an extremely strong dose. I have been sick for nearly an hour. That never happens. We must be travelling far – very far; possibly BC.' Topaz looked at the clock above the mantelpiece. 'We will reach the horizon point in less than thirty minutes, so you must leave immediately!'

Jake's head was swimming with confusion. 'Atomium? Horizon point? BC? What are you talking about?'

Topaz was losing patience. 'I am travelling with Zeldt, wherever he is going: Mesopotamia, Assyria, Egypt – who knows?'

'But you still have time to get out,' Jake protested, shaking his head.

Topaz clapped a hand to her forehead, then took a deep breath. 'This is a mission. I am on a *mission*.'

'Wh-what?' stammered Jake.

'Before we left Point Zero, Commander Goethe asked to speak to me, Nathan and Charlie on a private matter – you remember? It was agreed that, if I was taken prisoner, I would not resist. Our organization has no idea where the Zeldt dynasty is hiding. It could be in any century, anywhere in the world. This is our first real opportunity in years to discover where it might be.'

Now Jake understood why Nathan had insisted that they should not go and rescue Topaz. 'Then I'm coming with you,' he said resolutely. 'I have the atomium you gave me in Venice.' He fished out the little vial on the chain around his neck. 'I will take it now!' He started to unscrew the top.

'That's impossible, Jake!' Topaz took the vial and put it back inside his jacket. 'All the doses must be of exactly the same ratio of atomium. Even if I had the slightest idea what Zeldt's dosage is, or where we were going – which I don't – it would be insanely dangerous for a first-timer to travel back more than a thousand years. You'll end up killing yourself, not to mention the rest of us.' Her tone softened once again. 'Besides, I have to undertake this mission alone.'

'But you've lost your mind! Zeldt's not stupid. He'll find out what you're doing and he'll kill you.'

'He won't kill me, I can assure you.'

'How can you be so certain?'

'I just can!' said Topaz, so vehemently it made Jake a little frightened.

All at once Topaz felt bad. She reached out and stroked his hair. 'It's complicated,' she said softly.

'Complicated?' Jake repeated. That was the word

his mother had used. What were they all talking about?

There was the sound of a key turning in the lock. Topaz's eyes darted over to the door. With lightning reactions, she bundled Jake into a closet. 'Not a word, no heroics!' she commanded, and closed the door.

Mina Schlitz, as brittle-eyed as ever, stepped into the cabin.

Jake knelt down and looked through a crack. He could see Mina's black skirt and her red-backed snake wrapped around her forearm.

'What do you want?' asked Topaz coolly, displaying no fear of her adversary.

For a moment they stared at each other – two polar opposites: Mina in her tightly fitting uniform, granite gaze and jet-black hair as straight and severe as a guillotine blade; Topaz with her honeyed locks and wide indigo eyes that mirrored her ever-changing emotions.

'The prince will see you now,' said Mina in her passionless voice.

'Am I permitted to eat something first?' Topaz asked, feigning civility. 'So much atomium on an empty stomach would be nauseating even for you.'

Mina's snake had become restless. Its upper body was writhing towards the closet.

'Five minutes,' Mina spat as she turned back to the door. She stopped dead when she saw the crates of food on the floor. Then there was a banging from the oak chest.

In a flash, Mina had drawn her sword; she flew over to the chest and flung it open.

Jake acted on impulse. He sprang out of the closet and threw himself at Mina in an attempt to tackle her to the floor. She was too quick, blocking him with a sharp punch and bringing him down, then pressing her heel into his neck so firmly that it broke the skin.

'Truly, your persistence is starting to annoy me,' she said through gritted teeth.

Zeldt's private sitting room on the *Lindwurm* was sumptuously, monstrously decorated. An entire wall was made of glass cabinets containing the embalmed heads of an assortment of enemies. There were trophies from every era of history – old and young, some with hats and headdresses, some with blood-matted hair – but the faces all displayed that frozen look of horror before a cold-blooded execution. The cabin was dark except for an occasional cluster of black candles.

Zeldt, almost invisible in the shadows, sat at a desk covered with nautical charts. His captain stood beside him, awaiting final instructions for the journey.

The prince did not turn round when he heard Mina and two guards push Jake and Topaz into the room. Mina came to whisper in her master's ear. As he turned to listen, his pale face was lit by a sliver of light.

He remained expressionless as he turned back to the captain, passed him the charts and dismissed him. Dealing with a final piece of paperwork, he stood up and crossed the room until he was staring into Jake's eyes.

Jake spoke first. 'No luck in your mission, I'm afraid,' he said defiantly.

Zeldt was silent.

'Looks like the Renaissance is going ahead as planned,' the boy continued doggedly. 'Seems you can't put a good world-changing-event-of-supreme-human-advancement down.'

'Jake,' said Topaz softly, 'don't make this worse for yourself.'

432

There was a knock on the door and a stern-faced guard announced, 'Five minutes to horizon point.' He left, closing the door behind him.

'Usually I reserve places in my Compendium for truly worthy adversaries,' Zeldt said in calm, velvety tones as he swept a hand around his wall of severed heads. 'Enemies with a particular panache and intelligence. And although you clearly do not deserve that honour, it might amuse me for a while to see your pointless little visage there, with its misguided hope, frozen for all time. It will confirm my most resolute belief' – his voice sank even lower – 'that darkness will always prevail.' He pointed to one of the heads, the gory remains of an eighteenth-century aristocrat. 'That gentleman there is looking a little shabby – those Parisian embalmers leave so much to be desired . . . You will look very well in his place.'

Mina gave her evil smile as the prince opened a drawer laid out with exquisitely crafted weapons in silver and ebony. He ran his fingers over the contents before selecting a pistol.

'This is a clever device. As you may know, we are unable to travel with bona fide explosives, but this weapon discharges pellets of sulphuric acid through compressed air. It will rip a hole in your head and melt your brain at the same time.' Zeldt passed it to Mina. 'Set it to full velocity.'

Mina checked the gauge as she twisted the ratchet to its maximum setting, then passed the gun back.

Zeldt, in turn, passed it to Topaz.

She did not take it. He wrapped her limp fingers around the gun, then took a seat on a black ottoman in front of his diabolical wall of heads and crossed his legs.

'Shoot him please,' he uttered with chilling calm.

'*Non.*' Topaz shook her head. '*Vous êtes fou.* You're completely deranged.'

'Flattery will get you nowhere.'

Zeldt nodded at Mina, who took Jake's left hand – it was already raw from the rope – and held it tightly by the wrist. Then she plunged a dagger into his palm. Jake screamed in agony. Bile shot up his throat into the back of his mouth and his fingers twitched uncontrollably.

'He will die anyway. How painful do you wish it to be? It's your choice. Shoot him,' Zeldt insisted.

With the tip of her blade, Mina further explored the gash in Jake's quivering palm. The sharp edge came into contact with solid sinew. Mina's lips curled in delight as she pushed the dagger into the tendon, almost severing it. Jake choked; he felt sick with pain. He heard the red-backed snake hiss with delight.

'Stop!' cried Topaz, tears springing from her eyes. 'I'll do it. Stop hurting him, please!'

Zeldt raised his eyebrows at Jake. 'If I'm not mistaken, the minx likes you. You can carry that memory with you to your watery grave. Shoot him.'

Topaz's shaking hand held the pistol up to Jake's head.

His eyes widened in horror. He felt the cold metal of the gun's barrel touch his temple. 'T-Topaz?' he stuttered.

'I'm sorry – I'm so sorry.' A stream of tears poured from her eyes. 'But the torture will be unbearable.' Her finger tightened around the trigger.

Jake stopped breathing; electric pulses of fear paralysed his brain. A thousand images – of his parents, of his brother – flicked past at lightning speed.

Zeldt sat up in his seat. In the gloom, he resembled one of the frozen faces that lay behind him.

As Topaz squeezed the trigger, she suddenly swung the gun round, aimed and fired. The sulphuric pellet whistled past Zeldt's head and hit one of the glass cabinets, shattering it into a thousand pieces. As the prince turned in astonishment, the case spewed the corrosive embalming fluid into his face. He gasped and flailed around desperately, blinded by the acid. Meanwhile the head of a Persian warrior fell out and landed on the floor with a wet crunch.

'Run!' Topaz yelled to Jake as she kicked the dagger from Mina's hand. But Jake was feeling faint with agony, his head swimming; he could see the doorway, but he could not move.

Mina recovered herself, drew her sword and sliced it down at Topaz, ripping her cloak but barely grazing her skin.

Jake stumbled across the floor. It took all his strength to reach down, retrieve Mina's dagger from the floor and throw it to Topaz. She caught it in one hand and thrust it towards Mina.

The girl advanced, her sword held out in front of her. Topaz edged back, jabbing with her dagger.

'Run!' she commanded Jake again.

'I should have killed you when we were children,'

Mina whispered savagely. 'The spoiled little princess. We would all have been better off without you.'

'If you lay so much as a bony finger on me,' Topaz replied with scorn, 'your precious prince will not hesitate to cut you down.'

Zeldt, still blinded, heard Topaz's words. He reached up his hand and hissed, 'Mina, put it down! She is not to be harmed!'

Jake listened in bewilderment as he tore a strip of material from the sofa and tied it around his bleeding hand. Too late. Suddenly the pain engulfed him completely. He fell to the floor and lost consciousness.

As Mina hesitated, Topaz used the moment to seize a flickering candlestick and toss it across the room, igniting the pool of fluid that had gushed out of the broken cabinet. Flames spread across the floor. They licked around the embalmed head of the Persian warrior and up the wall.

Now Mina chose to disregard her orders; she let out a shriek and lunged for Topaz's heart. The latter parried with her dagger, grabbed Mina's snake by the neck and hurled it away. The serpent flew into the white-hot heart of the fire. It let out a screech as it writhed and twisted.

'*Noooo!*' Mina shrieked as she leaped across the room and thrust her hand into the inferno.

'Wake up, wake up!' Topaz commanded the unconscious Jake. There was no response.

Mina's scorched hand retrieved the seared body of her beloved serpent. It hissed as it stretched this way and that until its black, blistered skin cracked away from its flesh.

'It's all right – it's going to be all right,' she pleaded desperately, gathering it in her arms. The creature tried to reach out its blistered tongue. Then it died, hanging limply from Mina's hand. Her face filled with savage horror.

Even Topaz froze in momentary remorse, then turned back to Jake. 'Wake up!' she shouted once more. Jake's eyes opened and she pulled him to his feet.

'I will kill you! *Kill you!*' Mina roared at Topaz.

There was an explosion as the glass of another cabinet shattered in the heat. Within seconds they were all bursting, their contents flying everywhere.

As Mina went to help her wounded master, Topaz dragged Jake through the flames towards the door. She caught one last glance of the other girl's vengeful face before she yanked Jake out onto the deck.

The fire bell was sounding, and panicked guards were rushing down to help their master.

Topaz pulled Jake over to the main mast. 'The horizon point. We're approaching it.' She pointed to the gleaming Constantor at the stern. The discs were almost in alignment. 'Up is your only escape. Climb the mast!'

'Wh–what?' Jake stammered.

'The horizon point! The ship is about to disappear. A vortex of water will drag you down. Now climb!'

Jake shook his head. 'I can't leave you here,' he murmured helplessly.

'Well, you have to!' she shouted. 'There are no choices left!'

The *Lindwurm* had started to shake and judder. Jake, utterly dumbstruck, started to clamber up the mast. The salt water searing into his wound was agonizing, but it was a greater, rawer pain that compelled him to jump back down again and throw his arms around Topaz.

'I can't leave you here! I *can't*!' he cried over the loud creak of timbers. 'Mina will kill you.'

'Mina cannot kill me.'

'How can you know? *How?*' Jake yelled over the tumult.

Topaz looked Jake straight in the eye. It was time to utter the terrible truth. 'Because Zeldt . . . is family. He's *my* family. He is my *uncle*!'

Jake's eyes widened in horror, and he opened his mouth – but there was no more time. Every part of the ship was shaking now. Once more he climbed the mast, higher and higher. There was an extraordinary gathering of air from every part of the ocean. The *Lindwurm* shuddered to breaking point. The discs of the Constantor came into alignment.

'Topaz, I love you!' Jake yelled out to the small figure below.

There was a deafening explosion – and Topaz and the ship vanished beneath him. Jake cried out as he plunged into the sea below. He was sucked into the whirlpool. The ocean filled his lungs.

Jake tried to fight his way to the surface, but the current kept pulling him down, sending his limbs in every direction. Eventually he emerged above the waves. As he gasped for air, he became aware of the pain in his hand.

He looked around, and saw a wooden pallet,

dislodged from the ship's decks, floating by; he pulled himself up, collapsing exhausted onto his makeshift raft. He stared around, wide-eyed. He was alone in the middle of the rolling ocean. The *Lindwurm* had disappeared without trace.

As the waves started to settle, Jake became aware of another living creature panting beside himself. A dog was paddling furiously to stay afloat. Jake recognized the scarred, war-torn face of the mastiff, Felson.

On seeing Jake, the dog swam towards him; he looked half dead.

'You've been abandoned, have you?' Jake said to him. 'You want to be friends now?'

The dog's brow furrowed; he whimpered and reached out his tongue to lick Jake's face. The display of affection melted Jake's heart. His lips trembled and tears streamed from his eyes. He pulled Felson up onto the raft and held him tight.

'All right, we'll be friends,' he said softly.

30 PROMISES AND PROPOSALS

Jake and Felson were picked up by some Flemish fishermen. Having trawled the North Sea for over a month, they were returning home from Dogger Bank with a hold full of salted herring when they spotted the raft. They threw out a net and hauled Jake and his companion aboard.

The ruddy-faced men, who spoke Flemish with a strong sing-song accent, offered them plates of delicious cured fish and wooden cups – a large bowl for Felson – of a curious lemonade. One of them bandaged Jake's hand and showed off his own selection of scars.

The fishermen laughed and joked, drank from flagons and sang sea shanties all the way back to shore. They dropped Jake and Felson off at the harbour of Hellevoetsluis.

Jake found the *Aal* nestling amongst the many fishing craft in the harbour. Using some of the coins that Nathan had given him in Venice, he acquired fuel and water for the journey back and set off south again, back up the Rhine, steering his boat in the bright moonlight.

Jake's mind now turned to the shocking events on the *Lindwurm*. A succession of haunting flash-backs played out in his head: Topaz's strangeness, the showdown with Zeldt, the pistol, the fight, the fire, the fate of Mina's snake – and, of course, Topaz's astonishing revelation: that she was the niece, the very flesh and blood, of Zeldt himself.

As Jake had been dragged down by the ocean currents, so he now struggled with a vortex of con-flicting thoughts and fears. He felt desperately sorry for Topaz, but also appalled. His exhausted mind bombarded him with questions: had she ever been close to her family? If Zeldt was her uncle, who were her mother and father? What had Charlie said about them? One brother – hadn't he disappeared? And there was a sister who was more appalling even than Zeldt . . . Topaz must be the daughter of one of them? But under what circumstances had she been adopted? Jake felt nothing but love for Topaz, but he was now tormented by the most terrible question of all: *Was she, in any way, tainted by her family's evil?*

Just as Jake thought he was starting to go mad, he decided to block the subject from his mind until he was calm enough to think about it rationally.

The following morning, just before dawn, he arrived back in Cologne – where, before charging off to save Topaz, he had told his parents to wait. The grand square in front of the cathedral was almost deserted, but three familiar figures huddled together on the steps of the quay. One of them, sensing something, sat up. It was Miriam Djones. On seeing her beloved son, she leaped in the air, jumping for joy.

The Djoneses, Paolo Cozzo and Felson (who was timid and apprehensive at first, but soon warmed to Jake's family) set off after breakfast and made their way up the Rhine to the southern corner of Germany, until they could travel by water no more.

They stopped in the small town where Jake had stayed with Topaz and Charlie on their way to Castle Schwarzheim. As they made enquiries as to the best way to continue their journey to Venice, they were rewarded with the most unexpected piece of luck. The travelling players who had performed

Oedipus to an enraptured audience three nights previously were themselves heading for Italy. An acting troupe called the Commedia dell'Arte had been gathering rave reviews across the continent, and the players had decided to travel to Florence to learn from them first-hand. They had space to spare in their two rickety wagons.

It took three and half days to cross the Alps and traverse the plateau of northern Italy, but it was as fascinating and diverting a time as Jake had ever had. The players were an enthralling group of people, each playing a part: the world-weary king, the principled princess, the honourable soldier, the femme fatale, the pantomime villain and the fool. They rehearsed, debated, sang, danced, cried, and generally squeezed every atom of passion from even the dullest moments.

To everyone's bemused delight, the beautiful young ingénue of the troupe, Liliana, took a shine to Paolo. She was half a foot taller than him and two years his senior, but this did not stop her from blushing every time he so much as looked in her direction. Alan suggested that Paolo was 'emitting pheromones' following his heroics on top of Cologne Cathedral. By the time they arrived at

Venice, and had to go their separate ways, the poor young actress was completely smitten. She insisted on keeping a lock of Paolo's hair, which he gave her with poorly concealed reluctance.

The Djones family, Paolo and Felson made their way across the Venetian causeway and staggered, exhausted, into the bustling city. Though their heart was not in it, they passed some time window-shopping before the hour came to make their way to the Rialto and the agreed rendezvous with the others.

They ascended the steps of the ancient bridge in silence. As they reached the apex, all the bells of the city started to toll midday. If Nathan and Charlie had survived their mission, they would surely have already arrived in Venice. By 12.15 they had still not made an appearance.

'They must have been successful,' mused Alan, 'as everyone is still alive.' He swept his hand across the bustling crowds of people. 'So where are they?'

'You're splashing my silk organza!' boomed a voice below them. 'Venetian canal water is notoriously difficult to remove.'

The Djoneses stared at each other in delight. They rushed over to the parapet – to find Charlie

Chieverley, Mr Drake proudly perched on his shoulder, steering a golden gondola. The boat was elaborately carved with the figure of Neptune, along with adoring water nymphs and sea monsters, and there, on its velvet cushions, reclined Nathan, eating figs.

'Ahoy there!' He waved graciously at the four people leaning over the bridge. 'Missions accomplished. Three cheers for all of us. We'll dock over there at that taverna. We've booked a table for lunch. The ravioli is the best in the city, and the views of the Grand Canal are second to none.'

The six intrepid agents of the History Keepers' Secret Service had a sumptuous and noisy lunch in the sun-dappled taverna. (Once, that is, Mr Drake had made his peace with Felson.) They ate delicious pasta and swapped stories of their death-defying missions, with everyone at some point receiving at least one round of applause. Paolo, in particular, felt a warm glow inside at his new-found fame.

Nathan and Charlie also told the others what they'd done since intercepting the deadly books. They had carefully removed the miniature capsules of plague from each edition. Knowing they would have to take them to Point Zero for analysis and destruction, they had secured them for transportation.

After arriving in Venice, they had returned to the *Campana* and moved it, along with the *Mystère*, to a quiet quay beyond the Arsenale. They had visited the Venetian bureau and collected the spare Meslith machine, from which they had updated Point Zero on events so far. Finally they had freed all the kidnapped architects, who had been deserted by Zeldt's guards – they, it transpired, had fled the city.

After pudding they strolled along the busy network of canals until they arrived at the shadowy quayside where the History Keepers' ships were moored.

Nathan produced a map, whereupon there was a good deal of heated debate on the subject of which would be the best horizon point to head for. In the end Nathan reluctantly took Alan's advice and chose one due east of Ravenna. From this point they would be able to leap all the way to La Rochelle, cutting their journey time down considerably. As this route required a high level of atomium, it was also decided that Jake would travel with Nathan and Charlie, to make full use of their vigorously young valours.

The vials of plague were entrusted to Miriam, and everyone said their goodbyes to Paolo, who was returning to his aunt's house.

'So, will you stay with the History Keepers?' Jake asked him tentatively.

'Mmm . . . good question.' Paolo thought for a moment. 'Well, apart from being captured, chained up, tortured, locked in a cell with Nathan Wylder and forced to endure his sense of humour, thrown into a snake pit, savaged by black mambas and ordered to dangle from the highest building in the world . . . apart from all that' – a cheeky smile lit up his face – 'what's the worst that can happen?'

Jake and Paolo laughed out loud and gave each other a long and heartfelt hug.

Amidst much bellowing from Nathan, the ships set sail in tandem. Charlie sent Galliana a long Meslith message, informing her that they were on their way back, listing all the new developments and confirming that Topaz would not be with them as she had accompanied Zeldt to another, unknown part of history.

Within the hour, the ships were traversing the bright Adriatic. Jake watched his parents on the deck of the *Mystère*; laughing, arm in arm, the wind in their hair, they seemed a million miles away from the shambolic bathroom shop in south-east London.

Just after he had taken his sickening dose of atomium, Jake had finally plucked up the courage to approach Charlie at the helm and ask him, confidentially, about Topaz's history. He felt that Charlie would give him a straight answer.

'Of course, we've all known, ever since we were young, but it's rarely mentioned,' Charlie told him, his hands firm on the steering wheel.

'And who are her actual parents?' Jake was almost too frightened to ask.

'Her mother I have talked about – Agata, she is called. She is Zeldt's sister.'

'That's the one who tried to drown Zeldt in the freezing lake when he was a boy, and who burned her maid?' asked Jake.

'I'm afraid so,' murmured Charlie.

Jake heaved a sigh. 'And does Topaz look like her mother?'

'What's that got to do with anything?'

'Just tell me.'

It was Charlie's turn to sigh. 'I've never met her. Apparently there are some physical similarities.

But their personalities are galaxies apart.'

'And her father? Who is he?'

Charlie shrugged. 'No one knows, not even Topaz.'

Soon enough they reached the horizon point, and Nathan and Charlie flanked Jake closely as the Constantor aligned. Jake had assumed that he would have got used to the experience by now, but his tiredness seemed to make the effect more shocking and nauseating than ever. This time he closed his eyes as his alter ego shot up into the stratosphere. A second later, one after the other, the ships vanished from the seas of the sixteenth century.

Arriving back in 1820, they were met by dismal, driving rain. Mr Drake was appalled. He squawked and immediately flew below decks. The rain pelted down ceaselessly all afternoon, until they finally spied the distinctive conical silhouette of the Mont St Michel.

It was Rose who first spotted the two ships approaching across the rain-tossed sea. She ran about the castle, knocking on doors and telling everyone the exciting news. Only Oceane Noire, who was nursing 'a migraine from hell', failed to be sufficiently interested.

Gradually everyone assembled on the pier with their umbrellas: Galliana Goethe, Jupitus Cole, Signor Gondolfino, the costumier, and Truman and Betty Wylder – Nathan's parents, and Topaz's guardians. Before Topaz's departure from Point Zero days before, Truman and Betty had been informed of the mission their adopted daughter had been entrusted with. Now they knew that she would definitely not be returning. They'd come to offer their support, but hung back in the shadows, Betty dabbing her tears with a silk handkerchief.

The ships docked side by side, and there was a spontaneous round of applause as the agents emerged down the gangplanks. A great cheer went up for Alan and Miriam, and a greater one still for Jake, who was the last to step ashore.

'Welcome home, the Djones family!' Signor Gondolfino shouted at the top of his voice.

'Here, here!' everyone shouted in unison.

Miriam carefully handed Galliana the package containing the vials of plague. Nathan waited for everyone to settle down before delivering his 'impromptu' speech:

'We return victorious. All our agents played their parts magnificently. Disaster in Italy has been averted.' He held his arms aloft and proclaimed, 'The Renaissance remains intact.' Then he shook his mane of auburn hair, momentarily closed his eyes and adopted a more serious tone. 'However, in this moment of celebration, let us stop to remember Topaz St Honoré, who has bravely gone on to missions new.'

'Topaz St Honoré!' everyone murmured together.

Jupitus, who had been keeping very quiet, cleared his throat and said, 'Fruit cocktails and champagne will be served in the stateroom in one hour. I urge you all to attend as I have an announcement to make.'

Speeches over, Rose rushed across to her brother and sister-in-law, nearly squeezing the life out of them. 'That's the last time you go off on a mission without telling me,' she chided Alan. 'You're still my younger brother, remember?'

Galliana put her arm round a shell-shocked Jake. 'I've heard all about your bravery. Charlie says you are a keeper through and through. We're very proud of you.'

Jake smiled, but the commander could sense that he was overcome with emotion. She pulled him closer. 'I know, I know,' she whispered kindly. 'It can be magical beyond belief, but history can *also* be a very daunting place.'

When Jake arrived with his parents, the stateroom was humming with the chit-chat of all the History Keepers. The three of them had put on new clothes: Miriam her favourite dress from home in London, Alan his old corduroy trousers, both produced from the red suitcase. Jake wore *new* clothes of the 1820s: smart breeches, a buttoned waistcoat, a white shirt and a cravat tied in a bow. With his dark hair and big brown eyes, he looked every inch the romantic hero.

The room was lit with clusters of twinkling candles and decorated with fresh flowers. Through its four enormous windows, dusk was encroaching across the stormy vastness of the ocean.

Jupitus was filling champagne flutes. When he was satisfied that everyone was present, he silenced the excited buzz by tapping a spoon on his glass.

'I am a man of few words,' he announced, 'so I will keep this brief. I have happy news' – though there was not the vestige of a smile on his face – 'Oceane Noire and I are engaged to be married.'

A bewildered silence was succeeded by a slightly puzzled round of applause. Oceane, touching up her hair with her forefinger, stepped through the crowd and took her place next to Jupitus.

Rose did not clap; she was too stunned to even close her mouth. 'Good gracious,' she murmured as she pretended to search for something in her carpetbag. Jupitus flashed a glance at her. Only Rose and Galliana knew anything of his secret feelings, and neither was observing him now; so no one caught that look of profound wretchedness.

The news of Oceane and Jupitus's engagement washed over Jake; his thoughts were on weightier matters. His parents had been lost in history. Through dogged perseverance and sheer luck he had found them . . . but now he had lost Topaz. Haunting thoughts of her barged their way to the forefront of his mind. However much praise he received from Galliana and the other History Keepers, he knew he had failed in the mission he had set himself: to save her. He was tormented by the thought that he might never see her again. The world on its own was gigantic enough, but history, he now truly understood, was vast beyond all imagining – as infinite and complex as the universe itself, and filled with unimaginable darkness.

Jake breathed deeply to calm himself down. He wandered over to one of the huge windows and surveyed the wide horizon. Felson, who was waiting timidly by the door, padded over and stood by his side. The dog stared up at his new master, and then he too looked out to sea. Far, far off in the distance, a pulse of lightning illuminated a circle of ocean. Jake remembered how this whole adventure had started: a thunderstorm had heralded his entrance into this strange and thrilling universe. Almost every perception he had of the world had changed unalterably since then. Glory, duty, love and fear were now the entities that ruled his life.

He was a History Keeper.

There was no going back.

He made a solemn promise, whispering the words to himself, steaming up the window with a sigh of condensation.

'I will find you, Topaz. Wherever you are. In whatever place or time. If it is the last thing I do . . . I will find you . . .'

Acknowledgments

Firstly, thanks to all the *singular* ladies . . . Becky Stradwick, for really getting the ball rolling, and everything she's done since. Jo Unwin for her wisdom and character. Sue Cook for her immeasurable mind; and Rachel Holroyd and Sophie Dolan for all their great work and many laughs.

The book would not have been written without the help of the marvellous Morrisons, Ali Lowry, Richard Batty and all my noble friends who generously steered me from destitution!

A special thanks to Dick for picking me up from school, Dudley for always keeping an eye, to Rufo and to Justin, and finally my Mum for teaching me that humour is everything!

THE
HISTORY
KEEPERS
CIRCUS MAXIMUS

DAMIAN DIBBEN

Turn over for a special preview . . .

1 THE QUEEN OF THE NIGHT

The night Jake Djones brought total disgrace upon himself and jeopardized the very survival of the History Keepers' Secret Service was so unnaturally, bitterly cold that the Baltic Sea almost froze over.

From the rocky, windswept shores of Denmark in the west, to the frozen remoteness of Finland in the north, an endless expanse of ice – as thin as gossamer and a ghostly silver in the moonlight – curved across the horizon. A continual dusting of soft snow seemed to silence this far corner of the earth in an otherworldly hush.

A ship with blue sails broke through the veneer of ice even as it was forming, heading for the twinkling lights of Stockholm – a fairytale archipelago of bays, promontories and islets. The ship was called the *Tulip*, and at the creaking wheel stood a tall figure in a long fur coat. He reached out an elegant gloved hand and rang the bell. 'It's time, gentlemen,' he announced in a soft Charleston drawl.

Immediately two more silhouettes, both well wrapped up, came out of the snowy darkness and joined him at the helm, followed by a brightly coloured bird – a parrot – who nestled, shivering, on his master's shoulders. They gazed out eagerly through the snow as the ship sailed on towards the port. Their faces were slowly illuminated . . .

The figure in fur was strikingly handsome, a smile playing across his chiselled face. Next to him stood the owner of the parrot – a shorter boy with spectacles, his brows raised in a studious frown. The last person had olive skin, curly dark hair and big brown eyes that blinked with excitement. Three intrepid adolescents, young agents of the History Keepers' Secret Service: Nathan Wylder, Charlie Chieverley . . . and Jake Djones.

Charlie was the first to speak. 'Head for that central island there,' he said, pointing towards an isle of spires and towers. 'That's Stadsholmen, Stockholm's old town: the grand jewel of these islands, centre of the Swedish empire. Though sadly, of course, we're not arriving in the city's heyday. In 1710 our old friend the plague came here, taking out nearly a third of the population.'

'Not arriving in its heyday?' drawled Nathan, pulling his coat tighter against the snow. 'That's putting it mildly. Sweden in the winter of 1782 has got to be the most inhospitable place in history.' He produced a tiny box from his pocket and applied lip salve. 'If my lips get any drier, they'll turn to dust.'

'Hell's bells and Bathsheba, *92!*' Charlie exclaimed, closing his eyes and clenching his teeth in annoyance. 'We're in 1792. Honestly, Nathan, I sometimes wonder how you made it this far.' Mr Drake – that was the name of his pet parrot – squawked in agreement, fluttering his feathers indignantly at the American.

'I'm pulling your leg.' Nathan smirked. 'Do you really think I'd be wearing this ankle-length sable coat in 1782? Not to mention these buckle-less riding boots – so austere they're practically Napoleonic.' He turned to Jake. 'The 1790s are all about dressing down.' Nathan loved clothes almost as much as he loved an adventure.

'Buckle-less riding boots, my aunt,' Charlie muttered to himself, 'and don't even get me started on your sable coat. It's a work of barbaric savagery. Those poor animals had the right to a life as well, you know.'

As Jake listened to their banter, he felt a great swelling of pride that he belonged to the greatest and most mysterious organization of all time: the History Keepers' Secret Service.

Just a month had passed since his life had changed for ever. He had been kidnapped, taken to the London bureau and informed that his parents had been secretly working for the service for decades – and indeed had gone missing in sixteenth-century Italy!

From then on it had been a nonstop roller-coaster ride. He had travelled through time, first to Point Zero – the History Keepers' headquarters on the Mont St Michel in Normandy, 1820 – and then to Venice in 1506, as part of a team to find his mum and dad, and to stop the diabolical Prince Zeldt from destroying Europe with bubonic plague.

He had been reunited with his folks – but they had left behind Topaz, the mysterious and beautiful young agent to whom he had become devoted. Most extraordinary of all, he had discovered that his beloved brother Philip, who had apparently died in an accident abroad three years ago, had also been a History Keeper; there was a chance – a very slim chance – that he was actually alive somewhere in the past.

And now Jake was already on his second mission. Admittedly he had been selected more through luck than anything else (nearly everyone at Point Zero had come down with an appalling tummy bug after eating mussel soup, and agents were thin on the ground), and it was not a dangerous assignment – otherwise he would definitely not have been included, as he was still a novice. But nonetheless here he was, travelling to the Baltic in the 1790s to collect a consignment of atomium, the precious liquid that made travelling through history possible.

'So, tell me something about the person we're meeting?' he asked, trying to hide the tremor in his voice.

'Caspar Isaksen the Third?' Charlie shrugged. 'Not personally acquainted, but he's our age, I believe. I cooked a pumpkin tagine for his father once. He said it would live with him for ever.' (Charlie loved food with a passion and was an expert cook – although an experience in the kitchens of Imperial Paris had left him a staunch vegetarian.)

'*I've* been personally acquainted with Caspar Isaksen the Third. Twice,' drawled Nathan with a roll of his eyes. 'You can't really miss him; he eats cakes like they're going out of fashion, and never stops sneezing.'

'So what is the Isaksens' connection with atomium?' Jake persisted. He had learned all about this substance on his first voyage. To travel to a particular point in the past, agents had to drink a dilution of it, mixed with exact precision. Generally it worked only out at sea, in the magnetic maelstrom of a *horizon point*; and then only on the few humans with *valour* – an innate ability to travel through the ages. The History Keepers used it to watch over history, protecting the past from dark forces that sought to destroy it and plunge the world into darkness.

'The Isaksens *are* atomium,' replied Charlie. 'The family have been in charge of its production for more than two hundred years. As you know, it's notoriously tricky to make. To produce an effective batch, its ingredients – which themselves are kept a secret from all but a handful of keepers – have to be refined over a period of years . . .'

'Decades, I would say,' Nathan added.

'Quite,' Charlie concurred, 'and it must be created in freezing conditions. That's why Sejanus Poppoloe, the founder of the History Keepers, set up the laboratory in northern Sweden. After he had done so, he handed over all duties to Frederick Bruno Isaksen, the first of the line. To this very day, *all* atomium – exported to every bureau of the world, from China to Peru to Siberia – has been created in the Isaksens' laboratory.'

'So why are we meeting in Stockholm and not at the actual laboratory?' Jake asked.

'Dear me,' Charlie sighed, 'you *have* got a lot to learn. *No one* goes to the laboratory,' he explained. 'No one has the slightest idea where it is, not even Commander Goethe.'

Jake stared back in surprise. Surely if anyone knew where the laboratory was based, it would be Galliana Goethe – the commander of the History Keepers for the past three years.

'Only the Isaksens keep the secret and pass it on,' Charlie continued. 'Can you imagine the disaster if its location got into the wrong hands? Catastrophe times infinity!'

'There's a myth,' Nathan added, 'that it's hidden in a secret limestone cave, accessed through a mountain lake.'

'In any case,' Charlie concluded, 'when the atomium is ready, a member of the family delivers it to an arranged location. As Caspar Isaksen is a fan of the opera, like me, the opera house was the venue chosen on this occasion. And not a moment too soon,' he added sombrely. 'Atomium stocks at Point Zero are at an all-time low. This consignment is vital.'

'So no slip-ups from the new boy,' Nathan added mischievously, thumping Jake on the back.

Jake looked around at the port. There were ships everywhere, an intricate forest of masts and rigging. Along the shore, depots and warehouses teemed with activity as sailors and noisy tradesmen, their breath visible in the freezing air, worked into the evening, loading and unloading their cargoes: iron, copper and tin; crates of wax, resins and amber; sacks of rye and wheat; consignments of animal furs; and endless boxes of shining fish. Mr Drake surveyed the bustle with a keen eye, always intrigued – and just a touch nervous – when arriving at a new destination.

The *Tulip* docked in a narrow berth next to a huge

warship. Jake and Nathan gawped up at her, her great rounded hull punctuated by two cannon decks. High up on her starboard side a cluster of sailors, thick-necked and shaven-headed, stood talking in gruff voices.

Nathan caught their eye and lifted his fur hat in a flamboyant gesture. 'Lovely evening for the opera, wouldn't you say?' The sailors ignored him completely.

'You be a good boy and stay here.' Charlie stroked Mr Drake and gave him some peanuts. 'We shan't be long.' The parrot watched the three young agents jump down onto the quay.

They pulled their coats tight and, stepping carefully across the icy cobbles, made their way through the noisy bustle of people streaming along the dock. Jake glanced at the stalls selling cooked meats, salted fish, wooden cups of steaming cider. His attention was caught by a fortune-teller shrouded in a lace shawl, her wizened hand clutching tarot cards. She held them up to Jake, imploring him to listen to his destiny. He stopped briefly, his eye drawn by the card at the top of the pack: a smiling skeleton in front of a moonlit sea. The fortune-teller's eyes opened ominously, swimming in cloudy grey.

'Let's not get involved,' said Nathan, firmly taking Jake's arm and guiding him on. 'She probably works for the tourist office.'

The three of them skirted round the royal palace, then crossed a wide timber bridge into the formal square in front of the opera house – a graceful three-tiered building capped by a giant stone crown. A steady stream of carriages was arriving, out of which the cream of Stockholm's society – all wrapped in furs – disembarked and entered the building.

'Opera?' Nathan huffed. 'Is there anything more ridiculous? Overweight people warbling on about nothing! Couldn't that rogue Isaksen have arranged a rendezvous somewhere more appropriate?'

'How dare you, Nathan Wylder! How dare you!' Charlie fumed. 'This is a wonderful performance of Mozart's *The Magic Flute*. It was written only a year ago. The ink is barely dry on the manuscript and the great man is already dead – God rest his soul. It's a once-in-a-lifetime opportunity.'

Nathan pulled a guilty face at Jake and the three of them forged on through the crowds to the entrance.

Two figures on horseback emerged from the shadows on the other side of the square, their gaze fixed on the three agents. They dismounted, the first, dressed in a high-collared coat, stepping into the half-light of a street lantern. He was tall, upright, and had straight shoulder-length blond hair. His accomplice wore a dark cloak and a distinctive wide-brimmed hat. The blond man whispered something in his companion's ear, gave him charge of his horse, then hurried across the square in pursuit.

Jake's eyes lit up at the sight of the foyer. In contrast to the wintry gloom outside, it was an immense space of white marble and gilded mirrors, lit by constellations of chandeliers. Its inhabitants were as magnificent as the surroundings: poised, elegant people, the polished black boots of the men and the long silk dresses of the ladies reflected in the gleaming floor. Many were arranged in chattering clusters; others were ascending a grand staircase, their eyes eagerly scanning the crowds for the latest source of scandal.

Nathan was in his element. 'I genuinely think this might be one of fashion's all-time greatest moments,' he announced, sweeping off his fur coat to reveal a splendid ultramarine jacket and breeches. 'Look at the silhouettes, look at the detailing, the sheer pizzazz.

Their buttons alone could win prizes.'

An attendant wearing a coiffed wig, white gloves and an expression of loathing helped Jake and Charlie out of their coats. Jake's hand caught in his sleeve, and an undignified tussle was followed by the sound of the lining ripping.

'Ooops.' He blushed and tried to stifle a giggle as he passed it to the man. The attendant merely sighed, collected all three overcoats and exchanged them for ivory counters with golden numbers before he withdrew.

'And be careful with that,' Nathan called after him. 'It was worn by the Duke of Marlborough at the Battle of Blenheim.' He then confided in Jake, 'Not really, but you can never be too careful with vintage fur.'

A bell sounded and the opera-goers started making their way into the auditorium.

'Well, we might as well get it over with,' Nathan drawled. 'The opera is not going to bore itself. Where are our seats?'

'Royal circle, box M,' Charlie replied curtly, indicating the next tier. The three of them headed up the stairs, oblivious to the figure with long blond hair, who was watching them keenly from behind a pillar.

Another white-gloved attendant led them along a candle-lit corridor and through a door into their private box. It was a small room lined in dark red, with four gilt chairs and a spectacular view of the auditorium. Jake felt another surge of excitement – it was like being inside a giant jewellery case. Five tiers rose up from the stalls in a sweeping oval shape, each containing a succession of private boxes with a batch of gossiping aristocrats. Jake thought it looked like some crazy human zoo – everyone was looking around and whispering slyly to their neighbours.

'Well, where *is* Caspar Isaksen?' asked Nathan with a wry look at the empty chair. 'He's late.' He picked up a pair of silver opera glasses laid out on a side table. 'I suppose, while I am here, I may as well study some Swedish architecture . . .' He started to scan the space with the binoculars – and then stopped. 'Intriguing . . .'

Charlie turned to see that the object of Nathan's attention was a box containing three young ladies, coyly blushing at him from behind their fans.

'Oh, please concentrate,' he sighed. 'This is work,

remember.' He snatched the glasses and passed them to Jake. 'I'm sure *you'll* find something more interesting to look at.'

Jake examined the audience more closely. He half fancied inspecting Nathan's three beauties for himself, but felt it would be rude, so he started at the other end of the tier. He had never seen so much wealth, so many expensive clothes and glittering jewels. Suddenly his binoculars picked out a young girl in a white dress sitting on her own. There was something about her that reminded him of Topaz. He felt a pang as he remembered that dreadful night aboard the *Lindwurm* when she had disappeared, probably for ever, into the vortex of time. To take his mind off the memory, he swiftly continued along the row. Two stalls on, his gaze alighted upon a blond-haired man pointing a silver pistol directly towards him.

Jake gasped, dropped the binoculars, picked them up, looked through them again, shook his head, turned them the right way round and quickly returned to search for the box.

It was empty. The man was nowhere to be seen.

'What on earth is wrong with you?' Nathan asked.

'The box over there! There was a man pointing a gun.'

Nathan and Charlie examined the offending stall. An elderly gentleman and his wife were now taking their seats.

'He's gone now, but I promise you I saw him.'

Nathan and Charlie gave each other a look.

'You're new to this' – Nathan meant to be reassuring, but of course it came out as condescending – 'so you're jumpy, that's all. It's the opera; everyone is spying on everyone else. That's the name of the game.'

'He wasn't spying. He was pointing a gun, a silver gun,' Jake insisted.

'Silver?' Nathan noted. 'You're quite sure they weren't opera glasses?'

In truth, Jake wasn't one hundred per cent certain. The moment had been so fleeting.

'Besides, not a soul knows we're here. Only Commander Goethe has our exact time location, so let's not panic.' Nathan leaned over and whispered in Jake's ear, 'If I were you, I'd be more frightened of what's about to happen out there.' He pointed at the stage.

Jake nodded and tried to calm his thumping heart.

An excited hush descended around the theatre as the lights started to fade. A moment later, the orchestra suddenly struck up in a great fanfare of horns and bass drums. Jake once again scanned the tiers of people in search of the blond-haired man, but it was like looking for a needle in a haystack. Everyone was leaning forward, eyeglasses poised. Another blast of trumpets, and then the violins began.

Jake felt a chill go down his spine as the curtains slowly rose, revealing a dark landscape. At first this was difficult to make out, but a series of lighting effects, each one drawing sighs of admiration from the crowd, gradually illuminated the stage: in the background, a huge moon hung above mountains and pyramids; in the foreground stood palm trees and giant flowers.

'We're in Egypt,' Charlie whispered in awed tones, 'in the realm of the Queen of the Night. In a moment Tamino is going to enter, pursued by a giant serpent.'

'It's a roller coaster,' added Nathan, stifling a yawn.

There was a soft ripple of applause as the young hero materialized out of the desert mist, then fearful sighs as a giant snake curled down from above. At the sight of this, Jake froze. He knew the reptile was nothing but a piece of stage machinery – albeit a very convincing one – but memories quickly came flooding back. It was only a short time ago that he had been thrown into a hideous chamber of snakes and ladders. At the last minute he had been saved by two other History Keepers' agents – his mum and dad, actually – but the incident had left a scar.

Gradually the stage filled with curious characters: three mysterious ladies in veils, a man dressed as a bird – 'Mr Drake would have hooted with laughter,' Charlie commented – then, heralded by ominous claps of thunder, a majestic, fantastical figure took shape out of the stars.

'*That's* the Queen of the Night,' Charlie murmured as she emerged high above the others. 'She's going to ask Tamino to save her daughter from the clutches of the evil sorcerer Sarastro. It seems like she's this frightened mother,' he carried on breathlessly, 'but actually *she's* the villain and wants to steal the sun and plunge the world into darkness.'

'Don't they all? Mothers-in-law?' Nathan commented with a mischievous smile.

Jake was so hypnotized by this figure, so lost in her spine-tingling voice, so focused on her evil eyes, that when a knock came at the door behind him, he jumped in shock.

He and his companions turned to look at the door.

Another knock came, but this time it was followed by three sneezes and then a high voice: 'It's me, Caspar.'

All three of them gave sighs of relief. Nathan opened up and Caspar Isaksen squeezed himself into the box. Jake stared. Caspar was his age, but as wide as he was short, with ruddy cheeks, a runny nose and crazy blond hair going off in all directions. He had a worried smile and glistened with a layer of perspiration. He wore a bright turquoise jacket and breeches that were far too small for him, and Jake noticed that he had done up his buttons wrong.

'Sorry – so sorry I'm late,' he puffed, madly wiping his nose and dabbing his forehead with a handkerchief. 'Hello. Caspar Isaksen . . .' He shook Jake's hand, then Charlie's. 'Ah, Nathan! We've met, of course. As you can see, I didn't forget your advice – you said turquoise would do wonders for my figure.' He added with great pride, 'I *never* wear anything else.' He turned to show off his outfit from all sides and caught sight of the stage for the first time. 'Good heavens! The Queen of the Night is already on! Has she sent Tamino on his mission? She's a sly one, isn't she?'

Nathan was already losing patience. 'Yes, yes – but business first. I take it the atomium's in there?' he asked with a nod towards the holdall in Caspar's hand.

'The atomium is—' Caspar froze mid-sentence, holding up his finger. Jake was wondering what was going to happen next when suddenly he sneezed. Then again, and a third time for luck.

'Sorry, sorry,' Caspar sighed, wiping down his face with his snotty handkerchief. 'You're quite right – business first.' He knelt down, opened his case and started to remove the contents. Jake, Nathan and Charlie watched, bewildered, as he unloaded cake after cake after cake. 'I couldn't come to Stockholm without paying a visit to Sundbergs Konditori. Strawberry custard, cinnamon bun, Christmas knäck – yummy yummy,' he muttered as he laid them out one by one.

Finally, from the bottom of the bag, he retrieved a smart veneered box. He dusted off a layer of icing sugar, wiped off a dollop of cream and passed the box to Nathan. A concentrated stillness descended on the agents. Jake could see that the top of the box was inscribed with an elaborate I – for Isaksen. Nathan opened it, and a golden light shimmered across their faces.

Inside, in a midnight-blue casing, lay two crystal vials, each full to the brim of the infinitely precious liquid.

'That's one consignment for Point Zero,' said Caspar, in a more business-like tone, 'and one for the Chinese bureau.'

Nathan was just closing the case when Jake caught sight of a face in the crowd and his stomach turned to liquid. In the stalls, everyone was looking in the same direction, their faces bathed in light from the stage – everyone except for one person: the blond man seated in the far corner, who was staring fixedly up at them.

'There!' Jake shouted out, pointing at the man.

Nathan, Charlie and Caspar turned at once and saw the figure quickly rise from his seat, a silver pistol in his hand. Nathan snatched the opera glasses from Jake and used them to follow the man as he ran up the aisle and stormed through the double doors.

'We've been compromised!' he exclaimed. 'Back to the ship immediately!' He chucked the glasses back at Jake and carefully took hold of the box of atomium. He arranged something – Jake couldn't see what – inside, then flung open the door and looked both ways along the curving corridor: nothing but flickering candelabra. 'Charlie, you go that way. Whoever gets to the *Tulip* first, prepare to set sail straight away.'

In a heartbeat, Charlie was racing along the corridor and disappearing down the stairs at the end.

'Jake, Caspar, follow me!' Nathan barked. Caspar was hurriedly picking up his cakes and putting them back in his bag. 'Now!'

Nathan led the way, heading in the opposite direction to Charlie. Jake followed, with Caspar wheezing behind. Footsteps approached from the other end of the passage and a figure appeared.

The three agents froze. Time seemed to stand still as Jake saw their adversary clearly for the first time. He was the same age as Nathan – sixteen or thereabouts – and in many ways a crueller, blond version of him. He had striking features, a superior look in his eye and, judging by his tailored clothes, the same pride in his appearance. His hair, in particular, was a work of art: long, blond and perfectly straight.

Jake could see that Nathan had gone pale.

'Who in God's name is that?' the American started to say as the man raised his pistol – and fired.

MICHAEL SCOTT

The Secrets of the Immortal
Nicholas Flamel

THE BESTSELLING SERIES

THE
EMERALD
ATLAS

THE BOOKS OF BEGINNING

JOHN STEPHENS

THREE CHILDREN.
TWO WORLDS.
ONE PROPHECY.

A spellbinding, action-packed page-turner
in the epic tradition of C. S. Lewis and J. K. Rowling

FOLLOW FINN IN HIS FIRST
SPECIAL OPS MISSION

NORWAY, OCTOBER 1940

The Nazis have invaded Norway.

Finn and best friend, Loki, are determined
to fight back. They join the Resistance
carrying out dangerous missions. Soon vital
secrets fall into their hands and the enemy
is in hot pursuit.

Now they face their greatest challenge –
to steal a Nazi plane and fly it to freedom.

ISBN: 978-0-552-55674-3